AMY M. LE & LYNN THOMAS

One woman's journey through abuse and pain to find healing and self-love.

THE COPPER PHOENIX

THE COPPER PHOENIX

A NOVEL

AMY M. LE

LYNN THOMAS

THE COPPER PHOENIX

Jacket design by Virginia McKevitt

Manufactured in the United States of America

Library of Congress Control Number: 2021913553

ISBN: 978-1-7372037-1-1 (paperback)
ISBN: 978-1-7372037-2-8 (hardback)
ISBN: 978-1-7372037-3-5 (ebook)

Content Guidance

Warning: This novel explores aspects of psychology, mental health, and abuse. The story contains depictions of self-harm, substance abuse, eating disorders, suicide, racism, and physical and sexual abuse. Please read with care. There are scenes of rape and physical abuse and themes of addiction, domestic violence, and bigamy. This may trigger survivors of trauma.

The Copper Phoenix contains scenes that depict or mention the following:

- Child abuse/pedophilia/incest
- Eating disorders or fatphobia
- Kidnapping and abduction
- Mental illness and ableism
- Violence/Torture/Abuse
- Racism and racial slurs
- Miscarriages/Abortion
- Self-harm or suicide
- Sexual Assault/Rape
- PTSD/Trauma
- Nudity

Resources

Help is within reach.

Emergency

If you are in a crisis situation or a medical emergency, call 911 in the U.S.

Suicide and Crisis Lifeline

If you need a mental health professional today, call or text 988 to be connected with the 988 Suicide and Crisis Lifeline, formerly known as the National Suicide Prevention Lifeline. They are available 24/7. For more information, visit https://www.fcc.gov/988-suicide-and-crisis-lifeline

National Drug Helpline

If you are struggling with any addictive substance, including alcohol, professionals are available to help 24/7/365 at 1-844-289-0879. The National Drug Helpline is open to any individual dealing with addiction issues. For more information, visit https://www.help.org/drug-abuse-hotline/

National Human Trafficking Hotline

If you or someone you know is a victim of human trafficking, call or text the National Human Trafficking Hotline now. Call 1-888-373-7888 (TTY: 711)|*Text 233733 | For more information, visit https://humantraffickinghotline.org/

Rape, Abuse & Incest National Network (RAINN)

If you are or have been a victim of rape, sexual abuse, or incest, contact the National Sexual Assault Hotline at 800.656.HOPE (4673). It is never too late to report a crime. The Rape, Abuse, & Incest National Network (RAINN) will connect you to a local sexual assault service provider who will walk you through the process of getting help and reporting to law enforcement at your own pace. For more information, visit https://www.rainn.org/

Dedication

This work is dedicated to anyone who has experienced trauma and needs healing. Your story matters and you are worth fighting for. May you find the strength and courage to face your demons, seek help, and forge a path to recovery.

To the friends, family members, and community allies who work tirelessly to end abuse and open doors for better health, the authors of this book thank you deeply for the difficult work you do.

Acknowledgments

To our family who gave us the agency to write this story, your love and patience allowed us to heal through the power of words and storytelling.

To The Mighty Six Critique Team members (Kae Koontz, Marty Ludlum, Dee Britt, Uyen Hoang Beach, Susan Kite, and Matthew R. Corr), we are indebted to you for your commitment to going through this journey with the authors week after week to flesh out the story, the characters, the trauma, and the triumphs.

Thank you to our editors, Staci Mauney with Prestige Prose and Alicia Dean, Freelance Editor, for persevering through a tough manuscript.

To our beta readers, especially Jesica Owens, Kat Hansen, Carli Valentine, Julie Tran, and Jill Cochran, thank you for your courage to take this book on, and for providing invaluable feedback.

Finally, to all the people who work as humanitarians, doctors, therapists, healers, and advocates for mental, spiritual, emotional, and physical health, we are indebted to you. Thank you for your encouragement and commitment to a better tomorrow.

Praise for The Copper Phoenix

"I can't imagine the challenge of writing a story with such detail and depth as Claire's story, yet Le captures the heart-wrenching details beautifully; moving the reader to tears."—Jesica Fuller Owens, Book Enthusiast

"This is a sensitive, horrifying look at a child who lived through unspeakable evil and rose like a phoenix. Well written and riveting reading."—Susan Kite, Author of The Mendel Experiment

"Like a phoenix, Claire's life is marked by unimaginable pain & hardship, yet the strength she has gained because of it facilitates a rebirth that brings her to a place of love and safety."—Kat Hansen, Co-author of Hope and Courage: Six Life Lessons from the Parents of a Child with Congenital Heart Disease

"Wonderfully told and written! A tale of a woman that truly transforms into something absolutely amazing."—Carli Valentine, Author of Extra Special Heart and Children's Book Illustrator

"For those that have the privilege to read it, this story will undoubtedly serve as a useful tool to educate some and restore hope to others...The perseverance and resilience demonstrated through this story could, and should, facilitate a society that seeks to offer hope and security to survivors."—Jill Cochran, Freelance Editor

"Based on a true story, the situations Claire faces will break your heart over and over again. You will root for her and hope she can find just one adult she can count on."—Staci Hart Mauney, Owner/Editor at Prestige Prose and Author of Death by Dice: A Bunco Club Mystery

"The story takes you on an emotional roller coaster from sadness to horror to disbelief to hope and happiness. The story is very visceral and raw. It is a journey of triumph but reminds us that triumph is not without struggle and not without constant striving…hoping for better."—Dr. Julie Tran, Silicon Valley Natural Health and Co-author of Asian Women Trailblazers Who Boss Up

TABLE OF CONTENTS

1. LITTLE SUNSHINE

A violent tempest brewed in Bryant Baker's gut, swirling down and out through his groin, past his knees, and into his leather boots. He kicked the door down. Never mind he had the key to the house and it was unlocked.

Bryant stormed inside and pushed past his stepson. "Where is she?"

Michael gritted his teeth at his stepfather. "Mom?" The boy was almost thirteen years old and the man of the house ever since Bryant deserted them. Michael stood firm with his fists drawn, ready to fight.

Bryant Paul-Bunyaned over his stepdaughters, Lonnie, Cheryl, and Katie. With his hands balled tightly, Bryant charged down the hallway. His thick hair flew in different directions while his one nostril hair cuckooed in and out with every puff of his breath. He ordered the kids into their rooms. When they didn't move, he bellowed, "Now!"

The two littlest, Cheryl and Katie, did as they were told and scurried into their room. Lonnie burst into tears and screeched. In one swift stride, Bryant grabbed the two oldest by the collars and hauled them to their shared bedroom. The children were now helpless chicks in a seven-foot by ten-foot coop and Bryant had the only key. He locked the door and nipped over to the room he and Janet had once shared. Just as he suspected, she was planted face-down on the bed, passed out, her clothes stained and reeking of booze, wisps of hair plastered around her neck.

Lying next to Janet was his little sunshine, Claire. Her diaper swelled with urine. Bryant held his breath. The stench was almost unbearable. His baby smiled when he scooped her into his arms. His heart fluttered. Bryant scanned the room. "Where are the damn diapers?" He wrestled open the dresser drawers, all of which were off the tracks and broken. "I swear . . ." He muttered under his breath, and with one arm holding Claire, he tore the room upside down looking for clean diapers. Bryant kicked the stool and slammed his fist against the window.

The glass rattled and woke Janet. "What are you doing?"

Bryant faced his wife and was appalled by her appearance. Lips dry, makeup smeared, face pale… she looked like Batman's arch-nemesis. "Going as the Joker again?" Bryant couldn't resist the jab.

Janet leaped off the bed and steadied herself. "You're not taking her. Where are the kids?" As if on cue, muffled cries made their way to Janet's ears. Her children pounded on the door and wall, begging to be let out. "Bryant, what did you do? Why are the kids locked in their room?"

"They're fine. Where are the diapers?" Bryant asked.

"Why?" Janet asked.

Bryant took a step forward and held Claire up. "Look at her!"

Claire's diaper sagged below her belly button, so heavy and drenched in pee that it shimmied another inch below her hips. Bryant pulled the diaper off and tossed it at Janet. He wrapped a towel around his baby girl and raged out of the room with Janet scurrying behind him. She gripped his flannel shirt sleeve. "Give her to me! You can't take her. She's mine."

"The hell I can't." Bryant yanked his elbow from her grip. "I'm taking her, and there's nothing you can do about it."

"That's kidnapping," Janet screamed. "You won't get away with this."

"She's mine," Bryant argued. "I'm not leaving her with you. You can't even take care of yourself."

"You'll never get custody. I'll call the police, and they'll arrest your ass."

The fury inside Bryant intensified. He slugged Janet on her temple, and she stumbled back. Bryant advanced and slapped her face. Her ample skin felt soft against his calloused, gritty hands. Janet lunged at him, howling as she clumsily beat his chest. Red welts rose to her cheeks, making her look like a wild jungle monkey.

Bryant put Claire down on the couch and punched Janet in the jaw, stopping her in her tracks. She thrashed about and bit down on the soft fleshy part of his chest below his nipple. Bryant yelped in pain. He kicked her in the stomach and dragged her by the hair to the coffee table. He hammered her face against the oak. The louder she begged for mercy, the more annoyed he was with her high-pitched, pathetic voice.

Blood dripped down Janet's face. Bryant crinkled his nose. "Jeezus, even your blood smells like a used tampon. Clean up. You're a disgrace." He pivoted on his heel to get Claire, but the weight of Janet's sausage fingers pulled him back.

Janet had him by the neck. "You don't smell like roses, either, unless there's such a thing as whiskey roses." Her two-hundred-pound body anchored him to the carpet. Bryant tripped and fell backward. He crashed to the floor and knocked over the framed photos on the table.

Claire erupted into a scream. Her piercing cries escalated Bryant's anger and amplified his distress. The veins on his body flared. He slammed Janet against the kitchen doorframe. With one swift, herculean push, Bryant shoved Janet's head into the drywall and knocked her unconscious.

"Good riddance," Bryant muttered.

He picked Claire up and walked out the door. The last thing he saw as he drove away was Michael hopping out of the window and running toward the front door.

The autumn mist cloaked his truck as he sped out of town across state lines. He wouldn't see Rochester, Minnesota, again for two more years.

#

Claire's earliest memory was when she was three years old, screaming for her daddy as people wheeled him into the emergency room at a hospital in Rochester. Winter that year was unforgiving, but the biting cold stung less than the fear of losing her father.

"That's my daddy!" Claire cried. "Daddy!"

Claire squirmed to get away as the nurse scooped her up. Claire didn't like the nurse much. Her fingers dug into Claire's thighs, and her face looked like a horse's—long and narrow, with flaring nostrils and brown eyes set far apart.

Claire pushed at the nurse's bosom to free herself, but it was no use. Her father writhed on the gurney and clutched his chest. As the medical staff wheeled him through heavy double doors, Claire pleaded one last time, "Don't take Daddy!"

Claire kicked her nurse, expecting her to trot and follow. Instead, the doors closed. She pressed her face against the round window and watched her dad turn the corner and disappear. Claire didn't have it in her to fight anymore. The warmth of the nurse's bosom now comforted her. She rested her head there in defeat.

Two hours after they wheeled her father into the emergency room, Bryant charged out of Olmsted Medical Center.

"Mr. Baker, you're not free to go," the nurse called after him.

"The hell I'm not." Bryant signed the discharge papers against medical advice and left with Claire clinging to her father's neck.

"You all right, Daddy?" Claire asked.

"I'm fine, Sunshine," Bryant said. "This isn't my first rodeo."

Years later Claire learned her father often had angina spells. He described the pain as a dull burn that spread to his back, jaw, and stomach. Whenever an attack came on, he had the sensation of falling. The room would move, and he'd try to catch himself. If he got too dizzy and if the walls blurred out, he had five minutes to get to the hospital. Without fail, though, he always managed to charm a nurse or convince a doctor to give him nitroglycerin. Then he'd discharge himself against medical advice, same as always, and be back in the saddle again.

Claire and Bryant continued their travels, road-tripping from city to city, just the two of them on the open highway, singing their hearts out to outlaw country songs.

"How about some music, Claire Anne?" Bryant tapped his big hand on her shoulder.

"Okay, Daddy!"

Bryant put the eight-track tape into the deck of the 1970 GMC. Claire loved her father's Jimmy 4x4. The smell of the vinyl bucket seats and the roar of the V8 engine made her feel like she could fly. Although it was a used truck and had some rust, they were battle scars, her father told her, which made the truck special.

Claire loved the removable hardtop and watched her dad shift gears. It was like dancing in the open air with the wind and bugs fighting for real estate on her face. They both laughed if one of the bugs splattered on her teeth.

Kenny Rogers's commanding voice sang out strongly on the radio. Bryant sang deep, "Something's burnin'," and Claire echoed.

#

They passed through Jamestown, North Dakota, and rolled into a truck stop to fuel up and get something to eat. Inside the brightly lit diner, Bryant ordered coffee.

Their server sauntered over to their table and sat down. "Hello, Bryant. It's been a minute. What can I get you, other than coffee?" She winked at him.

"Your special for today." Bryant lit up a cigarette and put his hand on her lap. They had a gig coming up, and both father and daughter looked forward to singing together on stage. Bryant rarely splurged on treats, mainly because money wasn't easy to come by, but there was the promise of banking big in the next town. The old M&M was a reputable establishment that was swinging with heavy spenders and big tippers… or so they heard from truckers they'd met along the way.

"And what will the little lady have?" the server asked.

"Macaroni and cheese, please." Claire pointed to the server's blue eye shadow. "I like your eyes. I'm Claire. What's your name?"

"Why, aren't you cute? I'm Cindy. How old are you, Claire?"

"Three!" Claire volunteered. "How old are you?"

Cindy laughed. She pulled out a sucker from her pocket. "Here's a treat for you, for when you get back on the road."

"Bring her a slice of key lime pie too." Bryant patted Cindy on her bottom. "I'm going to celebrate my little sunshine's birthday." Bryant watched Cindy's backside as the server walked away.

#

Bryant and Claire got an early start in the morning for the gig in Montana. They drove for eight hours and stopped long enough to get gas and a snack or to use the bathroom. Sometimes Bryant didn't bother to get to a respectable bathroom. A bush on the side of the road was as good of a bathroom as any.

By nightfall, they had pulled into a parking lot next to a gas station. Bryant loved driving, but he was exhausted. "We're going to rest our heads here in Miles City, darlin', before heading to Butte tomorrow."

Claire yawned and jumped onto her daddy's back. "Can I take a bath tomorrow?"

"You know the rules." It was important to Bryant that they looked respectable. He wanted Claire to have pride in how she presented herself because one never knew when an opportunity might knock.

Claire nodded. "Bath every night so the bed bugs don't bite."

"And?" Bryant carried his daughter to the motel room. He couldn't tell if she was heavier because she was deadweight or if she had grown since last week.

"And brush my teeth so my smile sparkles."

"And?"

"Comb my hair because it's pretty."

Bryant felt guilty making Claire take baths when she was so tired, but he knew she'd sleep well after a good soak. Claire was only eleven months old when he took her from her mother. Janet was a morose woman who drowned her depression in so much alcohol, her sweat smelled of vodka. The curdled cellulite around her arms and thighs were second cousins to sour bleu cheese crumbles.

It didn't sit well with Bryant to leave his daughter with such a dysfunctional and amoral woman. Janet once left Claire at home in the care of his stepson and three stepdaughters so that she could party her décolleté off. The next morning, Janet was so hungover, she was oblivious to the neo-natal cries of Claire's hunger. Desperate to subdue her baby half-sister's screams, ten-year-old Lonnie filled a bottle with orange juice and fed it to Claire. She didn't know, of course, that it was heavily laced with vodka. When Bryant found out his baby nearly died of alcohol poisoning, it was quite clear what he had to do—divorce Janet and take Claire away from that toxic woman. That was September of 1972, and there he was, two years later, in a cheap motel, crossing state lines to find odd jobs and gigs wherever he could.

Little Claire Anne Baker was the ray of sunshine in Bryant's dreary world; she lit up his life in ways none of his other twenty or so offspring did. To be frank, he had lost count of how many rugrats he had. Every fling was inconsequential and he never stayed with any woman long enough to bond with his children. Claire, however, was stunning, with her copper hair, green eyes, and upturned nose. Bryant had melted the moment he saw her. Maybe it was because he never witnessed the birth of his other children or that all his kids had dark hair whereas Claire's was fire and gold.

Looking at his daughter asleep beside him, Bryant believed his daughter was one tough cookie. He remembered when she was three months old, Janet had brought her to visit him in an attempt to salvage their marriage. Claire was dressed in nothing but a diaper and a thin receiving blanket at the height of a harsh Minnesota winter. He had taken his wailing daughter in his arms and cradled her until she warmed up and stopped crying.

The memory of holding his baby, feeling her cold skin, hearing her blood-curdling screams, and then seeing her calm down in his arms, made his heart flutter with love.

#

By morning, Bryant and Claire were well-rested and full of energy. They drove another five hours, and at three in the afternoon, they arrived at the Town Pump in Butte.

A slender man with brown hair and thick caterpillar eyebrows came out to welcome them. "Hi, there. Minnesota plates, huh? What brings you to Montana?"

"Just exploring the country with my favorite girl." Bryant smiled and offered his hand. "I'm playing a few sets tonight—"

"We, Daddy," Claire corrected him. "I'm going to sing with my daddy."

Mr. Caterpillar Eyebrows bent down to get a good look at Claire. His mustache was as thick as his eyebrows. "Well, aren't you the prettiest redhead I've ever seen? What's your name, little one?"

"Claire Anne Baker."

"Well, isn't that something? My wife's name, before she married me, was Mary Ann Baker, but I bet you're the better singer."

"You should come to see us tonight at the ole M&M." Bryant lifted the handle to the fuel pump. "Self-service, I see."

The man grinned. "Wouldn't you rather pump gas yourself if it meant cheaper prices?"

Bryant agreed. "Every penny counts, especially with the gas shortage."

"The missus and I opened the first Town Pump twenty years ago. Now we have to cut back our hours of operation to make the gas last longer."

"It's a damn shame. I remember when gas was thirty cents a gallon," Bryant said.

The owner pointed to the service bay. "You have a long way to go if you're heading back to Minnesota after your gig. Why don't you pull her into the garage for an oil change? I can do it in three minutes or else it's free."

Bryant didn't believe him and couldn't resist the chance for a free oil change. He pulled the Jimmy into the service bay and lifted Claire out of the truck. The owner handed his wristwatch to Bryant. And just like that, he was done in less than three minutes.

"I'll be damned. Impressive. What did you say your name was?"

"Kenneally. Tim Kenneally."

"Bryant Baker." They shook hands. "Good luck with the business, Tim."

"Thanks. I reckon I'm goin' to have to see about importing gas from outside of the States now. This fuel crisis is hurtin' my business."

They waved goodbye to Mr. Kenneally and made their way to the M&M Bar with an hour to spare to freshen up.

Claire looked pretty wearing her little dress and white fur jacket. It was electrifying to sing on stage with his little girl and a whole band behind them. That night Claire sang Merle Haggard's "If We Make It Through December" while Bryant played his guitar. They ended the night with Bryant serenading "You Are My Sunshine" to his daughter. Claire was his whole heart. He knew she was special. Even though he was forty-three and his dirty blond hair was attracting silver dustings, he felt like the most handsome man in the world when she gave him her special smile.

2. THE REDHEADED WOMAN

The year Claire turned four years old, the winter was icy. Other than a pit stop in Bozeman, Montana, to get a bite to eat, father and daughter rolled along, content for the landscape to blur together into a haze of browns and greens.

Claire waited in the GMC Jimmy while her father made a call inside the phone booth. Soon, he hung up the telephone and hopped back into the 4x4. He fired up the car, and they headed east. The sound of the wind hitting the car and the tires pin-rolling on the pavement kept them awake, but in time the hum of the drive lulled Claire to sleep.

Hours later, Claire woke to a woman's breathy voice ebbing and flowing through her consciousness. "We will wake them." The voice sounded familiar.

Claire propped herself up off the shag carpet. She was in a dark closet inside a motel.

Her father's taut voice was one she knew well. "Take off your clothes, Janet."

"I haven't seen her since—"

"You can see her after we're done."

The woman's guttural protest went unanswered. Claire peeked through the sliding door to let the incandescent glow of the room spill into the dark closet. Her daddy was with a woman with large hips and a small bust. Her dark hair was red like Claire's, although not as fiery or long. She watched them until something brushed her ankle.

Claire slid the door open another inch to shine more light into the closet and was excited to see a baby next to her. He fixed his eyes on the bow in her hair.

She bundled the baby into her lap. "Hello, my baby dolly." She rocked him and let him suck on her finger. "I'll take care of you." Time passed quickly while she coddled him.

The moment the baby stopped babbling and started crying, the closet door slid wide open. Claire squinted until her eyes adjusted to the bright light.

The redheaded woman bent down to kiss both of them. "Come here, sweetheart." The woman took the baby and let him crawl beside her. "I'm Janet. You've grown up so much since we were last together." Tears welled up in Janet's eyes. She blinked away the wetness.

Claire was afraid of this redheaded woman. Her eye makeup was muddy, her lipstick caked her thin lips, and her hair was matted on one side as if she had lain in glue. The large Steppenwolf shirt draped her body like the excess skin of an obese woman who had lost a lot of weight.

As if reading Claire's mind, Bryant said, "You're a hot mess."

Janet glared at Bryant. "And you're no saint either, making me sleep with you."

"No one forced you."

"No? How else am I supposed to see my daughter? You disappear for months at a time and lure me to a sleazy motel—"

"Hurry up. I don't have all night." Bryant poured himself a shot of whiskey and lit up a cigarette. "You have ten minutes."

Janet sat cross-legged on the floor and lit up a marijuana joint. Bryant slapped her hand before she could take a toke. "It's pot," she screamed, "not heroin."

"Damn it, I don't give a shit. Put that out," Bryant said. "I said no drugs."

"That's not fair—"

"Nine minutes." Bryant turned on the radio. He strummed his guitar and sang Johnny Cash's "Walk the Line."

Janet turned her attention back to Claire and the baby. "That's Mark, your broth—"

Bryant slapped Janet on the head and gave her a crippling look with his steely eyes. Claire thought the woman's posture slumped into a strange curve.

"He's my baby dolly." Claire hugged Mark and kissed him.

"He's my son." Janet's voice quivered. "I also have four others, but they're not babies anymore." She laughed and then rifled through her big polyurethane purse. She flipped open her wallet to show Claire a picture. "This is Michael, my oldest." She pointed to a boy twelve years older than Claire. His hair was russet brown, like the potato, and layered, shaggy short on top and longer on the bottom, touching his collar. He had a self-reflective expression on his face, but his grin made him look goofy. Claire decided he was a mischievous boy. "Lonnie is my second. She's nine years older than you. And these two are Cheryl and Katie."

Lonnie's hair was feathered while Cheryl and Katie wore theirs straight with bangs. The three girls looked alike with their oval faces and brown eyes, but their brother Michael had brownish-green eyes.

"Where are they?" Claire was curious why they were not in the motel room with them. "Are they with their daddy?"

"Well, sweetheart, we are on our way to Missoula."

"You and my baby dolly?" Claire asked.

"Yes. Maybe you can come for a visit and meet them once we're all settled into our new home."

Claire pointed to the other photo in the wallet. She recognized Janet, but who was the baby girl with red hair?

"Do you have other babies for me to play with?"

"No, hon." Janet's eyes brimmed with wetness, and she flickered her lashes to dry them out. "I had a baby daughter. You remind me of her. She was taken—"

Bryant stood. "It's time to go." He snapped up his corduroy field jacket and took Claire by the hand. "Say goodbye, darlin'."

Claire waved to the redheaded woman and kissed her baby dolly on the cheek.

"Bryant, you can't go yet. Please, I need more time." Janet clung to Bryant's leg.

"We have places to go and people to see." Bryant snubbed out his cigarette and shook free of her. He helped Claire put on her coat. "I'll call you the next time we're in town."

Janet sprung to her feet and clutched his wrist with her jagged talons. The desperation on her face scared Claire, who sought protection behind her dad's leg.

Bryant freed himself from Janet's grip and left, exchanging the warmth of the room for the bitter cold of Montana. The soundtrack of Janet's sobbing played over and over in Claire's mind. She felt sorry for the redheaded woman and hoped she'd see baby Mark again.

#

From Billings, they headed south through the Crow Reservation and past the Bighorn National Forest. Along the way, pretty pine trees dotted the landscape, and wildlife, mostly deer or coyotes, lay flat on the side of the road. They spent some time in Cheyenne and Casper, Wyoming, that spring, where Bryant took a job as an auto mechanic. During the day, he worked on cars, and at night he joined a few jam sessions at the local taverns.

Claire only had to smile and sing a little diddy to charm her way into the tavern. If she told a joke, hearts softened, and she'd undoubtedly earn a free dessert or soda.

That was their life, on the road, across state lines, chasing the next big thing. Sometimes they'd stay in town long enough for Bryant to work, but then he'd itch to leave the auto shop. It didn't matter where he worked, every coworker was lazy and every boss was dumb. He could manage the business better than any of them. Unmotivated workers were a dime a dozen in his world.

There was a better job waiting for Bryant in Sioux Falls. They packed up their bags and headed east to South Dakota. At one of the truck stops Bryant saw a shirt that tickled him. It said *Big Cock Country* on it.

"What color should I get?" He held up two thick cotton shirts with long sleeves. "Red or orange?"

Claire pointed to the crew neck shirt with the bird on it.

"Red it is."

The shirt was on sale at half off, and that put springs under Bryant Baker's feet. He was a sucker for cheap deals.

Bryant loved being on the road with Claire. He'd tell outlandish stories that made her eyes pop open in disbelief or tell jokes that would spin her into hysterics. When they were out of stories or jokes, they filled the void by talking to truckers on the CB radio.

"Breaker one-nine for Tumbleweed." Bryant held his breath for a response. "Breaker one-nine. Tumbleweed, are you out there?"

Static crackled over the airwaves for a short period before a gruff, thunderous voice hee-hawed. "Tumbleweed here. Is that you, Cowboy?"

Bryant smiled. "Affirmative. And Sunshine too."

"This is Sunshine. What's your twenty, Mr. Tumbleweed?" Claire sounded so grown-up asking for his location, but her giggles got the best of her.

Tumbleweed choked and coughed. "Hot damn, Cowboy. She sounds young!"

Bryant bellowed with laughter. "Sunshine is my daughter. She was asleep last time."

"What's yer twenty, lil Sunshine?" Tumbleweed recovered from his spell.

"We're going to Daddy's new job, over."

Bryant chimed in. "Crossing the Missouri and heading to Sioux Falls."

"Roger that. Hey, Cowboy. Whatcha get when ya play country music back-asswards?" Tumbleweed left them in suspense for half a second before giving up the punchline. "Ya getcha truck, yer wife, and yer dog back." Tumbleweed wheezed a burst of laughter that sounded like he was huffing and puffing while suppressing a sneeze.

Bryant chuckled. "Did you hear that on Hee Haw?"

"Ten-four. What's the difference between a Mustang and a porcupine?"

"Uh, mustangs have hair," Bryant guffawed.

"Wrong. Porcupines have pricks on the outside." Tumbleweed roared. "Get it?"

A female voice interrupted their cacophony. "Breaker one-nine."

"Go ahead break," Bryant said.

"This is Vixen. Sounds like you boys are having a party."

"Negative," Tumbleweed responded and burst into stitches once more.

"Cowboy, I heard you and Sunshine just crossed the river on your way to Sioux Falls."

"Affirmative."

"I'm an hour ahead of all y'all," Vixen radioed. "Big accident coming your way. Gators all over the road. Smokey Bears everywhere. I suggest you pull in after the next yardstick for a snooze until it all clears up."

Bryant was grateful for the information. "Ten-four."

"Keep the shiny side up. Vixen out."

Claire tugged at Bryant's shirt. "What did she mean?"

"Keep the shiny side up means have a safe trip," Bryant said.

"No, about the accident."

"Gators, or alligators, are what we call rubber tire pieces on the road."

"And bears are the police," Claire stated.

"That's right. So are smokies. And at the next mile marker, we're going to exit and—"

"Get our nightgown on."

"That a girl. Now you're learning trucker talk." Bryant gave his daughter a wink. She caught on fast. He couldn't be more proud.

Tumbleweed interrupted their CB lingo lesson. "Shit, I've got a full-grown bear behind me. Tumbleweed out."

They signed off and wished Tumbleweed luck with the highway patrol. At the next rest area, they brushed their teeth and settled in for the night in the car.

"Daddy, what's in Sioux Falls?"

"Roofing. My new job is going to put a lot of money in our pockets."

"Can we get a dog?"

"Is that what you want this Christmas? How about a Barbie doll instead? You know we can't have a dog right now."

"Will Santa be able to find us?"

"Of course."

"I want my baby dolly. Can we visit that lady?"

The smile on Bryant's face faded. "I don't want to hear another word about that lady—"

"But Daddy—"

"Or about the baby dolly!" It saddened him to think his company was no longer enough, and he wanted Claire to erase any memory of her mother from her mind. "You hear me?"

"Yes, Daddy." The tears rolled down Claire's cheeks. She yanked the blanket over her shoulder and turned her back to him.

Maybe it was time to take root, Bryant thought. Maybe Claire needed stability. She was getting older and before long he'd have to enroll her in school. Maybe there'd be a woman for him in South Dakota, one who'd make a proper wife and be a wonderful mother to Claire.

3. GRANDMA'S HOUSE

Sioux Falls was a pretty town and an old one at that. Incorporated in the 1800s, it was named after both the Sioux Indians and the waterfalls of the Big Sioux River. In the city center, ancient burial mounds of Native American Indians were found at Sherman Park, which made Claire uneasy, but not nearly as perturbed as the enormous bronze statue of the naked man in the downtown area. It stood eighteen feet tall and was donated to the city in 1971, a year before Claire was born, by a millionaire named Thomas Fawick.

"That statue is a replica of *David*, a famous sculpture by the artist Michelangelo," Bryant said matter-of-factly.

"What is David holding?" Claire didn't like the intense glare on the statue's face. He looked mean. Bryant scooped Claire up in his arms for a better look. "It looks like a ball." She tried to read the sign on the base of the sculpture. "For the . . . en . . . joy . . . ment of the . . . kitty . . . zens and . . . stud . . . ents."

"Look at you, Sunshine, trying to read!" Bryant hugged his daughter tight and flagged down a woman walking by. "My Claire can read."

"But what does that mean?" Claire asked.

"It says this piece of art was gifted *for the enjoyment of the citizens and students*. It is here for people to admire."

"That's silly." It made little sense to Claire that people would want to stare at a naked statue in the middle of the city.

Things were going well in Sioux Falls. The roofing job was steady and so were the jam sessions. Bryant met Darlene, a brunette at one of his gigs who followed him around like a groupie. She talked too much, and Bryant's kisses were the only thing to silence her.

She had a mouth on her that made even Bryant blush. Many times Claire saw Darlene drink shot for shot with her father.

One night at Crawford's Bar, an incident occurred that had Bryant fuming. Claire sat in the kitchen eating a grilled cheese sandwich while Bryant wrapped up his gig with the last song of the night. From the kitchen, Claire watched Darlene sway side to side with her eyes closed.

Darlene was a few tequila shots and four Pabst beers into the night. She swiveled back and forth to the sound of Bryant's grizzly voice singing Waylon Jennings's "I'm a Ramblin' Man."

The bartender emptied the ashtray and lit Darlene's last cigarette. She chain-smoked the entire evening. While other women ran to the bathroom sick to their stomachs, Darlene stood flat-footed and continued to drink. She cheered as Bryant finished his set. She hopped off the barstool to kiss him but suddenly crashed to the floor.

Bryant jumped off the stage and charged past the patrons. He hoisted her to her feet. "Dammit, Darlene, get the hell up." He dragged her toward the kitchen.

"Slow down," Darlene pleaded. "You don't need to be huffy about it."

"When I want your opinion," Bryant said, "I'll ask a man for it." He pulled her along. Darlene tripped over her boots. She landed flat on her stomach. Her skirt flew up, giving a peekaboo view of her red underwear. People laughed. A man whistled. And Bryant threw the first punch. The two men exchanged jabs, and the fireworks began. Amber liquid flew and rained down on Darlene's legs. Shards of glass skated across the table and clung to a woman's cleavage. The server fell onto Bryant's guitar and crushed the soundboard. As swiftly as the trouble erupted, it quickly simmered with the sound of sirens crying in the distance.

Bryant grabbed his guitar and Claire's hand then dashed out the back door. "We're leaving Crawford's."

Darlene was close behind, stumbling but staying upright. The three of them climbed into the Jimmy and peeled off. Darlene thundered with laughter.

"You think this is funny?" Bryant elbowed her in the chest.

She howled in pain and slapped him. "Why did you do that?"

"You're an embarrassment. Look at you, drunk as hell."

She punched him in the knee. "Well, you're dumber than a dodo's dung!" Darlene burst into a fit of laughter.

Claire held her breath and clung tightly to the door handle in the back seat. The car swerved hard to the right, and Darlene's head hit the window.

They fought all the way home and by the time Claire put herself to bed, the yelling had been replaced by moaning and a bed creaking.

#

A couple of weeks after the Crawford's incident, Bryant packed their bags. "We're heading west to your grandma's house."

They left without saying goodbye to Darlene. Bryant had had enough of her lip and had worn out his welcome with the roofers. They harassed him whenever he'd show up late to work. Didn't they understand he worked late gigging? He had a child to raise, too, for chrissakes. Those boys could all go fuck themselves, and that was exactly what he told them. They fired him on the spot.

Claire and Bryant didn't get far before they pulled off I-80 and stopped at a Flying J gas station in a small Wyoming town called Evanston. Across the street was a lonely two-story brick building partially enclosed by a chain-link fence. The large empty parking lot and surrounding brown brush and weeds reminded Claire of a scary *Scooby-Doo* episode. She recognized the motel.

"Rut-roh." Claire pointed to the front tire—almost flat. Bryant kicked the tire and cursed his luck.

While he examined the tire and looked for the puncture, Claire pointed out a few other issues with Jimmy. "Daddy, there's a crack in the window." She pointed to the zigzag in the windshield.

"That crack is going to get bigger. Go on, Claire, show me the next flash card. What else?" Claire pointed to the ground at the bright green fluid. "Well, for fuck's sake." Bryant popped the hood. He stormed into the gas station with Claire right behind him. Bryant made a few phone calls to a nearby mechanic. "Looks like we're stuck here."

"Why, Daddy?"

"Everything's closed. The good news is that the leak is not coming from the radiator. Tomorrow I'll replace the hose and patch the tire and we'll be back on the road in no time."

As they exited the store, a semi-truck pulled into the station with loud country music blaring from the radio. A young man with a scruffy mustache and thick sideburns, wearing tight Levi jeans and an orange collared shirt, hopped out. He strutted over to them and pointed to the neon ooze. "Car trouble, *amigos*?"

"My daddy's hose is leaking." Claire volunteered the information to the handsome stranger with a funny accent. He laughed and tipped his hat.

Bryant eyed the stranger up and down. He didn't trust brown people, yellow people, black people, or anyone else unless they were white. The stranger was a smaller man than Bryant; he was confident he could send the brown-skinned man to his grave if he needed to.

"You wouldn't happen to have any cardboard?" Bryant asked. "I need something to catch the green drip from my truck."

"No, amigo, but I bet you can find some in the back. You sure it's not the head gasket?"

The stranger spoke in a sing-song way with inflections and pauses imposed at every third or fourth word. He pronounced each word succinctly, and his sentences were drawn out longer and slower than how most people talked.

Bryant shook his head and wiped the sweat from his brow. "It should be an easy fix. Right now, I just need a drink. And a clean place to spend the night." He turned his back to the stranger as a clue of dismissal.

"If you drive down Bear River Drive and turn right on Front Street, there's the City Bar next to Hotel Evanston. The hotel is very modern if you're looking for upscale lodging and food. They have a coffee shop and barber shop too. And all the rooms have telephones."

"There's a Motel 6 across the street." Claire pointed to the *Scooby-Doo*-esque building.

"Either your daughter can read or you've stayed at a few Motel 6s!" The young man patted Claire on the back.

Bryant stiffened and pulled his daughter close to him. "We'll be fine."

"That's where I'm staying tonight. All the eighteen-wheelers park in the back. It's cheap and clean. Easy to pull in and out. There's a laundry room and a vending machine too."

"What's your handle?" Claire asked. "I'm Sunshine. My daddy is Cowboy. We're going to visit my grandma in California. "

"Jalisco," he answered. "Maybe we can talk on the CB tomorrow when we're all back on the road."

"I don't think so," Bryant said. He was irritated now and curled his fingers into a fist.

"I know how to spell your name," Claire said. "H-O-L-I-S-K-O! What does it mean?"

"Say goodbye, Claire," Bryant said. "We best be on our way."

Jalisco laughed. He knelt on one knee so that he was eye-to-eye with Claire. "You're very close, but Jalisco is a state in Mexico where I am from, and it is spelled J-A-L-I-S-C-O. In Spanish, the J has an H sound."

Bryant grunted and swung open the door of his truck. It creaked, and Bryant thought, *Great, now I need WD-40.*

"Bye, Jalisco," Claire waved at him.

Jalisco stood and removed his hat. "Listen, let me buy you some beers, amigo. There's a group of us who meet up at Motel 6. It makes the truckin' less lonely. I usually play my guitar, the fellows sing, and we pass the time with some booze. Join us."

Claire bounced in her seat with excitement. "Daddy, you can play your guitar."

"What do you say?" Jalisco asked. "We have little, but what we have we share . . . usually hotdogs and corn dogs."

"You fellas have whiskey?" Bryant asked. He was warming up to this stranger, especially since he spoke Bryant's language—music and booze.

Jalisco grinned. "Whiskey, tequila, and if we're lucky, rice wine."

#

At the courtyard pool, three men sat around a table, animatedly sharing stories of their encounters on the road. Each one tried to up the other with machismo adventures. Four boxes of beer rested on the damp cement, and three glass bottles of liquor stood on the round table. Two were amber, and one was clear as water. A young girl around thirteen sat beside the pool with her legs dipped in the blue water, her pants rolled up to her knees.

"Awe, amigos," Jalisco said warmly. He pulled out an extra chair for Bryant and invited him to sit. "*Siéntate.*" He poured whisky into Bryant's cup. "This is Cowboy and his daughter Sunshine."

The other two men smiled and raised their cups. Bryant nodded. Never in a million years did Bryant think he'd find himself around a table with a Mexican, a Vietnamese, and another white man. Weren't all Mexicans illegal border-crossers there to steal jobs from hard-working Americans? And the only good Vietnamese was a dead one. *After all, they are all communists*, Bryant thought.

Jalisco introduced the Vietnamese man as Minh-Tri. He spoke little English, but he made good rice wine and laughed a lot. Minh-Tri never left home without a bottle of rice wine and a photo of his family. He had come to the United States with his wife, two daughters, and son. They were refugees from the Vietnam War.

"I served in the war. Got me a purple heart," Bryant said, stretching the truth a bit. He did serve in the military, just never in combat, and the closest thing to a purple heart was a bruised pec.

The other man was Frank, a Texan who moved to Oklahoma to be with his bride after they fell in love at a football game. His daughter, sitting by the pool, was Deanna Jean, who had just turned thirteen.

If it weren't for the fact that Bryant's truck needed repairs and these strangers had booze and a guitar, he would have been long gone from Evanston, Wyoming, and heading to the San Fernando Valley.

The girl by the pool came to join them. She was lanky, with short dark hair and an athletic build. She picked up Jalisco's guitar and strummed it, then tuned it and hummed an Erma Franklin song, "Piece of My Heart." When Deanna opened her mouth to sing the lyrics, her raspy, mezzo-soprano voice amazed Bryant. It was as if Janis Joplin's spirit rose from the dead and sang through the girl's voice box. Claire scooted closer to the young girl, clearly bewitched by her talent.

"That's my daughter!" Frank beamed with pride. "She may be a tomboy, but there's no mistaking that voice of an angel."

Minh-Tri nodded and scrunched his face as if he had bitten into something sour. He shook his head from side to side and with a thick Vietnamese accent, told them about his two daughters and son. "I have three children. When they sing, oh my god, they so bad! That why I truck driving!"

Frank and Jalisco roared. Bryant had to admit it was funny. Minh-Tri's thick Southern Vietnamese accent added a layer of hilarity to it. To Bryant, it sounded like a scratched vinyl record spinning on a turntable.

When Deanna finished singing, Claire clapped. As the evening wore on, Claire and Bryant learned Deanna's handle was Grasshopper. Her father was a driver for a hotdog company, and his trucker's name was HotLinx. A few times each year, Grasshopper and HotLinx cruised together on brief trips. Bryant liked the idea of another father-daughter team road-tripping around the states. He didn't feel as alone now, knowing they were driving beneath the same blanket of stars and canopy of sky.

Claire tapped Deanna's arm. "Does Santa bring you gifts at Christmas?" While the adults chatted, drank, and harmonized, Claire occupied herself with Grasshopper.

Deanna giggled. "Of course. Doesn't Santa visit you?"

Claire shook her head. She looked at her mismatched shoelaces. "How does Santa find you?"

"My dad and I have a house in Oklahoma. When I'm not in school, I sometimes go with him on his deliveries. It gives my mom a break."

"You're lucky," Claire said. "I wish I had a mommy and a house, but I'm going to go visit my grandma in California."

"Maybe Santa can send your gifts to your grandma's house."

"Oh, I can ask Santa to send that lady to the house and bring my baby dolly."

Hearing Claire talk about Janet and baby Mark again infuriated Bryant. It was best she erased any memory of her mother. He threw an empty beer can at his daughter. "Your mother is a mess. Forget her. And no more talk of your baby dolly. I mean it, Claire. You hear me?"

Claire flinched and leaned into Deanna. "Yes, Daddy."

For the rest of the night, Claire talked about her dream house and the foods she liked until eleven o'clock when her eyelids drooped like heavy sandbags. Bryant lifted her off the ground and carried her to a lawn chair, letting her sleep while he finished his beer.

The next morning a loud pounding at the door jolted Bryant awake. His face was wet. Why the hell was his face wet? His vision came into focus, and Claire's little face was inches from his. He felt the soft exhale from her lips and smelled the sourness of her breath.

Beer cans were scattered around the room. Claire rubbed his shoulder and tapped his face. "Daddy? Wake up." She jumped on the bed, and a soaked washcloth slapped his face.

Claire picked up the drenched cloth, sat on his chest, and wrung the dripping towel over Bryant's eyes. She giggled.

The knocking at the door sounded again, louder this time. "Check-out was at noon!" Bryant looked at the clock—nearly one o'clock.

It took them most of the afternoon to get the car road-worthy, but finally, Cowboy and Sunshine left Evanston and were off to Grandma's house.

#

Claire thought nothing was more fun than singing with her dad on the highway and watching the countryside unfold like a pop-up panorama book. Bryant popped a George Jones eight-track tape cartridge into the dash, and they sang "The Race Is On" as they crossed the California state line.

"Breaker one-nine." Jalisco's Spanish drawl was unmistakable. "Anyone on Sesame Street? Cowboy, you got your ears on?"

"Affirmative. What's your twenty, Jalisco?"

"Heading south on the double-nickel in Texas. Made it to Granny's yet?"

"Going triple digits to make it by supper." Bryant reached over and handed Claire the CB.

"Jalisco, this is Sunshine. What's for dinner tonight?"

"Road pizza's on the menu." Jalisco laughed. "I'm in the mood for something stinky."

"Ten-four. Skunk tonight?" Claire giggled at the thought of roadkill for dinner.

They bantered back and forth until a jolly voice interrupted them. "Break one-nine. Lil Sunshine. Is that you?"

"Hello, Tumbleweed. Come in. What's your twenty?"

"Passing the blue whale on Route Sixty-Six. Cowboy has been awfully quiet. He slithering with you?"

"My daddy is wasted. Just me and my rig passing the yardsticks."

Both Jalisco and Tumbleweed expelled a hearty laugh, but it was Jalisco's high-pitched whirlpool of air whistles from his larynx that had Bryant and Claire cracking ribs. Bryant threw in a couple of snorts too as if to Morse code his appreciation of Claire's sassiness.

"Glad to know you survived last night, amigos. Keep the rubber side down and the bugs off your glass," Jalisco said.

"Tumbleweed," Claire continued, "what's a podiatrist's favorite snack?"

"Ladyfingers?"

"No. Cheet-toes. Get it?" Claire hooted at her joke before Tumbleweed cackled back.

"I've got one," Bryant said. "How do you make a chipmunk yer best friend?"

Tumbleweed paused, then laughed so hard he choked. A couple of violent coughs later, he gave Bryant the answer. "Ya pull yer pants down and let him take yer nuts!"

And so it went for another twenty minutes, exchanging jokes to make the travel less lonely. They signed off just as Tumbleweed was getting pulled over again by a smokey bear.

"Keep the shiny side up and the dirty side down," Claire said.

#

At seven thirty in the evening, they stopped in front of a small one-story stucco home in the Sun Valley neighborhood of Los Angeles. The two-car detached garage sat to the left and slightly behind the house. It was a cookie-cutter home, but what made it charming was the beautiful blue larkspur flowers out front nestled behind lush blades of grass. The lawn was immaculately trimmed and edged, with no weeds or fertilizer burn. It was the nicest house Claire had ever seen, and her four-year-old self was keen to visit.

"Welcome to the San Fernando Valley, darlin'." Bryant checked himself in the mirror and wiped his palms on his trousers. "You're going to love it here." He jumped out of the Jimmy and smoothed out his trousers, then peeled his shirt away from his sweaty skin, fluffing it out to fan dry.

A tiny woman ran out the front door and flapped her arms in the air. She was a teacup at four feet, eleven inches tall, and although wizened in appearance, she exuded the animalistic energy of a jackrabbit. Her shoulder-length hair, straight as the horizon of an endless ocean, was dyed red, but in the evening sun, it looked construction-cone orange. Sharon gave her son a big squeeze and then dropped him like a soiled newspaper.

"Where's my granddaughter?" Grandma Sharon opened the car door and held out her arms. Her eyes were a piercing blue but full of warmth.

Claire leaned into her grandma's arms and folded into her bosom. "Grandma!" She smelled like Cocoa Puffs cereal.

Grandma Sharon's husband, Harold, stood at the stoop with his arms folded over his gorilla chest. "Well, don't just stand there! Let me get a good look at her." He loomed six feet tall and was built oxen-tough with his powerful arms and square jaw. He sasquatched over Grandma Sharon and looked menacing with his scowl.

"Hi, Grandpa." Claire was determined to win him over. "Look at what I can do." She twirled around in her pretty dress and showed him she could dance like a ballerina.

Grandpa Harold's face softened. He swung Claire up with one swift pull of his right arm, and she crashed into his barrel-chested embrace. "Welcome home, baby girl."

Bryant handed his mom a plastic trash bag. "Here's all her stuff."

"When will you be back?" Sharon did not take the bag, so Bryant tossed it on the La-Z-Boy recliner.

"I can't say." Bryant knelt and took hold of Claire's hands. "Claire Anne, you know you're my little sunshine, right?" Claire nodded. "There's something I need to do, and you can't go with me."

A large knot floated up to Claire's throat. Her heartbeat quickened, and her body temperature rose. She sensed something bad was happening. "Why?"

"You're going to stay with Grandma and Grandpa for a bit."

"How long?" Claire's voice quivered. Tears threatened to burst. She tried to be brave.

"Now, now, baby girl. Your daddy doesn't want you to be sad." Grandpa Harold patted her small shoulder and squeezed it. "We're going to have a lot of fun until he returns."

"That's right." Grandma Sharon wiped the tears that somersaulted down Claire's chin. "We have a surprise for you in the backyard."

Bryant hugged Claire and kissed her on the cheek. "Not long." He nodded to Harold and muttered thanks to Sharon.

Claire was confused. "Aren't you staying?" She panicked and shrieked, "Daddy!"

Bryant pulled open the front door and walked out. He looked directly at his truck and didn't look back.

Claire pushed off Grandpa Harold's chest and ran as fast as her little legs could carry. "Don't go! Please!" She felt herculean arms around her, stopping her in her tracks. She hated Grandpa Harold at that moment for holding her back. "Take me with you!"

Claire reached for her daddy, but within two bites of a starving dog, he disappeared. His truck raced down the street, drifted around the bend, and was gone.

4. LEMON TREES AND FIRE ANTS

Harold was an engineer and designed top-secret military aircraft at Lockheed. He'd leave for work before the sun came up and was home by mid-afternoon. "I tell ya, this job is goin' to drain the hops out of my system." He was a hard-working man and complained about his employer all the time. "They work me too much."

"Refuel with this." Sharon handed Harold a cold beer.

How he loved his wife. She was petite, but her size didn't stop her from being a fighter. Despite weathering an abusive marriage with her first husband, Sharon was all kerosene and metal, running on all cylinders with her wit. When it came to housewifery, she had a V8 motor, all roar and feminine power.

Harold loved chatting with his wife. They'd compare notes about their day until, try as he might to stay awake, he'd doze off for a pre-dinner nap. Lockheed worked him to the bone. His body and mind turned to rotten tomatoes after work. Sharon teased he was harder to wake than the San Andreas Fault.

Life was peaceful and predictable. They ate dinner together every night, and sometimes Sharon's daughter, Samantha, came over. Samantha and her husband, Brandon, had two children, but they rarely visited. On most nights after dinner, Harold watched television with his granddaughter while Sharon did the dishes. She'd join them once the kitchen was restored.

Sharon expected cleanliness, and Claire kept her room tidy. Their house had four small bedrooms, two bathrooms, and jalousie windows in each room. Claire's bedroom was decorated in colors of ivy green and white with a built-in bookcase of plywood and pressed wood cabinetry.

Books, photos, and stuffed animals filled the shelves, but Claire gravitated to the plastic box that held her costume jewelry.

Harold put Claire's bedroom together. He chose an emerald-green blanket dressed over a twin mattress. The bronze bedframe had a warm, natural patina finish. The cozy, brightly lit room had a view into the private backyard, where they could see the neighbor's lemon trees. Sometimes the citrus scent wafted through the open window into the room.

In the backyard was the surprise they bought for Claire—a plastic playhouse with a blue entrance door and a bay window in front. On the sides were windows with shutters where Claire sold pretend desserts.

"Would you like to buy a pie, Grandpa?" Claire greeted him. He was a regular and, dare he say, her favorite customer. "Today we have lemon pies."

Harold handed her a nickel. "Just a slice." He patted his stomach. "I have to watch my figure." Harold pretended to take a bite and puckered up. "Just the way I like my pies. Where do you buy your lemons?"

Claire pointed to the neighbor's trees. "Here's another slice, on the house." She handed him an invisible plate. "It's for Grandma."

Harold gulped his beer. "I better take it to her while it's warm and the beer is cold." He went into the house and let his granddaughter play for another hour. Every few minutes he checked on her through the kitchen window. Eventually, sleep claimed Harold, and he surrendered to a light snooze in his recliner.

#

Outside, Claire stomped her feet as tears streaked down her face. She screamed at the top of her lungs in pain. Sharon flew outside faster than a falcon hunting its prey. "What in tarnation?" Seeing the fire ants, Sharon immediately picked Claire up. "Harold, start a bath!"

Claire shook her leg. "It stings!"

Sharon burst into the house so fast, Claire's leg knocked over the empty beer cans on the kitchen table. The red welts on Claire's legs raised like razor cuts.

Sharon kicked Harold's foot. "For chrissakes, wake up, San Andreas! Fetch me a towel and a bag of ice!" Sharon gently put Claire in the tub. "I swear he can sleep through an earthquake."

Claire slapped the ants off her body and Grandma Sharon washed Claire's legs with soap and cold water.

Harold wrapped Claire in a towel and cradled the child tight. The cold compress brought their grandbaby instant relief. Sharon took Claire to her bedroom and sang until Claire fell asleep. All was peaceful again.

#

Aunt Samantha and her children came over one Saturday morning. Claire wasn't sure what to make of her. She was barely taller than Grandma, but the volume that came from her spitfire mouth made Claire think Aunt Samantha was a giant stuck in a little woman's body. She was an opinionated woman who didn't understand the concept of personal space. Claire sat with her cousins and Grandpa Harold to watch *The Pink Panther* cartoon while Grandma and Aunt Samantha gossiped.

"Have you heard from Bryant?" Aunt Samantha popped a piece of bacon in her mouth, then quickly shoved two more strips into her shredder teeth.

Grandma Sharon swallowed the last drop of her beer and crushed the can. "He's called once. He's in love."

Aunt Samantha rolled her eyes. "What does he know about love? He's probably whoring his way from coast to coast."

Grandpa Harold scowled at Aunt Samantha. "Watch what you say in front of the kids."

"Honestly, Ma, what kind of scumbag abandons his kid?" Aunt Samantha stood and disappeared into the kitchen, her voice carrying through the hallway. "I love my brother, but he's got a list of problems ten thousand miles long." She came back with three cold beers.

Grandma Sharon pried open the can and chugged it down like a thirsty desert nomad. "I'm sure he'll be back before we know it."

Aunt Samantha sat down on the floor next to Claire and tsked seeing the pus-filled lesions on her ankles. "Those ants sure got you good, little one."

Claire scratched at the blisters. "They itch."

Grandpa Harold shot out of the recliner and reached for the hydrocortisone. He gently rubbed the ointment on the pustules. The burn subsided.

The credits rolled on the *Pink Panther* episode, and Claire felt compelled to dance. She strutted across the living room and sashayed to the TV to change the channel. Grandpa Harold laughed.

Aunt Samantha frowned. "Don't encourage her. She probably learned that from one of his floozies. A four-year-old shouldn't know how to catwalk like she's a runway model."

Claire climbed onto Grandpa's lap and read the magazine on the TV tray table. "Aug . . . ust. One. Nine. Seven. Five. Redders . . . Dig . . . est. Seventy-five kents."

"Cents," Grandpa Harold corrected.

"What in tarnation?" Grandma Sharon raised her arms and rested her wrists on top of her head. She looked at Claire with eyes of gentle authority akin to *Mary Poppins*. Grandma's stance reminded Claire of an orangutan she once saw at a zoo.

"Sweet Jesus!" Aunt Samantha slapped the shag carpet beneath her. "Did you just read that magazine, little one?" Claire nodded. "She's reading the damn *Reader's Digest*. Good God Almighty."

"What does this say, baby girl?" Grandpa Harold pointed to the book section in the table of contents. "The first word, M and R followed by a period is short for 'mister.'"

Claire took her time sounding out the letters. "Mister. Mic . . . crack . . . en . . . goes to . . . sea."

"That's it. We're celebrating." Grandpa Harold's bear hug crushed Claire's insides, making her wince. "Sharon, heat some Hungry-Man trays." He drooled a wet kiss on Claire's forehead and made her laugh.

Grandma Sharon waltzed into the kitchen and pre-heated the oven. "TV dinners for lunch!" She ceremoniously took six cardboard boxes out of the freezer and lifted the corners of the aluminum foil covering. "I'm getting her tested. Our grandbaby is gifted."

Aunt Samantha lifted Claire off Grandpa Harold's lap and twirled her around. "Listen to your auntie, little one. All that smarts and all that beautiful you've got inside of you won't mean a damn thing if you don't know how to use it." Aunt Samantha shook her index finger. "Ain't no one special like you." She leaned her forehead into Claire's and whispered, "God gave you beauty and brains to do great things, so don't waste his gift."

Every day that summer with Grandma, Grandpa, and Aunt Samantha was filled with *joie de vivre*. In the years ahead, Claire pulled on those memories of Grandma's house to find comfort and an emotional haven.

#

Grandma Sharon had Claire tested, and one month before Claire's fifth birthday, she started kindergarten. Each morning, the two of them walked to school. By the afternoon, Claire's confetti-cannon mouth was ready to burst with stories, and she couldn't wait to spill her guts to Grandma on their walk home.

"I painted today." Claire took her grandma's hand. "Mandy said it was ugly, and she pulled my hair."

"Well, she was probably jealous of your painting." Grandma Sharon looked up and down Lewis Street before crossing it.

"She made me mess up. I was going to give it to Daddy."

"That's nice of you. Did Mandy make you cry?"

"Yes, but Tammy shared with me a Twinkie at lunch, and I wasn't sad anymore. And Mr. George made her say 'sorry.'"

"Well, we can't have Mandy ruining your paintings." Grandma stepped into a drugstore and meandered toward the toy section. "Just what we need." She grabbed a two-pack watercolor set. Each tin contained a palette of twelve colors and a paintbrush. "Why don't you pick out a paint book? We can't have you painting the walls or Grandpa's face now . . . or can we?" The thought of Grandpa's face covered in splotches of pink and purple polka dots amused Claire. She gave Grandma a mischievous grin.

They strolled the last three blocks of their ten-block walk with Claire holding proudly the new *Bugs Bunny Becomes a Star* coloring book. They had a few hours before Grandpa Harold came home, so Grandma got busy in the kitchen.

"Peanut butter and jelly sandwich or tomato soup with shells?" Grandma asked.

"You choose, Grandma."

"All right then, peanut butter and tomato soup sandwich, it is!" Sharon rushed over to give her grandbaby tickles. "After you eat, you can paint."

Grandma Sharon slathered a generous amount of strawberry jam on Claire's peanut butter sandwich and placed the plate in front of Claire.

Eager for a bite, Claire swiped the gooey sandwich off her plate. A glob of jam dribbled down the crust. "Rut-roh," Claire said.

"What in tarna—How did you get paint in your sandwich?" Grandma Sharon teased.

"That's not paint, Grandma! That's strawberry jelly." Claire licked her sandwich to prove it.

"Is that so? Well, we better get you washed up before Grandpa comes home."

While Claire took her bath, the jingle of keys signaled Grandpa Harold was home. She heard the clink when he tossed them on the table. Claire was restless to tell him about Mandy, so she climbed out of the tub. Sharon barely towel-dried her before Claire streaked naked into the kitchen. Grandpa Harold had his back to her and was unloading the groceries into the fridge.

Claire cleverly jumped into one of the empty brown paper bags and hunched down so he couldn't see her. She heard the 'pssst' of a beer can open and popped out of the bag to surprise him. "I'm your playboy bunny!" Grandpa Harold clutched his heart and laughed. "Did I scare you, Grandpa?"

"You sure did, baby girl." Grandpa patted her head. "Now go put your bunny furs on." Harold leaned down and kissed his little wife. "Good thing she doesn't know what a Playboy Bunny is."

Claire ran into her room and quickly dressed before joining them in the living room.

"Yes, but where did she hear that expression?" Sharon asked. "Oh, Samantha's coming over for dinner, dear."

"Again?" Harold plopped down on his favorite recliner. "She going to keep her opinions to herself this time?"

"No, but she's bringing beer and cupcakes."

Harold nodded and turned on the TV.

#

Claire loved playing with her dolls or reading her books in the living room while the adults talked. The white noise of their conversation comforted her knowing they were close by and all she needed to do to see them was lift her head. On one particular evening during the holidays, Aunt Samantha lingered to have a serious conversation with Grandma Sharon.

"Ma, grab some more beers," Aunt Samantha hooted. "Can't celebrate without the Bud. 'Sides, we need to talk."

"If it's about Bryant, no, I haven't heard a thing." Grandma Sharon sat down at the kitchen table. Her feet didn't touch the floor, so she crossed her ankles and swung her legs back and forth.

"He didn't even send her a present?"

Sharon shook her head. "No birthday or Christmas presents."

Samantha received her beer and held it like a crazed animal lover cuddling her cat. She drew a long sip and snuggled the can. "You should sue him for custody. He can't raise her, you know. She's five now. Imagine when she's a teenager. He's a man." Aunt Samantha wasn't holding back that night. "He's a drunk, and he's violent. She's just a little girl."

"You're right, but—"

"There is no 'but.' She's too precious, and he'll ruin her."

Sharon took a big gulp of her beer. "I love that ray of sunshine. Living on the road is not a life for a little girl."

"Exactly. It's not safe, and she needs stability. Plus, she's in school now."

"Hanging out in bars while he gigs . . ." Sharon swallowed the charcoal in her throat.

"Claire needs a safe, loving environment and a normal childhood." Samantha scooted her chair closer to her mother. "I know a lawyer. Doesn't hurt to inquire."

"No, I guess not," Sharon answered.

But it did hurt, and before long, Bryant showed up with his rage in tow.

5. MOTHER'S DAY

It was a warm afternoon with a pleasant breeze coming through the window. Wisps of Claire's hair framed her cheeks and tickled her chin. Life was peaceful, and school was exciting. Claire liked her teachers and made new friends. She read everything she could get her hands on and learned so much.

Grandma Sharon wanted to make plans for summer break. "Maybe we can go camping after you get out of kindergarten and we can see the redwoods." She peeled the last of the potatoes and plopped them into the pot of water before turning her attention to the hard-boiled eggs. "What do you think, Harold?"

Grandpa Harold stopped whistling his tune long enough to answer. "Do you think it's wise to make plans?"

"There's no reason we won't get custody. It's been nearly a year since he dropped her off and disappeared. He's abandoned her."

Grandpa Harold put down his newspaper. "I don't want you to get your hopes up."

A knock sounded at the door, but before Harold could get up, the door flung open.

"Hello!" It was Aunt Samantha and her kids. "I brought watermelon and beers!" They tumbled in and dispersed in different directions. "Happy Mother's Day." Aunt Samantha gave Grandma Sharon a peck on the cheek. "Claire, what are you reading?"

"*Mister Brown Can Moo! Can You?*" Claire answered. "It's another Doctor Seuss book." She flipped the book around so Aunt Samantha could see the pictures.

"Oh, the wonderful things Mr. Brown can do!" Aunt Samantha mooed like a cow.

Grandpa Harold joined in and buzzed like a bee while Grandma Sharon eeked and hooed. Before long, the kids joined, competing to be heard; they popped, slurped, sizzled, and cock-a-doodle-dooed. Grandma Sharon stood on the chair and raised her arms. She thundered and stomped her feet, then clucked like a chicken. They all fell about in hysterics.

Aunt Samantha ruffled Claire's hair. "You sure are a voracious reader!"

Suddenly the discord of screeching tires brought everyone's laughter to a halt. Aunt Samantha inhaled with a gasp and held her breath, her eyes wide open in alarm. "What was that?"

Grandma Sharon clutched her chest, mouth agape. Grandpa Harold raised one inquisitive eyebrow and bolted toward the living room. The front door slammed open. Heavy, fast footsteps charged into the kitchen.

"Where is she?" Bryant's angry voice bellowed. He snarled and clenched his fists. He strode past Harold and called out for Claire.

"Son—" Grandma Sharon stepped in front of Bryant and put her palm to his chest. The man standing in her kitchen was barely recognizable, drenched in sweat and disheveled like a beggar who hadn't showered, shaved, or eaten in days.

"She's mine! You can't have her!" Spit spewed from the corners of his mouth. He glared down at his diminutive mother.

"You're not fit to be a father." Aunt Samantha's voice rose to match Bryant's. "Look at you! You're a mess and a drunk. You can't even keep a job. What kind of father are you, chasing after every skirt in town—"

"Shut up!" Bryant jerked his head and slammed his hand onto the table. He curled his hand around the back of the chair to brace himself from shaking, then he kicked the chair and sent it sliding across the room.

Aunt Samantha stepped back and tripped on Grandpa Harold's foot. She would have fallen had it not been for Grandpa Harold's brawny arms steadying her.

"Son, please," Grandma Sharon begged, "you don't have to do this."

"Did you think you could get away with this? No one gets custody of her but me."

Claire was surprised to see her father inside the house. Her heart leaped to her throat and fluttered down to her stomach. "Daddy?"

"Go get your things," Bryant barked. "We're leaving!"

Claire blinked a few times, thinking he was a ghost. When she realized he was truly there, she grinned and jumped into his arms.

"Do as you're told." By the gritty tone in his voice, Claire knew her father meant business, but she was torn.

"But, Daddy—" She didn't want to leave Grandma and Grandpa, but she knew better than to defy him. Claire went dutifully into her room, her two cousins dragging their feet behind her. They helped her shove clothes and books into a backpack and pillowcase. There was a lot of yelling going on in the kitchen, but the children did their best to ignore the noise. They moved slowly, each child picking a stuffed animal or a toy off the floor to put into the bags.

By the time Claire reappeared in the kitchen, her father was pacing back and forth, swearing through gritted teeth. He grabbed Claire's hand and tugged hard. She winced and yanked it away. Claire stood, defiant and immobilized. She was happy to see her dad but wanted to stay. She was looking forward to a summer adventure in the redwoods, and she wanted to finish kindergarten at her school. She had friends who would miss her. She couldn't stop thinking about her little plastic house and the lemon trees in the backyard. Who would make Grandpa lemon pies? Who would read to Grandma?

Bryant scooped Claire up around the waist and carried her sideways. He did it with such swift force, Claire screamed in pain. His powerful forearms dug into her ribs.

Grandma Sharon, Grandpa Harold, and Aunt Samantha wailed in protest, but Bryant brushed past the pack of ululating fools. He drowned out their yowls by gruffly exhaling quick breaths as he stormed outside.

"Grandma!" Claire kicked and reached out. She squirmed and tried to free herself, but her efforts were useless.

Grandma Sharon chased after them, but Grandpa Harold pulled her back. "There is nothing we can do. He is her father."

Aunt Samantha jumped into the driver's seat of Bryant's car and refused to move. "You're not taking her. Dammit, Bryant, she's better off here."

Bryant tossed Claire into the backseat. "Don't move and be quiet." With both of his hands now free, he wrenched the driver's side door open and pulled Aunt Samantha roughly by the arm. He dragged her out of the car and quickly locked the doors. In the scuffle, the horn blared, and a neighbor came out to watch the commotion.

"Daddy, stop! Don't hurt Aunt Samantha." Claire's cries fell on deaf ears.

The car roared to life, and Bryant slammed on the gas pedal. Father and daughter pulled away from the curb and barreled down the street.

Aunt Samantha cursed and threw her shoe at the car. Grandma Sharon buried her face into Grandpa Harold's chest and cried. Claire wouldn't see them again for thirteen years.

#

For a short while, after they left California, Bryant and Claire lived in Rochester, Minnesota, where Claire finished kindergarten. Soon, Bryant's spirit outgrew that place. He drank too much and he knew it. He was turning into his old man, a drunk who beat his family, only Bryant swore he'd never beat his wife and kids. He remembered the violence of his deadbeat dad whipping his four-foot, eleven-inch mother viciously with a tree branch and then turning his rage onto Bryant.

He swore he'd never do that to his family and set off to prove it by finding himself a wife. Back to Billings, Montana, he and Claire went. There, in a small bar, a brunette named Gisela stumbled in.

Gisela had been married previously to an abusive alcoholic and was recently divorced when she and Bryant met. They were quite the egocentric pair, him being a textbook narcissist and Gisela a catalog psychopath. At five foot, nine inches tall, she was built like a semi-truck. Everything was big on that woman, from her bones to her boobs and her nose to her hips. She came complete—a turnkey wife, ready to bake, with her pots and pans, a set of young sons named Benjamin and Barry, some mighty fine crooked teeth, and broad shoulders worthy of the circus. There was nothing feminine about her. She didn't even apply makeup right, lining the foundation around the perimeter of her face like it was applied at mime school. Bryant married her anyway. He needed a woman to warm his bed and raise his child. He guessed he was a little old-fashioned that way. And now, Claire had two new brothers to play with. Benjamin was ten months younger than her and Barry was a couple of years younger.

#

To Gisela, Claire was nothing more than Bryant's redheaded bitch. She was a constant reminder that there had been another woman in Bryant's life. Every other weekend, Benjamin and Barry visited their paternal grandparents while Claire stayed home with Gisela. The boys often came home with presents, and it made Gisela happy that her boys enjoyed time with their grandparents doing fun things like going to the movies. Claire often got upset, complaining about how unfair life was. Several times, Gisela caught Claire playing with her sons' toys. To punish the child, Gisela sent Claire to her room and forbade her to come out until it was time to help with dinner.

That Christmas, Claire received gifts from her grandparents and Aunt Samantha, but Gisela sent them back. "They didn't send any gifts for Benjamin or Barry." Gisela fumed. "I'm returning them!"

Bryant didn't stop her. He adjudicated all domestic responsibilities to her, and she reveled in the authority. Claire quickly became Gisela's stagnant scum, loitering around being useless with her nose in books all the time.

They didn't stay in Billings for long. Bryant came home late one night and franticly packed up the car. "We have to leave. I got in another bar fight, but this time—"

"Leave?" Gisela screamed. "Now? We can't leave. Where are we gonna go?"

"Listen, I beat up this guy real bad . . . a cop . . . and put him in the hospital."

"What the hell?"

"Look, I was arrested, but instead of taking me to jail they took me to the hospital—"

Gisela wanted him to slow down and stop throwing clothes in a bag. She grabbed his wrist. "Did you have another heart spell?"

"If they catch me, I'll be sent to prison." Bryant darted up the stairs and turned on the bedroom light. He nudged Claire to wake. "Pack your things. Hurry. I don't have time to explain."

Bryant loaded up the car as Gisela begged him to stay. As much as she hated his temper flareups, his drunken stupor, his wild fantasies of threesomes, and his despicable daughter, she loved how kind, charming, and tender he could be when he was sober. Gisela had been married before. She didn't want to be alone, didn't want another failed marriage, and she needed a man to take care of her and her sons as much as Bryant needed a woman to warm his bed and mother his child.

"Bryant," Gisela pleaded, "the boys are asleep. I can't get them ready at a drop—"

"Claire and I are leaving. I'll send for you and the boys."

"When?" Gisela asked. "Where are you going?"

Claire shuffled down the stairs dragging a trash bag of her belongings and a backpack of books strapped to her back. The thump thump of the bags on the steps made Gisela want to push the child down the stairs to hurry her along.

Bryant ushered his daughter into the car and slammed the door. He gave Gisela a rough peck on the cheek and peeled away from the house. They took off like marked fugitives with bounties on their heads, leaving Gisela standing in the driveway crying.

A few weeks later, Gisela, Benjamin, and Barry joined them in a suburb of Phoenix, Arizona.

#

The Bakers were the poorest family in the school district. They lived off of processed government cheese and canned Vienna sausages, so pasty and high in preservatives, additives, and saturated fats, they were hard to swallow. The worst was canned potted meats. The slimy paste was nothing more than granulated, mechanically separated mystery meat. It was less repulsive on saltine crackers, but the sodium content always left Claire bloated and parched. They never had fresh vegetables, only canned stuff, and if there was fresh fruit, Claire had to be quick to claim her share. Tuna casseroles and Jell-O salads were staples in their household, but Claire didn't mind those as much.

More traumatizing than dinner was bath days.

"Claire, get in the tub now!" Gisela tugged off Claire's clothes and hoisted her into the scalding water.

Claire shrieked in pain and clawed like an angry cat to get out. "It's too hot!" She scratched Gisela's neck, which enraged her stepmother.

"Well, I can't have Barry taking a cold bath, can I? So deal with it!" Gisela forced Claire to sit in the scorching water. Claire hollered in pain. The hot water scorched her privates and seeped inside, burning her sensitive areas. Salty tears gushed out of Claire's eyes as if she had gremlins shooting a water hose behind her pupils. She wailed and attempted to stand.

Gisela pinned Claire down. They had to conserve the hot water to bathe all three of the kids. One bath to save on water, heat, and soap. By the time the youngest one took a bath, the water had to still be warm. Gisela did everything she could to scrub Claire's body and detangle her long locks, but it was like fighting an octopus. The harder Claire fought, the more force Gisela exerted to manhandle her.

Gisela jerked Claire out of the tub. "Do you know how exhausting it is to deal with your hair? Why, I ought to cut it off."

Tiny blisters bubbled over Claire's body, and a bruise appeared on her arm. Claire cried from the painful second-degree burn she endured. "I'm going to tell Daddy."

"You threatening me? If you say anything to him, I'll beat the shit out of you." In the days following each bath, Gisela forced Claire to wear pants and shirts to hide the bruises and burns.

Claire knew better than to complain, no matter how hot she was or how painfully raw her skin felt when the fibers rubbed against it. Her new mom frightened her. She suffered her terror in silence and tried to move as little as possible, which made Gisela furious. "Act normal, will ya? You act like it's so bad."

#

Gisela hated her stepdaughter and what she represented. Each time Claire complained, Gisela's body stiffened, and she imagined her heart and bones calcifying, her organs and mind hardening, and just when she thought she couldn't loathe this child any more than she already did, the brat raised Gisela's internal temperature to the point of spontaneous combustion.

Gisela had it in her mind to teach this ungrateful heathen to mind her manners and respect her elders. Claire spent a lot of time locked in closets. Whenever her father was out drinking and fraternizing, Gisela kept Claire in the dark until they heard the car door slam shut in the driveway.

Gisela hated being home with the kids, especially on the days when her period gave her bad cramps. Every month it seemed worse than the last. It was easier to let the children fend for themselves, and it was a reprieve for Gisela to not interact with her snotty, devil-haired stepchild.

By the time Claire was in second grade, Gisela gave Claire the role of caregiver, cook, maid, and babysitter. Gisela knew she had a distinct set of rules for Claire that were different than her sons. But if Claire was always getting beaten with a belt or grounded for the tiniest of infractions, it was because the girl deserved it, acting like she was smarter than everyone else, using big vocabulary words, and buttering Bryant up with her singing. Claire's sugary and melodramatic performances had Gisela checking her teeth to see if they were still there.

6. THE PROBLEMS WITH GISELA

There were no jobs for Bryant in Arizona, so once again, he packed up his family and moved back to Minnesota, where he was familiar with the people and landscape. This time, however, he returned to Minnesota with an extra bundle in the backseat. Gisela and Bryant welcomed baby Tanya to the Baker clan, born eight pounds, ten ounces, with eyes black like watermelon seeds.

The family was still poor, surviving on welfare, food stamps, and food banks. Bryant and Gisela found a dilapidated two-story house in Rochester that should have been condemned. The attic was unfinished and unbearably hot. There was little insulation. The slightly rotted beams and thin, damp plywood were playgrounds for spiders and mice. Their fate was often extinguished with steel-toed boots. It was the perfect home for Bryant though. The kids' bedrooms were upstairs while his and Janet's were downstairs. Being downstairs afforded him the privacy and luxury of coming and going with no disturbance. He had been obsessed lately with having a threesome and couldn't wait to invite another woman into his bed. It would be exciting to take his sexual relationship with his wife to the next level. Bryant loved his wife, and although she would never win first prize in a beauty pageant, Gisela was domesticated enough to fulfill his urges, keep Claire clothed and fed, and not ask questions when he came home late at night.

Shortly after they moved in, Claire had a birthday. It had been a while since they celebrated anything good, and Bryant had a good feeling things would change for the better back in his hometown of Rochester. On his way home, he picked up a pie to surprise his family.

\#

The front door slammed, and Claire flinched. She braced herself to receive whichever version of Dad was home. It was a crapshoot between the good, the bad, and the ugly depending on how much he'd had to drink.

"Set the table." Gisela opened the cupboards and pointed to the plates. "Break 'em, and I'll give you the belt." Claire obeyed and stepped onto the stool to reach the shelves. She diligently grabbed the plates two at a time, careful to keep her balance. "Set the table for five. Looks like your dad is joining us tonight."

In walked her dad with a six-pack of beer in one hand and a key lime pie in the other. "A little birdie told me someone's turning six today. I wonder who it is?"

The good version of Dad was there and not the bad or the ugly. Claire let out a sigh of relief. Bryant handed Claire the pie and kissed her on the head. "Turn up the radio."

Claire walked to the coffee table and tuned into KTCR in time to hear Smiling St. Pete announce the weather. "Fifty degrees right now with clear skies and about a twenty percent chance of precipitation later tonight. It's twenty-six minutes before eight o'clock. Congratulations to Leland Harris from Brooklyn Park who just won a Waylon Jennings I've Always Been Crazy album. Now, here's Kenny Rogers's latest hit, Daytime Friends."

She ran to collect her brothers for dinner, singing the chorus as she bounded up the stairs. She loved the lyrics about love and secret hideaways. It made her think of *The Secret Garden*, the book she had finished the day before. The book was too advanced for her, but she liked the cover, and her daddy had bought it for her at a yard sale. She would have to read it again.

She peeked into her room first to see if baby Tanya was still asleep in the crib. She was. Benjamin was in his room, sitting on his younger brother, forcing Barry to eat a booger. Poor Barry twisted his head from side to side with a ghastly expression on his face. Tears streamed down his face, but he didn't make a peep, too afraid of his big brother to complain.

Claire lunged forward and punched Benjamin in the arm. "Stop that."

"Make me," was all he said before he smeared the snot on Barry's forehead and leaped up to run downstairs.

Claire helped her little brother up and wiped away his tears. He lifted a corner of his shirt and rubbed the sticky mucus off his face. Together they headed into the kitchen, where Benjamin was already stuffing his face with Gisela's lasagna. The woman loved to bake but was a terrible cook.

"She hit me," Benjamin said, "and tripped me upstairs."

"I did not!" Claire defended herself.

"And she called me a swear word," Benjamin accused.

Claire was terrified to think that Gisela believed him and would lock her in the closet or give her the belt. It was a good thing her dad was home.

Gisela never abused Claire in front of Bryant. He was clueless, especially since she was forced to wear pants and long sleeve shirts to hide the marks.

"Well, maybe you deserved it." Bryant defended his daughter. "Did you provoke it?"

Gisela put the lasagna down emphatically and stared Claire squarely in the eyes. "I will not have any swearing in this house." How Judas of her to say when she and Bryant swore incessantly. "See those dishes?" Gisela pointed to the sink piled high with plates, pans, and bowls. "And those pots and pans? You're in charge of washing all of them from now on."

Benjamin laughed. "That's what you get."

"After dinner, every night, it'll be your responsibility to wash everything." Claire protested, but Gisela shot her a warning look. "Bryant, you have any problems with that?"

"If it helps you, then I don't see why not." Bryant chewed on his drippy, greasy dinner. It was mostly tomato sauce with a little cheese and low-grade sixty percent lean ground beef, but he didn't mind. That was what the beer was for—to wash it all down. "Tell me about school."

Claire was stunned that her father didn't stand up for her and push back on his wife. *It's ridiculous,* Claire thought, *that I have to wash all the mess that Gisela made.*

"Fine," Benjamin offered. "Mrs. Dowinger is nice."

"What about you, Claire? How are you settling in?"

Claire stabbed her not-so-meaty lasagna and forced herself to take a bite. "Some kids make fun of my glasses and call me names."

"Freckle-Faker Baker!" Benjamin yelled. "Glasses Molasses!" Her stupid brother laughed so hard he choked on his food and a piece of lasagna cannoned out of his mouth onto Claire's plate.

She flicked the chunk off her plate onto the table, disgusted by how gross boys could be. "One girl says I'm slow, and there's this boy who said I carried more bones on me than the cemetery." The tears threatened to roll in. "Why do we have to be so poor?" Her face burned and her eyes stung.

"Enough," Bryant said. "I work hard for this family. If you can't be grateful, there's the door."

They finished their dinner in silence. Bryant headed to the tavern right after a rushed birthday song and dessert. It took Claire an hour to hand-wash the mess Gisela left in the kitchen. By ten o'clock, Claire was tired and ready for bed.

"Where do you think you're going?" Gisela's grating voice sliced through Claire like a pack of razor blades carving through the tender flesh under her fingernails. "These dishes aren't clean." Gisela hurled a plastic cup at Claire's head. "Get back in there and rewash them!" She screamed and went ballistic, pulling out every pot, pan, serving dish, utensil, and kitchen accessory she could find in the drawers and cupboards. "You don't stop until every fucking dish is perfect with no spots or food on it!" Gisela dragged Claire to the sink and shoved the soggy sponge into her small hand. Gisela towered over Claire and continued belittling her. She inspected the dishes and made Claire clean them again and again until every speck of grease, every charred mark, every soggy crumb was nonexistent. "I'm going to bed. They better be spotless come morning, and if they ain't, you're getting a whippin' of a lifetime."

It was eighteen minutes past three when Claire slumped to the floor, exhausted and defeated, but confident that every speck was gone. The tear tracks on her face were long dried and flaked off by the time she tucked herself in.

Claire loathed doing the dishes from that day forth and swore she would have a dozen dishwashers one day when she was big enough to own a house and buy every appliance available.

#

Gisela got a job as a line cook at the Country Kitchen. For a while, her temper tapered off. Working gave her time away from her husband and the kids, as well as pocket money of her own. It gave her purpose and some independence. She even felt confident she could be the wife and mother her family deserved.

Before long, Gisela insisted Claire call her "Mom" because they were a family, after all. If Claire argued, acted up, didn't comply, or refused to call Gisela "Mom", Bryant punished her by making Claire stand in a corner with her arms outstretched twelve inches from the wall. He'd sit on the couch and watch Claire so she couldn't put her arms down. Every fifteen minutes he'd measure the distance from the wall to Claire's fingertips, and if it wasn't exactly a foot of space, he'd whip her with a belt.

Most of the time, Claire stayed clear of Gisela by listening to music or reading a book in her room. Sometimes she'd ask Gisela for permission to ride her bike around the block. Gisela always said yes and made it clear, "I don't need some other bitch's brat around."

#

One day, Claire went down the street to her friend Sara's house and stopped in for a bit. Her bike was in the front yard, just four houses down, but when she got home, Gisela laid into her about lying and riding her bike around the block. A week later, Benjamin did the same thing, but Gisela sighed and said, "Next time, you just need to tell me you're going to Johnny's."

Claire was small, fast, and nimble. Most of the time, she could outrun Gisela and catch the tail end of the belt instead of the entire length of it. For every couple of thrusts of the belt, one would make contact with her flesh. Sometimes, though, Claire was not so lucky and found herself locked in the closet until her dad got home.

The small, dark closet scared her. She imagined evil spirits and monsters lurking in the walls, their scaly claws ready to pull her into the depths of the foundation and pull her into the belly of the beast. She didn't want to spend an eternity in darkness in a monster's stomach. How would she escape? What would she do? How long would she be there? How would her daddy find her?

When she shifted her weight, the clothes brushed against her head, and Claire would frantically push them away like the cobwebs in the attic. The heat and blackness of the musty closet made her hyperventilate. Panic-stricken, Claire cried and screamed, kicked and clawed, until she passed out in defeat from exhaustion. Hours later, she'd feel the prick of fingernails digging into her arm as her stepmother yanked her off the floor and into the brightly lit room seconds before her father stepped into the house.

As much as Claire hated her stepmom, she sometimes felt sorry for her. One night, a loud thump woke Claire up. The bedroom door rattled. The sound of shattered glass frightened her. For a moment, she thought a stranger had broken into the house until she heard Gisela's cry. "Please, I'll quit my job and stay home. Stop! I'm sorry!"

"If I ever catch you flirting with the cook again, so help me God, Gisela, you'll be tasting blood for months," Bryant screamed.

"I wasn't flirting!" Gisela wailed.

"Bullshit!"

Claire tiptoed downstairs. The couch and coffee table were tipped over. Benjamin and Barry crept down the stairs behind her. The boys had been in their room playing under the blanket with a flashlight.

Gisela, crouched in a corner, was trapped between two walls with her husband standing before her, wielding a belt and whipping her with the buckle. The children were horrified. The baby cried. It was pandemonium. Claire ushered her brothers upstairs. She scooped Tanya in her arms and sang to drown out the noise.

Gisela's piercing screams permeated the walls and frightened the children. They huddled close to one another and tried to be brave. When Claire saw the mist in her brothers' eyes, she sang louder to comfort them.

#

That next day, after Bryant took off to heaven only knew where, Gisela packed a small suitcase. She wavered whether to take Claire with her. If she left Claire at home by herself, no doubt it would infuriate her husband. Gisela wasn't down to dealing with his wrath after the beating she had the previous night. What did it matter if she never saw Bryant and his wretched redhead again? She could leave Claire at home to fend for herself. Claire was six and used to being home alone. Nothing bad had ever happened before.

Why am I conflicted? Gisela wondered. *It might be days before Bryant comes home. Hell, he might be so drunk he wouldn't even notice we were gone.* In the end, her conscience got the better of her, and she pulled Claire's hand. "Let's go before I change my mind."

With the children in tow, they boarded the bus and rode across town to a women's shelter. The shelter was crowded and smelled of vanilla, hot chocolate, and body odor. The swirl of aromas made Claire dizzy. Gisela checked them in. After a quick tour and agreeing to the rules, they settled into their small room and waited for lunch to be served.

After a satisfying meal of rotisserie chicken and Caesar salad, the kids ran to the activity room to play while Gisela headed back to the room. She took one look at the lumpy mattress and flung herself onto the bed, exhausted, weathered, and beaten. She curled with her back against the wall and cried herself to sleep.

#

Claire woke to the sound of sirens. She peered outside the window to see two police officers in the parking lot. They headed into the shelter. A few minutes later, heavy footsteps approached their room and a loud knock rapped at the door.

Gisela opened the door. Two cops stood before her. The taller one had his right hand resting on his gun.

"We are here to escort Claire Baker home. As you are not the legal guardian of this minor, we could charge you with kidnapping."

"Take her," Gisela said. "She's nothing but a burden anyway."

Claire hugged her brothers and kissed baby Tanya, unsure when she'd see them again. She took hold of the officer's hand and quickly left the building.

The ride home in the backseat of the police vehicle felt strange to Claire, but when they got to her neighborhood, Claire sank deeper into the seat to avoid the stares. She recognized some kids and felt embarrassed. Her dry eyes burned, and her cheeks felt warm. The last thing she wanted was to return to school and hear the rumors of her being arrested and getting paraded through the neighborhood like a felon.

Claire saw her father standing in the doorframe as they pulled alongside the curb. He looked haggard and old to her, with his greasy hair and discolored shirt.

Bryant greeted his daughter at the door. "You're mine. She can't have you and has no right, you hear?" He spent the next week at home drunk on cheap whiskey.

A week later, Gisela came home with Tanya and the boys. The abuse got worse.

7. THERE ARE RAINBOWS

It was bath night again. Claire dreaded it and convinced Gisela to let Benjamin and Barry go first so they could enjoy the warm, clean water. She'd happily go last and sit in the cold, dirty gray water. Surprisingly, Gisela agreed, and when it was Claire's turn to get into the tub, she slowly stepped in, letting the cold, murky water rush between her toes and creep up her calves.

"I don't have all day," Gisela muttered under her breath. "Get in already." Gisela swiftly hoisted Claire up and dunked her in the tub, bottom first and legs in the air.

The sudden lift off her feet startled Claire, and when her butt was immersed in the tub, the cold water sent icy prickles up her spine and shockwaves throughout her body, like thousands of teeth marks chomping at her skin, eating her alive. "It's cold!" Claire flopped her arms, splashing water on Gisela's face and getting the linoleum floor wet.

"Whose idea was it to go last?" With one sturdy hand pinning Claire down and the other hand scooping a pitcher of bathwater, Gisela poured water over Claire's head and face. She yelped, snorted, and coughed as water rushed into her nose. The soapy water drenched her long hair. Claire couldn't see. Her thick locks clung to her face. She sputtered and tried to detangle the strands from her eyes.

Gisela scrubbed furiously, lifting Claire's arms to wash her armpits. She lifted Claire's chin to scrub her neck, and after a thorough wipe down, brushed her hair.

"Ouch!" Claire yelled. "You're hurting me."

"That's it." Gisela sighed with exasperation. "I'm tired of brushing your hair. We're cutting it." She threw the hairbrush on the floor.

"No!"

"Don't you backtalk to me!"

"Daddy likes my hair long." Claire picked up the hairbrush and ran it through her wet hair. The teeth caught on her knots and tangles. She winced in pain but continued slowly and deliberately, which made Gisela livid and impatient.

Gisela ripped the brush from Claire's hand and flung it to the floor. Clumps of hair tore from Claire's head and wrapped themselves around the bristles. Claire screamed in agony. Gisela sprung to her feet and grabbed the scissors from the drawer. "Sit still."

Claire lurched forward to escape, still naked from her bath, but Gisela was as wide as the door and blocked her exit. Arms flailing, head whipping side to side, Claire tried desperately to get away from her monstrous stepmother. "No! Don't cut my hair!" Claire's little heart beat faster. A lump formed in her throat. It was hard to breathe, hard to swallow. Rough, calloused hands clamped onto her arm as Gisela forcibly pinned her down. Claire saw the sharp scissors coming at her, and she wiggled and shimmied, squirmed, and crawled, anything to escape, but it was no use.

After that ordeal, Gisela retired to her room and left Claire in the bathroom, distraught, bawling at the top of her lungs. Claire looked at all the red strands on the floor. Some of her hair was clustered together in small clumps, some lay flat in varying lengths around her feet. She didn't recognize the pale girl in the mirror with her jagged short hair and sad, flushed face. *I hate you!* She silently screamed to herself and repeated it over and over in her mind. No one heard her pain.

Claire was afraid her dad would think she was ugly. He had told her on several occasions how he loved her red hair. If she no longer had that, what would there be left to love? She was sure he'd take one look at her and no longer see his sunshine. No doubt the kids at school would bully her more than they already did. She couldn't win. Not only was she the poor, skinny kid at school, but now she was the ugly kid too.

#

Claire, Benjamin, and Barry didn't see Gisela for days. It was that time of the month. Gisela stayed in her room the entire time, only getting up to use the bathroom. The kids were on their own to care for themselves. Bryant was on one of his binge-drinking benders. Claire knew the routine. Her dad drank for days, sometimes a week or two, and then sobered up for a few weeks before lapsing again. Sometimes she'd find him passed out in his car, keys in the ignition, the engine still running in the driveway, door open, with one foot out. On several occasions, Claire had to hit her dad so hard to wake him up that she swore she broke her hand. He was twice her size, and it was embarrassing when the neighbors stared as if the Bakers were their nightly gossip and entertainment show. No one ever interfered. Bryant had a reputation for being a violent drunk in the neighborhood, and if they reported the abuse, they'd have a reckoning on their hands.

In time, Claire learned how to cook simple meals for her brothers and herself. Spaghetti and meat sauce one week, macaroni and cheese the following week. At times like these, she missed her grandparents the most. What she wouldn't give to be sitting in the kitchen with Grandma Sharon, eating tomato soup with pasta shells or peanut butter and a homemade jam sandwich. Claire ached to feel Grandpa Harold's strong arms carrying her to bed and tucking her in. She missed her bedroom with the built-in bookcase, the stuffed animals she had left behind, and the comfy green blanket that shielded her from monsters. She wondered why they didn't come for her, didn't call, visit, or write. What were they doing? Claire imagined Aunt Samantha and Grandma Sharon drinking beers and talking in the kitchen while Grandpa Harold snoozed in his recliner.

She whispered a secret wish to Santa. "For Christmas, I want my grandma and grandpa and Aunt Samantha and my cousins. Please, Santa. That's all I want."

#

Sure as flies on garbage, the kids at school teased Claire for her "fifty-cent flea market" haircut. On top of that, her eyesight deteriorated, and Bryant allowed the school to give his daughter thick, plastic, gray reading glasses to wear so she could see the chalkboard. She was the skinniest, palest, smallest kid at school with a copper mullet and welfare glasses. The teachers loved Claire, however, for her politeness, intelligence, and advanced mastery of the English vocabulary. She carried a dictionary in her book bag because her dad always told her if she didn't understand a word, to learn it.

The school was Claire's sanctuary. Despite the teasing and lack of friends, the large brick building gave her purpose, whereas home gave her welts and boils.

One day, Mrs. Letterly pulled Claire out of math class with no explanation and escorted her to the nurse's office. Perhaps Mrs. Letterly knew about the persistent, throbbing pain inside her ear, which intensified with every step. Claire could only hope. Her ear had been giving her issues lately. Pain shot in her canal and pus lingered in the cavity of her eardrums. She suffered from ear infections because her Eustachian tubes were too small. The tubes were often blocked and swollen, causing fluids to build up with nowhere to drain. Germs festered, and without medical insurance or money for treatment, she dealt with the sting and discomfort, often screaming with tears of frustration.

As she walked a half step behind Mrs. Letterly, looking down at her old Mary Jane shoes that were scuffed and too small for her growing feet, a sense of doom embodied her. The clouds outside had somehow moved indoors and shrouded her in their gray sadness, dampening her mood.

They rounded the corner, and there was her dad, dressed in cowboy boots and a bright lime green polyester suit contrasted with a cherry red shirt. The huge block letters sprawled across his chest read "Big Cock Country." A belt with a gaudy buckle the size of a baby's head gave the finishing touch. His appearance mortified Claire, and she shrunk behind Mrs. Letterly's skirt.

"Sunshine, you've got a doctor's appointment," Bryant said.

Claire exhaled and stood tall, relieved to know she wasn't in trouble. She took her father's hand, and together they exited the school. "How did you know my ears hurt, Daddy?"

"They do?" Bryant squeezed his daughter's small hand. "I bet a daddy-daughter lunch date would make you feel better." Claire's eyes lit up, and she skipped to the truck to escape the raindrops. "Have you forgotten? Today's your birthday. How does it feel to be seven?"

"The same, I guess." Claire rubbed her ears. They still hurt, but she dismissed the discomfort. Somehow, knowing she would miss the rest of the school day made the pain more tolerable. "Where are we going?"

"Taco Bell," Bryant said. "If the drizzle lifts, we can eat at the park, and you can read. I got you a book at a yard sale."

"What about work?"

"Work can wait," Bryant said.

They got their burritos, and Bryant drove to the nearest park. The thought of spending the entire afternoon with her father was thrilling. It was like old times when she had her dad to herself. In that instant, he was her world again, and she was his sunshine. They found a large tree to sit under, and Bryant laid out a blanket. He presented her with *The Velveteen Rabbit* while he picked up a western novel.

Claire nuzzled into her dad to stay warm and tore into her bean burrito, famished, having had nothing but a few stale crackers and a large glass of water that morning. "Daddy? What are you eating?"

"A burrito like you, but it's spicy. You wouldn't like it. It has green habaneros and jalapeno sauce in it."

Claire insisted on having a bite and was confident she could handle the heat. She took a nibble, and seconds later, the burn on her tongue flared. Her throat tightened. Claire's mouth seized into a pucker, and moisture seeped around her eyes. Determined to prove that she could eat it, she took a larger bite. The burning sensation inflamed her nostrils and made her ear infection feel worse. Snot dripped down her nose and drool pooled around her gums.

"It's yummy," Claire said. Tears gushed down her cheeks. Swallowing was difficult, and she wished she had milk to douse the fire in her mouth.

"You don't have to eat that, sweetheart." Bryant shook his head.

"Yes, I do. I'm just like you."

Bryant laughed. "You sure are stubborn."

They resumed reading, and when it was time to leave, Claire felt compelled to address her father's lime-green suit, red shirt, and gaudy belt buckle. "Daddy? You need to burn your green suit."

"What's wrong with what I'm wearing?" Bryant teased.

Claire giggled. "It's embarrassing." She gave him a playful glare.

"Oh, come on," Bryant said. "A little embarrassment won't hurt you. It builds character. You picked this shirt. Remember?"

"That was before I could read," Claire said.

On the drive home, they sang Heaven's Just a Sin Away. Despite it being a chilly October day, the sun came out and shooed away the rain. A faint spectrum of colors swept across the sky, and Claire whispered, "Sometimes there are rainbows in October."

The two of them had a wonderful afternoon together, and with her dad in good spirits, Claire almost told him about the times Gisela hurt her. Would he defend Gisela and blame Claire? If he believed Claire, would he beat Gisela? Claire didn't want any more violence. She didn't like her stepmother, but she feared her father would pulverize Gisela's face into hamburger meat.

Claire shuddered. She hesitated to ruin the day they just had and kept her mouth shut.

#

Spring arrived early that year. The sun came out in her full glory, but she dragged the winter chill with her. Bryant thought it was the perfect day to go for a motorcycle ride. The Honda Gold Wing he had purchased last December was perfect for those long rides—comfortable, quiet, low-maintenance, and torquey as hell. It certainly was more affordable than a BMW or Harley-Davidson.

Bryant was pleased with how he negotiated the sale of the bike. A customer had brought his motorcycle in for service, intending to sell it so he could upgrade to another luxury bike. Bryant offered to purchase it. Working as a mechanic had its perks. He quoted an exorbitant price to fix the bike, then turned around and made a deal to take the repair burden off the owner.

"Claire," Bryant yelled. "Get your helmet."

"Where are you going?" Gisela asked. "I need—"

Claire ran down the stairs with her helmet tucked under her arm. "Let's go!"

With the sun on his back and the wind on his face, Bryant felt alive and energized. They cruised the entire day, explored unknown parts of the county they'd never been to before, and stopped at a diner for a milkshake.

"What do you say, for old-time's sake, we do a jam session together?" Bryant asked.

Claire flung her arms around her daddy and squealed with excitement. She nodded vigorously. "Now?"

Bryant nodded. "I know just the place."

#

They walked into a smoky dark tavern, a little hole in the wall known for its cheap whisky and cheaper burgers. It was still early and light outside, but the moment the door closed behind them, darkness prevailed.

"She can't be in here, Bryant." The bartender lit up a cigarette, her leathery face and raccoon eyes illuminated by the flame. She was rail-thin, but her face was puffy.

"This is my daughter," Bryant said. "How about you just turn your pretty face the other way?"

"And why would I do that?"

Bryant leaned close to the barmaid's face and whispered, "Didn't you say you wanted a ride?" Bryant knew Tara had been itching to have her way with him. She flirted unabashedly with him every time and pushed her breasts together with her arms to accentuate her cleavage to tempt him. Last week she brushed up against him and grabbed his crotch, then licked her lips and walked away as if nothing had happened. *Oh, I'll let you ride all right*, he thought.

Tara poured Bryant a whisky and turned away. Bryant scanned the room. Two patrons sat in the back, their faces shrouded in cigarette smoke, and a couple near the pool table groped each other playfully, grinding their bodies slowly to the melodies on the jukebox.

A trio on the small stage tuned their instruments, setting up for the live ditty that evening. Bryant took Claire's hand and led her to the stage.

"Well, if it ain't the Cowboy," Peter sang. He was a portly fellow with eyebrows as thick as his sideburns. "Who's this?"

"I'm Claire. My daddy and I are going to sing."

Peter winked at Bryant. "Your daughter is really pretty."

The other two men behind Peter put their instruments down and came for a closer look. One of them was old with wispy gray hair and a glass eye.

"Mind if I borrow your guitar?" Bryant asked. "My daughter and I want to sing a couple of songs for old-time's sake."

"Be my guest." Peter handed Bryant his guitar. "She's prime for the plucking . . . the guitar, I mean." Peter stepped off the stage and squeezed Claire's cheeks.

Claire inched closer to Bryant and found the microphone on the speaker. Taking her cue, she tapped her foot and recognized the tune immediately. She sang Waylon and Willie's song, "Mammas Don't Let Your Babies Grow Up to Be Cowboys." The room became quiet, the clinking of glass stilled, and all hushed to hear the sweet, innocent sound of Bryant's seven-year-old daughter. Everyone joined in at the chorus and swayed back and forth. When she finished, the room erupted in whistles and applause.

"More!" Peter slapped the bar counter and raised his beer high. "Another one!"

Claire soaked in the praise and grinned. "Daddy, can we do the new one?"

Bryant noticed the way Peter looked at his daughter—the same way Tara looked at him, with lust and ownership. It made him protective of his daughter and uneasy about the predators in the bar. He shook his head but Claire pleaded and pouted, so he gave in. "Last one, okay?"

"Ah, let her sing a few more," Peter yelled. "She's having a good time, and so am I."

Claire cleared her throat and sang "Good Ol' Boys." Once again, the room joined in at the chorus. It was a party. Even the old man with the glass eye removed the harmonica from his pocket and blew into the reeds.

Peter ordered a shot of vodka and downed it. "Sing your heart out, sweet girl. Woowie, you're gorgeous."

Claire lapped up the praise and the cheers. When their session was over, Peter hopped at the opportunity to compliment the little girl. He caressed her cheek. "You were so good."

Bryant picked up his daughter and carried her off the stage. He was tempted to pummel the other man's face. *Lights out for you, shithead.* He didn't want another man, a total stranger, touching his daughter. He sensed what was on the other man's mind, and he'd be damned if he let that man play out his fantasies. Bryant gruffly rushed past Peter and stopped at the bar to pay his tab.

Tara waved her hand. "On me today, but tomorrow . . . on you." She winked and bit her lower lip seductively.

"Hey, man," Peter said, "what's the rush? I didn't mean no disrespect. Hey, how long has she been singing?"

Bryant gritted his teeth. *Go ahead*, he thought, *say one more word about how pretty my daughter is, and you won't be shitting right for weeks.* It was getting hot inside the bar. Beads of sweat bubbled up around Bryant's forehead and temples. His chest felt tight, and his heartbeat pounded in his ears. Bryant swiveled to face Peter and let Claire slide down his leg. He clenched his fist and advanced one step. The snarling Rottweiler in him was ready for battle.

"Hey," Peter said, "I don't want any trouble. Sorry if I offended you." He raised his hands in defense and took a couple of steps away from Bryant.

Claire remembered the time her dad woke her up in the middle of the night and told her to pack. He had been in a bar fight and sent a cop to the hospital. They left Montana with Gisela standing flabbergasted in the rearview mirror. Claire tugged on her father's hand. "Let's go, Daddy. I don't feel good." It was true—she suddenly felt ill. She was hungry, and her ears ached.

Bryant gripped Claire's hand tight and stormed outside. He hoisted Claire roughly onto the motorcycle. "That's it, Claire. No more jam sessions."

They rode home in silence. Claire wept while Bryant tormented himself with destructive thoughts of hellfire and gasoline mutilating Peter's body.

8. THE TINIEST INFRACTIONS

The park down the block was a haven for Claire. She could swing back and forth to clear the cobwebs from her thoughts or sit under a tree to read a book. Riding her bike was a joy, and when the breeze hit just right, she felt free as a bird. She imagined herself soaring with the hawks away from her stepmother and her awful lasagna.

Freedom at the park came with stipulations. She had to let Benjamin tag along, and they had to be home by a designated time.

"I want you kids back by four to help me with dinner," Gisela said, "and Claire, Tanya needs a bath."

"I want to go too." Barry stomped his feet and pouted.

"You're too little," Claire said.

This made her brother cry. "I am not." Barry clung to his mother's skirt. Gisela huffed and swatted him on the butt to go inside the house.

"I'll race ya," Benjamin said. Claire jumped on her bike and zipped off. "Hey, I didn't say go yet."

Claire peddled fast. The breeze cooled her face and helped ease the pain in her ears. Benjamin yelled something, but she couldn't decipher what he was screeching about. The rush of coasting down the little hill thrilled her. She spread her arms out and laughed. "Yippee, I win."

Benjamin rode up beside Claire and punched her. "You cheated."

"Did not."

"Did too. I didn't say ready, set, go."

Claire shrugged. "Next time, just say it." She settled down on a patch of dry grass and opened *Black Beauty*. A few families were scattered around the park, but it was not crowded. Benjamin took off to the slides.

Claire made sure to keep an eye on her brother and glanced up when she got to the end of each page.

In the distance, Benjamin bounced around the swings, threatening to kiss some of the girls Claire recognized from school. They shrieked and ran away. Benjamin laughed and followed them to the monkey bars. He began dry-humping one of them and made her cry.

"Stop it," Claire yelled. "You're so warped, you freak!"

Benji ignored her and turned his attention to the blackberries at the edge of the park. Claire continued to read Anna Sewell's timeless novel when a loud shriek pulled her away. She recognized that scream. She had heard it many times—Benjamin's shrill cry when he didn't get his way, when he got reprimanded, and when he was afraid.

She smelled the smoke before she saw the fire. Claire dropped her book and ran to Benjamin. A few of the adults scurried over, their children behind them. One man took off his sweatshirt to beat back the fire. A woman used a small blanket to help him. Another adult poured what little water he had left in his water bottle.

Claire watched helplessly while the adults contained the fire and ultimately extinguished it. One of them asked Benjamin what happened. He was mute and burst into tears. His lips quivered, and in between the sobs, he hiccupped words of *not my fault* and *I didn't mean to*. One of the women scowled and told them to go home.

Claire took her brother's hand and walked back to the tree to retrieve her book. A small box dropped from Benjamin's pant leg, and it was clear what had happened.

"Benjamin," Claire exclaimed. "Where did you get those matches?"

Benjamin wiped his tears with the back of his hand. "I found them in the garage."

"Wait until your mom finds out."

Benjamin wailed. "You can't tell her. Please."

This was Claire's opportunity to get Benjamin in trouble. For once, he'd get a beating and not her. Gisela's precious son wasn't that innocent. He wasn't an angel. This time, Claire was determined to make Gisela see that.

Benjamin pulled away from Claire and ran to the park trash can. He threw the matches in there and folded his arms in victory.

"That's not going to save you," Claire said, although she worried it just might. It would be her word against his. She hot-potatoed the idea of whether to tell or not. She had one block's ride to decide.

Benjamin rushed through the door and immediately sprinted up the stairs to his room. He slammed the bedroom door with such great force that a picture skewed.

"I told you four o'clock," Gisela screamed. "It's ten minutes past. If dinner is not ready by the time your father—"

"Benjamin started a fire." The words propelled from her lips, and it was too late to shove them back.

"He what?"

Claire lengthened her spine and challenged her stepmother by looking directly into her eyes. *God, she is an ugly, big woman.* Claire defiantly put her hands on her hips. "Benji brought matches to the park, and he started a fire. It took three adults to put the fire out." Surely Gisela would discipline her son now.

Gisela rose higher than a bear on its hind legs and hurled a wooden spoon at Claire. It happened so fast that Claire didn't have time to dodge it. The spoon whacked her squarely on her collarbone. It pricked like a bee sting. The demonic look on her stepmother's face startled her. She pivoted to run.

Gisela charged at Claire. "This is your fault." She grabbed the broom and swung it at Claire. "You're older and should know better. It's your job to keep him out of trouble!"

Claire bounded up the stairs. She barely made it three steps before fat fingers curled around her bony wrist and yanked her backward. Gisela was swift and strong for a woman her size. She flung Claire to the ground, sending her crashing onto the hard floor. A sharp pain hammered her tailbone. Shockwaves snaked up her neck.

Gisela pinned Claire down with one foot. "You stupid ingrate." She jabbed the broom handle into Claire's stomach. "It was your job to watch over my Benji." Gisela leaned forward to crush Claire with her weight. "He could have been seriously hurt. He could have burned himself." Gisela was livid.

Claire swallowed the vomit that threatened to escape her throat. She wriggled from under Gisela's foot and jumped to her feet. Claire ran to the living room to put distance between them. Gisela swung the broom like a madman killing a swarm of mosquitos. Occasionally the wooden handle made contact with Claire's wrist or the back of her knee, and she flinched in pain. They ran around the couch a couple of times before Claire leaped toward the kitchen, intending to dash out the front door.

In her haste, Claire misjudged the corner and slammed into the pillar near the entryway. She lost her footing and braced herself for the fall. Gisela was on her faster than a pack of wolves. Claire took the beating blow after blow. Her stepmother's fury was insidious, the way her teeth clenched, her eyes darkened, and her face reddened. Gisela's brittle, unyielding hair flared like hissing snakes each time she hammered down on Claire's chest.

"And you're fucking late!" Gisela screeched. "I told you four fucking o'clock, you little cunt." She shook her head. "You're a worthless piece of shit. Look at you. Ugly, stupid, and rail-thin like a twig. You can't do anything right. You might as well be dead for all I care. Nobody would miss you. You are worthless. I can't even depend on you." Gisela huffed and snarled with every lashing. And when Claire no longer fought back and her body went limp, Gisela dragged her up to the attic. She shoved her onto the hard plywood. "You stay, dog, until your master lets you out."

Claire's eyes fluttered. Things were blurry, but she knew where she was. There was only one place that hot and humid. *I'm in the attic.* A mouse scurried past her nose. The plywood felt good—cool—against her cheek. She rolled onto her back and stared at the rotting beams. The world spun. She was acutely aware of how dry her throat and mouth were. What she wouldn't give to have a sip of cold water from the garden hose.

Another mouse scurried past, but Claire didn't care. She let it use her body as a bridge and felt its tiny nails dig into her leg as it scurried to the other side. Claire didn't know if she ought to laugh or cry. She felt delirious. Had that happened? Benjamin started a fire and nearly burned the blackberry bushes. Heck, he could have destroyed the whole park. Yet she got the punishment. She was the one with cuts and bruises. Claire realized there were different sets of rules for her than for Gisela's boys.

She was always getting beaten or grounded for the tiniest infractions. It was not fair. Claire hated her stepmother, and it seemed the feeling was mutual.

#

Another year around the sun . . . It was June, Bryant's birthday, and Gisela wanted to make a big deal of it. She would cook him something nice, maybe pork chops, and bake an apple pie.

The sun was shining. Not a cloud in the sky. Gisela hummed a tune as she glided into her bedroom in search of her purse. Outside her window, Benjamin and Barry hunched over an orange and black caterpillar that inched its way up a tree. She smiled, happy to see her boys enjoying the sunshine, exploring nature in the yard, and living their childhood.

On that particular morning, Gisela felt light on her feet. She wasn't feeling bloated, and her husband had given her good loving twice last night. She knew the way to his heart was through his stomach, but of course, it meant starting through his pants. Yes, home-baked apple pie would do the trick. Nothing was going to spoil her day, not even Bryant's wretched redhead, and she was determined to make Bryant's birthday special.

Gisela spotted her purse hanging on the closet doorknob and pulled out a five-dollar bill. She inhaled and yelled, "Claire, get in here!" She waited for a second and yelled again. "Get your nose out of them books and get in here! Now!"

She waited, and when Claire did not appear, Gisela huffed and waddled out of the bedroom, down the hall, and stomped up the stairs. She didn't knock of course. It was her house. The door was ajar, so Gisela kicked the door open.

The loud crash of the door slamming against the wall and Gisela's sudden appearance made Claire flinch. Gisela lurched over to the bed and ripped the Sony Walkman off Claire's head. The sound of Prince screaming, "I wanna be your lover," trickled out of her headset before it was silenced on the pillow.

Gisela tossed Claire a five-dollar bill. "Take the boys to Long's and get a gift for your dad."

#

Claire collected her brothers for the fifteen-block walk to Long's Drugstore.

"I don't want to go," Barry declared. "It's too far."

"Can we ride our bikes?" Benjamin asked.

"Yeah, can we?" Barry asked. "My feet is gonna hurt."

Claire corrected her little brother. "Are, not is. My feet *are* gonna hurt. And no, we can't ride our bikes. It's not safe. There are cars and busy streets to cross."

"Well, then," Benjamin said, "we'll just walk our bike across."

"And what if our bikes get stolen while we're inside?" Claire stopped to face her whining brothers. She rested her hands on her hips and spread her stance, channeling her inner Ramona Quimby character. Claire's favorite author at the time was Beverly Cleary, and oh how she wanted to get away with mischief like Ramona. "Listen, motor mouths, we are walking. It's Dad's birthday, and tomorrow is the start of summer, so you better enjoy this weather before winter hits you sideways."

Benjamin and Barry shut their mouth and continued walking. Claire was pleased with herself and allowed a little smile to curve around her nose.

Rochester was nice in June. Kids were out of school and enjoyed their freedom running through the sprinklers or playing foursquare in the driveway. In summer, you couldn't tell the poor kids from the rich kids. Everyone wore flip-flops, ripped shorts, and tattered tank tops. People ate corn and watermelon and tossed rocks for fun. There was no pressure to buy school supplies and new clothes or shoes or get haircuts and perms. Claire breathed in the fresh air and soaked up the warmth of the sun. Being a redhead, though, she had to be careful not to overexpose her sensitive skin to the UV rays.

They approached a strip mall, and Claire pointed to the IGA grocery store. "Let's walk through there. It's cool inside."

As they approached the store entrance, Claire noticed a little girl sitting alone in an idling car. There was no one else in the car with her. Suddenly the vehicle moved and rolled back. The little girl shrieked, and her fear was evident. The Nova wasn't moving fast, but if it wasn't stopped, it would roll out across the street and into the lake.

Claire had seen her dad operate a truck for years when they used to drive cross-country. Confident she could stop the Chevy, she rushed to the driver's side and opened the door, running along with the rolling vehicle. Somehow the little girl managed to shift it into neutral. Claire hopped in and pulled the emergency brake. The car came to a slow stop. The little girl stared at Claire in shock.

"Hurray, we stopped the car," Benjamin cheered. Both he and Barry were behind the car with their arms extended, believing their mighty strength stopped the car from rolling.

Claire hopped out of the car. A strong hand rested on her shoulder, and she followed that hand until it connected to a man's face.

"Thank you," he said. "Oh, thank you! You kids saved my daughter."

"You shouldn't leave your car running, mister," Claire said.

"You're right," he said. "I was only going to be a minute."

"Yeah," Benjamin added, "she could've been kidnapped or something."

The man nodded. "You kids are so brave and smart. Your parents would be proud. They're doing a fine job raising you." He patted Claire on the head and rustled the boys' hair.

Claire grinned. She felt proud. She was a hero.

They continued their walk to the drugstore, and once inside the boys immediately rushed to the candy aisle.

"Let's get Dad licorice," Benjamin said.

"No, gum," Barry said.

"Dad isn't going to want candy," Claire said. "We're here to get him a birthday present. Help me find something nice."

They walked over to the next aisle where they found puzzles and games. Benjamin and Barry busied themselves with the Rubik's Cube and Magic Eight ball. Claire saw a watercolor set with two paintbrushes. Her heart was freefalling into the pit of her stomach. A lump formed in her throat. An overwhelming sense of homesickness and sadness hit her like a ton of packed snow. She couldn't breathe. Her eyes stung, and she realized she missed Grandma Sharon and Grandpa Harold so much. She could see clear as the blue sky Grandpa's face as he dozed in his La-Z-Boy recliner while Grandma baked a pie and Aunt Samantha spouted gossip while chugging her beer.

Claire darted over to the next aisle of bandages and cold medicine. She didn't want the boys to see her cry. *Would Ramona cry?* Claire asked herself. *No, she's too tough to cry. She makes other kids cry.*

"Hey," Barry said, "let's get Dad a puzzle. We can put it together."

"Yeah, or how about this?" Benjamin asked.

Claire took a deep breath and wiped her eyes. She returned to the toy aisle to see what Benjamin was talking about. He handed her a plastic guitar pick.

"Well, he does play," Claire said. "Maybe he needs another one of these."

"Do we have enough money?" Benjamin asked.

The kids took the pick and the puzzle to the cashier. "That'll be $4.90."

Claire handed the clerk five dollars and got a dime back.

"Can we get some candy, please?" Barry asked. "We have a dime left over."

"We've got some penny candies over there." The clerk nodded to the counter three feet to his left.

Barry's face lit up. He bounced to the candy jar. "Oh, look, they have Jolly Ranchers and Tootsie Rolls and Bazookas . . . and Twizzlers. Ooh, and they have Smarties and Sweethearts. Can we get some? Please?"

Benjamin joined his brother's frenzy. "I want a Hershey's Kiss or maybe Bit-O-Honey. Oh, wait, maybe a root beer barrel."

At least twenty jars of candy contained assortments of colors, flavors, and textures. It was hard to choose. Claire thought it would be nice to have something to chew or suck on for the walk home. They did, after all, rescue that little girl in the IGA parking lot. *Heroes deserved rewards*, she reasoned. Claire caved in and spent the dime on some candy. She didn't want to hear Barry beg relentlessly for Royal Caramels or cry incessantly all the way home if he didn't get his way. Worse yet, what if Gisela gave her a whipping because she denied him a treat?

The walk home was uneventful. A stray dog walked with them for half a block but discovered chasing cats was more fun. Claire took the guitar pick out of her pocket and admired it. They had chosen a nice one. She loved how it bathed in the sun's shimmer and glistened when she turned it side to side.

When they got home, Barry rattled off their adventure to his mom. "We saved a girl from near death, Mommy. If we didn't come along, she would have drowned in the lake or got smooshed by a truck. I stopped the car."

"Me too," Benjamin said.

"And look, we got Dad these—a puzzle we can do together, and a pick for his guitar." Barry grabbed the pick from Claire's hand and shoved it three inches from his mother's face. "I picked it out. I was the first to see it."

"You were not," Benjamin said.

"I were too!"

"Were not!"

"Were too!"

Gisela laughed. "Boys! It doesn't matter. You both got Dad great presents. He's gonna love it."

"Yeah, he's gonna love it," Barry said.

"Was there any change leftover?" Gisela asked the boys but locked eyes with Claire. Both Barry and Benjamin responded at the same time, but one said yes while the other said no. "Well, which one was it? Yes or no?"

"The cost was $4.90," Claire said.

"So there was ten cents leftover," Gisela said. Claire nodded. Gisela held out her hand. "Well, where is it?"

"We bought candy, Mommy," Barry said. "Claire let us get some Jolly Ranchers."

"I see." Gisela's tone dropped noticeably lower. "Kids, go play outside." Claire took a half step back. "Not you, Claire."

Benjamin and Barry scooted outside to play kickball while Claire stood rooted in place. She knew a lecture was coming, but for what, she didn't know. Gisela calmly rose from her chair. "Stay. You are not to move, you hear me?"

Claire bit her lip and watched her stepmother disappear through the doorframe. She felt hot. Her body temperature rose, not because of the heat, but because of the nervous tension of the unknown. Perhaps for once, her stepmother would show her kindness and reward her for being a good girl. She had saved a kid from a moving car. She and the boys got nice presents for Dad, returned safely, and stayed out of trouble. She used the money wisely and spoiled the boys with candy. Wouldn't her stepmother appreciate that?

The few minutes it took Gisela to return felt longer to Claire as she waited for that heavyset stepmother of hers to shuffle back to the kitchen. Claire let her thoughts meander. *Oh, why won't you lose some weight?* She thought about Gisela's big frame, which made her think of food and how they never had enough. She switched gears to daydreaming about television shows, her favorites being *The Dukes of Hazard, Three's Company*, and *Happy Days*. Fonzie was pretty cute. For cartoons, it was *The Jetsons* or the new *Tom and Jerry* show. She couldn't decide which one she liked better.

The sweet, cinnamon smell of apple pie baking in the oven was the only thing keeping Claire company. She saw in her mind's eye the golden sugar bubbling out of the slits in the flaky crust. Her mouth watered. *It wouldn't hurt to take a peek*. Even though her stepmother told her to stay and not move, there wouldn't be any harm in checking the oven. She could be nimble and return to her position before Gisela came back.

Claire quickly scurried to the oven and pulled the door six inches. There it was, crispy and golden like she envisioned. She inhaled a deep current of cinnamon, brown sugar, and butter, then closed it to return to her post, right in the nick of time.

Gisela sauntered into the kitchen, with one hand behind her back and one wicked smile on her crooked-toothed mouth. "I have something for you, girl."

She lifted her arm, and Claire saw the leather belt buckle swoop down. She felt the pain and heard the crack before she saw the slash on her collarbone. Claire fell to her knees in excruciating pain and wailed aloud, her voice a gurgling, primal scream. Tears gushed from her eyes as she endured a second lash. Claire didn't know what to do, but with the third whip, she bit Gisela's ankle and sunk her teeth in deep and shook like a rabid dog.

Gisela stumbled back and crashed down on the chair, breaking one of its legs. She fell gracelessly to the floor, her arms and head thumping the wall with a booming thwack. "You bitch! You little shit!"

Claire laughed. Her body throbbed and ached, but she didn't care. She had been to this bruising dance before. She knew how it would end, but not without a fight. Claire felt devilish and delirious, yet oddly satisfied knowing she had branded her stepmother's ankle with teeth marks.

Once again a cat-and-mouse chase ensued. Gisela got her good across the back, shoulders, and buttocks . . . all the places that could be discreetly covered with long-sleeve shirts and pants.

The one question Claire had in her mind was how the finale would go—locked in the closet or dragged to the attic?

In the end, Claire found herself dragged by the wrist up to the attic. Her body went limp, not because she could no longer stand, but because she was going to make her stepmother work for it. She anchored her dead-weight body to the floor and smiled as Gisela grunted from the exertion.

The sweltering attic was a familiar friend to Claire now. How ironic that she was warming up to the crawl space. The bugs and tiny click-clacks of mice no longer bothered her.

She lay flat on her stomach and watched a mouse gnaw at a wood chip. She twirled her fingers and said, "Bibbidi Bobbidi Boo," but the mouse didn't turn into a horse.

Claire closed her eyes and let sleep and exhaustion claim her. She needed to rest. It would be another three hours before her father came home.

9. NEW BEGINNINGS

The phone rang. Gisela hesitated to answer but thought, *What if it's the Publisher's Clearing House?* She had been trying for the past two years to win the million-dollar sweepstakes. "Hello?"

"Am I speaking with Mrs. Bryant Baker?"

"Speaking."

"This is the Methodist Hospital, ma'am. Your husband was admitted early this morning, and he is in critical condition."

Gisela's heart raced. She loosened her grip on the phone and pulled up a chair to sit. "What happened? Is he going to be all right?" Wetness brimmed around her eyes. A dozen thoughts raced through her mind, and questions vied for her attention. What if he didn't make it? What would she do? Oh Lord, what if he was in a coma for years and never woke up? What if he became incapacitated and she had to watch him deteriorate? What if she had to take care of him? Oh, geez, what if she was stuck with his brat until she was eighteen?

"Mrs. Bryant?"

"What? Sorry, yes, I'm here."

"He is in ICU. You may want to get his affairs in order in case . . ."

"Yes. Thank you." Gisela hung up before the voice on the line finished talking.

A few days passed before Gisela was given the news that her husband was awake. She gathered up the children and drove to the hospital. Would he be maimed? Scarred? Disabled? She thought of the worst-case scenarios. The last thing she wanted to do was take care of a bedridden, Quasimodo man.

When they got to the hospital, there he was, tethered to tubes, monitored by beeping machines, mummified in bandages and a leg cast. Gisela gasped. *Oh, God, what if he is paralyzed?*

Bryant's breathing was labored. He huffed, then stopped breathing momentarily, before letting out a gurgling of forced air through his mouth. He wheezed as his chest rose and collapsed. How fragile, small, and vulnerable her husband looked. His face was swollen, bruised, and unrecognizable.

Claire ran to Bryant but stopped short to stare at him. Tears raced down her cheeks.

"Mrs. Bryant?" Gisela, Claire, Benjamin, and Barry swiveled around to acknowledge the new presence in the room. "Hi, I'm Nancy. We spoke on the phone."

Nurse Nancy was young, with beautiful, thick blonde hair, slender arms, toned calves, and almond-shaped eyes. She was exotic-looking. Gisela didn't know what ethnicity she was but was thankful her husband hadn't been conscious to meet his nurse.

"What happened to my husband?" Gisela asked.

"Your husband crashed his motorcycle into a guardrail. His alcohol content was quite high. He's lucky to be alive."

"Well, is he going to be deformed? Retarded?" Gisela asked.

"Doctor Mansfeld thinks he'll have a full recovery." Nurse Nancy smiled at the cute children. She knelt to speak to them. "Your daddy is going to be fine. He's going to need you all to be strong and help your mommy around the house while he gets better. Can you do that for him?"

Benjamin and Barry nodded. Claire stared blankly at the nurse.

In the end, Bryant was in the hospital for three weeks, and when he was released, he repaired his motorcycle and told his family not to wait up. "I need to get right back on the horse. I can't let this accident stop me from living my life."

"Where are you going?" Benjamin asked.

Bryant didn't answer. He strapped on his helmet and rode off.

#

"Daddy's home!" Barry dashed through the front door and tracked dirt into the kitchen where Claire was dusting the ceramic pots and fake house plants. Baby Tanya watched her big sister throw the dust feather at their brother.

"Barry, I just mopped the floor!" Claire frowned seeing the specks of mud and clumps of dirt. A part of her worried Gisela would beat her for the dirty floors, and for a fleeting moment, she scurried to grab the mop.

The excitement of having Dad home, however, trumped her fear and the call of duty. She picked Tanya up and followed Barry into the living room.

Bryant tossed his helmet and sagged into the couch.

"Daddy!" Claire put Tanya down and jumped into his lap.

Bryant chuckled. "Sunshine, you're too old to be jumping on me like that."

"Your face is dirty! Where did you go?" Claire asked. "Did you bring us anything? You were gone an awfully long time."

"Yeah, did you bring me anything?" Barry plopped onto Bryant's other lap.

"Where's your mom?"

Barry shrugged. "I haven't seen her all day."

"She's on her period again and has been in bed since Friday," Claire said. "Cramps."

"Again? Seems like she's always on her damn period." Bryant frowned.

"Benjamin is down the street with his friend, George. I told him to be home by six for dinner," Claire said.

"I got some groceries. Why don't you cook us dinner? There's stuff to make tacos and spaghetti."

"Ooh, spaghetti," Barry exclaimed.

"No," Claire said. "I'm making tacos."

"It's not taco Tuesday," Barry said.

"You kids decide. I need a shower." Bryant grabbed a cold beer from the plastic bag and shuffled down the hallway. The kids scurried off to the kitchen with the bags, debating on whether spaghetti or tacos sounded better.

#

Bryant opened the bedroom door to reveal a dark room. The curtains were closed. The air was stale and stuffy with a hint of vinegar. Something was sour. He opened the single-paned window to air it out. Bryant glanced at the lump in bed that was his wife. The blanket rose and fell slowly, quietly, and Bryant knew Gisela was sleeping. He tiptoed to the bed and watched her. Surprisingly, he missed her. He didn't care if she was on her period or not. He was feeling frisky and was set on having his way with her later. It had been two weeks since he'd been with anyone, too sore from his motorcycle accident to bother hooking up with the women he met at the bars and motels. The devil knew there were plenty of loose ones on the open highway, but he resisted. He was proud of himself for being faithful and celibate, although he still dreamed of a threesome.

Bryant kissed Gisela lightly on the forehead and stripped off his clothes. He took a big swig of his cold beer and strutted down the hallway to the bathroom buck naked. The water hit his skin, and he exhaled. He felt ten years younger, twenty pounds lighter, and five days cleaner. The stress of the accident, the weight of the world, and the burdens of all the yesterdays swirled down the drain with the dirt and grime. Bryant was ready to change his ways. He made up his mind to stop drinking, be the breadwinner his family deserved, and spend more time at home. Being on the open road allowed his mind to wander and his senses to gather.

Alcohol and motorcycles did not mix. He realized that. Never again would he find himself slammed against a guardrail or let anyone discover him lying unconscious alongside a road. Three weeks in the hospital was three weeks too long. His little girl was growing up fast, and he didn't want to miss another moment. Bryant smiled, thinking about the good old days when Claire was three and four years old, teaching her CB lingo and showing her off at jam sessions. His little girl could sing. She was smart, articulate, beautiful, precocious, and responsible. He was proud of her.

Little Barry was still young and innocent. Maybe Bryant could be a father to him and teach him about cars and music. Benjamin wasn't so bad either. He needed a strong male figure in his life. He had a reckless streak to him, which wasn't so bad if he harnessed it and used it the right way.

Bryant stepped out of the shower and dried himself off. He felt like a new man. Perhaps being close to death does that to a man.

The smells of sweet yellow onions and ground beef lured Bryant out of the bathroom. He quickly got dressed and nudged Gisela to wake.

She rolled over and smiled at him. "You're home."

Bryant planted a sweet, soft kiss on his wife's full lips. "Get up. Let's have dinner. Claire's cooking."

"What are we having?"

"Your guess is as good as mine."

They both laughed. Gisela rolled out of bed and brushed her hair. She freshened up in the bathroom and rinsed with mouthwash she had left over from the women's shelter. The food smelled heavenly. They hadn't had a decent meal in weeks. It was good to have her husband home.

Benjamin arrived on schedule. His eyes lit up seeing his mom awake and out of the room. Bryant was home and there was food on the table. "Oh man, what are we having? Smells like burgers."

"Spaghetti," Claire and Barry said in unison.

"Go wash your hands," Bryant said. All three kids ran to the kitchen sink and quickly rubbed their hands under the cold water. The boys wiped their hands on their shirts and darted to the table. They both wanted to sit next to Bryant.

Claire wiped her hands on an old shirt that had been promoted to a kitchen towel last week when she caught a rat chewing a hole in the chest pocket. She placed the spaghetti on the table close to her father so he could serve himself first.

"This looks good, sweetheart," Bryant said. "You're getting to be quite the cook. What do you know how to cook now?"

Claire beamed. "Well, spaghetti and lasagna was—"

"Were, not was." Bryant corrected his daughter.

"Were the last things you taught me." Claire served herself a big scoop of noodles.

"What else?"

"Tacos, of course, and tuna noodle casseroles. I know how to make tomato soup with pasta shells too like Grandma used to."

"Well, I know how to make peanut butter and jelly sandwiches," Benjamin said.

"Have you all been good while I was gone?" Bryant asked.

Barry nodded. "I helped fold clothes and put them away."

Benjamin slurped his noodles and added, "Yeah, and we helped with dusting. We got the lower parts, and Claire got the higher parts that we couldn't reach. And I vacuumed the floors."

"All your shirts are clean, Daddy," Claire said proudly, "and they're hung just the way you like them, all facing the same way and color-coded too."

"And my pants?" Bryant asked.

"Yup," Claire said. "And shoes, too, all lined up, exactly the way you showed me, Daddy." This pleased Bryant. He liked order. The military had taught him that. "I help Benjamin and Barry in the mornings to get ready for school, and I cook breakfast too."

"Yuck," Barry said. He stuck out his tongue and pretended to faint. Benjamin and Gisela laughed at his impression. "Your oatmeal is so thick."

"It is not," Claire said. "At least it's not soggy like—" She almost said *your mom's* but she bit her tongue. Gisela's oatmeal was bland, runny, and simply gross.

"Like what?" Gisela asked.

Claire shoveled more spaghetti in her mouth so she didn't have to answer with her mouth full.

"And how was school?" Bryant asked.

"Claire got a C in math class." Benjamin sneered.

Bryant frowned. "I am so disappointed in you. You are capable of so much more than this."

Claire knew where this conversation would go if she did not redirect it. She'd end up in her room to think about how she could do better. To lighten the mood, she changed the subject to music. "I want to play the viola."

Gisela shot Claire a look as if to say *over my dead body*. "No, you're not playing the viola."

Benjamin laughed. "I told you so. She told me she wanted to play the viola, and I told her no way."

"If she wants to play the viola," Bryant said, "she can play the viola."

Claire narrowed her eyes, shot Gisela a smug look, and thought, *My daddy's home, and you can't have it your way now.* When everyone was busy dishing up food or drinking juice, Claire stuck her tongue out at her stepmother.

Gisela threw her fork at Claire, which narrowly missed her cheek and ricocheted off her shoulder. "You're not fucking playing the viola. We already had this conversation. Benji, get me another fork."

Bryant slammed his palm on the table, which made the baby whimper. "What was that? Gisela, control your temper, or I'll control it for you. It could have struck her in the eye and blinded her."

Claire's face heated up from the tears brewing under her lashes. It wasn't sadness or defeat she felt. It was anger and frustration. Empowered by her father's presence, Claire spoke louder and challenged Gisela with confidence. "Why can't I play?"

Gisela calmly accepted the fork from Benjamin. "Claire, for one thing, we don't have the money. We're not spending a penny on your instrument or lessons."

"But—"

"And I don't want to hear you screeching away. I already have migraines as it is."

"I'll play in the backyard so you don't have to hear it."

"Absolutely not. No! Besides, I need your help taking care of your brothers and Tanya. You have your chores, not to mention homework and keeping up with your grades. You wouldn't have time anyway. My foot is down. You are not wasting your time scratching strings."

"I'll practice when you're not around. I want to play." Claire looked at her dad. "Please. Daddy, I bet the school will loan me one for free. It wouldn't cost you anything. Daddy, you play the guitar. Let me learn the viola. It's important to me. We can jam together like we used to."

Gisela pounded her fist on the table. "I said no, Claire, and that's that."

"Now wait a minute," Bryant said. "This is not your call. You can't tell my daughter she can't play an instrument. Who do you think you are? If Claire can keep up with her studies and chores and help you when you need it, I don't see why she can't take on an extracurricular activity."

"I'll take good care of the instrument, and I'll keep up on my chores," Claire said. "I promise. And I'll get good grades. I'll study hard and not let you down."

And that was that. Gisela was cross, but there was nothing she could say to change Bryant's decision.

10. THE LOVE HOMESTEAD

Seasons came and went, and with each passing year, Gisela let herself go more and more. Nothing brought her joy. They were living hand to mouth, slipping further into debt. Work was hard to come by, and when it did, Bryant's paychecks didn't stretch farther than the dive bar around the block. Funny how there was money for libations at the pub but not food for the cupboards or milk for the fridge. Time stood still for Gisela. It was the same slop every day—oatmeal and ramen.

Abdominal cramps crippled her, and fatigue weighed her down. She didn't have the energy to get out of bed most days or the motivation to do anything productive. Lately, her gut gurgled in the mornings and her sense of smell picked up the faintest odors, the worst being Bryant's morning breath.

Nauseated by the smell of sweat permeating from her husband's skin one night, Gisela lurched out of bed and rushed to the bathroom, barely making it down the hall before green chunky liquid sloshed out of her mouth.

"This the second time you've thrown up," Bryant said. "You're not pregnant, are you?"

Gisela didn't know what to think about Bryant's question. The idea was absurd. Tanya was barely three years old, and the last thing she wanted was another child. "I doubt I'm pregnant. I didn't have any symptoms with Benjamin or Barry, or Tanya for that matter. It's probably just a bug."

"It better be. We can't afford another mouth to feed. Besides, we need to find another place to live."

"Why?"

One look from her husband told Gisela everything she needed to know. The raised eyebrows, the pursed lips, the slight cock of his head, and the subtle shrug of his shoulders meant they had missed one too many payments on their rent.

"It's not looking good," Bryant said. "I've been asking around. Nothing is available, and everything is getting too damn expensive."

Gisela wanted to say, *Well, maybe you oughtta stop drinking and get off your lazy ass to find a decent job.* Instead, she proposed an idea that had a fifty-fifty chance of getting accepted. "What do you say we move back to Montana? My folks have property out there, and the oil industry is boomin'. You could get a job in the oil fields. It pays good money. We could live with them for a bit until you get a job, and then we can venture out on our own. We can be like the Clampetts."

Bryant laughed at her comparison to the TV show *The Beverly Hillbillies.* "You mean, us hillbillies striking it rich in oil and living among the posh?"

Gisela shrugged. "What do you say?"

Bryant weighed the pros and cons. He liked Minnesota. Rochester was home. It was where Claire had been born and where he felt most comfortable. Jobs, however, were scarce, and he had exhausted most of his connections. Gisela reminded him that Montana was where they first met, and wouldn't it be romantic to return? She took his hands and placed his palms on her breasts, rubbing the back of his hands to massage her nipples. Gisela stepped closer to her husband and swayed side to side, rubbing her front against his growing manhood, hard and emboldened with lust.

"Damn it, woman," Bryant whispered. "What are you doing to me?"

"Remember that little dive bar in Billings?" Gisela asked. "Remember how I sat down next to you and you said, 'You look like you just killed a man'?"

"Yeah," Bryant said.

"And you made me laugh because, ironically, I had just walked away from an abusive relationship. I was there to take a victory shot. I didn't kill him but wanted to hurt him real bad."

"You had this strange grimace on your face like you were in physical pain. Then you smiled as if to gloat. I thought you were beautiful and so assured."

"It was all those things. I wasn't sure leaving Benji and Barry's father was the right thing to do but proud that I walked away from that bastard. And sure, I was in pain. He beat me just about every day."

"You want to go back to Billings, huh?"

"Well, Hardin, actually. That's where my parents are. It's a small town east of Billings. We'll have the convenience of big-city living and the privacy of small-town life."

Gisela kissed Bryant softly on the lips and fluttered her way to his neck. Leaving a trail of butterfly kisses on his collarbone and the hollow softness between his clavicles, she worked her way to his earlobe, nibbling it playfully and licking his ear. She breathed softly and unbuttoned her shirt, offering the lush, creamy mounds of her cleavage to him.

They surrendered to one another, and in the aftermath of their lovemaking, Bryant and Gisela agreed to start their new family adventure in Montana.

#

The town of Hardin was less than three square miles. Nestled on the banks of the Bighorn River and the northern edge of the Crow Indian Reservation, the population was almost evenly split between Native Americans and Caucasians. The nearest general store from Gisela's parents' home was fifteen miles away. Billings was an hour's drive west of the podunk community which meant country life was rudimentary, routine, and predictable.

Claire finished fourth grade at Hardin Primary and skidded into summer excited to explore all that Grandma Gertrude and Grandpa Jerry's ranch had to offer. Acres of land stretched beyond the limits of Claire's imagination. The farm was populated by rows of herbs and vegetables with mini orchards of fruit dotted throughout the property. Claire thought this was what sleeping with a full stomach looked like. There was livestock too . . . chickens and cows. Claire imagined a thousand of Grandma Sharon and Grandpa Harold's houses fitting on the Love Homestead land, which was what Grandma Gertrude named the ranch.

Unlike Grandma Sharon, who was so petite she was pocket-size, Grandma Gertrude was a woman of great girth, tall, and as strong as a hay bale tractor. She wasn't mean like Gisela, but she wasn't tenderhearted either. She ruled the roost, and everyone had to earn their keep. It didn't matter how small you were, how old you were, or how tired you were. There was always work to be done.

Grandpa Jerry was loud and proud like a rooster. He set precedence each day, getting up before dawn, toiling the land, and protecting his flock and family. He'd respond to any threat on his property by swinging a shotgun over one shoulder and an ax over the other. He was lean and lopsided too, with one leg a couple of inches shorter than the other. He was born that way, he said.

Life on the ranch was great for Claire on the weekdays. She passed the time helping in the kitchen canning fruits and vegetables, prepping meals, and washing dishes. In the evenings, she would unwind and watch sitcoms like *Happy Days* and *Laverne & Shirley*.

The weekends, however, were a different matter. The Sabbath period began at sunset on Friday and lasted until sunset on Saturday. After church, the whole family spent the day sitting on the couch doing nothing. It was unbearable. The kids couldn't talk, couldn't watch TV, couldn't even read a book. They certainly couldn't sleep to pass the time. It was unfair the adults could talk but the kids had to remain silent. It was permissible to get up to use the toilet if one asked politely to be excused, but of course, they couldn't dilly-dally more than a few minutes. Grandma Gertrude once hissed at Claire for spending too much time in the bathroom. "Quit your lollygagging. Disrespecting God on the Sabbath will get you nowhere you wanna be."

One Sunday morning, Benjamin, Claire, and Grandma Gertrude were getting ready to walk the highways in search of aluminum cans—a Sunday ritual. Every penny counted on the homestead, and everything was accounted for, down to the last juice box in the refrigerator.

Claire grabbed a white trash bag and buttoned her sweater. "Grandma, what's a Seventh-day Adventist?"

Grandma Gertrude frowned. "Gisela, don't you teach the children anything?" Before Gisela responded, Grandma Gertrude explained. "Adventists are Protestant Christians. Do you accept Christ as Lord and Savior?"

Was that a trick question? Claire wasn't sure. "Well, who's Christ, exactly, and what's he lord over?"

"My goodness, child. No one ever told you about God?" Claire shook her head. "Well, haven't you learned anything at church?"

"Well, I know God is our creator and the Bible is his Holy Word."

"That's right. God is the Father, Son, and Holy Spirit."

Claire was confused. "But what does that mean?"

Gertrude held out the lunch sack for Claire. "Grab the PBJs." Claire did as she was told and put the peanut butter and jelly sandwiches into the bag along with a juice box. She filled the water bottles with tap water and put them in as well. "I'll explain later. Go get Benji."

Grandma Gertrude drove Benjamin and Claire a mile down the road and hopped onto the highway. Every Sunday the kids were dropped off at a certain mile marker, and with their trash bags in hand, they walked in opposite directions for miles, searching for aluminum cans so Gertrude could give them to the scrapyard for pennies on the pound. It was important to her to maximize their profits and stretch their dollars. Living through the Great Depression taught her to pinch every penny and waste nothing.

"Grandma," Benjamin said, "My feet still hurt from last time." He pulled off his shoes and rubbed his feet. Last Sunday they had walked for five hours looking for aluminum cans along the highway, down in the ditches, and along the valley. Each time they'd cover a different stretch of land, sometimes heading east, other times heading west. "And my legs hurt too. Can we go home after lunch?"

Gertrude ignored her grandson. She thought he was the most rotten, spoiled, and noncompliant child she'd ever met. No grandchild of hers was going to be weak and lazy. "Quit your complaining. Fill those bags. The faster you both work and the more cans you find, the sooner you'll be done. I'll find you both around noon, and we can eat our sandwiches. And I'll tell you more about the Trinity and what it means to be a good Christian."

Gertrude dropped Benjamin and Claire off at the same spot as last Sunday but on the opposite side of the highway. The summers in Montana felt warmer than in Minnesota to Claire. Perhaps it was because she had to walk for miles all day, every Sunday, to collect a hundred cans. Claire dreaded the weekends, spending Saturdays in silence on the couch and Sundays roaming the roads like nomads. It was backbreaking, water-blistering, cotton-mouth work, but she supposed that was better than getting beaten on the weekends for small infractions.

Without a watch, it was difficult to know how much time had passed between the first spotted aluminum can to the next. Claire occupied her thoughts with songs she'd make up, tales she'd spin, and daydreams she'd weave, hoping one of them would become reality one day. Humming along the highway, she'd occasionally catch a car slowing down to watch her, the drivers curious to see a fair-skinned, freckled-faced girl with red hair and scuffed shoes walking alone along the bank of the freeway. Thank goodness no one bothered her or meant her harm. Claire didn't know what she'd do if someone tried to kidnap her, spit on her, or make crude gestures. Benji wasn't as lucky. He had been hit a few times by litter that people had thrown out the window, stuff like shoes, scrunched-up McDonald's paper bags, and even beer cans.

Lost in her quiet world, she sang the refrain of her made-up song out loud, testing her vocal cords to see if the lyrics sounded as pretty as they did in her head.

"Gonna walk this road, gonna carry my load," Claire sang, "Gonna pick up cans, with my cold, cold hands. And when I'm done, gonna see the sun. Shining down on me, she'll set me free."

By the time Claire collected thirty-two cans, she knew she had a pound of aluminum, which was worth about ten cents. It didn't seem right to work in the heat for hours. Her feet hurt from stomping on the cans to crush them, and her back ached. The throbbing in her temples didn't help either. Her stomach rumbled.

Claire stopped to rest on a big rock and scanned the road behind her. She spotted Benjamin, his small silhouette a mile down the grassy fields. He was an orange dot that moved slowly away from her. As annoying as her brother was, she felt pity for him. She felt sorry for both of them. While Barry was home hanging out with Grandpa Jerry, tinkering with machines, both she and Benjamin had to shuffle along in the dirt, trip over debris, and have random objects flying at them as they ricocheted off cars roaring by. In the distance, Claire saw a strip of rubber from a blown tire. *Alligators*, she remembered.

"Breaker one-nine for Tumbleweed," Claire said. "Are you there, Tumbleweed?" Silence. Claire cocked her head. A semi-truck approached. Claire pumped her right arm, and the trucker obliged. He honked his horn and waved. She grinned and waved back.

She wondered where Tumbleweed was now. *Probably getting pulled over by a bear*. Thinking about their trucker days and the kind people she met warmed her spirit. She imagined Jalisco at a Motel 6 somewhere, drinking with HotLinx and that other Asian man, Minh-Tri. Would Deanna be with them? She really liked Grasshopper and hoped the father-daughter duo was well. Wetness brimmed around Claire's eyes. Imagining HotLinx and Grasshopper traveling on the open highway made her miss the days of Cowboy and Sunshine.

Claire couldn't help it. Her chest heaved with sadness and longing. She fought to suppress the overwhelming depression that blanketed her. Why was she here? What was the point? Sparks of remembrances fired from her memory bank. Grandma Sharon cooking pasta. Grandpa Harold snoring on the La-Z-Boy. Waves of faces flooded her mind. Her baby dolly and that redheaded woman in the hotel. The creepy man at the bar who said she was pretty. Mr. Kenneally who did an oil change in three minutes or less. Daddy's old hot-mess girlfriend, Darlene.

Her legs crumbled like broken matchsticks, no longer strong enough to support her frail body. She plopped to the ground. Her body shook, and she cried uncontrollable tears. So alone. So defeated. Why didn't she have a friend in the world? Why didn't she have a mother who loved her? What did she ever do to deserve the bruises and scars on her body? She wanted her daddy, not the drunken daddy who beat women, but the sober one who used to rock her when she was sick and read to her at bedtime.

Gisela's menacing scowl flashed clearly in Claire's mind. It jarred her. The anger uncorked. She thrashed her fists against her legs and crushed the dirt with her knuckles. A litany of profanity spewed from her nine-year-old mouth. Spit frothed at the corners of her parched lips. "You're a horrible mother. I hate you. I hate you. I hate you."

Claire hoisted herself up and kicked the bag of crumpled cans. The aluminum clanged about as they scattered in different directions. She stomped them a second and third time, making sure to dig her heel hard into the ground, wishing the dirt would swallow the cans and take her with them.

"Ugly lunatic! Bitch! Stupid, ugly bitch!" Slanderous defamation seethed and frothed from Claire's mouth. The hatred slithering in her veins found its way out of her pores. Tiny molecules of pain and atoms of solitude seeped into the weed-infested highway. She thrashed her body like a bird impaling itself against the thorns. She wanted to die.

Grandma Gertrude's car pulled behind her on the shoulder. "What in God's name are you doing, child? Stop your meltdown and get in the car before you hurt yourself. And pick up those cans."

11. FRY, CHICKEN LITTLE

Claire sat in the car next to Grandma Gertrude while Benjamin sat in the back with the window rolled down. They ate their peanut butter and jelly sandwiches in silence.

Sweat glistened at Claire's temple. She took a swig of water and felt the cool liquid trickle down her throat. Grandma Gertrude ate slowly and savored her PBJ while Claire and Benjamin scarfed theirs down like rabid animals gnawing on their leg to free themselves from a trap.

"Grandma," Claire said, "will you tell us about the Trinity and what Seventh-Day Adventists believe in?"

Gertrude huffed, incredulous at the thought of Gisela not teaching these children anything. "The Trinity is the Father, Son, and Holy Spirit."

"Can I have the other half of your sandwich, Grandma?" Benjamin asked. She was eating so slowly that it was torture to him.

Gertrude handed Benji the rest of her sandwich, and he snatched it like a starved dog.

"Why do we sit in the living room on Saturdays after church and do nothing?" Claire asked. "Isn't church on Sundays anyway?"

Gertrude gasped and shook her head. "Claire, God created the world in seven days. He finished creation on the seventh day and rested. That's why Saturday is the Sabbath. Answer me this. What day does our week start?"

"Sunday," Benjamin exclaimed.

"Right," Gertrude said. "And the seventh day, the holy day, is Saturday. Why those other Christians moved it to Sunday is . . . well, it's just unbiblical. I mean, just because Sunday was the day of his resurrection doesn't mean Sunday is the Sabbath. No, God rested on the seventh day, so we rest on the seventh day. It's a time to relax and reflect, not work. And no distractions like television. A good Christian gives all of herself to God."

Benjamin rolled his eyes. Claire nodded. She still had so many questions. "What else? Like, how come you don't drink coffee or beer or pop like Daddy and Gisela? And how come you don't eat pork?"

"My child, our bodies are holy temples made by God's grace. We have to eat healthily. That's why our ranch has an abundance of fruits and vegetables. Things like alcohol, tobacco, and drugs poison our bodies."

Claire nodded in agreement. She wondered if Grandma Gertrude knew about Daddy's drinking and smoking habits. What would she do if she knew he disappeared to taverns every day for his cigarette and whisky fix? "But, Grandma, we're not vegetarians. We eat a lot of hamburgers and chicken."

"Well, sugar, that's all right. You just can't eat dirty animals, like pigs and rabbits. And shellfish is completely out of the question."

"But why are rabbits dirty? Don't they eat just lettuce?"

"Rabbits have a very large cecum, which is a pouch near the large intestine. A rabbit has to eat a lot of plants to get enough nutrients and has to ferment the food to pass it. The cecum is the fermentation chamber. Rabbits don't have a pre-stomach as a cow does. And because the cecum is between the rabbit's gut and rectum—"

"What's a rectum?" Benjamin asked.

Claire turned in her seat and sighed, thinking her little brother didn't know anything. "It's the butt, doofus, where poop comes out."

"Eww." Benjamin scrunched his face and stuck his finger in his mouth as if to vomit.

"That's right," Gertrude said. "The rabbit re-digests the food material and basically eats its own excrement."

"Excrement means dung," Claire said.

"I know what dung is," Benjamin said.

"Yeah, but I bet you didn't know what excrement was," Claire said, proudly rubbing it in. "Maybe if you read more your vocabulary would be bigger and you wouldn't be so dumb."

"Claire!" Gertrude frowned. "It's not okay to talk to anyone like that."

"Well, I'm never eating rabbit," Benjamin said. "Gross."

"The rabbit is too toxic and hence dirty," Gertrude said.

"What happens when we die?" Benjamin asked. "Will I go to heaven? And what's heaven like?"

Gertrude patted Benji on his head. He was a hellion at times, but still innocent and young. "Benji, have you been a good boy? Do you listen to your parents?" Benjamin nodded. "And do you try your best in school?" Again, he nodded. "And you carry God and his teachings in your heart?" He nodded vigorously.

Claire rolled her eyes. "You are terrible at school, and you don't listen at all. Tell the truth, Benji."

Benji hit his sister. "Take that back."

"Children," Gertrude said, "there will be only one judgment. When we die, we go into a long, unconscious slumber. Only Christ can resurrect us. He will descend from heaven to earth, and those who are redeemed will live forever on a New Earth while the condemned will be destroyed by fire."

Benjamin shuddered. "If I died from plain old age, like when I'm sixty, would I get resurrected sooner?"

"When the second coming is here, we all get judged at the same time," Gertrude said.

"Yeah, but what if I killed someone or stole something? Wouldn't I have to sleep longer before being judged, since I did something really bad?"

"No," Claire said, "that's not how it works. Didn't you hear what Grandma just said?"

Benjamin stuck out his tongue at his sister.

"All right, kids, time to get back to work. We're having chicken for dinner, and you kids are going to help."

Gertrude dropped the kids off to continue the menial task of picking up cans while she returned to the homestead to prepare dinner.

#

Gisela waddled out of the house. She had gained a lot of weight in the past few months. She was certain it was the baby growing inside of her, not the fried chicken she'd been eating. Living with her parents wasn't all it was cracked up to be. She forgot how strict her mother was and how her father never rested. He worked before sun up and into the night, tending to the cattle, fishing, hunting, or fixing farm equipment . . . it never stopped. She resented her parents for her crappy childhood.

When she was ten years old, she wanted to get her ears pierced. All her friends were doing it. They'd show off the earrings that they got at the craft fairs and gabbed about what jewelry paired with what outfit.

"We don't wear jewelry," Gisela's mother had said. "We are here to serve God, not ourselves. A good Christian lives a simple, humble life through God's grace. How do you want to portray yourself to the world? Natural beauty is that of a woman bathed in sunlight and adorned only by his teachings. No daughter of mine is going to be a harlot and wear shimmering things. No, you will not be on display for the pleasure of other people. You are here to serve God."

When there was a school dance, Gisela wanted to go, but again, her mother robbed her of that joy.

"Dancing is for worship, to praise our God. The kind of dancing those kids do is sacrilegious. No daughter of mine is going to rub herself up against a boy and get herself pregnant."

On Saturdays, Gisela played the deaf and mute child, forced to sit on the couch with her hands tucked beneath her thighs and not make a sound. If she sighed and fidgeted to show her discomfort and resentment, she'd get a stinging slap across her cheek.

Over the years, she resented her parents more and more. Instead of exploring the wonders of the farm, climbing trees, and tormenting potato bugs, caterpillars, and grasshoppers, she was forced to help her mother bake and canned fruits and vegetables. If she wasn't confined to the kitchen, she was helping her father skin an animal or hold a chicken down while her father executed the poor fowl with his machete.

Dating was completely out of the question. "You must live a pious life," her mother always said. Gisela remembered when she met Miles at a gas station. He was the cutest boy she had ever met with his chestnut eyes and stubble. He looked both boyish and manly at the same time. She knew he was her ticket out of the Love Homestead. Miles was the first boy to pay attention to her, so when she got pregnant, she was relieved. They married, and the two of them started a new family away from this godforsaken town.

"Mumma," Tanya said.

Gisela scooped her daughter onto her hips. "You're getting too big for me to carry."

Little Tanya pointed at Gisela's stomach. "Baby."

"Yes, baby. You're going to be a big sister." Tanya beamed and pointed to the driveway. The old Ford truck rumbled closer, and Gisela could see her mother's straw hat before she saw her face. "Looks like they're home from can-picking."

Bryant came up behind Gisela and held up a chicken by her legs. "Good timing. The kids need to learn how to prepare the chicken."

Gisela's stomach turned. She had flashbacks of the horror she felt watching the chickens run in different directions while her dad chased them with his machete in hand. Their squawking and frantic wing-flapping gave her nightmares for a whole year.

Claire hopped out of the truck with her big bag of crushed aluminum. "Hi, Daddy." She handed Grandma Gertrude the bag and skipped over to kiss Tanya. "Hi, Ton-ton."

"Benji, go get your brother," Bryant said. "I'm going to show you kids how to decapitate a chicken." He chuckled, placing a mental bet on which one of his kids would puke or cry first. For sure it would not be his Claire. No, she was tough as nails. His bet was on Barry. He handed the chicken to Claire. "Here, hold her while I grab the ax."

The chicken writhed and protested hanging upside down. Claire stretched her arm out to distance herself, afraid the chicken might peck her eyes out.

Benjamin laughed. "It's going to bite you."

"Chickens don't have teeth, stupid," Claire said.

Tanya squealed and reached for the chicken.

"No, Ton-ton," Barry said. "Don't touch it. It'll bite you."

Benjamin slapped his little brother on the head. "Chickens don't have teeth, you moron."

Bryant waved the children over to the wooden table he had built specifically for the slaughter. "Kids, come here." The contraption was a plank of wood with two nails protruding, wide apart enough to hold the chicken's neck.

Claire, Benjamin, Barry, and Tanya gave Bryant their full attention.

"Can I hold the chicken?" Barry asked.

"I'll tell you what," Bryant said, "we'll go in order by age. The next time we have chicken, Benjamin can hold it, and then you're next."

"Okay, Daddy, what do I do?" Claire asked.

"We're going to lay her down on this board. You're going to put her neck between these nails and hold her legs down while I sever it here." Bryant pointed to the chicken's jugular. "You have to slice it at the right spot on the veins. If you don't, you leave the brain stem and cerebellum intact, which doesn't kill the animal."

The chicken squirmed as Claire approached the table. She wrapped her fingers around the chicken's neck while firmly holding its legs. The animal clucked in protest. Claire tightened her grip.

The kids all held their breath and nodded except Tanya, who clung to Claire's leg and cried. Bryant raised the ax. Claire squeezed her eyes shut. In one swift blow, the blade chopped the chicken into two pieces. Claire screamed.

The chicken's body convulsed violently and jumped out of Claire's hand. It rolled off the plank and landed on Tanya's feet. Tanya shrieked and kicked it. The headless chicken bobbled and ran aimlessly, bouncing into Tanya's legs before hitting a post.

The poor toddler was terrified and screamed at the top of her lungs. Benjamin laughed. Claire picked Tanya up to comfort her. "It's okay."

Bryant grabbed the chicken. "Shit. Maybe I cut it too high. Tanya, it's all right. The chicken's dead . . . just the nerves are still—"

Tanya howled louder. Her big teardrops sprinkled Claire's arm. The two sisters clung to one another for dear life.

"All right, go in the house," Bryant said. "That's enough adventure for one day. Boys, help me clean up, and I'll show you how to boil and pluck the feathers."

#

"What are we having for dinner?" Barry asked.

Benjamin jabbed Barry in the ribs. "Duh, chicken."

Barry scrambled to poke Benjamin back, but he wasn't quick enough. Benjamin reached into Barry's pants and yanked up his brother's underwear, giving him a wedgie.

Tears brimmed at the edge of Barry's eyes. He quickly adjusted his underwear and kicked Benjamin in the shin. "How does that feel?"

Benjamin winced and fluttered his eyelashes to hold back the tears. The boys wrestled to the ground, and Benjamin put Barry into a headlock. Benji balled up his right hand and rubbed it hard on his brother's head. "Want a knuckle sandwich? I got a good noogie for you! That's what you get for asking a dumb question and kicking me, turd."

Barry yelled at the top of his lungs. "I was talking about what we're having with dinner, not for dinner, you jerk."

"That's not what you said."

The two boys scuttled back and forth with wet willies, more wedgies, and Charlie horses. While the boys tumbled, Claire went to the kitchen to batter the freshly-killed chicken. She didn't like the rubbery feel of the skin, but she loved her grandmother's fried chicken. The skin always came out crispy.

She worked alongside Gisela and Grandma Gertrude, washing the zucchini and yellow squash and cutting up the vegetables while Grandma put the rolls in the oven. Gisela turned on the stove and poured the peanut oil into the frying pan.

While the oil heated up, Claire watched Grandma Gertrude dredge the chicken. "Grandma, what's the secret to your fried chicken?"

"Well, you first need a fresh chicken."

Claire giggled. "We definitely have that."

"Yes, and you want to trim off all the fat. We want a thin skin for crispy chicken. Then you wash the chicken in very cold water and let it soak in cold water for five minutes before draining it. Never use warm or hot water."

"Why?"

"I suppose putting a cold chicken into a hot pan is like electrocuting the chicken to a crisp and shocking the meat." Gertrude stiffened her body and stretched her arms out to mimic the bride of Frankenstein. Claire laughed and thought Grandma Gertrude wasn't so bad after all. She was strict, and she didn't like monkey business, but she was fair and a little funny. "Meanwhile, you put a splash of vinegar, a teaspoon of salt, a pinch of black pepper, some garlic cloves, and a yellow onion into a pot of water. You'll want to boil the brine for five minutes before putting the chicken in. Now, if we had time, you'd soak the chicken in the brine overnight, but a flash brine will do to make sure the chicken comes out juicy. It melts off the fat, makes the skin thin, and cuts the frying time so you don't have to worry about burning the skin and having raw meat."

"What about the seasonings?" Claire asked.

"You're getting ahead of yourself," Grandma Gertrude said. "Every step is a secret. It's important to not overcook the chicken in the brine. You have to monitor it. As soon as the meat is cooked, you drain it into the colander and rinse it."

"—in cold water," Claire said.

Gertrude nodded. "And then pat it dry with paper towels before coating it with potato starch. That's important."

"The drying or the starch?"

"Both. The dryer, the better, because you don't want wet, clumpy flour. It also locks in the juices of the chicken and has a high heat tolerance."

"What about cornstarch?" Gisela asked.

"You can use cornstarch if you don't have potato starch," Gertrude said, "but the potato has more flavor than corn. It's a little cheaper and has more nutrients."

Gertrude turned the stovetop to medium heat and placed a saucepan on the front burner. Claire watched her grandma coat the pan with a dark sauce, some vinegar, garlic, honey, brown sugar, paprika, and black pepper. Gertrude stirred the sauce as it melted. She tasted the glaze and nodded. One by one, she pan-fried the chicken and then transferred it to the hot oil. "This is how we lock in the flavor and fry the chicken, Claire. It's already cooked, so we just need to fry it for a couple of minutes until it's nice and golden. You must use an oil with a high smoke point when deep-frying because not all oils are the same."

Gertrude went on to talk about the differences between sunflower oil, avocado oil, vegetable oil, and olive oil and how people also make oils out of coconuts, grapeseeds, and sesame seeds.

"What's your favorite oil for fried chicken?" Claire asked.

Gisela's head throbbed. The brat asked too many questions, and her mother's incessant droning about oils agitated her.

"I like sunflower oil because it's got a buttery flavor," Gertrude said. "But we don't have any, so peanut oil it is. Claire, do you think you can handle the frying while I go to the bathroom?"

"You're going to trust a child with hot oil?" Gisela was irritated. Her mother should be asking her to take over, not a nine-year-old who never did anything right.

"Gisela," Gertrude said, "she's already proven herself around the kitchen." Gertrude winked at Claire before excusing herself.

Being alone in the kitchen with Claire gave Gisela the opportunity to observe the child critically as she fried the drumstick in the sauce, making sure to coat the entire piece of meat before slowly dropping it into the hot oil. The sizzle made Gisela hungry, and the smell of honey wafted up to her nostrils, making her salivate.

The pace at which Claire was going made Gisela impatient. "A sloth can move faster than you. Here, give me that." She grabbed the tongs out of Claire's hand and dropped the wings and breast meat into the saucepan. "At the rate you're going, we'll be eating next Sabbath." She plopped the chicken into the hot oil. The grease splattered on Gisela's apron and trickled down the sides of the pan.

Claire screamed. Splatterings of oil landed on Claire's shirt and scorched her skin. "It burns." She lifted her shirt to see her stomach inflamed with red splotches.

"Quit your bitchin', you little shit," Gisela seethed with clenched teeth. "You're so dramatic. It's not like it's acid." Gisela grabbed butter from the counter and slathered it on Claire's stomach. "You'll be fine."

"I want my daddy!"

"Shut your mouth, you fucking baby," Gisela screamed. She couldn't take any more of this little scum who was a constant reminder her husband had been with another woman before her. "Sit down and stay there." Gisela stared at the selfish little tart who held all of Bryant's heart, leaving only crumbs of it for her and her children. *You may have my mother fooled, but you'll pay for your sinful, deceitful games.*

"Gisela!"

The sound of her mother's voice grated her ears and shredded her heart. Gisela turned to see the whole family staring at her. Gertrude ran to the stove and removed the burnt chicken.

"What happened?" Bryant asked. Claire lifted her shirt to show her father the red marks on her body. "My god." He grabbed a kitchen towel and drenched it in cool water. Bryant gently wiped off the butter and placed the cool towel on Claire's stomach. He rocked her and kissed her tear-stained cheeks.

"It was her fault," Gisela said. "If she wasn't going so slow and deliberately trying to irritate me—"

"She's just a child." Gertrude shook her head. "Claire, let's get you into a cool shower."

All eyes were on Gisela, the coldest pair belonging to her husband. Gisela stormed out of the kitchen and slammed the bedroom door. She wanted to choke that child for turning everyone against her and making her look like the villain. *You're going to fry, Chicken Little. Oh, you're going to beg for death when I get my hands on you.*

12. NOT AGAIN

Two months at the Love Homestead was more than Bryant could take. No smoking, no caffeine, no alcohol. Hell, he couldn't even take a piss on Sabbath day without Gisela's mother questioning his dash to the restroom. The novelty of living on the open range quickly wore off. When Gisela's cousin, Martin, offered him a job at an oil field in Casper, he couldn't resist. It meant more money and less preachy judgment from Gisela's folks. His in-laws were good people who worked hard. They meant well, but dammit, he was a man. A man had to take care of his family. A man needed privacy when he was in bed with his wife. A man should be able to visit the crapper without feeling pressured to hurry up and get to hauling hay in the barn. No, he didn't need anyone putting rules around how to adult.

"We're going to Wyoming," Bryant announced.

"What?" Gisela asked.

"Yep," Bryant said. "Got me a damn good job in the oil field. Great pay. Good benefits. Your cousin, Marty, hooked me up."

"This news is better than apple pie on a Sunday morning as far as I'm concerned," Gisela said.

"When are you leaving?" Jerry asked.

"Two weeks," Bryant said. "They're even setting us up with temporary housing for a month until we find our own place."

"I was getting used to having you all around" Jerry said.

"Well, this calls for a celebration." Gisela sat on Bryant's lap and wrapped her arms around his neck. "What'll it be? Key lime pie? Lasagna?" Gisela planted several kisses on Bryant's forehead.

"Not again! I don't want to leave," Claire said. "Daddy, we move too much. I want to stay here for fifth grade."

"Sorry, Sunshine. It's a done deal. We leave in two weeks."

Claire pushed her chair back and crossed her arms. "Can't you go and I stay? I like being in the kitchen with Grandma Gertrude. She's teaching me to knead dough and can peaches and bake pies and garden—"

"Your dad's made his decision," Gisela said.

#

Claire started fifth grade at Pineview Elementary School in Natrona County. The large school with over three hundred students had small classrooms with a ratio of twelve students for every teacher. Interestingly, the building had an attached facility with fourteen rooms that hosted programs for deaf students. Across the street from her school sat a mid-century modern home that became the Wyoming School for the Deaf. In the first month of attending Pineview, she got a tour of that house with its irregular, star-shaped floor plan and low, hovering roof of zigzagging gables. The single-story home was constructed of steel beams, with a round room in the center, surrounded by classrooms and offices. Sunlight flooded the house through the ceiling skylights and large windows in the classrooms. It was like stepping into a palace made in heaven.

Everything about Casper, Wyoming, was amazing. The house her father found, sprawled between two neighborhood streets with a fenced backyard, was spacious and modern. Claire's bedroom was in the basement, away from her parents, the boys, and Tanya. She had privacy and minimal interaction with Gisela. She learned American Sign Language so she could communicate with deaf students. On top of that, her dad permitted her to resume viola lessons and take on the saxophone.

Perhaps the two best things about Casper were the morning coffees with her dad and meeting Zachary, a shy boy with nutmeg-colored eyes and round glasses. Zachary was deaf. The two of them paired up to make macrame plant hangers and other projects at school. They quickly became friends and had many laughs over charades as Zachary tried to interpret Claire's hand gestures. The two friends quickly became Tweedle Dee and Tweedle Dum, bosom friends who traded sandwiches every day. Claire hated her PBJ sandwiches and craved meat while Zachary hated pastrami and wanted the sweet gooey taste of jam and peanut butter. It was perfect.

As for the morning coffees . . . While everyone slept, Claire woke each morning at six to spend fifteen minutes with her dad before he went to work. Although her coffee was heavily diluted with water and milk, she felt grown up sipping the brew and talking to her dad about school and his work in the oil fields. After he left, Claire got herself ready for school, then woke her brothers up to get them ready.

Bryant was making good money in the oil industry, and for once, the refrigerator was full of food with milk and cheeses—not the processed government kind, but real cheddar, mozzarella, and Swiss. On occasion, there'd be apple pie or cold rotisserie chicken in the fridge.

#

As Gisela's pregnancy progressed and her stomach grew, so did Bryant's sexual appetite. His wife's energy level had diminished, and her willingness to mess around waned, which made him impatient and frustrated. Gisela's mood swings kept Bryant away from the house more and more each week. With Gisela too tired for anything, she spent most of her days sequestered in her room. This allowed Bryant to taste the local flavors of Casper, Wyoming, and he liked what was on tap. It wasn't just the endless beer but the steady flow of beauties flowing in and out of the bars. Since the baby wasn't due for another three months, Bryant decided inviting another woman into their bed would spice up their love life.

"You've got some nerve, Bryant!" Gisela hurled a candy dish at Bryant's head, narrowly missing him before it shattered into a hundred pieces. "I'm carrying your child, practically bedridden for the next three months, and you thought it'd be fun to have a threesome?" Gisela kicked Tanya's plastic chair and sent it flying toward the androgynous woman Bryant had brought home.

This woman, with her edgy haircut and leather pants, looking like she could grace the cover of *Vogue* magazine, intrigued Bryant the second he saw her at the bar. She had the kind of look a man and woman could appreciate.

Gisela clenched her teeth and clawed at her husband. "Never again, Bryant. You hear me?"

Bryant was embarrassed by his wife's temper tantrum. "This is insane." He didn't see what the big deal was. It had been weeks since his wife had pleasured him. Was it too much to ask to let Christie join them and take over where Gisela couldn't?

"Call it hormones or call it jealousy, but don't call it insane." Gisela threw a shoe at her husband. "Get out." She ripped his shirts off the hangers and threw whatever she could at Bryant.

"It's not like I'm cheating on you, woman. What's wrong with both of us enjoying Christie together? We can tag her in and—"

Gisela punched the wall. "Tag her in? This isn't WWF, and you're not Vince McMahon."

Bryant had had enough of his wife's mouth. She was a raving mess, and no one was allowed to speak to him that way. He curled his fingers into a fist and clocked Gisela squarely in the chin. She stumbled backward and tripped on one of Tanya's toys. Gisela wailed loudly so Bryant kicked her to shut her up. Bryant grabbed Christie's hand and strode outside. He took one last look at the house before driving back to the honky-tonk.

#

Gisela hissed in anguish with each contraction. It felt like Paul Bunyan stepped on her back while a gorilla slammed a Samsonite suitcase against the walls of her abdomen. "Get this damn baby out of me!"

Bryant ushered his wife into the car and slammed the door shut. "Claire, we'll be back." He fired up the truck and roared down the road, leaving his four children standing on the porch.

Claire ushered her siblings back inside the house and locked the door.

"Can you make macaroni and cheese with little smokies?" Benjamin asked.

"Sure," Claire said.

"But I'm hungry now." Barry helped himself to a banana and then peeled another one for his little sister. "Here, Ton-ton."

For the next two days, the children fended for themselves. Luckily it was a weekend, and there was no school. Claire read her books, practiced her instruments, and bathed Tanya. She played mother by feeding, playing, and assuring her little sister that everything was going to be okay. Claire was in charge. Even her brothers behaved, as much as seven- and eight-year-old boys do.

They passed the time playing hide-n-seek and card games, but Barry's favorite was playing house. While Benjamin and Claire took on the role of mommy and daddy, Barry was the baby.

"Waa." Barry pretended to cry. "Baby hungry."

Claire handed Baby Barry an empty bottle. He sucked on it like there was real milk in it.

"I'm going out," Daddy Benjamin said. "Don't wait for me." He slipped into a pair of Bryant's cowboy boots and pretended to light up a cigarette.

"Be back for dinner," Mommy Claire said. "We're having tacos."

"Maybe, maybe not," Daddy Benjamin said. He closed a pretend door and drove off in his imaginary car.

Mommy Claire shook her head.

"They're home!" Barry ran to the window.

The crunch of the gravel announced someone was there. Claire peeked out the curtains, and sure enough, her daddy's car was parked crooked and a good fifteen feet from the door. The engine was running with the driver's side door open. She could see her father's left shoe, but he didn't get out.

"Not again," Claire mumbled. She walked out to the car to find her daddy passed out in the front seat, reeking of alcohol, with a lit cigarette dangling from his lips.

Claire snubbed the cigarette out on the ground and turned off the engine. The children shook Bryant repeatedly and called out to him until he was lucid enough to get out of the car. Benjamin and Claire pulled on Bryant's wrists while Barry pushed from behind.

With their neighbors witnessing the ordeal, Claire's embarrassment grew when Bryant crashed to the ground and crawled the rest of the way into the house. Once he passed the threshold, Claire quickly locked the door.

Bryant didn't make it farther than the couch. He groaned and mumbled something incoherent, waving his hand like King Mongkut of Siam in *The King and I.*

"Where's Mommy?" Barry whispered. "And the baby?"

Benjamin shrugged. "I guess we better get to bed. School tomorrow."

The boys took Tanya's hand and shuffled to the bathroom to brush their teeth. Claire looked at her father. He was completely unconscious. No snoring, no wheezing, just short, irregular, labored breaths. How small and pathetic he looked, a grown man slumped on the couch looking like a ragamuffin. Claire felt sorry for him.

13. BACK ON TRACK

Claire fell in love the moment she held little Shannon in her arms. Her new baby sister smelled of honey-dipped roses and looked like a baby dolly with her pink heart-shaped lips, slightly translucent skin, round chubby cheeks, and big almond eyes.

The baby scrunched up her face and squirmed. Claire giggled. "You have a big poopie?" She kissed her sister on her forehead and cheeks while caressing her tiny, stubby fingers and toes. Claire now had two little sisters in her care. She made it her mission to love and protect Tanya and Shannon with all her might.

"I'm hungry," Barry said.

"Me, too," Benjamin agreed.

Claire gently put Shannon in the crib they had found at a yard sale and picked up Tanya. "I suppose you're hungry too."

In the kitchen, Bryant was reading a newspaper and smoking his morning cigarette. "Hey, Sunshine. Why don't you cook us some eggs?" Bryant took Tanya onto his lap and read the paper out loud to his little girl while Claire made scrambled eggs. He kissed Tanya and bounced her on his knee. Little Ton-ton squealed and giggled.

"Remember when you used to read to me, Daddy? And when you'd sometimes surprise me at school and we'd go read a book at the park?" Claire took a sip of her daddy's coffee and kissed him on the cheek. "Can we do that again soon?" Bryant nodded and mm-hmmed. She opened the fridge to get milk. "Bacon!" Claire reached for the package and cut it open. She couldn't remember a better Sunday. Gisela was asleep, Shannon was peacefully tucked in her crib, and Claire was sharing quality time with her father, who was in a playfully good mood. "How's work?"

Bryant snubbed his cigarette and lifted Tanya in the air. He swung her around and tossed her up a couple of times. "Work has never been better."

"Again, Papa," Tanya demanded.

Claire placed a plate of eggs on the table. Barry and Benjamin flew to their chairs and helped themselves to the fluffy scramble. While the bacon was frying, Claire poured a generous amount of milk into her coffee. "So what do you do as an oilfield operator?"

"Well, I make sure operations run smoothly with the oil wells and that the production is optimal. And if there are mechanical failures, I make sure the equipment is fixed."

"That sounds like an important job," Claire said. She was so proud of her father. He hadn't had a drink in over a month. For once, they had a big, nice house, newer clothes, and a stocked kitchen. Gisela slept a lot, so there had been less friction between them.

"How's fifth grade?" Bryant asked. "You still like playing the viola and saxophone?"

"Oh yes! And my friend, Zachary . . . he's deaf. We have so much fun together at school. I'm learning sign language." Claire signed a few words to show her father what she learned. "That means 'your pogo stick is crooked.'" Bryant chuckled. Claire signed again. "That means 'your slinky is broken.'"

Bryant roared. "I've never heard that before." He checked his crotch. "Yep, all good."

Claire blushed. "Daddy!"

They both had a good laugh and spent the next half hour eating eggs and bacon, drinking coffee, and daydreaming about the future.

#

Life was good in Casper for a while, but then Bryant went on a bender shortly after celebrating Claire's tenth birthday. Things quickly spiraled out of control. Bryant went on drinking sprees, splurging his paychecks on top-shelf whisky. Although he didn't eat much and got little sleep, he felt alive and celebrated his good fortune. Bryant knew Claire and Gisela would always be there to take care of him if he came home drunk.

He was a lucky man, and he knew it. When he stumbled home and passed out on the couch, he'd wake with a blanket draped over him and his shoes next to the door. Claire kept the household running, mothering his children better than Gisela. Bryant knew his family deserved better. He tried to quit drinking, but life was stressful. Every once in a while when he was feeling down, he'd remember how his old man used to beat him and how Bryant had tried to protect his mother, Sharon. She was tiny, being a whole foot smaller than his dad, but Bryant had to give her respect. She was fierce and ultimately found the courage to leave the abusive relationship, taking Bryant and his sister, Samantha, with her. Then Sharon met Harold, and what a blessing. Bryant's stepfather was a hardworking man who took care of his family, and that was who Bryant tried to emulate.

Bryant looked at his daughter, Claire, sleeping soundly on her bed. She was his perfect, beautiful angel. Bryant stroked Claire's hair and caressed her small hand. He hated himself at that moment and felt ashamed. "I'll do better," Bryant whispered. "You deserve the best of me." He sat on Claire's bed and wept. "My new year's resolution for 1983 will be no more drinking." Bryant kissed his sweet sunshine on the forehead and drifted off to sleep holding her hand.

#

"Happy New Year!"

The Bakers rang in 1983 by dancing to Kool & the Gang's song, "Celebration." Bryant had been sober for two months, and he hadn't had an angina spell for a long time. Life was back on track. Work in the oil industry was lucrative and steady, albeit stressful at times. The boss could be a hardass who demanded punctuality, perfection, and optimal production. Still, Bryant was making more money than ever and spending more time with his family.

"How about a private concert?" Bryant asked. "Claire, show us what you've learned."

Claire beamed. She grabbed her viola and the sheet music. "I just learned 'More Than a Feeling' by Boston."

"Good ole rock music," Bryant said. "Let's hear it."

Claire secured the instrument to her collarbone and found the playing position. She took a deep breath and exhaled as the bow glided across the strings. The low, deep sounds of the viola put Claire in an immediate trance, and she closed her eyes, letting the vibration of the notes send her to another realm. Nothing existed except the music.

Bryant picked up his guitar and joined his daughter. Together they played and sang. Benjamin, Barry, and Tanya curled around Gisela and listened contently. Their eyes drooped, and Tanya let out a big yawn.

Father and daughter jammed a couple more songs before the kids were sent to bed.

"I don't want to go to bed yet," Benji said.

Bryant scowled. "Git."

The kids all filed into their rooms. Bryant took Gisela's hand and lead her to their bedroom. Nothing got him friskier than the seduction of music. He stripped off his pants and pulled Gisela's gown over her head. She eased herself onto the bed and spread her legs for him. They went at it fast and hard, yowling like cats in heat, changing positions every ten minutes.

In the next room, Benji heard his parents grunting. He couldn't sleep with the bed squeaking and the walls rattling. He tiptoed out of bed and slipped into the closet that adjoined his parent's room. Through the crack of the door, he watched his father ramming himself repeatedly into his mother as she braced herself against the wall.

"What are you doing?"

Benji jumped seeing Claire in the closet with him. He placed his finger over his lips and whispered, "Shh. Look, Claire. They're doing it."

Claire peeked through the closet door to see her dad and stepmother having sex. "Benji, you can't watch."

"I couldn't sleep."

"That's their private time."

"I watch them do it all the time."

"That's wrong, Benji."

"But—"

"We can't watch that."

Suddenly the closet door flung open. Claire and Benji froze.

"What the hell are you two kids doing?" Bryant pulled Benjamin by the ear and yanked Claire up by the arm. "What do we have here? A couple of peeping Toms?" Bryant's calloused hand came down hard on Benji's cheek. "Gisela, get my belt."

Claire held her breath. She knew what was in store for them both. Unlike her stepmother, Claire's father did not discriminate. He didn't think twice about punishing any of his children for their insolence. Benji wailed and screeched with every lash of the belt. Claire bit her lip and closed her eyes. She screamed silently for mercy as her flesh burned. While the tears soaked her face, she clenched her teeth and didn't dare make a sound.

#

By spring, the steep fall in oil prices forced some of the national refineries to close their Casper operations. The population of Wyoming saw a big dip as people moved out of state in search of jobs. Homes and storefronts stood empty. Bryant once again found himself without a job.

"Damn it. They laid me off. I can't catch a fucking break!" Bryant kicked the trash can and hurled his stainless steel cup, an Alcatraz replica he got at a yard sale. Coffee splattered all over the window and counter. The baby woke with a start and cried.

Gisela cradled Shannon in her arms and bounced up and down to hush the baby. "Bryant, you'll find something. Maybe Texaco or Sinclair Oil has an opening. Or Amoco?"

"Even if they did, do you know how many guys I'd be competing with for that job? I only have six months under my belt. Those other guys have way more experience."

Gisela rubbed her husband's shoulder. "How do you know if you don't try? Experience is not everything. I know you'll find something. You always do. Maybe my cousin can—"

"No. I don't want to feel like I owe Marty anything. Besides, nothing is going to be better than this. We're going to have to give up this house."

"Maybe I can get a j—"

"No," Bryant bellowed. "You're not getting a goddamn job." He slammed his fist on the table.

Shannon wailed louder. Gisela stopped rubbing Bryant's shoulder. "Great, see what you've done?"

"I need to think." Bryant grabbed his flannel shirt and slipped on his boots.

"Where are you going?"

"Don't wait up." Bryant slammed the door shut and hopped into his truck.

"Daddy!" Claire ran outside, barefoot and in her pajamas. "Where are you going? Can I come?"

Bryant shook his head. "Stay here and take care of your brothers and sisters. I won't be long. Go on now, get inside." Bryant didn't want to listen to her pleas, and he certainly didn't have the patience to deal with a screaming baby and incompetent wife. He backed out of the driveway and headed in the one direction he knew could provide solace . . . Smoky J's Pub.

Claire fumed and kicked the dirt. She ran back into the house and slammed the door.

There was Gisela, bouncing Shannon up and down, yelling at the baby. "Stop your bitching, you little shit."

"You're going to make her throw up," Claire said. "That's not how you do it." Claire reached for her baby sister. "She doesn't like that."

Gisela pushed Claire's hand away and slapped her face. "Don't you tell me what to do." Gisela put Shannon down on the carpet and grabbed the fly swatter. "This is all your fault."

Claire stepped back and nearly tripped on Barry's shoe. "Take that back. Daddy was doing so good, and now he's going back to the bar, back to drinking. I just know it, and it's because of you. You did something or said something to upset him."

"You don't know shit. You're the reason he drinks. Are you even his daughter? Think about it. Anyone here has rusted hair like yours? Your daddy has dark hair. My kids have dark hair. You're the only one with red flames coming out of your scalp like the devil's spawn. You're a burden, and you don't belong in this family."

"That's not true," Claire whispered. "Daddy loves me. I'm his sunshine." Claire wiped the corners of her eyes with her sleeve.

Gisela laughed. "You think your hair is red like you're something special? Like you were kissed by God's light?" Gisela snickered. "It's red because it came out of a red-soaked pussy. Your mother was a whore. Your daddy felt sorry for you. I bet he's slumped over a bottle of whisky right now regretting the day you were born. Hell, he's scheming right now on how to get rid of you, like the last time he left you in California. One day, you're going to come home to an empty house, and there ain't no one gonna be here." Claire was speechless. Gisela pushed Claire aside. "Get out of my sight before I whip you good."

Claire lost her balance and fell hard on her tailbone. She winced in pain and shot up to her feet. "You have to catch me first, you big, ugly, fat cow." Claire stuck out her tongue and ran down to her room in the basement. Gisela was right at her heels. On the last step, Gisela mistook the landing and fell flat on her belly.

Claire half laughed, half cried. Gisela got up and chased after Claire. Around the room they went, Gisela not letting her limp slow her down. She gasped for air. Exasperated, Gisela grabbed a book and threw it at her stepdaughter. Claire ducked but as she hunched down, the book hit her on the side of the face. The pages sliced into her temple near her eye and she yelped.

Gisela saw the Sony Walkman on Claire's bed and lunged for it. "You won't be needing this."

"No! Put that down. Give it to me. Please. I'm sorry."

"Too late." Gisela grabbed Claire's Best Violist trophy from the nightstand and smashed the cassette player.

Claire sobbed. She jumped on her deranged stepmother, but Claire's eighty pounds was no match for Gisela's 190. Gisela ripped the cassette tape out of the player and pulled out the ribbon. When she was satisfied the tape and player were destroyed, Gisela tossed them at Claire. "You're not to leave this room until your father comes home. I don't care if that's hours or days. And if I hear one peep from this room, you'll be sorry."

Gisela stomped up the stairs, took one look at Shannon crying on the floor, and went straight to her bedroom, leaving the poor babe writhing on the carpet to self-soothe. Gisela reached for her Valium and popped a couple of pills. She lay down and waited for her anxiety to subside before turning out the lights. She didn't know it, but she was suffering from postpartum depression.

Downstairs in her room, Claire could hear her baby sister crying. She looked at the ceiling and tracked the sound of Gisela's footsteps as her stepmother walked to the bedroom. Every creak in the floorboards above told Claire that Gisela was going to bed. She waited for the thump that signaled her stepmother was on the mattress and undoubtedly wouldn't be up again until tomorrow.

Ever so softly, Claire butterflied up the stairs and scooped Shannon in her arms. She cradled the baby and rocked Shannon for what seemed like forever before the baby hushed. Claire let her sister suck on her thumb, and together they fell asleep on the floor, with Bryant's jacket wrapped around their bodies to stay warm.

14. SICK TO DEATH

The summer before sixth grade, Claire lived in a small three-bedroom, one-bath trailer with a gravel parking spot near Billings, Montana. The family surrendered the nice rental home in Casper, sold whatever they could for spending money, and drove to Laurel, a town fourteen miles southwest of Billings. They were close enough to Gisela's parents if they needed anything but far enough not to breathe the same stifling air.

Soon, Bryant got a job in the transportation department of the Laurel School District, maintaining the buses and occasionally driving one when they were short on drivers. It didn't pay much, but no one bothered him.

Laurel Middle School was like any other school before Pineview Elementary—riddled with stuck-up kids who looked down at Claire for the way she dressed and her copper hair. She was a freak in their eyes with her pale skin, welfare reading glasses, and bony arms and legs. Oh, how she missed her friend, Zachary. They had cried rivers signing their farewell, promising to write once a month.

There was little to do in Laurel except go to school and come straight home to help Gisela care for Shannon and Tanya. The daily grind of living and constantly being on the go took a toll on Claire's health.

"Get out of bed," Gisela exclaimed. "The dishes are dirty, and I can't do anything with the mess in the kitchen."

Claire squeezed her eyes shut and pulled the blanket over her head. She groaned and curled into a ball, hugging her knees. "I don't feel good." It was so cold. She hadn't slept well, and no matter how many layers she put on, she couldn't warm up. She tried snuggling with Shannon and

Tanya to siphon their body heat, but it didn't help. The three girls shared the same bedroom and slept together on the full-size mattress on the floor.

Gisela kicked the mattress. "Don't be so lazy." Gisela knelt on the floor and rolled Claire over. She threw off the blanket and saw Claire's ghostly pale face, eyes rimmed with redness, sweat glistening along her hairline.

Claire wheezed and scrambled to pull the covers back over her. Her breathing was erratic. She coughed again and could not stop. With each puff of air expelled, her throat burned and her abdomen cramped up. Her throat and lungs were on fire. Her body convulsed as the cough came in rapid succession. Her chest tightened. Her throat constricted into a knot and her stomach seized up. With each burst of air came phlegm. Too cold and too weak to run to the bathroom, Claire swallowed the mucus and shivered.

"What's wrong?" Bryant asked from the doorway.

Gisela shrugged. "Looks like death is coming to claim her."

Bryant's eyes widened in shock. "My God, she's shaking like she's having a seizure." He scooped up Claire in his arms, blanket and all, and hurried to the car. "I'm taking her to the hospital."

Bryant rolled through every stop sign and sped up at each intersection to get to the nearest medical center. Claire let out a moan and fluttered in and out of consciousness. The jerky movement of the car made her nauseated.

Bryant came to an abrupt stop and pulled into the closest parking space, not caring that the truck was crooked with one tire over the line. He scooted Claire out of the truck and ran inside the sterile medical building.

"Something's wrong with my daughter," Bryant said. He had never felt so scared in his life.

The triage nurse leaped into action and asked for Claire's medical history. "When did her symptoms first occur?"

"I guess since Wednesday. She was sluggish and ate very little last night. She complained of body aches."

"Any diarrhea?" the nurse asked.

"Not that I know of."

"She's burning up. We're going to admit her. I think she has pneumonia," the nurse surmised.

Dr. Sunnly came by twenty minutes later to conduct a physical exam. He placed his stethoscope on Claire's chest and back. "Take a deep breath for me, Claire." It hurt too much, but Claire did her best to inhale deeply and exhale as the handsome doctor listened to her lungs. "Good girl. Again."

"Well?" Bryant asked. "Is it pneumonia?"

"I can hear crackling at the base of her lungs. When rales are present, that's a sign something is seriously wrong. We need to do a chest X-ray to determine the extent of the inflammation. The nurse will also get a blood and mucus sample so we can analyze the cause of the infection. A CT scan would be good, too, so we know what we are looking at to determine the best way to treat her."

"How much is this all going to cost? Can't you just give her antibiotics or something and send us on our way?"

"Mr. Baker, this is serious. I want to keep her here for a week—"

"A week?" Bryant vehemently shook his head. "No."

"Your daughter needs to be on an IV drip and—"

"Absolutely not," Bryant hollered. "I'm checking her out."

Dr. Sunnly frowned and raised his voice. "She may not make it!"

"She's strong. She will either make it or she won't, but I'm taking her home and will care for her myself."

Bryant checked Claire out against medical advice and took his daughter home. He tucked her in bed and let her sleep.

"Well?" Gisela asked.

"What's wrong with her?" Benjamin asked.

"She's got pneumonia," Bryant said. "Take care of her will ya?" Bryant grabbed his keys. "I'm going out."

"Out?" Gisela asked. "Out where?"

Bryant didn't answer. He needed some air and time to think. Seeing Claire that sick worried him, but it also stressed him out. He closed the front door and disappeared down the road.

Gisela begrudgingly warmed up chicken broth and had Benjamin deliver it to Claire's room. Claire managed to sip a third of the semi-warm broth as Ton-ton stroked Claire's hair and planted soft kisses on her cheek. "I'll take care of you, Mommy."

#

Claire's health slowly improved, but Tanya's took a turn for the worse, starting with little sneezes and progressing to congestion, runny nose, sore throat, and coughing.

"This is all your fault." Gisela slapped Claire over the head. "You got her sick." She pounded her fist against Claire's body, striking her in the chest.

Tanya was horrified and screamed, "Don't hurt Mommy!"

Gisela stopped. "What?" She kicked Claire in the back. "How dare you turn my child against me?"

Claire scrambled to get away. She was still too tired and weak from her illness to fight.

Benjamin and Barry stood motionless, watching the chaos unfold. Tanya's cries triggered Shannon to wail, which made Claire burst into tears. She simply did not have the energy to run or fight. She slid her back down the wall in defeat and sat on her haunches. With her hands over her head, Claire took the beating as it came until she fell over. Gisela dragged Claire to the water heater closet and tossed her inside. She glared at the child cowering before her and closed the door.

"Serves you right," Gisela huffed.

Claire didn't dare open the closet even though it wasn't locked. She'd been to this dance before and knew to stay until her dad got home. She wiped her tears and blinked a few times to adjust to the darkness. Only a sliver of light from beneath the closet door gave Claire comfort. The damp, musty room was stifling. The hum of the water heater purred loudly, but she could hear Gisela yelling at Tanya.

"Go to your room!"

Inside the closet, Claire tried to find a comfortable position. There was barely enough room for a heater, much less a human, even if it was a small child. The cramped room was cluttered with cleaning supplies, shoes, and who knew what else. Something grazed against Claire's arm, and she jumped. Her imagination got the better of her as she visualized red eyes glowing and arms reaching out to clutch her to the depths of hell. Claire screamed in terror. Her heartbeat quickened, and her head throbbed. She flailed her arms and kicked the heater. The thrashing caused so much ruckus that the closet door flung open. A nanosecond of relief was snuffed out by Gisela's grip around Claire's throat.

"Quiet!" Gisela shoved Claire back inside and slammed the closet. "Don't you make a sound!"

Claire could hear Gisela dragging something to the hallway and pushing it up against the door. *Is it a chair? Maybe the nightstand?* She couldn't stand, couldn't sit, couldn't lie down. She leaned against the wall, her body bent into a V-shape at a thirty-degree angle, and there Claire stood for what seemed like days. Her back was sore. Her legs were numb. Her feet felt like lead when she tried to move and wiggle her toes. It was as if currents of electricity zapped her skin and coursed throughout her body, tapping her tailbone, squeezing her fingers, and sending tingles up to her head. She couldn't breathe. Her throat burned with dryness. She was hyperventilating. Claire wanted to tell her daddy about Gisela's mistreatment of her, but would he believe her? And if he did, he'd surely beat Gisela, who'd no doubt retaliate by sending Claire to her grave.

Claire licked her lips and bit her lower lip. She was so tired. Tired of half-standing. Tired from lack of sleep. Tired of carrying the weight of the world on her back. She closed her eyes to rest. The dull glow from beneath the door turned to black, and Claire slumped sideways.

#

The weeks dragged on slowly with only one highlight that Claire couldn't wait to share. She was ecstatic and skipped all the way home. Claire burst into the house and immediately went to work cleaning the dishes. She sang as she prepared a nice ramen noodle dinner, dressed with boiled chicken breasts and chopped green onions.

"Daddy," Claire said, "guess what?"

"Let me see," Bryant said, "Ed McMahon called, and you won the Publisher's Clearing House prize."

Claire giggled. "Guess again."

"You found treasure at the end of the rainbow," Barry chimed in.

"No," Claire said.

"Well, spit it out already," Gisela said dryly. "We don't have all day."

"I won the spelling bee!" Claire held her breath for her father's congratulatory praise. "It was down to Brian and me, and—"

"Well, I can't imagine it was that hard, seeing there's only, what, fifty or sixty kids in your grade?" Gisela asked.

Claire ignored her stepmother. She wasn't going to let Gisela pour cold water on her accomplishments. "I won with *onomatopoeia*."

Benjamin laughed. "Anna wanna pee on ya!"

Barry joined his brother and cackled. "I wanna pee on ya."

"I bet you couldn't spell it," Claire said. "You don't even know what onomatopoeia means."

Hearing that word again put Benjamin and Barry in stitches. They hugged their bellies and played off each other.

"I know what it means," Barry said.

"Yeah," Benjamins said. "It means someone's getting pissed on." Benjamin thought he was so clever and couldn't stop laughing.

Gisela joined in. "What a ridiculous word."

Bryant chuckled. "Winning the spelling bee at your school isn't the same as winning at the national level," Bryant said. "Keep working at it, and you'll improve. You're never going to be the best if you don't keep working at it."

Claire put her fork down. The ramen tasted bland to her. She lost her appetite. Being the best in her grade wasn't good enough. Her father made that clear. She had to be the national spelling bee champion to make him proud.

"I bet you can't spell *supercalifragilisticexpialidocious*," Benjamin said.

Claire rolled her eyes. "Not like you can either."

Claire felt humiliated. That night she tossed and turned as letters swirled around her mind and words danced in her dreams. She tried to catch them, but they evaded her grasp. *Will I ever be good enough?*

15. ENOUGH WAS ENOUGH

Autumn arrived, and the vibrant leaves put Gisela in a good mood. Bryant made love to her the night before. It was one of those rare occasions when their bedroom play wasn't rushed. Bryant came home with the smell of whisky and cigarettes on his breath, but she didn't mind. He was seductive and alluring, teasing her with his ear nibbling and nipple pinching. She wanted to be mad at him for coming home drunk, but his kisses were tender. His hot breath and soft lips covered every part of her and brought out the woman in her. There was an urgency in his thrusts that left her pining for more. It was times like these when she remembered why she loved him.

In the glow of the morning light, Gisela bathed in its warmth emanating from the and punched her in the shoulder window. Birds flew overhead as squirrels jostled their morsels of food. Not a cloud in the sky. Gisela opened the window and breathed in the cold, fresh air. The butterscotch scent of ponderosa pine trees kissed her nose while a soft breeze gingerly caressed her face. She hummed as she boiled water to make oatmeal for breakfast.

Tanya was the first to pitter-patter into the kitchen. Gisela frowned. "Ton-ton, when are you going to be potty-trained?" The wet diaper bulged below the toddler's belly button. "You're three years old. No more diapers. You need big girl underwear." Gisela stripped the soiled diaper off and tossed it in the trash. It landed with a heavy thump.

Gisela went into the girls' bedroom and grabbed one of Claire's underwear. She helped Tanya slip into it and found a safety pin to cinch it tight. Seeing Claire still in bed, Gisela threw a sock at Claire's head. "Get up, you lazy girl."

Claire rolled over. "I don't feel good."

"Don't lie to me," Gisela said. "You're fine. Now get up."

Gisela stormed out of the room with Tanya waddling behind her. Claire propped herself on one hand and slowly stood. She swayed side to side and stopped midstride to the closet. Her stomach lurched to her throat. Claire covered her mouth to suppress the urge to vomit. She got dressed and took extra time in the bathroom brushing her teeth, washing her face, and combing her hair.

At the table, Benji and Barry gobbled up their oatmeal like hogs at a trough. Claire sat down and stared into the bowl of brown mush. She took a small bite of the cold and soggy goo. It took everything she had to swallow the gross slop.

"What's wrong with you? Hurry up and eat," Gisela said. "You'll be late for school."

Claire lifted her spoon and shoved a heap of oatmeal into her mouth, but the texture was the consistency of diarrhea. Claire gagged. She shut her eyes, pinched her nose, and swallowed.

Gisela threw a wooden spoon at Claire. "Don't be so dramatic. You better not waste one bite, kid."

Claire scooped another spoonful of oatmeal into her mouth, but before she could swallow, a big glob of slop spewed out of her mouth and splashed into her bowl. Curdles of oats dripped from her lips down to her chin. More chunks of brown lava flowed from her tongue to the table.

Gisela shrieked. "Are you fucking kidding me?"

Barry scrunched up his nose. "Eww, yuck!"

"That's gross," Benjamin said.

Claire covered her mouth. "I'm sorry. I didn't mean to—"

"You're gonna clean that up," Gisela said.

Claire pushed her chair back to get a kitchen rag, but before she could take a step, Gisela pushed her back into her seat.

"What do you think you're doing?"

"I was going to get a towel—"

"No, you're not."

"But you said to clean—"

"That's right. Start eating. We don't waste food. You're going to swallow every bite of what's in front of you." Barry stared with his mouth agape. "I'd hurry up and eat that if I were you." Gisela's voice grated Claire's ears. "Otherwise it'll be waiting for you after school."

"You have to eat your puke," Benji laughed.

Claire let the soft tears slither down her cheeks. She forced herself to swallow the barf-oatmeal mixture and managed to keep the waves of vomit down.

#

High-pitched screams reached Claire's ears before the trailer came into sight. She recognized that cry—Tanya shrieked hysterically. Claire tossed her backpack to Benjamin and ran to the house. The door was wide open. Claire burst through the entrance and stopped dead in her tracks. Gisela had Tanya by one arm and was whipping her little sister with a belt.

Claire couldn't believe her eyes. Bloody welts branded Tanya's arms and legs like she was a candy cane. Her sister screamed in agony. Tanya's body swelled beet-red. Tears and drool drenched her little sister's tank top. Yellow stains drenched her underwear. Tanya had wet herself.

Claire hated Gisela so much. She prayed for someone to rob their house and shoot her stepmother. She imagined Gisela trying to run from the gunman, tripping, and staring down a barrel of a rifle. She could see a congregation of alligators swarming in to eat her alive as she took her last breath. And just for good measure, a parade of elephants would stampede over her body to crush the last remnants of life left in her. It would be good riddance. They all would be better without her.

"You're not a goddamn baby anymore," Gisela screamed.

Fire rose inside of Claire. She grabbed Tanya and handed her over to Benjamin and Barry, who arrived just before the next lashing.

"Go next door," Claire barked, "and don't you dare come back until I get you." The boys took their sister's hand and ran out the door. Claire turned to face her stepmother. "Who do you think you are?" Gisela didn't answer. Claire didn't expect her to. Claire ran to the kitchen, and Gisela bolted after her.

"You little shit," Gisela yelled.

Claire pulled the top kitchen drawer open and hurled a chef's knife at Gisela. "Beating me is one thing—" Claire grabbed another knife and chucked it at Gisela. "But she is just a baby." Claire snapped her wrist and sent a paring knife at Gisela like it was a ninja star and followed it with a carving knife. Claire sailed one knife after another at Gisela with every word that flew out of her rampant mouth. "You. Fucking. Stupid. Cunt!"

"Are you fucking mad?" Gisela screamed. She ducked and managed to dodge almost all of the knives. "You should have been committed a long time ago, you crazy bitch! I knew you were a deranged demon-child the moment I saw you. Even the devil cast you out of hell, you wretched spawn."

Everything from a butter knife to a steak knife and bread knife was heaved in Gisela's direction. One of them pricked Gisela's arm and another bounced off her palm. None of them pierced her skin deep enough to do damage.

The last knife in the drawer was a cleaver. Claire held it high in the air. Her nostrils flared with every exhale as her chest heaved. She stood to her full height and took a deliberate step forward. With each advance, Gisela took a step back.

"Don't you dare," Gisela croaked.

"If you ever lay a hand on Ton-ton again," Claire threatened, "I will kill you."

Claire ran toward Gisela, who darted down the hall. Gisela slammed the bedroom door shut and quickly locked it. "You're a lunatic!" She collapsed to the floor. Her heart bashed against the chambers of her rib cage and echoed in her eardrums.

Claire smiled but didn't allow herself a victory dance. She may have won the battle, but the war still waged on. Claire picked up all the knives and put them back in the drawer. She held onto the cleaver, just in case, and went next door to retrieve her siblings. Enough was enough.

16. THIS IS GOODBYE

After the knife-throwing fiasco, Gisela had had enough. She was convinced Bryant's brat was possessed. How could anyone love that wretched child? These past few years she had given him everything. She took care of his kid, cooked his meals, and laundered his clothes . . . and for what? She admitted Bryant was great between the sheets, but she couldn't build a home on sex alone. He was a drunk, a cheat, and an unreliable provider. His dependability was sporadic at best.

Gisela was exasperated. She loved him though. He was charming and handsome. He wasn't always violent. When he was sober, he was very loving. Bryant might be old-fashioned about gender roles, but so was she. A man's job was to work and provide for his family. A wife's job was to run the household and raise the children.

She just couldn't get over her husband's obsession with threesomes. Sharing their bed with a stranger was unnatural. He saw it as a carefree adventure. Gisela saw it as degrading. The idea of him with another woman gave her brain hemorrhoids if there was such a thing.

I'll decide once I get to the women's shelter. She dialed her neighbor, Jake, and made arrangements to be dropped off at the shelter that afternoon.

Gisela pulled out the old suitcase and unlatched it. The same worn suitcase she'd packed when she left her ex-husband . . . the one she took to the women's shelter the first time Bryant beat her. This suitcase had almost as much mileage on it as she did but was twice as weathered. She stared at the empty suitcase for a long time, trying to convince herself to stay.

What would she do to support herself and the kids? She didn't have any skills to speak of, and the thought of working in a greasy diner appalled her. An overweight woman with no job, no education, no money, and four children under the age of eleven was a walking billboard for America's Least Desirable. She'd have to apply for welfare.

Tanya and Shannon needed their father. Didn't they? Would she be a bad mother to rob them of their father? What about the boys? They had grown attached to Bryant, and he was the only father they knew. Would Bryant look for them and drag them home?

Gisela imagined his wrath once he discovered they were gone. She wouldn't put it past him to call the police and report her kidnapping his girls. Heaven forbid if he caught up with her. He'd turn her face and body into the hunchback of Notre Dame.

Gisela shuddered and packed her clothes into the suitcase. She grabbed a large trash bag and carelessly tossed the kids' clothes into it.

The more she thought about it, the more excited Gisela got imagining Claire and Bryant coming home to an empty house. Good riddance. They deserved each other. She hated Claire. If that child could be so mean-spirited and uncontrollable as to throw sharp objects at her, the devil only knew what harm she was capable of as she grew older. Gisela would never yield to her stepdaughter and wasn't going to stick around to raise Bryant's heathen child another day.

Voices outside spilled into the living room. The kids were home from school. She tossed the bag of clothes into her room and ran to the kitchen to prepare ham and mayonnaise sandwiches.

"Hi, Mom," Benjamin said.

"How was school?" Gisela asked.

"Good," Barry said. "I got a gold star on my map drawing."

"Good for you." Gisela handed the boys their sandwiches. "Claire, I need you to run down to Circle K and get a pack of cigarettes."

Two days had passed since the knife-throwing rampage. Gisela and Claire had barely spoken more than three words to each other. Claire salivated seeing her brothers scarf down their sandwiches. She took the two dollars and headed out the front door, taking her sweet time walking to the store, giving her time to be in her head and think.

#

The knife scene replayed in Claire's mind. Guilt from losing her temper mixed with satisfaction seeing Gisela cower in fear gave Claire a conflicted feeling. What if one of them had pierced her stepmother in the heart or lungs? What if it had punctured an artery or plunged into her stomach? As much as Gisela deserved to die a slow and painful death, Claire didn't want to go to jail. She remembered being in the back of the cop car when she returned home from the women's shelter. It was embarrassing. If she had killed her stepmother with one of the knives, she'd be dragged away in handcuffs and placed in the backseat of a police car again. She wouldn't be able to face her dad with that shame. And if she was in prison, who would take care of Shannon and Ton-ton? Who'd get the boys up and ready for school? Who'd cook for Daddy?

Claire opened the door and walked into the bright store. Her favorite cashier was working.

"Well, hello, Miss Claire," Jennifer said, her voice so smothered in honey that Claire's teeth ached. "Back for cigs?"

Claire nodded. "Are you having any sales today on candy?"

"I'm afraid not, sugar."

Claire lowered her eyes. "Okay, well, just a pack of cigarettes then."

"That will be a dollar and fifteen cents." Jennifer handed Claire a pack of Benson & Hedges and gave her the change. With the coins was a Jolly Rancher candy. Claire's sun-kissed, freckled face lit up. Jennifer winked. "Our little secret."

Claire skipped out of the store and strolled home, timing her arrival by how long it took to suck down the candy. When she got back to the mobile home park, her dad's truck was in the driveway. He was home early. She smiled and ran the rest of the way.

"Daddy!" Claire swung the front door open, but no one was in the living room. She immediately sensed something was wrong. It was too quiet. Claire rushed to her room, expecting to see Ton-ton playing with a doll and Shannon taking her afternoon nap, but they were not there. Perhaps they were at a neighbor's house.

She walked to her brothers' room, and it, too, was vacant. A sinking feeling enveloped her as she walked trepidatiously toward her father's room. Her pulse quickened. Her palms became moist. She was acutely aware of her dry lips and throat. Claire held her breath and strained to listen for sounds from the room. Nothing. She pushed the door ajar wider and scanned the room.

Bryant sat on the floor, propped against the bed, a bottle of whisky in hand. Half the bottle was gone.

A folded piece of paper lay on the floor next to his knee. Claire had been gone less than an hour. He must have gotten home while she was at the store.

"What happened, Daddy?" Claire asked. "Where is everybody?"

Bryant grimaced and put his head in his hand. "They're gone."

"Gone? Gone where? What do you mean?"

Bryant handed Claire the note. She unfolded the paper and recognized Gisela's curvy handwriting.

Bryant, this is goodbye. I can't do this anymore. The drinking, the cheating, the bouncing around from house to house. Not to mention Claire hates me despite everything I do for her. I'll file for divorce once I'm settled.

Gisela

That was it. Short and to the point. Claire folded the note in half and knelt beside her father. She didn't know whether to throw herself a rainbow party or a pity party. Claire stayed silent and claimed ignorance of Gisela's disappearance. What would her father think if he knew she was the reason they had packed up? That her going berserk was the hammer that sealed the deal?

"I'm sure they'll be back." Claire placed her hand on Bryant's shoulder to comfort him. As much as she hoped to never see Gisela again, Claire's heart throbbed as if it were being forced through the eye of a needle. This was her fault.

The mist in her eyes swelled into big tears and slithered down her cheeks. It hit her that she might never see Ton-ton or baby Shannon again. If they truly never came back, she'd even miss her stupid brothers. Who would protect them when Gisela's temper flared? Who'd take care of them when Gisela spent her monthly cycles in bed with cramps and self-pity? Guilt clung to her shoulders like a heavy, rain-soaked cloak. She shouldn't have thrown those knives at Gisela. She shouldn't have said all those nasty things and called her stepmother the C-word. Claire curled next to her father and cried.

Bryant took a swig of his whiskey and slurred his words as he spoke. "What do you say we move back to Rochester Let's go back to where you were born. Just you and me. There's nothing for us here."

Claire place her cool hands on Bryant's arm and her warm cheek against his shoulder. "That's a good idea." They could use a fresh start. Her gut told her Gisela was gone for good. She didn't want to live in that house and come home each day to see traces of Gisela in the house, strands of her hair, an old sweater, or the nearly empty bottle of an Avon fragrance sample. "Or we can live by Grandma and Grandpa and Aunt Samantha!"

Bryant frowned. "Claire, we're not living in a state full of Mexicans and Chinese."

"Why?" Claire asked.

"They're all thieves. If they're not stealing my job, they're stealing the shirt off my back." Bryant shifted his weight and pivoted around to face his daughter. "Worse yet, they're always staring at you with their judgy little eyes. They think they're all smarter than us. We stick to our kind, you got it?" Claire nodded and held her breath. Her father was drunk and reeked of alcohol. "Birds of a feather flock together. Why they stay in the good old U-S-of-A boggles me when they have their own country they can go back to."

Claire wondered if she had ever met a Chinese person. She remembered that trucker friend of Jalisco's back at Motel 6. She couldn't remember his name or his face. "But Jalisco was nice. "You remember him, Daddy? Isn't he Mexican?"

"I still wouldn't trust him farther than I can throw him." Bryant chucked his empty whisky bottle at the painting Gisela had insisted on buying at a garage sale, saying it might be worth something. Seeing the ugly thing made Claire taste bitterness on her tongue.

Bryant hugged his daughter. "At least I still have my sunshine." He stood up and steadied himself. "I need a shower beer. Grab me one, will ya?" Bryant took a step and lost his balance. He landed flat on his back on the bed and stared at the ceiling. "Hello, Henry."

"What?" Claire asked.

Bryant pointed at the large brown stain shaped like a squirrel. Bryant smiled and pointed at the stain. "That looks like a squirrel. I just named him Henry. Now go get me that beer. And start dinner. I'm hungry."

Claire did as she was told, but when she came back to the bedroom, her father was snoring. She nudged him, shook him, and yelled at him with no response. Claire pulled her father's boots off and picked up the Famous Grouse whisky bottle. She trudged to the kitchen and tossed the empty bottle away then put the beer back into the fridge. Her tummy rumbled and reminded her she hadn't eaten since breakfast.

Claire fried up a couple of eggs for dinner and sat alone at the kitchen table eating her over-easy eggs. She replayed in her mind the knife attack. Her hand twitched as she relived the anger that bubbled in her. Seeing Tanya's red face screaming in pain, helpless to do anything but endure the lashings, made Claire distressed. She threw her fork at the sink and sobbed. She pounded her fist on the table repeatedly. Why? Why had she done that? Why did she have to lose it and throw those knives? Couldn't she have thrown something else? Shoes or spoons? She longed to hear her sister's voice and ached to hold baby Shannon in her arms and swaddle her tight. She saw Barry's round face and sweet smile whenever she'd give him something sweet. Even Benji, as annoying as he was, had been her partner in crime and someone to talk to when she was bored. She missed her brothers and sisters so much and never felt such hollowness in her stomach. She wanted to tear at her chest and rip her heart out.

"I will never be cruel to my children," she declared under her breath. "They will know love and kindness, and I'll play with them. We will laugh all the time and be silly, and I'll protect them from anyone bad."

Claire crossed her arms on the table and laid her head down to weep. She promised to never be anything like Gisela.

17. THREE'S COMPANY

What didn't fit in the truck got left behind. Claire packed her clothes, toiletries, a few books, including her dictionary, and a couple of photos she had of her siblings. Bryant abandoned everything except the essentials—his clothes and his guitar.

Back in Rochester, Minnesota, Bryant found a dinky two-bedroom apartment on the west side of slum town. For weeks, Claire ate dinner alone. She sat in front of the window each night, crying and waiting for her father to come home. Was he lost? Hurt? In jail? Her imagination ran wild, envisioning her daddy in a bar fight, drunk at the wheel, hit by a semi-truck, and crashing into a guardrail on the highway. Sometimes he'd come home at ten o'clock at night and other times, much later, after she'd passed out from anxiety and fear.

On those nights, Claire missed her grandparents the most. Her father never called them or wrote to them, so she had no way of getting in touch with them. When Gisela was in their lives, she made sure any presents, letters, or phone calls from Grandma Sharon or Grandpa Harold were deflected. She hoped they hadn't forgotten her. With the constant moving from one address to another, it was impossible to track their whereabouts. How Claire missed them and hoped to see them again.

Bryant was back on a bender, feeling sorry for himself that Gisela had left him. Without fail, Claire found her father passed out in his car. It was a miracle he made it home. Claire's routine consisted of walking to school, coming home, doing her homework, and living her life independently of her father.

Before long, they moved out of their small apartment and into another place on the south side of Rochester. Bryant responded to a room for rent ad, and the next thing Claire knew, they were sharing an apartment with a woman in her thirties named Candy.

She was a fetching redhead with freckles, skinny like Claire, and responsible too . . . everything Gisela was not. Claire liked her immediately. The two of them spent a lot of time together since Bryant was rarely home.

"Hey, you want to go to the mall?" Candy asked.

Claire nodded. "What are you going to get?"

"I need a new alarm clock, and maybe I'll get something for my date," Candy said. "You can help me pick something nice."

They meandered around the mall, popping into the big department stores like Sears and JCPenney, but Candy didn't try anything on.

"Do you know where you're going with Jason?" Claire asked. She was looking forward to meeting Candy's boyfriend. "Maybe that will help us pick something just right."

"Good point," Candy said. "He mentioned dinner and a movie at the drive-in, then night boating on the lake."

"You definitely want to be comfortable if you're sitting in a car for two hours," Claire said. "And be warm out on the boat."

Candy nodded. "Probably cover my legs, too, in case of the bugs. I guess no dress for me."

"Maybe a pantsuit with a sweater?"

"Yeah, but pantsuits aren't the easiest to get off when—"

"Oh," Claire gasped. "You mean when you get to second base . . ."

Candy laughed. "No. I mean . . . well, yes, that . . . but I was going to say when I need to use the bathroom."

Claire blushed. The two of them burst into laughter and had the giggles for the rest of the afternoon. Each time they passed a mannequin wearing a romper or pantsuit, they'd look at each other and chuckle.

"Oh, can we go into Waldenbooks?" Claire asked. "And maybe Tower Records too? Just to look?"

The two of them wandered the aisles, flipped through the pages of Sweet Valley High books, perused the poster racks, and listened to a couple of vinyl records from R.E.M. and The Police.

"You hungry?" Candy asked. "There's a new restaurant in the food court called Panda Express, and it's so good. I just love Chinese food."

Claire and Candy grabbed lunch and talked endlessly about dreamy movie stars and what they wanted in life. Candy shared she wanted kids but couldn't have any. "I never had a regular menstrual cycle and have been underweight my whole life. I'm thirty-three now and have to accept I'll never have children of my own."

"Does your boyfriend want kids?" Claire asked. She didn't want the day to end. She felt normal, safe, happy, and important. She could listen to Candy talk forever and not get bored.

"Jason has a daughter from a previous relationship so he's good not having another child. I, however, have been seeing a psychologist for the past year, trying to come to terms that I will never be a mother."

Candy put her fork down and pushed her plate of chow mein noodles aside. She looked past Claire to the Sbarro pizza sign and rapidly blinked to fan the moisture away.

Claire noticed the change in mood. "I'm sorry you can't have kids." Claire got out of her chair and hugged Candy. "You have me though."

"Yes, and I am having a wonderful time getting to know you."

"What does a psychologist do?"

"Well, they're like a counselor. They listen to your problems and help you figure out what you can do to not be screwed up anymore. Anyway, let's enjoy our afternoon. C'mon, I want to buy you a shirt or something. There's nothing like shopping to cheer a girl up."

Claire eagerly followed Candy to Benetton and Esprit. They modeled for each other some clothes and ultimately left the mall with bags from Kinney Shoes, Casual Corner, and Suncoast Motion Picture.

Halfway home, Claire realized they forgot something. "Didn't you need an alarm clock? We forgot to go to RadioShack."

"Dang it," Candy said. "Oh well. That'll give us another excuse to go to the mall again soon."

#

"Hey, it's Friday night," Candy said, "and I got paid." She shimmied over to Bryant and kicked his foot. "Getting paid and getting laid." She let out a low, raspy laugh. "What about you, old man? What are you doing tonight?"

Bryant flicked his cigarette ash at his roommate. "None of your business. And for the record, I may be fifty, but I've got plenty of mileage here." Bryant pointed at his crotch. "Enough to keep the ladies begging for more."

"Come out tonight with Jason and me. I want to witness all these ladies begging for more." Candy laughed. She slipped her fingers around Bryant's cigarette, took a drag, and didn't hand it back to him. "Claire will be fine for a few hours."

"I know," Bryant said.

"Well then?"

Bryant lit a fresh cigarette with the cherry end of Candy's cigarette and took a big puff before agreeing. He was ready for some devilish fun.

An hour later they were at the smokey honky-tonk on the other side of town. It was much bigger inside than it appeared outside. Perhaps it was the panel of mirrors behind the bar that gave the illusion of space. Bryant admired himself in the mirrors and liked seeing the bar entrance behind him. From the reflection, he surveyed the crowd and appreciated the slender legs ubiquitously present around him. He had to admit, the crowd was good-looking.

A blonde beauty with ripped jeans, cowboy boots, and an untucked V-neck T-shirt approached the bar. Her hair flowed like wheat fields and smelled like honey. She gave him a sideways glance and smiled.

"You smell good. What are you wearing?" The blonde didn't wait for Bryant's response. "Let me guess. Stetson."

Bryant nodded. Never mind that an hour before he had rubbed some random cowboy scent from an Avon catalog on his neck. "Aren't you a bit young to be in a pub?"

"I'm twenty-six."

Bryant pulled out the barstool and invited her to sit. "Can I buy you a drink?"

She gave him her hand. "I'm Shoshana. Well, Shana, actually."

"Bryant."

Shana leaned against the bar rail, letting her cleavage flag the bartender's attention. "Alabama Slammer, please."

Bryant noticed she wasn't wearing a bra. "You can put the lady's drink on my tab."

"I haven't seen you here before," Shana said.

"So you're a regular here?"

Shana giggled. She took out a cigarette, and Bryant was quick to light it. "Thank you. This is the best bar on this side of town. I come here on Fridays to unwind. You here with anybody?"

Bryant nodded to the pool table where Candy and Jason were racking balls. "That's Candy, my roommate, and her boyfriend, Jason."

"Roommate?" Shana raised her eyebrows.

Bryant didn't like anyone second-guessing him. If she wasn't so cute, he'd walk away and not give her a second of his time. What a shame she dressed more like a farmer than a farmer's daughter. Bryant wondered what curves hid beneath her baggy jeans and oversized T-shirt.

"Well, I just moved back here not too long ago."

"From?"

"Montana."

Shana accepted her cocktail from the bartender and crossed her legs. "What was in Montana?"

Memories of Gisela bubbled up, but Bryant quickly dismissed his ex-wife. *She left me*, he reminded himself. Besides, he was a man who did what he wanted, and it was clear the woman in front of him was not to be ignored. He liked that she was easy to talk to. "There was nothing in Montana."

Shana flashed a flirtatious smile. "But the ski resorts—"

"I don't ski."

"And Yellowstone—"

"I don't hike."

"Well, what do you do then?" Shana asked.

"I ride—" Bryant said.

"Horses?"

"No, my bike," Bryant said, "and I like to play my guitar and sing."

Shana laughed and gently slapped his knee. "Not all at the same time, I hope."

Bryant felt a sharp prick on his neck and was surprised to see Candy behind him. She stabbed him again with her fingernails. "She's off-limits."

"Candy!" Shoshana hopped off the stool to hug her friend.

"You gotta be shitting me," Bryant said. "You two know each other?"

The two women wrapped their arms around each other's waist and toasted their glasses together.

"Shana, girlfriend, go prowl somewhere else," Candy said. "Bryant's too old for you." She pointed to a tall blond at the jukebox next to Jason. "He's more your speed."

Bryant shook his head. "You mean Mr. Henley shirt over there who's all brawns and no brains? Look at him. He looks like he's waiting for that jukebox to give him change like it's a damn vending machine. Shana, would you rather have a boy or a man?"

Candy took the orange slice from the rim of her Blue Lagoon drink and threw it playfully at Bryant. "Don't answer that. This one has an ego." She poked Bryant's shoulder and winked. The three of them joined Jason at the pool table, and as the night wore on, the four of them worked the room, playing darts, shooting pool, and throwing coins at the jukebox. They danced. They flirted. And when it was the last call for alcohol, they went their separate ways—Bryant back to Shana's rambler and Jason back to Candy's for a frolicking good time.

Oh, how wonderful it felt to be untethered and free, Bryant thought, as he fell asleep in a tangle of arms and legs.

#

Bryant woke to find Shana's cat eyes three inches from his face. Her sensual lips curved into a Cheshire grin. "Not bad for an old man."

"Who are you calling old?" Bryant pulled back the covers and slapped Shana's bare skin. He yearned to kiss her, taste her mouth, play with her tongue, and ravage every inch of her flawless body again. *I'm going to make you mine.*

"I had fun last night," Shana said. "And boy, can you sing!" She grabbed his cowboy hat and swayed provocatively at the foot of the bed.

Bryant reached for her but she moved out of reach. With his hat on her tousled hair, she sang "Islands in the Stream." When she got to the chorus, Bryant piped in, changing the lyrics to "Move in with me . . . to another place . . ."

"What?" Shana exclaimed.

"Move in with Candy and me," Bryant said. "It'll be fun."

"We just met last night!"

He tugged at her hips and nuzzled his face into the mounds of her flesh. "So?"

Shana moaned. "Okay, but I get to be Chrissy."

Bryant stopped kissing her. "What?"

She giggled. "You know, the show, *Three's Company*. Candy can be Janet and you can be—"

"Don't you dare say Jack or Mr. Furley." Bryant picked Shana up and tossed her onto the bed. He rubbed his whiskers on her neck and tickled her, sending her into bouts of uncontrollable laughter.

"Mercy! Mercy!" Shana rolled over to catch her breath. She straddled her new lover and caressed his jawline with her finger.

"Does this mean yes?" Bryant asked. He held his breath for her reply. He knew it was insane to move in together after one night, but they had a strong, undeniable attraction. He wanted to wake up every morning next to her, feeling alive and full of joy, playful and well-rested. Could he be in love? Bryant didn't recall ever feeling this way about anyone before. Shana brought out a vitality he thought he had lost, a hunger for sex that she satisfied, and a passion for role-playing that he always fantasized about.

Shana kissed Bryant and whispered, "It's a maybe."

#

Weeks went by, and Claire didn't see her father. Candy said not to worry, that he was out sowing his oats. With Candy home every night, Claire took comfort in knowing an adult was there to keep her safe. She didn't stay up late each night looking out the window, wondering when her father would come home or if he'd come home at all.

For three weeks, Claire's days were filled with schoolwork, and her nights were consumed with books and music. Sometimes Candy took her to the mall or out to eat. Occasionally Jason came over, and the three of them sat on the couch to watch TV or on the floor to play board games. Claire loved Candy, who was the first strong role model she ever had. The relationship Jason and Candy had with each other was relaxed, tender, and playful. Claire developed a little crush on Jason but kept that secret close to her heart. She hoped one day she'd find a good boyfriend like Jason to marry—someone tall, handsome, strong, funny, and loving.

"Claire, sweetie," Candy said, "guess what Jason brought over? Popcorn and the new *Star Trek* movie."

Claire jumped to her feet and clasped her hands together. "The second one?"

"Yup," Jason said. "*Wrath of Khan*! I bought the video. It was forty dollars, but I can't have the first one without owning the second one."

"That's expensive," Claire said.

"It's worth it," Jason said. "We can watch it over and over as much as we want. Here, put it in while I make some popcorn."

Claire pulled the video out of the sleeve and pushed it into the VHS recorder. The tape played automatically, so she hit the pause button and waited on Jason.

"Come sit with me." Candy patted the sofa cushion. "Your hair is getting long, and it's as copper as mine. Want me to braid it?"

Claire nodded. "Candy, are you still seeing a psychologist?"

Candy scooped Claire's long strands into the palm of her hand and began braiding. "Yeah, I see her off and on still, but probably not much longer. I can't have kids, no matter how desperately I want them, so I should move on and accept it."

"Can I ask a favor? Do you think your counselor would see me?"

"Why?"

"I don't want to become screwed up like my dad."

Candy stopped braiding. "Oh, honey, trust me, you've got a good head on your shoulders."

"Please?" Claire didn't have the words to explain how she felt but believed a counselor could help her. She loved her father but sometimes, his drunken behavior and how he treated people embarrassed her.

. She wanted him to be well, to be normal, and she wanted to have the kind of life people on *Diff'rent Strokes* and *The Facts of Life* had. None of them beat their kids or disappeared for weeks at a time. None of them moved every few months or got drunk and took their anger out on their family.

Candy thought about it for a couple of seconds and conceded. "All right, I'll give Sunrise a call and see what they say."

18. SUNRISE

Candy pulled into the parking space in front of Sunrise Youth and Family Counseling but kept the engine running. Claire fidgeted in the passenger seat, biting her lip and gazing out the window—anything to avoid eye contact with Candy. Claire tucked her hands underneath her legs to keep still.

Candy patted Claire's thigh. "We don't have to go inside."

Claire shook her head. "No, I want to go." As nervous as she was, Claire knew she needed to get a few things off her chest. She wanted the counselor to tell her everything was going to be all right. She needed to hear she wouldn't grow up to be messed up like her dad . . . or Gisela, for that matter.

Inside the small Sunrise building, Claire's nose was assaulted by the sweet and pungent scent of mothballs. Only one person sat in the waiting room. A teenage boy sulked in the corner, his ripped black jeans exposing a scraped knee with dried, burgundy trails of blood. His legs sprawled apart in front of him while his head rested against the floral-print wallpaper. He looked dead.

"Sign in, please." The receptionist pointed to the clipboard on the counter. Her name tag read *Barbara*.

Candy checked Claire into her appointment and picked a seat far away from the sleeping boy to finish filling out the intake form. They waited in silence and watched Barbara until it was their turn. Behind the desk, Barbara moved in stealth mode, rising to the copier and fax machine, swiveling to the file cabinet, and falling back to her seat where she juggled the phone and the PC in front of her. Clickety-clack went Barbara's fingertips as she entered Claire's information into the IBM console that was her personal computer.

A gentleman appeared from the back office and briefly looked at Claire before turning his attention to the teenager in the corner. "Jacob?"

The boy opened his eyes and shot out of his seat, nimble and swift. He nodded and followed the man down the hall.

"Will you be in the office with me?" Claire asked.

"Would you like me to?" Candy asked.

Claire hesitated. She didn't know what to expect and, for that reason, wanted Candy there. At the same time, she didn't want Candy to think less of her if she heard the secrets of her heart.

"Oh, you can't go in there," Barbara said. "It's strictly confidential."

Candy squeezed Claire's hand. "You'll be fine. Just speak from your heart. No one will know what you say except your counselor."

Five minutes later, a woman entered the room and smiled warmly at Claire. "I'm Rita. You ready to come talk to me?"

Claire rose slowly and wiped her clammy hands on her pants. She nodded and followed Rita down the hall to the third door on the left.

Rita motioned for Claire to sit.Claire shuffled and slithered to the couch as if numb and already defeated.

"Would you like some juice or water? Maybe a snack?" Rita offered. "It's free. You can take whatever you want from that basket in front of you."

Claire surveyed the wicker basket. There was Capri Sun fruit juice in an assortment of flavors, Fruit Roll-Ups, potato chips, and Handi-Snacks. She reached for the Handi-Snacks and put one in each of her coat pockets, then opened the apple juice and potato chips.

"Claire, you are in sixth grade?" Rita asked. Claire nodded and squeaked out a yes. "Why don't you tell me how you're feeling today."

Claire shrugged. "Fine, I guess."

"Is there anything specific you want to talk about today?"

Claire didn't know where to start. Should she start with Gisela and how her stepmother ruined everything? Or should she talk about Ton-ton and Shannon and how much she missed her sisters? Should she start with her grandparents and how she missed them? Maybe going straight to how she felt about her dad's drinking was the right approach.

The dull ache in her chest flared up again as guilt settled into her stomach. Claire saw vividly the knives flying at Gisela's head. She remembered how good it felt to thrust the blades as fast and as hard as she could. The cold handles of the knife transferred their energy to her arm and made her feel powerful. The torment of knowing it was Claire's fault that Gisela left and that she'd never see her siblings again made her want to throw herself into a lake.

When Claire didn't respond, Rita took a sip of her coffee and said, "It says in my notes that you're worried about your dad and that you don't want to end up like him." Claire stopped crunching on her chips and met the psychologist's eyes. "So can you tell me what you mean?"

Claire swallowed her chips and tossed the empty bag on the coffee table. "My daddy drinks a lot. He's going to end up killing himself someday."

"Are you worried he is going to get into an accident?"

"Yes, or he'll get beaten up, or have one of his heart spells and die in the hospital."

"How many times has this happened?"

Claire had to think about that. She tried to count on her fingers the many times he had his angina spells, the time he crashed his bike and spent three weeks in the hospital, the bar fight he had in Montana when they ran from the cops in the middle of the night, leaving Gisela and her siblings behind . . . In the end, Claire blurted, "Too many."

"How does that make you feel?"

"Like I'm the parent, I guess. But he's the adult. It's his job to take care of me."

"That's very perceptive, Claire. You are right. Parents need to take care of their children."

"Sometimes he comes home drunk and passes out in his car, with the door wide open, and I have to help him inside. The whole neighborhood watches, and it's embarrassing. And sometimes he's so hungry he'll make something to eat, like eggs, but he'll burn them. The smoke detector goes off, and I think he'll burn down the kitchen. But he doesn't care. He'll sit and eat half of his burnt eggs, light a cigarette, and then pass out with a lit cigarette in his hand. I have to put it out or else he'll burn the house down. There've been times when he's so drunk, he can barely hold his fork, and I have to put his plate on the counter before he knocks it to the floor." Claire took a breath and willed her tears to go back where they came from. It was no use. One escaped, and the rest followed.

Rita handed Claire a tissue. "Claire, have you told your dad your feelings?"

Claire shook her head. "It's no use. He won't listen or care."

"I'm sorry you feel this way. Tell me what you like about your father."

"Well, when he's not drunk, he can be fun. He takes me riding on his motorcycle, and sometimes we go to garage sales. He used to surprise me at school and take me out to eat, and we'd spend the afternoon reading together at a park. He tells me I'm his sunshine, and he doesn't treat me like a baby." Claire tried to think of more things. "I know he loves me, but when he drinks, he can be mean."

Rita furiously wrote down notes and listened intently. "You're very perceptive and mature for your age, Claire." The hour went by quickly, and they scheduled a follow-up session for a couple of weeks later.

On the drive home, Candy didn't ask questions, and Claire didn't share any information. "Hey, my birthday is coming up," Candy said. "Jason is taking me to a nice Chinese restaurant to celebrate. We're inviting a few friends, and I want you and your daddy to come."

Claire sat up straighter in her seat and smiled with excitement. She had never been to a nice restaurant before. Back when they traveled cross-country together, she and her dad ate at cheap diners, grabbed food at gas stations, or stopped at McDonald's and Taco Bell for quick bites. This would be a real treat to sit down at a fancy restaurant, order from a big menu, eat from real china plates, and celebrate Candy's special day. She couldn't wait.

#

The day arrived, and Claire surveyed the clothes she had in her drawers. She tried on different shirts and pant combinations, but nothing was pretty enough. She wished she had a nice dress to wear to the restaurant. She dug through the drawers and scoped out the dirty laundry pile. Nothing. If it didn't smell, then it had rips or stains on it. She shuffled her tops around, half expecting a nice outfit would miraculously appear.

"Hurry up, Claire," Bryant said. "We have to pick up Shana before heading to the restaurant."

Claire hadn't met her father's new girlfriend yet and wasn't looking forward to it. She didn't like that he disappeared for weeks without any phone calls, entrusting her to Candy's care while he was out doing who knew what and with whom. At least Claire didn't have to witness any drunken episodes. She finally settled on the nice shirt Candy had bought her at the mall and slipped on black cotton pants that were a tad too short.

"I'm ready," Claire called out. She met her father in the living room and stopped in her tracks. "Daddy, you look handsome."

"Thanks, Sunshine. Let's go."

In the car, Bryant turned on the radio. The two of them sang to the tunes on the radio like old times with Claire belting from the backseat. When they pulled up to an old rambler, a young woman stepped out to greet them.

Claire could not believe her eyes. Her dad's new girlfriend was half his age. She was young and skinny, with honey-wheat-colored hair and a sharp, pointy nose. She was pretty with boyish features. Her eyebrows were thick and a bit unruly. She reminded Claire of the actress and model Brooke Shields, only the male version with lighter hair. If Ms. Shields had a twin brother, Dad's new girlfriend was him. She wore no makeup. Her hair was tied in a messy ponytail. Her clothes were anything but feminine or coordinated. She wore denim overalls, mud boots, and a big long-sleeve orange crewneck shirt.

Shoshana slid into the front seat and lathered kisses all over Bryant's face. "Hiya."

"Hiya, yourself," Bryant said. He turned to Claire and introduced Shana to his daughter. "I think you two are going to get along just fine!"

Claire was speechless. Shana looked like she was in high school.

"I've heard so many wonderful things about you," Shana said. "Your father told me you play the viola and you love to read. I love books too." Shana continued to ramble. She talked fast and nonstop all the way to the restaurant. "So what's your favorite book, Claire?"

"I'm reading—"

"We're here," Bryant said. "I'm starving. I hope they're not serving dog and weird shit like jellyfish."

Shana laughed. "I'm sure it all tastes like chicken."

"Well, if we suddenly notice all the stray animals are missing . . ." Bryant grabbed Shana's butt and squeezed her cheeks hard. He planted a rough kiss on her full lips and chuckled. It was still swollen from their lovemaking last night. Finally, he had met his match—someone who could keep up with his sexual appetite. Shana was in her twenties, and although she dressed like a boy, at least her ass and breasts were firm like a teenager's. She was a wildcat in bed. The sex was so good—lights on or off, it didn't matter. Anywhere, anytime, and in any position, she was ready for him. Bryant was smitten.

Inside the Chinese restaurant, a slender woman in a yellow cheongsam with gold accents greeted them. "Welcome to Imperial Garden. How many?"

"We're meeting friends here," Shana said. "Oh, I see them." Shana pointed to the far corner where Candy and Jason were seated around a circular table with three other people. There were eight black lacquered chairs with red cushions, and all but three were occupied.

The hostess escorted them to their semi-private section. Claire followed behind, admiring the silk dress with the high slits on either side. The gold phoenix design on the dress shimmered with each step as the hostess swayed her hips from side to side.

"Claire, I saved you a seat next to me," Candy said. Claire eagerly went to sit next to her.

"Hey, birthday girl," Bryant said.

Candy made the introductions around the table to her mother, father, and brother. The eight of them chitchatted about the latest blockbuster movie, *Tootsie*.

"Golly," Jason said. "Can you imagine playing that role? Dustin Hoffman was amazing."

"And hot," Candy's dad, Jerry, said, which made everyone but Claire laugh.

"Do you think he had to lose weight and wear a girdle to play Tootsie?" Candy's mom asked.

"Bea, of course, he did," Jerry said. "Honey, the man had an hourglass figure. I wonder how they tucked the . . . you know . . . so that you couldn't see his bulge."

"Duct tape," Bryant said. "Lots and lots of duct tape."

Everyone laughed. Since Claire hadn't seen the movie, she had no interest in their conversation. She continued scanning the menu.

Candy leaned over and whispered, "Do you know what you want to order?"

"No," Claire answered. "What are you having?"

"Well, I was thinking we can do family-style and order a few dishes and all share. That way we can taste different things, and you can see what you like."

Claire nodded. "I'm so hungry I can eat a horse. I want to try everything!"

The adults ordered, and twenty minutes later, platters of steaming hot food came out on a cart. The waiter placed each dish on the table and presented them with chicken chow mein noodles, Mongolian beef, egg fried rice, Beijing roasted duck, and honey shrimp. The food looked so colorful and smelled divine. Claire's mouth watered. Candy helped Claire by dishing up a little bit of everything onto her plate.

The sound of glass clinking pulled Claire's attention away from her noodles.

"I have an announcement." Bryant grinned and took hold of Shana's hand. "Shana and I got married."

"What?" Candy asked. "For reals?"

"Wait," Jason said, "you just met last month."

"Well, when you know, you know," Shana said.

Claire let out a low groan. Bea raised her eyebrows. Everyone was quiet. Jerry broke the silence and congratulated the newlyweds. Everyone around the table muttered the same. Everyone but Claire. She glared at her father. This time she wanted to throw a knife at *him*. The whole time he was gone, he was out with Shana, a woman he barely knew, and not once did he care to let her in on what was happening in his life. Claire didn't need another mother. Shana was only fifteen years older than Claire. She was barely an adult.

Claire crossed her arms and scowled at her father, daring him to meet her eyes. Her breathing became short and fast. This was Candy's special night. It was her birthday. They were there to celebrate her, yet her father managed to make it all about him. It hit her that her father was a self-centered man with terrible timing.

"Why so glum?" Bryant asked. "C'mon, Sunshine. I know this is a surprise, but you'll love Shana. She's great. And she's excited to be a part of our family, to be your friend." Claire didn't know what to say. Words competed to come out, but her mouth flatlined. "What's the matter? Cat got your tongue?"

"How could you?" Claire stood and put her hands on her hips. "You're ruining Candy's birthday dinner."

Candy patted Claire on the arm. "It's okay. There's room for more celebrations tonight." Candy tugged at Claire's arm and coaxed her to sit down. To keep the mood light, Candy joked, "So when are you moving out, Bryant?"

Claire sat and stared intently at her father and Shana. She wished she had the power to telekinetically drill holes into both of them.

Shana clasped her hands and leaned in, elbows on top of the table. "We'll look for a place after our honeymoon. We're going to—" Shana looked at little Claire, who was banging her spoon on the table. "As I was saying, we're driving to either Iowa or Wisconsin to explore a bit."

"For how long?" Claire asked.

"One, maybe two weeks," Bryant said. "We'll bring you back a souvenir." Claire rolled her eyes but made sure her father didn't see. "You too, Candy. I'd appreciate you keeping an eye on my girl a little longer until we're back."

"Wow, Bryant, I guess I better start looking for another roommate," Candy said.

"Why don't you and Jason move in together?" Shana asked.

Jerry and Bea looked at one another at Shana's suggestion. Jerry's face drew a blank but Bea smiled and nodded.

"We both still have time on our leases," Jason said.

Shana batted her eyelashes. "Don't wait too long." She kissed Bryant and rubbed his crotch underneath the table. "Good men don't stick around long, so you have to snatch them up while you can."

Despite their age difference, Shana found Bryant irresistible. He was smart, sexy, funny, and charming. His prowess in bed brought out the seductress in her. Shana hadn't had much experience with men growing up. Her days and nights were filled with farm chores, running the tractor, baling hay, feeding the livestock, and fixing broken equipment. She was too busy to notice boys and too masculine to attract anyone's attention. How she caught Bryant's eye was a mystery to her.

Claire ate her food in silence and melted into the background of the conversations at the table. The food was delicious, and she enjoyed every dish, but it would have tasted better without the bitter news. While the adults talked, she sank deeper into her chair and ate as loudly as she could, smacking her lips, slurping her soup, and clanging her utensils against her bowl. She wanted to make sure they all understood how she felt about the marriage and her father ruining the birthday dinner.

19. HOW STARS DIED

Bryant and Shana left town Wednesday night and headed to Winterset, Iowa, the birthplace of John Wayne. That suited Claire just fine, who was still upset with her father and needed space from him, even though he had just returned from a three-week romp with Shana.

Friday quickly came around. Claire met up with her pal, Becky, and the two of them walked to school together. The girls had become friends in English class when they discovered they had several things in common. They both loved to read and lived in the same apartment complex, only Claire's building was in the front and Becky's was in the back, and they both hated oatmeal with a passion.

"Wanna sleep over tonight?" Becky's chirpy voice put a smile on Claire's face. "My mom said I could have a friend over."

"I have to ask Candy when she gets home from her shift. She's usually home by six. If I'm not over by seven, then it would mean I can't come over."

"Okay," Becky said. "I hope she says yes."

#

Candy called home at 6:05 p.m. The phone rang twice before Claire picked it up. "Hello?"

"Hey, kiddo."

"Hi, Candy."

"I'm running a little late. I can get us a pizza on my way home."

"Actually, " Claire said, "can I stay at Becky's tonight?"

"Sure," Candy said. "I guess I can stay at Jason's then. Have fun, and I'll see you tomorrow around lunchtime."

"Okay," Claire said. "Thank you."

Claire hung up the phone and peeked into the fridge—bare with one egg, wilting lettuce, half a dozen beers, and expired milk. She looked at the clock. It was 6:08 p.m. She didn't feel like frying the egg for dinner. She remembered she had a couple of dollars in her backpack. *I'll go to the quickie mart and get a soda and snack first.* Claire grabbed her backpack and shoved in her clothes, toothbrush, comb, and as an afterthought, the new book she got at the library.

Outside, the dark and cold night was typical of a Minnesota winter, but at least it wasn't windy. The sun had set over an hour ago. Claire zipped up her coat and pulled the strings on her hoodie. Her backpack helped to keep her warm. She walked briskly to the convenience store, excited to get to Becky's as soon as possible. Claire turned the corner and meandered through the neighborhood streets. She knew Rochester well, having ridden her bike all over town to run errands for her dad, go to the library, and get groceries for Candy.

There was one house on the corner of Baton and Cotton that creeped her out. Kids at school told stories about old crazy Ruford who had lived there since his birth in 1785. He was the last surviving son in the Williams lineage, and after his wife died from meningitis, he went cuckoo. So deranged, it was rumored, that he killed and ate his son to spare his child from getting the meningococcal bacteria. Old man Ruford also believed that if he ate little children, he'd absorb their youth, immunity, and vitality, thus escaping the disease. He finally died at the age of 101, but his ghost lingered on, and every so often, people claimed to see him in the window. The house sat empty and condemned for years after the last inhabitant claimed Old Ruford came to their daughter's room in the middle of the night and nibbled on her ankle. As Claire approached the old, unkempt house, chills coursed up her spine and throughout her head.

She willed herself to look at the windows. Her heart raced and zipped around in her chest. She half wanted to see the ghost but prayed she'd see nothing. Instead, in her peripheral vision, she was vaguely aware of a vehicle approaching from behind. It stopped. A white man jumped out. Startled by the sudden appearance of the stranger, Claire stopped in her tracks. Something hit her on the head. Was it a rock? His fist? Thick arms wrapped around her. Her ribs hurt. *Too tight.* Her feet were off the ground. She couldn't breathe. She smelled oil. It was his hand. His thick, calloused hand, covered her mouth and nose. Claire squirmed and kicked. She tried to yell.

The man shoved her inside his driver's side door. She scrambled to roll over and reach for the door handle. He lunged to lock the passenger side door. She screamed. Another hit on her right temple. This time she knew it was his fist. The car sped off.

"Stop!" Claire cried. "Let me go!" She punched his arm and kicked his thighs. She aimed for his face, but he caught her wrist. He pulled her toward him and then thrust her hard against the window. Her head throbbed. Her vision became blurred. The streetlamps blipped past. A couple of traffic lights and neon signs glowed overhead, reflected in the windshield.

"Be a good girl," the man said. His voice was deep, low, and gruff.

Claire went in and out of consciousness, dazed by the repeated hits to the head. The last thing she saw was his sideburns before the night went black.

#

Claire opened her eyes. Someone carried her. She was slung over a man's shoulder, but only for a moment. A door creaked, and with one swift move, she landed with a thud on her back. Darkness engulfed her. No street lamps. No neon signs. No traffic lights. She was in a small space. The cold fabric under her hand was rough. Vinyl seats. She was in the backseat of a car.

"Someone's awake." The same curt voice. The same gruff hands. The same smell of oil as he clamped Claire's mouth shut. A sharp pain rippled between her crotch as jagged fingernails scraped against her soft flesh. His fingers pried and manipulated the folds of her vagina. Suddenly they were inside of her. Claire closed her eyes and blinked back the tears. She screamed silently in her mind. *No. No. No.*

Her chest heaved. His weight crushed her. Claire was afraid she'd pass out again. His breath was so hot. With each thrust her head jerked back, her hair caught underneath her shoulders, and the strands yanked at her scalp. She was trapped. Thoughts of being locked in the closet by Gisela came rushing back. The monster with the scary eyes was real. She couldn't stop looking into his eyes. Dark with no whites to them.

Claire arched her body to get out from under him. She lifted her chin to ease the pain of her hair trapped underneath her back. This only excited the man more as he grunted and smiled. A bead of sweat dripped onto her forehead. Or was it his saliva? He took his hand off her face to tug her pants down further. Claire curled her legs so he couldn't get them past her knees.

"Dammit," he muttered.

The door creaked and a gust of cold air whooshed into the back cabin of the car. Strong hands gripped her ankle and slid her out of the car.

The man dragged her away from the vehicle. They were in the woods somewhere. The only sounds came from his footsteps and labored breathing. Branches snapped. Brush rustled. Claire's heart thumped 120 beats per minute.

She found her voice. "Stop. Let me go."

"Shut up."

"Please. I won't tell anyone."

"I said, shut up."

Four hundred heartbeats later they were in a field of weeds, clumps of dirt, and moss. The man towered over her five-foot frame. He shoved her to the ground and straddled her. He outweighed her by nearly a hundred pounds. Claire was eleven years old and seventy pounds soaking wet. She was no match for him. One look at his piercing gaze and Claire knew. His look cemented his intentions. He wasn't done with her yet and meant to do her further harm.

With her arms pinned at her sides between his legs, there was nothing Claire could do. Everything about this man was evil, from his greasy, wavy, obsidian hair to his narrow eyes and enlarged pupils.

He smirked, a menacing sneer etched across his face. "I've been watching you." He held her down and ripped off all her clothes, casting them carelessly aside. He tugged and pulled until her forest green hoodie purchased at the Goodwill camouflaged as one with the moss. The jeans she had begged her father to get at the yard sale kept company with the dirt. The T-shirt Candy got her on one of their shopping trips suffocated the weeds ten yards away. Her small underwear with pink trim and pretty butterflies fluttering around the front and back were scrunched beside her feet. Even her socks and shoes were one with the field. Her coat . . . where was her coat?

For a few minutes, the man did nothing, only looked her up and down. He touched her flat chest and rubbed the soft white flesh of her tummy. He raised her arms over her head and smiled, pleased at what he saw.

Claire went into the recess of her mind and called out silently for her father to save her. *Daddy!* Over and over she called out to him in her thoughts. *Daddy!*

The man shook her violently. "Why don't you scream?"

Claire knew screaming would do no good. Who would hear her? Gisela's face flashed across her thoughts. Oh, how her stepmother loved seeing the fear in her eyes with every whipping, every belt thrashing, every closet entrapment. Claire was not going to give this man her fear.

She was not going to give him that one power over her that she still controlled.

The stranger got off of Claire and held her down with a restraint across her neck. His scrutiny traveled from her face down to her vagina. She hadn't gone through puberty yet. There was no fuzz on her armpits, no pubic hair covering her privates, and no bristles on her smooth legs.

"Ripe for the picking," he said. And in his cruelty, he roughly pried her legs apart and mounted her.

The penetration of his erection ruptured Claire's cervix. She had never felt pain as intense, as excruciating, or as traumatizing. This was beyond the fire ants that crawled up her legs at Grandma Sharon's house. Beyond the scorching heat of the scalding water that Gisela forced her to bathe in to save on the utility bill. Incomparable to the hot oil that coated her skin from frying chicken at Grandma Gertrude's homestead.

A geyser of tears gushed out of Claire's eyes. The knot in her throat expanded until it blocked her windpipe. The agony of asphyxiation lasted an eternity as the pressure on her throat deepened. Claire gasped and coughed but no relief came. His chokehold took her in and out of consciousness.

The man slapped her across the face. "If you scream, I'll make your ending easier. C'mon, little girl, just one little yelp, and this will all be over."

Throughout the night, Claire went in and out of consciousness. She was punched, slapped, and manipulated in different positions to quench a thirst that this demon stranger needed satiating. For Claire, it was agony in perpetuity. At any moment her legs could snap and her body be ripped in two.

Anguish. Shame. Disgust. Words could not succinctly describe Claire's fright. It was a chilling twenty degrees outside, but her body was on fire. And when she went limp, the man hit her in the ribs to wake her.

The hours wore on. It was as if a thousand electric eels found their way into the forest that night, each hungry to devour her flesh and shock her body into comatose oblivion. They traveled up and down her body, exited her extremities, and re-entered her flesh to do more carnage. Wave after wave of electricity pumped through her veins and seeped into the crown of her head down to the tips of her toes.

For five hours this man tortured Claire. Those five long hours felt like five lifetimes.

#

Claire didn't know how much time had passed, where she was, or what day it was. She only knew something bad happened.

She stared at the faint murmur of light in the sky. The stars flickered, but their shine was dim. A shooting star flashed across the heavens. Claire had read about how stars died. Several billion years after its life begins, a star loses its fuel. It contracts under the weight of gravity and heats up like internal combustion. In seconds, the core collapses as the heat intensifies until it explodes, sending fragments of itself into space. It will never be whole again.

Claire imagined herself as a shooting star. Her light would never shine as bright again. Instead, a black hole would take its place in the vast emptiness of space and time.

She lay there on the damp clumps of filth for another thirty minutes, letting the bugs crawl in and out of her. She was but a hindrance . . . an obstacle in their nightly routine. Slowly her senses rolled back, and Claire realized she had to get home before Candy came home. She slowly brought her legs together and winced at the soreness that ached all over. Claire rolled over to her side. Her ribs protested at the sudden disruption, and she sat still. She suspected her ribs were broken or, at a minimum, bruised. Signs of bruising on her body emerged and, even in the dim glow of the moon and stars, she saw the black trails of dried blood caked on her inner thighs.

Her pelvis seized into hypersensitive cramps. She didn't understand what was happening inside her body, but in reality, she was hemorrhaging. She scanned the field. She was alone. A shiver sent tremors to her hand as she slowly gathered her clothes. She shimmied her underwear up her legs and then crawled to collect her shirt and pants. Once Claire was fully clothed, she hugged her knees and rocked to and fro. She knew she had to get home, but how? Her legs failed her. They didn't want to extend or stand or support her weight.

In time she found the strength to stand and survey her surroundings. Disoriented, Claire looked at the stars as if they could navigate her home. Her legs twitched, and she followed in the direction they took her . . . She came across her backpack and coat and put them on. One foot in front of the other she traveled until the skyline came into sight. Rochester had never looked so pretty with its city lights flickering in shades of red, green, blue, and white. Every step toward town tormented her, for it hurt so much to move.

Claire carried on and found the edge of town. She recognized her surroundings. Two blocks straight. Right turn. Three blocks to Cotton

Street, past Old Ruford's eerie house, a left, and then a straight shot home. No one was in sight as Claire made her way to the apartment. The cold wisps of air kept her alert while her body went numb. What felt like a million steps later, Claire arrived at her apartment complex. She fumbled in her pocket and exhaled to feel the cold brass metal and contour of her keys. Quietly she slipped into the apartment and went straight to the bathroom.

The bright light hurt her eyes. She squinted and blinked until her eyes adjusted. Staring back at her in the mirror was a thing with hollow eyes, unrecognizable as ever being human. This monster reflected in the glass condemned her, judged her, and hated her. Claire's copper tresses were tangled with stems and leaves sticking out in every direction. Her jaw was reddish-purple. She loathed the person in the mirror.

Her insides were inflamed, and all she could think was *Get off of me!*

On came the hot water. The steam rose as the clear liquid fell from the showerhead into the drain. Claire stepped into the tub and pulled the curtains closed. The water was hot but not hot enough. Claire wanted her outsides to level up to the same intensity of heat as her insides. Only then would the burn go away. She believed it would help her feel balanced and normal. It would bring relief.

She grabbed the washcloth and scrubbed the blood off her legs. *Get off of me.* She rubbed the wet cotton between her legs repeatedly until it was inflamed more than it already was. *Get off of me.* No amount of scrubbing made her feel clean, wholesome, or satisfied. Claire repeated again and again, "Get off of me!"

The hot water became warm and then ran cool. Claire sat in the bathtub and stared at the dirty vinyl tub. Nothing mattered except the black smear on the bottom of the bathtub. And when the cold water eased her back to reality, Claire shivered and turned the faucet to the left.

She stepped out of the tub, gathered her soiled clothes, stuffed them into a plastic grocery bag, and stuffed them into her backpack. She would discard them on the way to school on Monday.

Inside her bedroom, Claire felt small and alienated. *Is this my bedroom? Am I in the right apartment? How did I get here?* She vaguely remembered walking through the neighborhoods. Claire grabbed her pillow and blanket off the bed, turned off the lights, and crawled under her bed. With her back against the hard surface of the wall, she curled into a ball and willed herself to sleep.

20. THE INCUBUS

Candy stayed with Jason for the weekend after Claire assured her she could stay at Becky's. In reality, Claire spent the entire weekend in her bedroom, frozen in fear, staring at her closet, reliving the horrors of Friday night.

The children outside laughed and yelled as they played in the snow. She wanted to yell at them but was afraid if she screamed, she'd never stop. Claire would lose her sanity forever. Every sound was excruciatingly loud, even the hum of the baseboard heater. Her body felt heavy with the burden of carrying this secret. It pinned her down and immobilized her. This secret would become the incubus of Claire's life, sucking traces of her existence into an unknown abyss, holding her hostage in the confines of her mental hell.

Getting out of bed took too much effort. Cocooned in her blanket, Claire withdrew into the deep recess of her intellectual self and shut off her emotions. Too fatigued and weathered to do anything else, she closed her eyes tight and visualized expelling her soul from her body. She wanted to be the black hole that was once a star.

#

On Monday, Claire walked the few blocks to school with Becky. She dropped the bag of soiled clothes into one of the dumpsters along the way. She didn't want any reminders and thought discarding evidence would bring her some relief. It didn't.

"What'd you throw away?" Becky asked.

"Just old, stinky clothes," Claire said. "I forgot I had them in my bag."

Becky, of unassured feet and mousy voice, nodded and plodded along. She tripped on the uneven sidewalk and giggled. "Sorry you couldn't come to the sleepover."

"Yeah, sorry," Claire said. How could Claire tell anyone what had happened? Who would believe her? She was still here, wasn't she? Claire wanted things to be back to normal, even if normal meant an absent father and a new stepmother. At least she had school. School was safe. Books were a refuge. Music was a sanctuary. What else did she need?

The girls continued their walk. Becky did most of the talking, but all Claire heard was the jeer of *I've been watching you.* His face sneered at her. His hot garbage breath suffocated her. Claire shuddered ever so slightly. "Yeah," Becky said, "it seems every winter it gets colder and colder."

Claire nodded, letting Becky believe she shivered because of the chill in the air. Claire scanned the brown and white canvas of Rochester before her. Her gaze pinballed from cars to trees to houses to parking lots. Was he lurking somewhere? Would she find him on the gnarly stoop of Ruford's haunted house? Her head swiveled as she remembered that man's touch. Tugging. Punching. Penetrating. Shaking.

#

Bryant and Shana came back from their honeymoon in Winterset, Iowa, ten days later. For once, Claire was thankful for Minnesota's harsh winters. She covered herself up in sweatpants, turtleneck sweaters, hoodies, and oversized coats. Even though the bruising and swelling had subsided by then, Claire needed to protect her body from exposure.

Every day after school, she rushed home to do her chores before her dad and Candy came home, then locked herself away in her room.

"Hey, Sunshine." Bryant peeked into his daughter's room. "I haven't seen you much since I got back. You doing okay?"

Claire wanted to tell her father he sucked, that he was never there for her when she needed him, and that he was too wrapped up in his interests. Instead, she said, "I'm fine. Just got lots of homework. You should go spend time with Shana."

"All right, study away then." Bryant closed the door but then propped it back open. "Honey, you're getting to that age . . . One day you will become a woman, and you'll know when that day comes. And when it comes, you will need to find a woman to talk to. Okay? Shana or Candy or maybe one of your teachers." Father and daughter stared at each other awkwardly for a few seconds. "Well, I'm gonna go see Shana now. Oh, by the way, I saw a babysitting ad posted at the store. Here." Bryant handed

Claire a crinkled piece of paper with a name and phone number. "Thought you'd want to make some money." He closed the door until the latch clicked and took off toward Shana's rambler.

The days slipped into weeks, and Claire passed the time chilling in her room, listening to music, reading, and doing her homework. On occasion, she babysat for the couple a few blocks down the road.

Daytime was manageable. She had school to keep her busy, and every waking moment was spent completing homework that wasn't due until weeks later. Her teachers gave her advanced work before it was even assigned. Soon, Claire completed the sixth-grade curriculum two months early. She spent the last part of sixth grade sitting in the back of the class working on other things, mostly journaling and doodling, which isolated her further. Even Becky and Claire ran out of things to talk about, and the pair drifted apart.

Nightfall brought on distress as Claire relived the agony each night. The trauma consumed her. Night tremors. Gasps for air. Cold sweats. In her slumber, she was an animal tethered to a post, ready for the slaughterhouse. She couldn't move. She felt weak and helpless. No matter what Claire tried to do, she couldn't change the ending. The demon had her in his clutches.

#

The day finally arrived to say goodbye to Candy. Bryant and Shana found a small apartment northwest of Rochester in Silver Lake. It was a tearful farewell for Claire, who clung to Candy and promised to call often.

"I wish I could stay with you," Claire said.

"Me too," Candy said. "You have my number. Call me, and we'll have a girls' day."

Silver Lake, with a population of 700 people and almost as many geese, was a sleepy town stuck in the 1960s. A coal-burning power plant discharged water into the lake, making the water five degrees warmer than usual. Heating the lake allowed the water to stay open all year round, even during the harsh Minnesota winters, but of course, one had to share it with the giant Canadian geese.

No sooner had they settled into the tiny apartment than they were forced to leave. The apartment was getting torn down, and a hardware store was being built. During one of her walks to the store to get her father cigarettes, Claire noticed a lonely house that should have been condemned. The perimeter was completely trashed with a lopsided desk and two tires in the front yard. The front screen door was off its hinges, and shards of glass stood straight up from the dirt and weeds. A For Rent sign was displayed in the window. Claire told her dad about it.

A week later they moved in, and in exchange for fixing the place up, Bryant got a great deal on the rent. The interior of the house was pretty trashed. They hauled away junk, including a dusty, broken couch. Fecal matter was everywhere, some of it fresh from mice and stray dogs, and some so dry Shana picked one up mistaking it for a twig. Having lived on a farm and used to dirty grunt work, Shana wasn't bothered by the petrified poop. She tossed it into the garbage and wiped her fingers on her jeans. It took three weeks to air out the house and dissolve the foul odors of piss, mold, and shit.

Summers in Minnesota were like sweatshops inside wet saunas. The heat and musty air brought on stomach cramps. Claire's abdomen twisted in knots as if it were put through a wringer. She dropped to her knees and clutched her stomach. It felt like someone had sucker-punched her. She found herself thinking of Gisela and the spells of pain that afflicted her stepmother each month. Thoughts of that awful woman turned into thoughts of Ton-ton, Shannon, Benji, and Barry. She'd give anything to see them again.

To distract herself from the pain, Claire picked up her book, *Captive Woman*, and continued reading where she last earmarked the pages. Every day she sat in her room, too afraid to go anywhere and too anxious to open the window. A small fan and a ton of Lindsey Johnson's romance books were her only companions. She wondered what love was supposed to be like. In *Captive Woman* an French woman got kidnapped by a ruler and became his slave. The king humiliated her, stripped her of her spirit and pride, and ravished her night after night. On every page, the heroine was deathly afraid of the man's anger, and yet she fell in love with him in the end. Each page took Claire to the corner of Clueless and Disgust.

"No way!" Claire yelled. She vehemently hurled the book at the wall. "That's stupid. He forces himself on her, and she falls madly in love with him? In what world?" Claire couldn't fathom how a woman could fall in love with her rapist and how the book was a bestselling novel. "You're selling a lie!"

Claire wiped the sweat from her face and took a long drink of water from her glass. She questioned if all men, including her father, were that way. She decided no more romance novels for her, and perhaps psychology books were the way to go to understand the meaning of love.

She then noticed a red spot on her sheets—blood. Panic-stricken, Claire imagined her insides spilling out of her. The redness soaked through her knickers. She ran to the bathroom and shoved wads of toilet paper in her underwear. *This is it.* She concluded the assault must have rotted her guts, and it was only a matter of time before she died. The bugs harboring inside her would soon find their way out. Claire picked up the phone to call Candy but didn't know what she'd say. She hung up the receiver and shuffled back to her room.

Eventually, days later, the bleeding stopped, only to return a month later. Claire rolled up her bedsheet and bloodied underwear and soaked them in the tub. She poured shampoo on the stains and rubbed the fabric together to scrub out the blemish. Tears flowed. She decided she had to tell someone.

After dinner, Claire whispered to Shana, "Can I talk to you?"

Shana gave a wintry nod and followed Claire outside. They sat on the stoop and looked at nothing in particular. Both of them were silent and pondered what to say.

"Sorry about dinner," Shana said. "I'm not a good cook. Canned tuna and mashed potatoes are as fancy as it gets. Your dad tells me you make great lasagna and casseroles."

"I can show you next time," Claire said. She leaned forward and picked up a stick. Her hands were restless.

"I know our marriage must have been a shock to you," Shana continued, "but I want you to know I love your dad. I hope we can be friends." When Claire didn't respond, Shana talked about her visit to Iowa and how surreal it was to be in the same city where John Wayne was born. "Do you like western movies?" Claire shrugged. "Well, I grew up on a farm and lived around horses my whole life. Pigs, chickens, cows . . . you name it, we had it."

"Alligators?" Claire asked.

"Why, yes," Shana said. Claire stopped tracing the dirt with her stick and looked at Shana. A smile percolated on Shana's face. "Gotcha."

Claire released a crooked smile for the first time in months.

"I think I'm sick," Claire said. "I might be dying."

Shana gasped. She took Claire's small hand into hers and squeezed it. "Tell me why you think so. What happened?"

Claire inhaled and held her breath before slowly exhaling. The warmth of Shana's hand brought her comfort. "Shana, I've been bleeding . . . a lot . . . down here." Claire pointed to her crotch.

"When did this start?"

"A couple of months ago."

"Does it hurt?"

"Yes, a lot. Mostly in my stomach though."

Shana exhaled with relief. "How long does it last?"

"A few days," Claire said.

"Darling," Shana said, "you're not dying. You're turning into a butterfly."

"I am?"

"Well, not literally," Shana said, "but your metamorphosis is beginning." Shana explained the female anatomy and what happened to all women as they hit puberty, transitioning from a girl to a woman. "Claire, now that your body is fertile, you have to do your best to protect yourself and not let any boys touch you down there. You can get pregnant and have babies. One day, when you're married, you'll want to start a family with your husband, but not before then. You understand?"

Claire wrapped her arms around Shana and cried. She was relieved she wasn't dying. Even though her heart and head ached each day, she couldn't imagine leaving her dad to fend for himself. It was true he had Shana now, but Shana was a terrible cook.

21. SLOW BURN

Months passed, and the honeymoon was over. Claire noticed her dad returned to his usual ways. He spoke curtly to Shana, criticized her cooking, and degraded her for the way she dressed.

"You can't be going braless whenever you feel like it," Bryant said. "You dress like a man. Don't you own a dress?"

"I'm a farmer's daughter, remember?" Shana asked. "I grew up in jeans, T-shirts, and boots, working the fields and tossing bales of hay. You never had a problem before with me going braless."

"Well, you went to nursing school, didn't ya?" Bryant asked. "Don't nurses wear dresses?" He didn't let Shana answer. "My daughter is going to take you shopping and teach you how a girl should dress. It's like I'm married to a boy." He rolled his eyes.

Claire noticed Shana flinch and felt sorry for her. Bryant disappeared into the bedroom and came out with a wad of cash in his hands. Claire wondered where it came from. They never had money.

"Here's two hundred dollars," Bryant said. Shana extended her hand, but it was Claire who received the money. "Buy her a feminine wardrobe. And while you're at it, teach her how to cook. I can't take any more of her mac and cheese."

This time it was Claire who cringed. Shana knew only one way to cook macaroni and cheese—lumpy, with curdled American cheese. "What do you want to have for dinner, Daddy? Meatloaf?"

"You decide, Sunshine."

Claire and Shana hopped into the truck and headed to the thrift shop on the other side of the tracks. They rode in silence and listened to the radio. T.G. Shepphard's song "Slow Burn" came on the airwaves, and Claire sang along.

"Wow," Shana said, "you know your songs."

"I've always listened to country music," Claire said. "Dad and I used to drive all over the country together. We'd listen to music, sing together, and when we got bored, we'd get on the CB radio and talk to other truckers."

"Really? He never told me. It's like I don't even know him."

Claire wanted to say, *That's because you married him after two months*, but she kept quiet.

"Well, anyway, you have a beautiful voice," Shana said.

Claire thanked Shana and resumed singing. Music was one thing she trusted in this world. She got lost in the songs, the melodies, and the lyrics. When the songs were happy, she allowed herself to feel joy. When they were sad, she took comfort in knowing it was someone else's pain, not hers.

They pulled into the parking lot of the Rag Tag Thrift, but Shana left the engine running. Claire cocked her head. "Are you okay?"

Shana's lips curled as her eyes cast down. "Your dad is slipping away from me. I hope me wearing a dress will make him happy."

Claire patted Shana's leg. "My dad never spends money on anyone. He loves you." Whether that was still true or not, Claire wanted to cheer Shana up. "I don't know where he got all this money—"

"Oh, he hustled it shooting pool," Shana said. "He's a real shark."

"Well, let's get you some nice outfits. And save some of it to buy dinner."

Shana's eyes lit up. "Can you teach me to cook? Maybe a nice stew or something?"

"Sure," Claire said.

Inside the Rag Tag, shoppers darted into dressing rooms, children begged for toys, and men tinkered with electronics. It was deceptively large inside with mirrors strategically placed along the walls to give the illusion of space. Claire noticed the bulletin board had a babysitter wanted sign and pulled it off the board. She folded the paper in half and then shoved it into her pocket.

Shana scanned the room and bit her lower lip. Her brows furrowed. She shifted her weight and took a half step backward.

Claire sensed her restlessness and held Shana's hand. She led her to the women's section. "Don't worry."

"It's so overwhelming," Shana said.

"Dad wanted dresses. Let's start with dresses!"

Shana nodded and pursed her lips tight. She clutched her chest and stopped. "Oh my gosh, I forgot to put on a bra. How am I supposed to try on clothes without a bra?"

"Okay, then let's go get bras first."

They turned right and headed to the southwest corner, passing a boy with rosy cheeks and a runny nose. The snot perched at the tip of his lip.

Don't do it. And then the kid did it. He licked the mucus and smiled. Claire shuddered.

"Oh my gosh." Shana once again stopped in her tracks. She pointed at her reflection in one of the mirrors.

Claire noticed what Shana saw. Sure enough, through her T-shirt were two peaks where her nipples stood erect. The thin material left nothing to the imagination.

They quickly darted to the undergarment racks. Shana indiscriminately pulled brassieres of different sizes and bunched them across her chest as if she were hugging a pillow.

"What size are you?" Claire asked.

Shana shrugged. "Dunno."

"Well," Claire said, "I think we can put this one back." She gingerly took one of the bras from Shana's arms. "Unless you plan on using this as a watermelon sling . . ."

Shana laughed. The size 38DD cups were as big as Claire's head. Taking license with the mirth and absurdity of it all, Claire hooked the bra under her chin and pulled on the side straps. "Greetings, Earthling. I come in peace."

They meandered throughout the entire women's section looking for skirts, dresses, and wedge sandals that could go with any outfit. It was hard finding something to accentuate the curves Shana didn't have. She was rail thin with hips smaller than her shoulders. In the end, they found a couple of A-line dresses that flared out below the waist. They were quite flattering on Shana's athletic frame. Bright halter tops with thick straps and skirts that ruched and draped below her belly button completed the ensemble. At the checkout line, Shana spotted some jumpsuits hanging on the sales rack. One had a V-neck and the other a scoop neck.

"Claire, look." Shana pointed. "What about those?"

"I like the denim one," Claire said. The denim pantsuit with the V-neckline was nice. It came with a thick red belt to cinch the midsection.

Claire got out of line to check the price. It was fifty percent off. Perfect. And it was a size small. Double perfect.

They left the thrift shop with a lot of money left over. It was time to go to the grocery store. On the way home, they swung into Save-a-Dime and browsed the meat section.

Shana suddenly laughed. "You know what's funny? Here I am, twenty-six years old, learning how to dress and cook from an eleven-year-old." Claire wasn't sure if Shana was mocking the situation, but her eyes twinkled with genuine merriment. "You and I are going to be good friends, Claire. I have much to learn."

Claire grinned. She didn't have any friends and welcomed the idea. "I'm almost twelve, you know." Spending the day with Shana was a nice distraction from her lonely, self-loathing day.

They returned home to find Bryant gone. Shana shrugged her shoulders and turned on the radio. "Let's get cooking and surprise your daddy when he gets home."

They finished the stew not a moment too soon. The hum of Bryant's truck signaled his return. Shana ran into the bedroom and giggled like a schoolgirl. She quickly slipped out of her shorts and T-shirt and donned the denim jumpsuit.

"Ta-da," Shana exclaimed. She slowly twirled around and let her husband soak in the new look. "Do you approve, honey?"

Bryant whistled. "I approve." He pulled her into his arms and kissed her passionately, then patted Shana's rear. "Where's the change?"

"On the table," Shana said. "We spent fifty dollars today."

That evening they had a lovely dinner together, and as the weeks slipped into months, Shana learned to cook stew, spaghetti, tacos, and macaroni and cheese.

#

Boredom soon kicked down their marriage door again. Bryant and Shana argued more often, with him storming out of the house, leaving tire marks at the four-way stop down the street. As soon as he was gone, a distraught Shana shuffled into Claire's room and crawled into the bed. Her tears and running nose left stains on Claire's pillow.

"Did you fight over the house?" Claire asked.

Shana sniffed. "It started with that. I don't know what he expects. I keep the house clean. I pick up after him."

Shana's idea of clean was nowhere near Bryant's definition of clean. Claire experienced time and time again what her father expected. Clothes had to be hung and organized by color, facing the same direction.

Dishes had to be spotless, dry, and put in their proper place. Her dad expected perfection. He didn't like clutter and didn't tolerate greasy stoves, sticky countertops, unswept floors, or dusty furniture.

"Can I be honest with you about something?" Claire asked. "My dad is a neat freak."

"You're telling me." Shana sat up and wiped her eyes with the back of her hand like a toddler. "Anyway, that wasn't what our fight was about this time."

"Oh," Claire breathed.

"Yeah, your dad keeps bringing women into our bedroom."

"Oh!" Claire said. She was sure Shana was going to say something about the way she dressed or how she needed to look less masculine.

"He thinks if I don't let him have a threesome, then I don't love him." The tears threatened to roll again. "I don't think he loves me anymore. I'm not enough for him."

"What are you going to do?"

"Can you talk to him?"

"Me?" Claire asked. "He won't—"

"Yes, he will! You're the only one he'll listen to."

"Shana, I don't know."

The tears escaped one by one down Shana's cheeks. "Sorry, you're right. This is my problem, not yours."

#

As the months passed, Claire stayed busy with school and babysitting to make extra money. She started noticing random visitors coming to the house. Most of the time she stayed isolated in her room and didn't get a good look at their guests. However, she heard their voices. They were always women. Of course, Claire thought they were Shana's friends until one evening she heard yelling, crying, and furniture slamming against the walls.

"Get out," Bryant yelled.

The door down the hall creaked, and then Claire heard a thud.

A woman howled in pain. It wasn't Shana's voice. "Oh, c'mon!"

"Get the fuck out!" Bryant yelled. The door slammed hard.

Footsteps shuffled down the hallway and stopped at Claire's door. Claire sat up and stared at the doorknob. Sure enough, it slowly turned and a woman peeked in. Claire's heart pounded against the chamber of her chest and leaped to her throat. From the moonlight casting its glow into the room, Claire saw a raven-haired woman, her skin white and freckled, with dark, theatrical makeup caked on her face like a porcelain doll. Claire froze and could not find her voice.

"Hey there, little lady." The woman's voice was raspy.

Claire stuttered. "Who are you? What do you want?"

"Ever been licked by a woman?" The woman stepped into the room uninvited and closed the door.

"Get out," Claire hissed.

"You'll like it. Let me lick your pu—"

"Get out!" Claire spoke louder this time.

"Let me go down on you. I promise you'll love it. I'll make you feel so good."

Claire jumped off her bed and turned on the lamp. She almost wished she hadn't. Kneeling beside the foot of her bed was a young, gaunt, pale-faced woman. She looked like a vampire. Claire guessed she was eighteen and high on drugs. The girl's black pupils eclipsed her hazel eyes, making them appear bulged and buggy. A sliver of white shined in the center of the dilation . . . a reflection of the lightbulb from Claire's nightstand. Even her dried, cracked lips freaked Claire out. Her face looked like it was melting with the smeared lipstick and dripping mascara.

Despite the cool air, Claire's hands became clammy. Her body temperature rose. "Leave," Claire said, "or I'll scream, and my dad will throw you out."

The woman's eyes widened. She sniffed and swayed back and forth with excitability. "I can't leave. I don't have a car, and I'm far from home. It would take me hours to get home." The woman reached for Claire's hand. Her boney fingers wrapped around Claire's wrist and trembled.

Claire yanked her arm away. "That's not my problem. You better start walking." Claire darted past the woman and opened her bedroom door. She pointed to the front entrance of the house. "Go!"

The two stared at each other. Claire didn't back down. She glared at the young woman, willing her to walk out the front door.

"Do you have any money?"

Claire ran to the kitchen and grabbed a rolling pin. She raised it above her head. "Leave! And don't you dare come back, or I'll bash your head in."

Defeated, the drug-strung vampire left. Claire slammed the front door and locked it. Her chest heaved rapidly as she slumped to the floor. Ten minutes passed before her heart rate tapered to a normal rhythm.

Claire couldn't believe what had just happened, but she swore to lock her bedroom door each night after that.

#

Claire's twelfth birthday slid in quietly without much ado. She was glad Shana and her dad didn't make a fuss. They were too wrapped up in their drama anyway, and Claire needed to shut the world out. If she didn't leave the house or interact with anyone, she wouldn't run the risk of seeing her attacker again.

Winter break came. The days and nights overlapped and swirled together like clothes in a dryer. Nightfall brought flashbacks of waking up alone in the open field, cold, naked, and in pain. She slept during the day and remained vigilant at night. Cars slowing down at the four-way stop by her house made her suspicious. Every man walking past their house on the sidewalk was a threat. Every dark car was a potential trap.

As if the paranoia wasn't bad enough, the bickering between her dad and Shana sent Claire over the edge. She wanted the noise to stop. Out came the books or on came the headphones. She squeezed her eyes shut to drown out the rage in her head, but it was no use.

Claire's bedroom door suddenly flung open. Claire jumped and ripped her headphones off.

"I can't. I just can't!" Shana exclaimed. Woeful tears encrusted her face. She threw herself on Claire's bed. Through hiccups and a jagged, trembling voice, Shana blurted out, "He's at it again. Your dad brought home another side chick." She curled her body around Claire's pillow and muffled something indistinguishable into the polyester fibers.

"What?" Claire asked. "I can't understand what you're saying."

Shana arched her back and lifted her head off the pillow. "Side chick is downstairs."

Shana's pleading eyes enveloped Claire with pity and sadness. *This had gone long enough*, Claire thought. "Okay, Shana, I'll talk to him."

Hope and gratitude sprung into Shana's eyes. "You will?"

The two of them went downstairs with Claire leading the way. Her father sat in the living room next to a woman with bleached blonde hair and ink on her arm that read "Dillon Forever." The two of them were chuckling at a private joke.

"You think it's funny, Dad?" Claire said.

Their heads swiveled around to focus on Claire and Shana. The stunned look on their faces empowered Claire to take control of the moment. Before her father could recover from the shock, Claire sat down opposite him and took a deep breath. With steely eyes, Claire cast the blonde a look as if to say, *Don't speak.* "Dad, Shana came and talked to me. I know you like threesomes, but you know, you keep bringing so many women into this house. I've heard you brag about sleeping with so many women, and frankly, Dad, it disgusts me, and I'm disappointed in you." Claire didn't pause. She knew any hesitation would open the door for her father to sweet talk himself out of the situation, or worse, hulk himself over the women in the room. "Is Shana not enough for you? You're a grown man who needs his kudos and kibbles from so many women to feel good about yourself." Claire took a deep breath and swallowed the spit at the base of her throat. She was surprised her father didn't yell back, stand up, throw something, or hit her. She hoped he felt embarrassed.

His silence gave her the confidence to continue. She had his attention. One look at Shana's stony face gave Claire the courage to go on. "Why do you bother getting married? Why don't you just fuck around?" The word *fuck* tasted good on Claire's lips. She had never spoken to her dad that way before, but she didn't care. His disrespect toward Shana was a gratuitous slow burn on the family, and that pissed her off. "You don't honor your wives. You never have. Constantly bringing other women into your bed does not honor your wife."

Claire couldn't believe her eyes. Tears streamed down her father's face. She hoped her words drove nails into his heart and that the shame and guilt leaked out with every teardrop. His shoulders drooped and shuddered. "You need to take a hard look at yourself, Dad. And by the way . . . two months ago, you kicked a chick out of your bedroom, and you know what she did? She came into my room and offered to lick my pussy. Her words, not mine. She begged to lick me. She wanted to go down on me. She asked if I ever had a woman taste me. Told me I'd love it. Don't you think having random strangers here puts our safety at risk?"

Claire stood and crossed her arms over her chest. Her father was reduced to a sobbing mess. "I don't get it, Dad. I once heard you bragging about having two women in the hospital having your babies at the same time. How many brothers and sisters do I have out there? Your sleeping around is teaching me that when I grow up, it's okay for a man to cheat on me or knock me up and abandon me, or beat me when I can't make him happy. But isn't that on you, Dad? Isn't your happiness on you?"

Claire didn't know what else to say. She was fuming. She knew she was taking her anger and fears out on her dad. The memories of the rape, the dark secrets that burdened her soul, the beatings inflicted upon her by Gisela . . . they all stacked on her neck, shoulders, and back and pinned her below the ocean floor, drowning her. On top of all that, she missed her siblings and pined for her grandparents.

Claire was prepared to die with her words. She braced herself for her father's fist. She would leave this world swinging, if not for herself, then for Shana.

Bryant's swinging fist never came . . . at least not that night.

22. PREDATORS

There was something beautiful about seeing Shana waddle into the kitchen to get a glass of water. Claire admired the roundness of Shana's belly and couldn't wait to meet her baby brother or sister. She didn't care if it was a boy or girl; she just wanted a baby dolly to love and nurture.

Despite Shana's hair looking greasy and knotted, her face radiated with joy. Her skin, flawless and smooth, glistened in the sunlight. *She even smells good.*

"Good morning," Shana said. "Do you think you can braid my hair today? Maybe even help me with makeup?"

"Sure," Clair answered. "Are you and Dad going out?"

Shana sipped her water and shook her head. "Your dad invited some people across the street over for a party tonight. He wants me to do my hair and makeup . . . you know, look presentable. And we need to prepare some food."

"Do I have to be at the party?"

Shana rubbed her belly and sat down. "I think he wants us there to serve and keep the gravy train going."

"Can't I hang out in my room during the party? Please?" Claire pulled out a chair and plopped down. "How about I clean and get the house ready? I'll even cook and set up the trays. You can play hostess, and I'll be quiet in my room. No one is going to notice I'm not there."

"It's not up to me, Claire."

#

The two of them got busy decluttering the living room area while chicken drumsticks and wings baked in the oven. The scent of sweet honey barbecue sauce wafted through the rooms and teased Claire's senses. Her stomach made an obscenely loud gurgle while her mouth salivated.

Shana whistled as she dusted the shelves, wiped down the windows, and cleaned the kitchen counter. Claire dragged her feet as she vacuumed the carpet and mopped the linoleum.

By four o'clock they had enough food to feed a small army even though only half a dozen people were invited. The house smelled like pine needles, and it was so spotless an army drill sergeant would have been hard-pressed to find something unacceptable.

Bryant walked through the front door and smiled. In one arm he carried a brown bag filled with whisky, beers, and cigarettes; in the other was a box of donuts, lady fingers cookies, and potato chips. "Hi, girls. Smells good in here. What are we having?" Bryant leaned in for a kiss, and Shana obliged.

"Claire and I made spaghetti, pigs in a blanket, chicken wings and drumsticks, tater tots, and grilled cheese sandwich squares."

"Dad," Claire said, "do I have to be at the party?"

"Yes, you need to help Shana. Look at her. She's going to burst any minute. I need you to help serve and fetch."

"Please, Dad? I'll just be in the way." Bryant gave her a look that stopped Claire in her tracks. It was a cross between the stare Bert gave on Sesame Street and Dr. David Banner's angry furrow on *The Incredible Hulk* TV show right before he raged into a green monster.

She turned her back on him and rolled her eyes. "Fine. I'll go shower and change."

"Can you braid my hair and help me with some makeup before you do that?" Shana reached for Claire's arm. "Please?"

The two of them disappeared into the bedroom while Bryant put the beers in the refrigerator. He popped a warm tater tot in his mouth and poured himself a glass of Jack Daniels on the rocks. Across the room, the face of Bobbie Gentry on the cover of her *Fancy* album beckoned to him. Bryant lit up a cigarette and removed the vinyl from its sleeve. He gently put the needle on the record and closed his eyes. Bobbie's sultry voice soothed Bryant's soul. He leaned back on the couch and sang along. Just as he got to the chorus, the front door swung open.

"Honey, I'm home!" Floyd Phillips stood in the doorway holding a fifth of gin and a deck of cards. Like any drunk sixty-year-old man, he moved like a wounded, geriatric escapee from Alcatraz.

"Floyd, you dirty dog," Bryant said. "You're early. The party isn't until another half hour."

Floyd grinned. "Here I thought I was fashionably late." He shifted his gaze from Bryant to Claire, who stood in the hallway staring at him. "I didn't know you had a daughter."

Oh, the ugly stick hit you good. Claire had never seen him before. By the smell of him, he was already a few drinks in. Floyd swayed from side to side and slurred a *hello, how do you do,* then attempted a mock, chivalrous bow as he removed an imaginary hat. He tripped forward and caught himself by the coat rack.

"This is my daughter, Claire," Bryant said. "Shana should be out in a bit. You know how women are." The two men shook hands and laughed.

Bryant offered Floyd a cigarette, and Claire held her breath to see if Floyd's wet brain would catch fire.

"See something you like?" Floyd asked.

Claire realized she was staring. She blinked and scurried to the bathroom to take a quick shower before the party.

No sooner was the door locked and the water running than Claire heard more voices in the living room as people trickled in. She heard one woman's voice and a few lower, gruff voices. The volume quickly escalated from a 1920s speakeasy to a rowdy bull-riding arena. Claire hopped in the shower and took her time soaking in the hot water.

Twenty minutes later, she made herself presentable and joined the adults. A quick survey of the room brought her attention to a young man with toothpick legs and cowboy boots. He stood six feet, eight inches tall, sported a fresh military haircut, and flaunted his manufactured-in-a-laboratory muscles. His neck was unusually long and slender and his large nose protruded forward as if searching for iron, steel, or anything magnetic. Claire couldn't help but think he looked like a Foghorn Leghorn PEZ dispenser.

A light tap pricked Claire's shoulder, and she flinched. She swiveled to find Shana mouthing *help* and pointing to the kitchen. Claire followed her and grabbed a tray of food. The two of them reentered the living room with grilled cheese sandwich bites and previously frozen hotdogs wrapped in pastry dough. The men busied themselves with drinks and upmanship of whose car was better while Shana and the other woman chit-chatted about finger foods tasting better if you actually ate with your fingers.

Claire wished she had a rope to put herself out of her misery. Soon, the folksy sounds of Bobbie Gentry simmered into the walls, and the chatter of adults talking about stupid things ping-ponged around the room.

Claire walked to the turntable and flipped the record over to the B side. Foghorn Leghorn-Skinny Neck guy waved Claire over and patted the seat next to him."Come. Sit. I'm Kenny, by the way."

Claire wrinkled her nose. He smelled as if Gloria Vanderbilt and a horse farrier had a baby while mucking stalls at an equestrian Kentucky Derby stable. That is to say, he reeked of manure and cheap perfume.

"I'm Claire."

Kenny and Claire talked about nothing in particular. He asked her questions, and she answered politely, never giving him more than a few words.

"How old are you?" Foghorn Leghorn asked.

"Twelve and a half," Claire answered.

"You like school?"

Claire shrugged. "It's all right."

Kenny suddenly lurched forward and put his hand on Claire's knee.

"Oh, sorry. Did I bump you?" It was the woman who was talking to Shana. She held one drumstick in her liver-spotted hand and a plastic animal sippy cup in the other. As she talked, the cigarette dangling from her lips bounced up and down as if trying to escape her thin, five-layered, lipsticked mouth. If ever there was a sallow woman, it was this lady whose jaundiced skin camouflaged her green shirt and brought out the grayness of her fake pearls.

"I almost spilled my drink on poor Claire here," Foghorn Leghorn said and squeezed her knee before he placed his hand back on his lap.

"I said I was sorry, Kenny," the woman said and then resumed talking to Shana.

As the evening wore on, a haze of smoke engulfed the stale air. Shana and the other woman gnawed on what was left of the chicken like rabid rats. The men got belligerent, gesturing in big motions as they made racist comments and mimicked the migrant workers at Sloppy Joe's Tavern. Claire learned Kenny had a tank of piranhas in his apartment for no other reason than to impress the ladies. Bryant bragged nonstop about his music career and playing on all types of stages across the country.

By midnight she couldn't take it anymore. Claire opened the window to let fresh air in. A stinging sensation rocked her bottom, and she let out a yelp. Someone had spanked her, but she didn't know who. Floyd and Kenny were the closest to her. She eyed them suspiciously, but neither of them took notice. Befuddled, she slipped into her bedroom and waited for everyone to leave or pass out.

It was after three in the morning when she left her room to get a cup of water, stepping over her wasted father, who had a pig-in-a-blanket still in his mouth.

#

On a dreary Tuesday morning, Shana's water burst and a frenzy ensued to get to the hospital. Bryant scrambled to get the clothes and other necessities together but in the end yelled, "Fuck it," and dashed out the door.

Shana moaned and hissed the entire ride. "Go faster."

Claire held on for dear life as her father zipped through the neighborhood and then merged onto the freeway at seventy miles an hour. The highway speed limit was fifty-five.

"Slow down," Shana screamed. "You're going to kill us."

"First you said go faster. Now it's slow down?" Bryant yelled. "Make up your damn mind. You're not having this baby in the car."

When they finally arrived and checked in to the hospital, it was a hurry-up-and-wait game as the nurses got Shana prepped. Claire sat helplessly and stared at Shana's contorted face. When Shana huffed and puffed, Claire mirrored her, sucking in short gulps of air and exhaling rapidly. When Shana's eyebrows furrowed and she gritted her teeth, Claire did the same.

Claire realized her chest was heaving in rhythm with Shana's breathing. She winced and clenched her fists. She was exhausted and slumped into a nearby chair. Her jaw ached. She must have been biting down the whole time.

As the nurse wheeled Shana down the hall with Bryant scurrying alongside, Claire sat numb and stared at the television. She was filled with nervous excitement to meet her baby brother or sister. Her stomach growled, and her eyes drooped heavily, but she didn't dare make a fuss. A *Highlights* magazine caught her eye. Claire passed the time flipping through the pages, solving the problems and riddles in the activities pages, and reading the short stories. Five magazines later, fatigue took over, and she wilted over the side of the chair, letting sleep claim her.

#

Jason Andrew Baker was born at 4:56 p.m. weighing eight pounds, twelve ounces, and looking like a big grape with his oblong head and purple, sinewy arms and legs.

Claire stood in the hospital room and stared at her baby brother. She gently stroked his cheeks and admired his long eyelashes. He was perfect in her eyes.

"Come take care of me," Bryant said.

"What?" Shana asked. "Now?"

Shana propped herself up in bed. Her swollen body and feet made it difficult for her to sit upright. She licked her dried lips and hooked loose strands of hair behind her ears.

Bryant stood in the doorframe of the bathroom. "Come on."

"I just had a ba—"

"I've been neglected for too long," Bryant said. "You're going to give me what I want, when I want. And I want it now."

"What's happening?" Claire asked.

"Stay with Jason," Bryant said. "We're going into the bathroom for a minute."

Shana heaved herself out of bed and shuffled to the bathroom. The door closed. Claire heard a *buh-voop* sound followed by the clang of her dad's belt buckle hitting the floor. This wasn't the first time she had heard her father having sex. Claire turned her attention to baby Jason and sang him a lullaby to drown out the moans and groans coming from behind the bathroom door

Bryant and Shana were in the bathroom for a solid half hour before they emerged. Shana wiped her mouth and crawled into bed. She brought the covers up to her neck and closed her eyes.

Bryant left the room without saying a word. Claire continued to watch over her baby brother and wished she could rock him to sleep. A distant memory ebbed into her consciousness, and a warm, comforting feeling enveloped her. She could see Grandpa Harold asleep in his La-Z-Boy chair and feel Grandma Sharon's tender kisses. She hadn't thought of them in a long time and wished she were back in California.

Her heart sank. Even though she was in the room with Shana and little Jason, she felt so alone and invisible.

#

One Saturday afternoon Shana and Bryant went out for some bread, eggs, and other items. Claire stayed home to babysit.

"Who's the cutest?" Claire cooed. She wiggled Jason's toes and tickled his feet.

Jason squirmed and squealed with laughter. Claire loved her baby brother's laugh. He drooled a lot and wriggled like a grub when he was happy. Sometimes he laughed so uncontrollably he'd scrunch up his face and squeeze out a fart.

Jason's rattle was within reach, and just as Claire stretched to get it off the couch, the door burst open. A loud bang got Claire's heart racing up and down her neck. She fell back so hard she bounced.

In barged wet-brained Floyd. He slammed the door closed with the heel of his boot and strode over to Claire in two strides.

"You—" Floyd said.

Claire screamed. She scrambled to her feet. "Get out."

"Your daddy home?"

"He'll be back soon," Claire hissed.

"Where?" Floyd stumbled forward, so drunk he slurred his words and didn't make sense. "Where he be? Be home."

Claire stepped back to put some distance between them. Little Jason lay on the floor wide-eyed and watched. She was worried this man was going to do something stupid and hurt the baby. Claire darted around Floyd and lunged to the floor to pick up Jason. She wasn't fast enough. He was a wide man and not easy to get around.

Floyd wrapped his burly, hairy arm around Claire's waist and pinned her to the wall. He burped and then hiccupped. His clothes reeked of gunpowder and cigarettes. His hot breath doused her face like kerosene as his lips touched the tendrils of hair above her ear.

A hardness pressed up against her back as Floyd rubbed his front side to side between the middle of her back. With one hand groping her budding nipples, Floyd let his other hand roam freely, first massaging Claire's thighs and then squeezing the soft flesh between her legs. His clutch tightened.

"You know what I'm going to do to you?" Floyd breathed.

Claire sucked in a big gulp of air and let out a blood-curdling, high-pitched scream. It was enough to startle Floyd, and he loosened his grip on her body.

She whipped around to face him. "My dad is gonna kill you," Claire screamed. "Get out."

"Don't tell him—"

"He's going to beat you so bad when he finds out!"

"All right, all right." Floyd held up his hands in surrender and staggered out the door. Claire locked it and double-checked that it was latched, bolted, and secure.

Her legs crumbled, and she crawled to Jason. "You're okay. He's gone. The bad man is gone."

It was another forty-five minutes before Shana and Bryant came home carrying three bags of groceries. Claire told her daddy what happened.

"He wasn't going to do anything, Claire," Bryant said. "He was probably just messing with you. He's not even going to remember this happened."

"But, Dad, he—"

"Go wash your hands and help Shana with the meatloaf."

"The man was feeling up my body," Claire argued.

"Honey," Bryant said, "you have to understand, he has a wet brain."

"I don't have to understand anything."

"You need to have more compassion. Now go."

And that was that. Her father dismissed her with a flick of his wrist and a pivot on his heels.

Claire bit her lip and muttered under her breath, "I hate you."

#

Weeks had passed since the Floyd incident, and Claire made sure to always lock the doors and windows when she was home alone. She immersed herself in music and books and took to journaling in her diary. Other than going to school and doing her chores, which included taking care of Jason when the adults went out, Claire stayed shrink-wrapped in her bedroom.

"Claire?" Her father's voice boomed from down the hall and slipped under her door.

"Yeah?" Claire yelled back.

"What are you doing?"

"Homework," she lied.

"Go outside."

"Why?" Claire asked. "I don't want to."

Moments later her bedroom door creaked open. Bryant's head poked in. "You've been cooped up inside too long. I want you to get some fresh air."

"But—"

"Go outside and play."

"Dad—"

"I'm not asking," Bryant said. "You're always in your room. Stop being a hermit and go play outside."

Claire hmphed and earmarked her book. She tossed it on her desk and slithered out of bed. Off came the pajamas and on came the shorts and tank top.

It was a warm sixty-eight degrees outside. Claire squinted and instinctively shielded her eyes from the sun with her palms outstretched. The mizzle from the day before had left a faint smell of damp earth that lingered in the air. The neighborhood was quiet. A curious squirrel watched her dump her chalk out onto the concrete and scurried up the tree when it realized she didn't have nuts to offer.

Across the street were rows of apartments as far as her eyes could see. She wondered which building Floyd and some of her father's friends lived in. At the four-way stop up the road, a couple walked, their arms linked as they engrossed themselves in deep conversation.

Claire picked up a white chalk and drew a tic-tac-toe grid. She placed Xs and Os with blue and pink chalk neatly in the squares and after five games of coming to a draw, she switched to something else.

She scrawled a hopscotch board on the sidewalk and looked for a pebble. It had to be the right size . . . not too small that it would bounce off the board if she threw it too hard, and not too heavy that it'd land on the same square each time. It had to be the right shape, also, otherwise, it could roll away.

After a few minutes of tossing, hopping, bending, and repeating, Claire took refuge in the shade. She was about to go inside to get a glass of water when, in the distance, a man waved his orangutan arms in her direction. As he approached, Claire recognized him immediately. How could she forget the six-foot-eight skyscraper with Popeye arms? His military haircut was shaggier than when she last saw him, but his nose was still searching for something magnetic.

"Hello, girlie-girl," Foghorn Leghorn PEZ-dispenser guy said. "You remember me? Kenny?"

And before she could respond, Kenny hooked his index finger under her tank top and pulled it up. Claire froze. He licked his lips and whistled. "Hmmm, you're going to be sweet in a couple of years."

Claire swatted his hand and pulled her shirt down. She ran as fast as she could into her house and slammed the door as hard as she could.

Why? Claire asked. *Why are they all disgusting animals?*

23. A FRIEND FOR CLAIRE

School started like any other new school year. Claire threw on an old pair of faded blue jeans a little too short but not quite highwaters if she wore blue socks to camouflage with the jeans. She pulled the burnt-orange sweater out of the hamper and gave it a good sniff. The faint smell of rubber and wet leather assaulted her nose. It still had the sale sticker on the sleeve from the Rag Tag Thrift store's clearance extravaganza. Had she been wearing it with the sticker attached this whole time?

Draped over her top drawer was a green turtleneck sweater worn for a few hours two days ago. It was good enough to re-wear. This year was going to be different. Claire could feel it. It was going to be better because, in less than two months, she'd turn thirteen. She wasn't a child anymore. Two small mounds protruded where her flat nipples used to rest, and her monthly flow came regularly each month. Her body told her to quickly grow up, but Claire desperately wanted to hold on to the early years of childhood when it was simple with the stretch of highway, the CB radio, the truck stops, and outlaw country music on the airwaves.

Now, there would be dances, pimples, and hormonal boys to *not* look forward to . . . a bridge to adulthood that everyone crossed if they lived long enough. And Claire had lived long enough.

She had paid her dues and deserved to cross that bridge to a better tomorrow. She endured the fire ants and the fried chicken grease burns. She survived Gisela's wrath and the Love Homestead's Sabbath rituals. She even survived that awful night in the field, left for dead, smelling like the stench of the stranger's rotting soul.

Claire freed her mind and headed to the kitchen to make toast. Shana and Jason were still asleep, and her dad either hadn't come home last night or was already at work. She didn't see his truck outside.

The bread popped up, and Claire slathered a generous amount of butter on it before taking a Cujo-bite. Perfect. Not too crisp. Not too soft.

The walk to school invigorated her. A light breeze whispered sweet nothings in her ear and pricked her freckles as she walked briskly to school. Maybe she'd make friends this year . . . find solidarity with others who were in their last year of junior high and would soon start over again at the bottom of the social ladder in high school.

Living in Rochester where there were about fifty-five thousand people, most of whom were affluent because of the Mayo Clinic or IBM, Claire accepted she'd never fit in. Walking among the rich technology or medical professionals' kids felt like living life as spent gum under someone's shoe. Claire was acutely aware of the line between the haves and have-nots. Even though the kids wore the same things—jeans, T-shirts, and running shoes—there was a difference between thrift store shirts and department store shirts. And if you walked to school, you were below the poverty line. If you got dropped off at school, you were likely to be voted most popular, best dressed, or most likely to be rich and famous.

In lickety-split time, Claire arrived at Willow Creek Junior High. She ambled through the crosswalk toward the drop-off line; her eyes fixated on a black and tan Lincoln Continental Mark VI sedan that had just pulled in. Behind it came a blue Mercedes Benz 500SEL.

One day I'll be able to afford one of those cars. Her father used to tell her, back when they traveled the countryside together, that education was the key to unlocking shackles and chains. And while her father was an intelligent and charming man when he was sober, education couldn't save him from his demons. Claire knew dropping out of school was never an option.

"After you turn eighteen," Bryant had said, "my financial obligations end. You better be able to support yourself, and education is the answer."

Two boys got out of the vehicles, and upon seeing each other, they high-fived.

"Up high," the blond boy said.

"Down low," the other one responded.

"Check out our new Mark Six," the blond said, referring to the new Lincoln Continental. "Gnarly isn't it?

"Totally tubular."

Claire watched as the two boys entered the building together. The blond one was Paul Bergerhackle. He walked funny like he had a pet squirrel in his pants, but because his family was rich and he could afford expensive gadgets, he was the most popular kid in school. With a name like Bergerhackle, he had to be either rich or good-looking to survive life.

They were in a class together last year, and because seats were assigned by last names in alphabetical order, Paul Bergerhackle sat behind her. Sometimes he'd swat her head with his thumb and middle finger like he was flicking a gnat. Other times it was a spitball or something small that the teachers wouldn't notice.

On one occasion Claire found over a dozen tiny staples in the back of her hair while she was in the shower.

Gawd, please let me not have any classes with him this year.

The first day of school was uneventful. Even lunch period was tolerable. No one paid attention to her, and she was grateful. Then came the fourth period with French and the fifth period with math. In both classes, Paul Bergerhackle and his friend, Nick, sat behind Claire. She could feel their eyes boring holes into her, and she felt conspicuous like a naked person at a masquerade ball.

In the second week of school, Paul strolled into math class wearing a new jean jacket. The only thing new Claire ever got was underwear. He stood in front of the classroom surveying the class like a king surveying his subjects. It was as if he wanted to make sure everyone saw his new clothes.

Claire immediately turned her back to him and grabbed her book out of her backpack. She stacked the math book on her binder and Pee Chee where it rested for two seconds.

Paul swiped Claire's books off the table and whispered, "What's up, Gingersnap?"

The book and binder thumped on the ground as Paul nonchalantly walked to his seat. Chuckles from some of the kids in the room echoed between the walls.

"You know, you need to grow up," Claire muttered.

A moment later, the teacher walked into her classroom and began roll call. "Welcome to advance math," Mrs. Burkinshaw said. "Let's begin."

"Ashleigh Arnold?" Mrs. Burkinshaw asked. "Claire Baker?"

"Here," Claire answered.

"Paul Bergerhackle?" One by one she checked their names off. "Nick Darling?"

Paul's friend, the one who had stepped out of the Mercedes earlier, raised his hand.

Claire stiffened. Was he a darling? Claire smirked. *Highly doubt it,* she thought, and tensed up, anticipating trouble was brewing.

"Christine Lopez?" Mrs. Burkinshaw called.

"Present," came a soft voice behind her. Claire recognized that voice and looked over.

Christine and Claire had been schoolmates since sixth grade, but they never talked. On that day, however, the tone of Christine's voice made Claire think of cotton candy and root beer . . . sweet and supercharged with sugary elixirs.

Christine was beautiful with her olive skin and dark hair with thick curls framing her Spanish features. She had been pretty back in sixth grade, but now, she was a vixen. The braces were gone, and her chest was fuller. Claire made a bet Christine's hips curved out just enough to accentuate her small waist and give her the hourglass figure that gave boys twitches in their pants.

Days turned into weeks. Worse than math class was her woodworking and metal shop class where Paul, Nick, and his cronies ruled the hour. Their teacher, Mr. Ogawa, a small Japanese man who had survived the internment camps, had no control over his class. Kids got away with everything.

Nick Darling approached Claire with a mischievous smile. He flipped a penny on her desk while Mr. Ogawa was on the other side of the room helping a student. "Here. That's about all you're worth, right?"

Claire grimaced. "Fuck you."

"Wouldn't you like to?" he asked. "Nah, I don't want to do you."

"Listen, fucktard," Claire hissed, "no girl would ever be with you."

The bell rang, and Claire stood up to leave. Nick shoved Claire's head into a saw. Luckily it was not on. "Bitch, you want to take me on? Shall I turn on the saw?"

Claire's legs turned to whispy wafers. Her foot went numb, and her mouth puckered in pain. She locked eyes with Mr. Ogawa, who looked away.

Nick released her head and laughed. "Just remember, I can turn on the saw."

"Didn't your mama raise you any better than that?" Claire asked.

And so it went the first month. Paul, Nick, and their friends taunted Claire and called her everything from Carrots to Cheetos-head. In math, Paul continued to knock her books off the desk every chance he got.

"Paul, one of these days, the teacher is going to catch you," Claire said. And then one day, Mrs. Burkinshaw did catch him.

For a petite woman, she moved fast. To Claire's astonishment, Mrs. Burkinshaw wrapped her slender fingers around Paul's neck and applied enough pressure to force him to look down. "You pick up her books right now. Do it again, and you're going to wish you hadn't."

Claire made the mistake of telling her father about Paul and Nick and how they treated her in the classes, to which her dad laughed and said, "How dare you think you're smart enough for advanced math? And why the hell are you taking French? You'll never use it. If you want to live in this country, learn Spanish."

Bryant called the school and had her placed in Spanish. He let her keep advanced math even though he made it clear he was doubtful she'd pass it. For someone who used to stress the importance of education and how dropping out was never an option, his doubts about her math abilities dumbfounded her. She realized her father was a walking contradiction. Intelligent yet clueless. Charming yet abusive. Loving yet self-centered.

After the first month of school, the boys resorted to calling her Copperhead, Copper, Coppertop, and sometimes Duracell.

"Hey, Claire . . ." Claire scanned upward to see Christine in front of her wearing a Bon Jovi T-shirt. Her mouth curved into an apologetic smile, meeting her brown eyes and long lashes. "Those stupid boys threw your purse out the window." Claire checked the back of her chair, and sure enough, her purse was missing. "I talked to Mrs. Burkinshaw, and she said we can go get it."

The two of them went outside and took their sweet time walking to the field behind the math building. Claire did her best to avoid staring at Christine. She was too pretty. "Thanks for telling me," Claire said to make small talk.

"They're a bunch of jerks," Christine said. "So where do you live?"

"Off Twenty-ninth and Simpson Road. You?"

"Opposite." Christine pointed toward the fields. "We're on the other side of McQuillian Fields. We should hang out sometime."

"Sure," Claire said, wishing she had known Christine last year. Perhaps she could have walked to Christine's house after that godawful night instead of stumbling all the way home alone.

The two of them collected Claire's purse and headed back to class.

By the second month of school, Christine and Claire had become intertwined like licorice vines in a Twizzler package. They found each other at recess, in the bathroom, at assemblies, and in the hallways. There was always something to talk about, and the one thing they had in common was their love of music.

At last, a friend for Claire. Together the two girls increased their circumference of friends, and soon, there were five of them who shared one common bond, unbeknownst to one another—they all came from dysfunctional, broken, abused households and yearned to belong.

24. ORONOCO

A couple of weeks after Claire's twelfth birthday, she ambled downstairs to find a pretty blonde girl sitting in the living room. She looked to be about sixteen years old.

"Shana and I want to go out for dinner. You're going to go for pizza and a movie with Laurie."

"I don't want to go," Claire said.

"You're going, and she's taking you," Bryant insisted. "Laurie is staying with us for a while because she's having some problems at home."

"So you're going to send me off with a total stranger?" Claire asked. "I don't even know her."

"Claire, this is Laurie," Bryant said. "Laurie, this is my daughter, Claire. Now go." Bryant handed the blonde girl a twenty-dollar bill. "That should be enough."

"Where's Jason?" Claire asked. "I'll watch him while you and Shana go out."

"He's at the sitter's," Bryant said. "I'm tired of you being cooped up inside the house. You're stinking up the bedroom."

"Dad—"

"Enough, Claire." Bryant waved his hand in dismissal. "Go."

Claire stomped up the stairs and grabbed her coat. Once inside Laurie's old Volkswagon Beetle, which smelled of halitosis, they took off down the road going forty miles per hour. *Way too fast*, Claire thought, considering the national speed limit was fifty-five miles per hour on the highways. Laurie made a sharp turn around the corner, and Claire tipped over in the backseat. *Any faster and this car will skid into town sideways.*

"Where are we going?" Claire asked.

Laurie took the last drag of her cigarette and flicked it out the window. She let the smoke linger in her mouth before exhaling. "Need to pick up my friend, Steph."

They pulled in front of a blue house with white trim and Christmas lights strung around the windows. It was early November. Claire wondered if the lights had been there since last year.

Laurie honked her horn, and a petite girl bounced out of the front door. She looked a little older than Laurie and not nearly as pretty. Her makeup was too dark, and she had bright purple lipstick that, under the dome light of the car, made her lips light up like a neon sign.

Up went the volume in the car as the two teen girls sang "Pretty Woman" by Van Halen.

Twenty minutes later they pulled into a trailer park in the small town of Oronoco. One house was lit up like the Fourth of July. Heavy metal music blared with Bon Jovi's voice screaming from the speakers, "She's a runaway."

A few people loitered outside, laughing and passing a doobie. Trucks, cars, and motorcycles were parked outside with no regard for the carport or gravel parkway.

"What are we doing here?" Claire asked.

"Steph just needs to stop in and get something." Laurie pulled down the visor and reapplied her lip gloss. "We'll get dinner and see the movie after this."

"I'll just wait in the car then." Claire's heartbeat quickened. Chills ran up and down her neck and arms. She pulled the coat tighter and shivered. It was cold outside, but the goosebumps pricked her temples, and Claire knew this was a bad crowd.

"No, you have to come in," Steph said. "It's not safe for you to sit here alone at night in the car. We're going to be too long for you to sit here, but we'll be as quick as possible."

"Laurie can wait with me then while you go in." Claire sunk deeper into the backseat.

"No, I'm going in too," Laurie said. "You can just sit in the living room awhile and wait. Besides, it's cold out here."

The two girls wouldn't let up and demanded she come. Against her better judgment, Claire followed them inside.

They walked past the few men loitering on the front porch. Claire felt small as they towered over her. The men smiled, but their eyes did not convey warmth or friendliness.

Inside the double-wide trailer were a dozen men, most of them wearing T-shirts and leather jackets. Two women huddled in a corner and poured over a photo album with a beer in one hand and a joint in the other. Claire couldn't tell their age with their drug-ridden faces, black eyeliner, and blue eye shadow, but she guessed perhaps late teens or early twenties. One of the women looked vaguely familiar. It dawned on Claire the woman was the same girl who had come into her bedroom a year ago and offered to give Claire a vaginal cleanse with her tongue.

Dumbfounded, Claire sat down on the couch and looked everywhere but at that girl. She scanned the room and saw two people necking; the man groped the woman's breast while the woman fondled his enlarged member. Claire quickly looked away.

"Hey." Face to face with the one person she tried to avoid, Claire sank into the couch and said hey back. "Remember me?" the girl asked. "Pauline. You fucking made me walk home that night."

"No one invited you into my room," Claire boldly said. Remembering Pauline in her room that night offering to lick her made Claire sick. She would have vomited if there had been anything in her stomach to throw up. Claire looked for Laurie and Steph only to find them both disappearing into a room with a guy.

Pauline's words grated and brought Claire's attention back to her. "Whatever. Let bygones be bygones. Want a beer?"

Claire shook her head, but Pauline thrust a cold can into her hands anyway. There she sat, beer in hand, not daring to move, hoping to not bring attention to herself. Pauline tried to talk to her, but Claire gave short one-word replies. She kept watch and hoped Laurie and Steph would return soon. Five headbanging songs later, Claire thought about running to the car to see if it was unlocked. Maybe she could get into the car, lock it, and wait. *Eventually, they'll come looking for me.*

Pressure pushed against Claire's bladder, and she decided to relieve herself first before heading to the car. "Where's the bathroom?"

Pauline pointed toward the two bedrooms where Laurie and Steph disappeared into. "Down the hall, last door on the left."

Inside the bathroom, it took her a minute to relax enough for the stream to flow. When she opened the door, one of the biker guys stood in front of her blocking the exit. He stood five feet, eleven inches, and towered over her five-foot frame.

Claire froze for a split second before finding her voice. "Oh, the bathroom is all yours."

The biker guy smiled. "Oh, it's okay. Actually, I was looking for you. You're pretty. Come talk to me."

"We're leaving soon," Claire said, hoping it was true.

"Yeah, I know," he said. "Come on, just for a few minutes." He stepped to the side as Laurie exited one of the bedrooms with her arm draped loosely around a guy's neck.

"Laurie," Claire yelled, loud enough to compete with the vocals of another heavy metal ballad.

"Hey," Laurie said, "looks like Mark wants to talk to you!" Laurie ushered Claire into the dark bedroom. It happened so quickly, she didn't have time to gather her thoughts or her courage to fight back. The door closed, and the light switched on. It was just the two of them.

"You don't have to be afraid," Mark said. "I'm not going to do anything. You are safe. You're fine. I just want to chitchat. No big deal."

Mark gently took Claire by the hand and led her to the bed. She tried to control her breathing as her heart pummelled through her ribs. With every beat, her heart drummed against her chest cavity, making dents against her bones.

"What's your name? What school do you go to?" Mark asked. "This must be strange for you."

"I don't know what we're doing here," Claire said.

Mark scooted a little closer. "Hey, relax. Laurie just wants to get her groove on, and I thought you could use a break from all those people out there. Here, have a seat." He patted the bed.

"I don't want to sit."

"No, really, it's okay. It's just you and me in here, and you're fine." He patted the mattress again. "I'm Mark, by the way. What's your name?"

Claire slowly sat on the corner's edge farthest from him, making sure her feet touched the floor in case she needed to bolt. "Claire," she answered.

"You like your classes?"

"Some."

"Claire, you're so pretty. Have you ever been kissed before?"

"No."

"A pretty girl like you? Would you like to try?"

"Someday, maybe, but I don't have a boyfriend."

"Can I kiss you?" Mark leaned over and kissed her before she could answer. He rubbed her arm and stroked her neck with his fingertips.

Claire pushed on his chest. "No. I don't want to be kissed."

"Sweetheart, I just want to kiss you." Mark stood up and walked toward the door. A breath escaped Claire's lips. She realized she hadn't been breathing. The rush of relief abruptly ended when the room went dark and Mark was immediately on top of her.

His kisses were more forced, urgent, as his lips crushed hers and his tongue worked to pry her mouth open. Claire didn't know what to do. He was heavy. She felt his hardness pressed against her inner thigh as he gyrated his hips and rubbed his penis on her legs.

Claire squirmed and tried to slip out from under him, but he was too big. His talons wrapped around her bony wrists. He pushed her arms up above her head. Mark clasped his fingers through hers and pinned her hands against the bed. He let out a husky exhale and groaned. His kisses traveled around her face and neck and when he released one of her hands, she wrestled to push him off.

"Whoa, whoa. It's okay." Mark looked at her, his face inches from her. His breath smelled of beer and weed. From the sliver of light coming through the window curtains, she saw his eyes. Dark and big, like whales, staring at her with curiosity and intensity, but not malice and anger. He smiled and relaxed.

Claire peeled off the bedspread and ran out of the room. The music pierced her ears. The bright light hurt her eyes. She ran outside and spotted the beetle, but the car was locked. Claire saw another trailer sixty feet away with lights on. She ran toward it, looking back once to see if anyone was following her.

"Claire!" It was Laurie.

"C'mon, get back here!" This time it was Steph.

Claire continued toward the other trailer with its front porch light illuminating the single-wide mobile home.

"For fuck's sake, calm down." It was another girl's voice. Pauline. Who else could it be?

Claire rapped on the trailer door. She peered back at the three girls running toward her. She banged harder. Complete silence on the other side of the door. Claire kicked the door. No one was home. The three girls surrounded her.

"You need to calm down," Laurie said. "We'll get you home. Don't worry."

The air outside was ice cold. A soft wind blew, but it pricked her eyes. Claire blinked several times. "I have to go home. This is not where I need to be."

"Hey," Laurie said, "Mark likes you. It's okay if he is interested and you're not."

"Take me home!" Claire screamed.

"Soon," Steph said. "We're going to be just a little while longer. Just come in and sit in the living room. You don't have to leave the living room."

"No," Claire said adamantly. "No!"

"Listen," Pauline said, "Stop being a brat. You're such a baby. Quit your bitching."

Claire felt the sting of her words. She willed herself not to cry. She wasn't a baby. It was freezing outside. These people were strangers. Only druggies, thieves, and bad people listened to heavy metal while drinking and smoking pot. Oronoco was a small town, less than three square miles and twenty minutes from home. With a population of less than a thousand people, it had been incorporated as a city only fifteen years ago in 1968. Claire only knew this because it was mentioned in history class when they covered Olmstead County's historical events. Her teacher had referred to it as a bedroom community outside of Rochester, and that term alone now had Claire feeling claustrophobic and afraid. The only way in and out of Oronoco was on US Highway 52 unless she swam the Zumbro River. Claire was trapped.

"We have to go home. There's a certain time we have to be home, or my dad is going to be mad."

"We're almost done in there," Steph said. "Just sit on the couch for another fifteen minutes while I finish my shit."

"You're fine," Laurie said. "We're supposed to be at a movie by now. Your dad's not expecting us home for at least another hour."

Claire was at the mercy of these girls. She couldn't walk home. They were in the middle of nowhere. She could already hear her father's gruff voice hammering down at her.

Back inside the loud, bright, warm living room, Claire sat pressed against the armrest of the couch. She willed herself to be stiff, dead weight. Claire did not budge, not even when a sleazy-looking guy with an unkempt beard sat in a chair beside her. He smiled at her and offered her drugs.

"No, that's okay," Claire said, trying to be polite but wishing she could smash his face in.

Her untouched can of beer was where she had left it. She held it until it went warm.

Thirty minutes went by. "When are we going to leave?" Claire asked.

Laurie shrugged and went back into one of the bedrooms with a different guy. Steph did the same.

"I have to go to the bathroom again," Claire said to Pauline. "Will you go with me?"

Pauline rolled her eyes. "Fine. Make it quick."

After peeing, Claire debated whether she should just stay locked inside the bathroom, but she was afraid Laurie and Steph would leave without her. She opened the door to find a half-naked Laurie stumbling out of the bedroom.

"Pauline," Laurie said, "you can leave. You don't need to babysit her."

"Are we leaving now?" Claire asked.

Laurie blocked Claire in the hallway. "Don't be such a prude."

Behind Laurie stood Mark. Same guy as before with his dark brown curly hair, brown eyes, narrow face, and lanky body. His smile this time was mischievous. In one swift movement, he picked Claire up and took her back into the same bedroom.

"No!" Claire yelled. "What the fuck? No! I need to go home! I'm not supposed to be here."

25. PAYMENT

Inside the room, a sliver of light from the window cast shadows on the walls. Mark pulled Claire's shirt swiftly over her head and tossed it on the floor. He tugged at her pants and peeled them off so hard her shoes thumped against the baseboard heater.

She cried out, "No. Get off me."

"I'm not going to hurt you. I'll be gentle." Mark said. "Laurie and Steph owe me, and you're my prize."

Claire shivered, feeling awkward with her naked body on display. Mark mounted her. His skin was hot. He moved in and out gently, slowly at first, and then faster and faster. With each thrust he made, Claire's pain subsided; her fingers and toes tingled.

"No!" Claire whispered. She didn't have the strength to yell.

"Don't fight it, and you won't get hurt."

Mark lifted her leg over his should and resumed, taking pleasure however he could with her.

The bedroom door suddenly flung open and the lights went on. An onslaught of men spilled in. Claire's eyes opened wide. Her heart hopscotched down to her stomach and back up to her throat as her chest rose and fell rapidly. Beads of sweat percolated on her upper lip and hairline. She became hyperfocused on the unfamiliar faces.

"Don't fight me," Mark said. "If you do, the rest of them will join in."

His words hit her like a thousand daggers beneath the arctic ocean floor. She went into stone-cold shock. Her brain shut down. Claire lay paralyzed by fear. She closed her eyes and instantly felt weightless. Her mind disassociated until she floated above all of them. Up, up, up . . .

The men stood at the foot of the bed cheering Mark on. "Show her what it takes to become a woman."

Claire watched and listened helplessly.

"Fuck her," they jeered. "Break her in."

Time stood still. Claire's vision blurred. Their voices echoed in the background. Mark's moans became distant. Vibrating between her ears were rhythmic squeaks of the box spring. And then . . . nothingness. He finished, but it wasn't over.

"See?" Mark said. "Sex isn't so bad."

Everyone left the room. Claire fell back into her body with a crash and curled up on her side. A cold pair of hands pulled her up into a sitting position. Rough fibers scorched her face as her shirt slid down her head. Someone slipped Claire's arms through two round openings. Her torso was now covered.

"You know," Laurie said, "Mark just wanted to pop your cherry. It's not a big deal."

Claire looked at Laurie but saw past her. Steph picked up the pants and helped Claire get dressed. One moment they were in the trailer; the next they were in Pauline's house. Claire didn't remember the ride there or how she was naked once again.

"A hot soak in the tub will snap you out of it."

Who said that? Claire didn't know nor did she care. The sponge scraped against her hot skin like sea urchins propelling their spines across the ocean floor. The roughness awakened her senses as her body came out of the coma. Claire found her voice. "I want to go home."

"You should take her somewhere first and get her something to eat," Pauline said. "You can't bring her home like this."

Claire desperately wanted to crawl into her bed and lay there forever. She imagined suffocating herself with her blanket and pillow.

Laurie, Steph, and Claire piled into the Volkswagen Beetle as Pauline waved goodbye. Instead of going home, they arrived at Denny's restaurant.

"I'm starving," Laurie said and dragged Claire out of the car.

Inside the diner, Claire noticed the clock on the wall—nearly three in the morning. An elderly couple stared at the girls and tsked as they walked by. They were seated adjacent to the old couple at a corner booth in the back.

"Oh my god, can you believe that little girl sitting in the booth next to us? No child should be out this late."

Claire wanted to scream back at her. *Lady, I don't want to fucking be here!*

"They're up to no good," the lady's companion said.

The girls ordered food, and even though Claire was not hungry, they ordered her an All-American Slam. She pushed her eggs around but couldn't muster the strength to take a bite. She was exhausted and craved the comfort of her bedroom with its musty blanket and mildewed windows.

Steph shoveled a Moons Over My Hammy sandwich in her mouth and said, "You're acting like the fucking world just ended. So you got laid for the first time. It's no big deal."

"Listen," Laurie said, "if it makes you feel any better, I'm sorry. I needed some drugs, and Mark wanted your virginity as payment."

"You sold me for drugs?" Claire asked.

"She didn't sell you," Steph said. "It's not like we're pimps. Mark just took what he felt was—"

"And you were going to stay at the trailer as long as it took to—"

"Lighten up, Claire," Steph said.

"He's a grown man!" Claire exclaimed. "Oh my god, guys, what if I got pregnant?"

The girls laughed.

"He would take care of it." Laurie cut into her Grand Slam pancakes and shoveled them into her mouth. "He'd pay for an abortion."

#

After Denny's, Laurie dropped Steph off and drove home to Claire's house. In the astronomical twilight, the sky illuminated just enough light for Claire to see the faint stars and planets flickering above the town. It would be another two or three hours before the sun rose. One light was on in the house. Claire braced herself and walked in.

"Where the fuck have you been?" Bryant charged over to the girls before Laurie could close the door. Shana sat on the couch. Her face contorted with fear. "Goddammit, do you know what time it is? Fucking five o'clock!" Bryant clenched his teeth. "Claire, what do you have to say for yourself? How can you make me worry like this? My god. I thought you were raped or lying in the ditch somewhere! Explain yourself. You couldn't pick up the phone and call?"

"We don't have a phone," Claire answered.

A sharp, stinging sensation shot up Claire's jawline and into her eyes. She stumbled backward and hit her head against the wall. Her father's fist came swift and hard. She righted herself and held onto the wall for support. Her knees trembled, her mouth ached, and everything below her waist was dead.

Bryant backhanded his daughter again and knocked Claire across the room.

"How come you're not screaming at her?" Claire yelled and pointed at Laurie. "She's the one who took me out. I didn't want to go."

Bryant punched his daughter in the chest, and Claire dropped to her knees.

Laurie interjected. "Bryant, we—"

"Get the hell out of my house," Bryant fumed. "Don't you ever come back!" Laurie smirked and slammed the door as she left. Claire ran upstairs before her father could punch her again. "You're grounded for a fucking year!"

Claire crawled under the covers and curled into a ball, a fetal position she was well-accustomed to now, only this time, no matter how tightly she held her knees to her chest, she still felt exposed, weak, and vulnerable. She wanted to scream and let all her anger, fear, frustrations, and pain out. The tears didn't come, and she was proud of herself for not crying. Rage steamed out of her bones and simmered beneath her skin.

I hate you. You ruined my life. I trusted you. How could you? You're no father at all. You're supposed to protect me. You're supposed to love me. You're supposed to fight for me. You're supposed to hold me and tell me everything is going to be all right. You used to love me. We used to have fun together. I was your sunshine. Well, fuck you, Dad, you drunk, racist, male chauvinistic, narcissistic asshole.

Claire screamed in silence. She squeezed her eyes shut to suppress the tears from escaping and locked the turmoil deep within the cavity where her heart resided. In defeat, she succumbed to the numbing agent that would be the salve of protection from ever feeling joy and wonder again. She vowed to trust no one. Every rotten person in the world had ulterior motives. Every man was a demon, a pedophile, a danger to society. And every woman was a man's pawn or a trapped and caged animal.

Well, Claire was ready to step into the arena and fight with claws drawn and fangs out. *To hell with this life and everyone in it. I'll make everyone pay.*

#

By morning, Claire had begun her prison sentence of being grounded. She dusted, mopped, scrubbed, and vacuumed until the house was spotless. Shana tried to cheer her up but soon gave up after receiving only one-word replies. Bryant avoided eye contact and gave her the silent treatment, which was fine by Claire. She threw invisible daggers at him when he wasn't looking. She welcomed the stench of his rotting soul and wanted a front-row seat to his descent into hell.

That night, Claire grabbed a slice of buttered toast and ate her dinner in her bedroom. By midnight, the house was still. The longer Claire lay in bed, the more claustrophobic she felt in her tomb. Her body ached, but her mind raced a mile a minute. She had to get out of her crypt and never come back to this toxic wasteland that was her home.

Claire shoved her belongings into her backpack and climbed out the window. The polar air felt good against her face. She wondered if this was what it felt like to free-fall out of a plane or plunge into an Alaskan lake. It invigorated her. She imagined her veins turning into icicles, her heart hardening until it stopped beating. She didn't know who to call or where to go. She had no plan, except to never step into this house again.

The neighborhood was eerily quiet. Only one flickering porch light lit the street. Claire thought about walking the two blocks to the house she babysat for. Mrs. Linden was probably asleep, but maybe there was a chance she'd hear Claire knock and let her in. It was worth a try.

As she walked toward Cotton Street near the haunted house where the ghost of Old Ruford lurked, Claire's imagination got the best of her. Shadows jumped out of the brick walls, and black mist rose from the damp ground. The bark and mulch turned over to stare at her as the trees tiptoed behind her, their branches ready to snatch her up and break her neck.

Claire picked up her pace and hastened to get to Mrs. Linden's house. She had been babysitting little Beth off and on for the past two years and had managed to save thirty dollars from the last few visits. A light was on in the kitchen. To Claire's relief, she saw movement inside. She knocked lightly at first, then urgently the second time.

The door opened, and a man peered from behind the door—Mrs. Linden's younger brother, Perry, who lived with her. He was in his late twenties, with dishwater blond hair, crooked teeth, and freckles all over his face and arms. His eyes opened wide.

"Claire!" Perry opened the door a little wider. "God, come in. What are you doing here? What's wrong? It's late!"

She stepped into the warm house. It felt like a furnace compared to the Rochester streets.

"Is Mrs. Linden here?" Claire asked.

"No," Perry said, "it's just Beth and me. She's sleeping. Do you want to wait?"

Claire hesitated.

"My sister should be home soon," Perry added.

Claire nodded and put her backpack down. She took off her coat and sat down on the couch.

"Are you hungry? Thirsty?" Perry asked.

Claire nodded.

"Okay, I'll be right back."

Claire watched as Perry disappeared into the kitchen, his joggers hanging loose on his body while his T-shirt clung to his torso. Claire slipped her hands beneath her thighs to warm them up and surveyed her surroundings. The all-too-familiar house was covered with framed photos of the family and landscapes of places they had visited. Some of the frames were small, others were big. Some had wooden frames, others in plastic or shiny metal . . . all were mosaically hung and askew. She scanned the frames to see if there were any new pictures since her last babysitting gig at the house.

"I hope you like peanut butter jelly sandwiches and hot chocolate." Perry handed Claire the plate and placed the mug on the coffee table. He grinned and sat down next to her on the sofa. "You've grown up since I last saw you. Mind telling me what happened to your face and what you're doing out this late at night all by yourself?"

Claire imagined she must look haggard with her bruised face. She took a bite of her sandwich instead of answering him. The chunky peanut butter contrasted with the smooth grape jelly and tasted nostalgic on her tongue. It was like being home with Grandma Sharon and Grandpa Harold. Oh, how she missed them. If only she had their number. If only her father kept in touch with them.

In between mouthfuls, she opened up to Perry about going to Oronoco against her will and how Laurie and Steph took her to Denny's to eat after the party. She skipped the part about Mark and going to Pauline's house to get cleaned. "When we got home, my dad was so mad, he beat me and threw me up against the wall." To mask her quivering voice, Claire sipped her hot chocolate. She blinked back the tears and whispered, "It wasn't my fault. Now I'm grounded for a year."

"I'm sorry." Perry cupped her face and pulled back the loose strands around her ears. "Things will be better tomorrow." He gently wrapped his arms around her and held her tight.

It felt good to be held. Claire needed to feel safe. She needed his comfort. She felt warm and cared for in his embrace. Claire let out a big exhale and leaned into his chest. The dam broke, and she could no longer choke back the tears. She sobbed and wailed. Her body convulsed. Perry lifted her onto his lap, and she didn't fight him. He rubbed her back and stroked her hair. She didn't stop him. He kissed her forehead, her nose, and her lips. She hungered for the closeness and tenderness. The pulse in his neck soothed her, and she let him take her upstairs to tuck her into bed.

Perry put on some music to calm her. Air Supply spun on the needle as Perry climbed into his bed and pressed his body next to hers. His gentle strokes helped Claire disconnect as he took off her clothes and made her forget. Making love out of nothing at all . . .

The sex was quick and gentle. Claire realized it had been an hour since she had gotten to the house, and they were still alone. "Shouldn't Mrs. Linden be home by now?"

"Actually," Perry said as he held her chin between his thumb and index finger, "she's working all night and won't be home until seven."

Claire stiffened. She scrambled out of bed and threw her clothes on. Realizing she had been duped and hating herself for being easy prey, she ran out of the house with her shoes untied, her coat unzipped, and her backpack bouncing against her back. She cursed herself. *So much for claws drawn and fangs out! How could you be so stupid?*

26. CHRISTINE TO THE RESCUE

Claire wandered around town, making sure to stay clear of places where her dad or Shana might go for gas, food, or beers. She made her dollars stretch and got a bean burrito at Taco Bell. She found a tree to sit under, and a gush of memories flooded her thoughts . . . memories of her father pulling her out of school so they could sit at a park and read together . . . memories of singing outlaw country songs on the open stretch of highway and doing gigs at honky tonks . . . memories of trying to be brave and eat that spicy burrito on her birthday when Dad gave her *The Velveteen Rabbit* to read while he read a western book.

Wanting desperately to get her life back on track, Claire went to a pay phone and called the police. Maybe if she reported the rape, Mark would get arrested, her dad would understand, and they'd make amends.

"Olmstead County Sheriff's Department."

Claire stuttered but managed to get the words out. "Hi. How . . . how do I go about reporting a rape?"

"Was the victim you in this incident?" the voice on the other end asked.

"Yes," Claire whispered.

"How were you dressed?"

"I don't . . . I don't remember."

"Well, were you doing drugs?"

"No."

"Had you been drinking?"

"No."

"Was there anything you did to bring it on?"

"Ma'am, I am only twelve."

"Yeah, but did you egg him on?"

Claire slammed the phone down and hung up. She kicked the pay phone door and ran out of the booth. She ran until her chest and throat burned and the salty tears tasted bitter on her lips. Filled with anguish and loneliness, Claire dropped to the ground underneath a big tree and hugged her knees. She buried her head between her arms and sobbed. She ached for someone to show her kindness, to believe her, to listen, and not judge.

The evening wore on sloth-like, and eventually, Claire kept moving to stay warm. She darted in and out of stores to take advantage of the heat. By nine that night, her stomach growled. She sat down at the park bench and watched some boys play basketball under the lights. A girl with dark hair sat by the court. Claire's heart skipped a beat. Was it Christine? She walked along the chainlink fence to get a closer look. It wasn't her.

Claire crossed the street to a phone booth and fumbled in her pocket for the change from Taco Bell. She picked up the receiver. The dial tone was loud. Claire slipped two dimes and a nickel into the pay phone and dialed her best friend's number, praying she remembered it correctly.

We're sorry. You have reached a number that has been disconnected or is no longer in service. If you feel you've reached this recording in error, please check the number and try your call again.

Claire hung up the phone and retrieved her coins in the return slot. She tried again, this time punching the number three digit instead of five. The phone rang. On the fourth ring, Christine's voice came through the earpiece. "Hello?"

"It's Claire. I ran away from home."

"What?" Christine's voice went up a pitch. "Where are you? Are you okay? What happened?"

"I'm in front of Ace Hardware."

"By Bear Creek or Joyce Park?"

"Joyce," Claire said. She shivered and slipped her hands into her coat pockets, cradling the phone with her left ear and shoulder. "Can I stay with you for a while?"

"My grandma won't allow it. Stay put. I'm going to come and get you. It's going to take me some time to get there."

"How are you going to get me?"

"I'm going to ride there. Just don't go anywhere. I'm gonna call Jackie first. Maybe you can stay with her tonight, and then we'll figure it out in the morning."

"Okay," Claire said. "Thanks, Chris."

Claire sat under the street lamp on the corner parking lot and leaned against the phone booth. An hour passed before she saw the silhouette of a girl pedaling frantically across the street. Christine stood on her bike and pumped her legs quickly, her dark curls bouncing behind her black parka. Chris jumped off the bike, and the two girls hugged.

"I can't believe you rode all across town to get me," Claire said, grateful to have a friend to rescue her.

"Hop on," Christine said. "Jackie said to come to her house."

Claire straddled the Schwinn "Sting Ray" chopper bike and held on to the back bar of the banana seat. Off they raced up a few blocks until they got to Jackie's house.

Jackie's mom answered the door and ushered the girls inside. Mrs. Clemmons fretted about and handed them a soda and a warm bowl of chili before disappearing into the living room. Jackie sat with them to keep them company.

"Thanks, Jackie," Claire said. "You look sleepy. Did we wake you?"

Jackie yawned and covered her mouth full of braces. She rubbed her eyes and nodded. 'It's eleven! I was already in bed."

"I'm sorry," Claire said.

"So what happened?" Jackie asked. "Did your dad really hit you? Did you run away?"

"What do you think?" Chris asked. "Look at her face. It's black and blue. Of course, he hit her."

"But why?" Jackie asked.

"It's a long story," Claire said.

"All I know is she can't go back home," Chris said. "And I know my grandma won't let her stay with us. We were hoping she could stay with you for a while."

Mrs. Clemmons reappeared in the kitchen. "Sorry, but I can't be responsible for you. I've called social services. They're on their way to get you."

Claire jumped up and nearly knocked her chair over. "I can't go back home. They're just going to take me back home. Please, I can't—"

"No," Mrs. Clemmons said, "they're not. They'll make sure you have a safe place to stay and—"

"And then what?" Claire asked. "Will I still get to go to school?"

Mrs. Clemmons sat down and folded her hands on the table. "Of course, you'll continue with school. The important thing is you'll be safe until this is all sorted out."

By 11:30 p.m. a social worker had shown up at the house. Claire had only a few minutes to say goodbye to Chris and Jackie and thank Mrs. Clemmons for the chili. At the police station, they took photos of her bruised face and the cuts inside her mouth. They asked a few questions, completed a couple of forms, and assigned a lawyer to the case. By midnight, she was officially a foster kid in the custody of the state.

Claire was dropped off at a house on the other side of town near Chris's house by McQuillan Fields. Her new foster parents were Dick and Janet. Claire was too tired to get a good look at them. She was shown to her bedroom where she crashed onto the pillows and slumbered deeply until the next morning.

#

A voice permeated through the door before it was pushed ajar. Claire stared at the man before her. He looked like a skinny Santa Claus. For a second Claire forgot where she was. She was lying on a child's twin bed with dinosaur prints, stickers, and clay sculptures all around the room. She was literally in the *Land of the Lost* TV series.

"See you in five minutes," Dick said. "Breakfast is ready."

Claire followed the voices and walked to the kitchen. Dick sat at the head of the table with his newspaper open.

Janet smiled and invited Claire to take a seat. Claire noticed the age difference between her foster parents. Whereas Dick's head and face were covered in white and his thin frame looked like he had survived the great famine of the North Pole, Janet was tan and young, as if she were still in college, and had teeth as white as her pearl earrings.

Janet placed a bottle of maple syrup on the table. "Don't be shy. There's plenty of pancakes and eggs."

"There are," Claire said softly.

"What's that?" Janet asked.

"Nothing," Claire said, not wanting to get in trouble for correcting Janet's grammar. "Anything interesting in the news?"

"I'm actually looking at the classifieds," Dick said. "I'm a principal at a nearby school but looking for a change. You know, Claire, we don't usually take kids your age, only young ones between six and eight years old. Your stay here is temporary. They're going to find you another foster home. We only agreed to take you in on short notice given the circumstances."

"In the meantime," Janet said, "we'll make sure your stay with us is comfortable."

"Tonight, Janet and I have a prior engagement to go to," Dick said.

"Yes," Janet said, "a party."

"Do I have to go?" Claire asked.

"Our social event is for adults only, so you'll stay here by yourself," Janet said.

"Can we trust you," Dick asked, "to behave for a few hours?" Dick lowered his newspaper and raised one eyebrow. Claire nodded. "Good. Now finish your breakfast. I'll take you to school, and we'll pick you up after."

That night, on Friday the thirteenth of all nights, Claire found herself alone in a strange home filled with awards, trophies, and certificates showcasing all the accomplishments Dick had achieved as an educator. While he and Janet were at their party, Claire moped around in the kitchen. Looking for a snack, she grabbed a bag of chips and poured herself a tall glass of Kool-Aid fruit punch.

She turned on the television and clicked through the channels. Every station had commercials. The emptiness in the pit of her stomach ballooned into a mass of loneliness and despair. She sat on the floor and leaned against the couch. Nothing but darkness enveloped her mind. Claire wanted to die. She wanted to vanish and not exist or feel anymore. The self-hatred seeped into her bones like death's venom. It poisoned her thoughts and rotted her body. She wanted to forget, to numb the pain and wipe out every memory of violence in her life, from Gisela's whippings to her father's beatings, from the violent rape by the stranger in the field to the rushed violation from Mark in the trailer park. The weight of it all crushed her twelve-year-old shoulders and smothered her in vile dejection.

With tears somersaulting down her face, Claire remembered the bottle of vodka in the liquor cabinet she had seen earlier. She helped herself to a heavy pour of the clear liquid in her Kool-Aid. Fifteen minutes in, her surroundings became a kaleidoscope of shifting colors. The walls danced on the ceiling while the couch moved toward her until she tripped and fell on the soft cushions. Her body was still yet the room rocked like gentle waves and seesawed her body up and down.

After she finished her drink, Claire stumbled to the kitchen to refill her fruit punch and added more vodka to the cup. She swayed and shuffled to her dinosaur bedroom, feeling her way along the hall like a blind girl reading the braille of the popcorn walls. Curled between the T-rex blanket and sheets, under the pterodactyl sky, Claire squeezed her eyes shut and let out a primal scream. She cried rivers of tears as she bit down on her lip and punched her small fists into the pillow.

The more she drank, the thicker her tears became. The room spun, and when all the dinosaurs in the room swirled around her, she finally surrender to the swoosh of the world flushing her down the drain until her consciousness was no more.

#

Saturday arrived and social services came to pick Claire up. Dick and Janet didn't say anything about the half-empty vodka bottle. Perhaps they didn't notice. With a wave and a "good luck," the foster parents dismissed Claire and closed their front door.

Ten minutes later Claire was introduced to Steven and Lorraine, who had a child around Claire's age. Their son, Emery, was a neanderthal who shoveled his food into his mouth, dropped bits of vegetables onto the floor, and chugged milk like it was a treasure to hoard. Both Steven and Lorraine walked with their chins up and their arms hanging unnaturally by their sides as if they were propped up by a puppeteer.

"Today's Saturday," Lorraine said, "and we have game night on Saturdays."

"That's right," Steven added. "We expect you to join in family game night. Emery picked Uno tonight."

Claire wanted to scream at them. *Have you seen my face? I was just raped and beaten, and my mouth is cut up inside, and you want me to fucking play Uno?*

"Claire dear," Lorraine said, "we expect you to acknowledge us when we talk to you. A simple yes, ma'am, or yes, sir, will do. Steven doesn't like repeating himself, and when you don't answer, he thinks you didn't hear him."

Claire looked at Steven and Lorraine in disbelief. Was she in the twilight zone? She didn't understand the point of pretending to be one happy family. "I don't feel well. I'd rather rest in my room and—"

"We're not asking you. We're telling you," Lorraine said. "It's family game night. You're here. This is where you're going to be. You have to blend in with our family."

Steven said, "Oh, and bedtime is at nine tonight. We have church in the morning, so get out your best dress."

"I don't want to go," Claire said.

"Don't be ridiculous," Lorraine said. "Of course, you're going."

"What denomination are you?" Claire asked. It didn't matter what they were; she was determined to get out of going. The jackhammer in her head had been going nonstop since she woke up, and her mouth was still sore from where her father punched her.

"We're Lutherans," Steven said, "but it doesn't matter what religion we embrace. We're good Christians who serve God, and while you're staying with us, you will learn the Word of our Lord."

Claire crossed her arms around her chest. "I'm not going."

"You don't have a choice," Lorraine said. "You will go."

The hell I am. Claire looked and felt like shit. She had nothing decent to wear at church anyway, and the last thing she wanted to do was play house with these Bible-thumping strangers.

That night they played Uno, and it was agonizing. Emery was a poor loser and an even worse winner. He gloated and rubbed the cards in her face every chance he got.

"Can I go spend the night at my friend Jackie's house?" Claire asked. "I can come back tomorrow."

"You have to call your social worker," Steven said.

Claire called CPS, and of course, her social worker said no. When it was finally bedtime, Claire lay in her bed and slowed her breathing to focus on the snores that eventually came from across the hall.

Claire quietly gathered her belongings and tiptoed out the front door. She walked three miles to Jackie's house. Claire tapped on Jackie's window and hoped her friend was awake. The last thing she needed was for Mrs. Clemmons to catch her and call social services again.

The curtain pulled back, and Jackie's pale face stared at her. Slowly, the window slid open. "Claire," Jackie whispered, "what are you doing here?"

"Can I stay with you tonight?" Claire asked. "Let me in. It's freezing." The screen popped off, and Claire climbed in.

"You can crash here tonight, but you can't stay."

"I know. Can I just leave my stuff here and maybe come by every once in a while to shower?"

"Sure," Jackie said.

And with that, the girls said nothing more except good night and went to sleep. Tomorrow would be a new day.

27. BACK ON THE STREETS

For the next forty-five days, life did not change much for Claire except she was no longer confined inside four walls. The moon and stars were her ceilings, and the park bench and damp ground became her mattress. If she wasn't sleeping under a bush, behind a dumpster, or underneath bleachers, she wandered the streets and did whatever she could to survive. Going to school was out of the question for fear her dad or social services would find her and put her right back to where she didn't want to be. Every few days, Jackie snuck Claire into the house for a shower and some food.

"They're looking for you," Jackie said.

"Who?" Claire asked. She had just gotten out of the shower, hair still dripping wet, when Jackie handed her a plate of food and a soda.

"The police," Jackie said. "They're going house to house looking for you, asking if we've seen you."

"What did you say?" Claire asked as she gobbled her sandwich.

"I said no, of course. I told them I hadn't seen you for a couple of months."

At that moment, Jackie's bedroom window slid open, and Christine climbed in. She was out of breath, her nose bright red from the chill outside.

"Hey," Christine said. "Jackie called me when you were in the shower. I hauled ass over here. I can't stay long. I brought you some socks and a few things I stole from my grandma's kitchen." Jackie tossed the bag to Claire, who rummaged through it to take inventory of her prize—two pairs of socks, mittens, saltine crackers, juice boxes, canned sardines, one bagel, and two apples.

"Thanks, Chris," Claire said.

"You can't keep this up much longer, Claire," Jackie said. "What are you going to do?"

"Actually," Christine said, "she won't have to. I have a friend—his name is Christopher—and he's got an apartment nearby. He says you can stay with him for a few days. At least it will get you out of the cold and off the streets. Maybe he can help you find a job, or maybe he has a friend who can help. Meet me at Joyce Park later today at six, and I'll bring you to his place."

"I . . . I don't know, Chris," Claire said. "I don't know him."

Christine hugged Claire. "You're my best friend. I've got you. Trust me, Christopher is a good person."

"You've got to get off the streets," Jackie said.

"Okay," Claire said.

Christine reached into her pocket and handed Claire a few dollars. "Here. I took some money from my piggy bank."

"Your babysitting money?" Claire asked.

Christine shrugged. "It's only five dollars, so don't get all sappy."

"Yeah, but it's five dollars of your hard-earned money," Claire said.

Later that evening at six o'clock sharp, Christine came streaking by Joyce Park on her bike. Together they rode a few miles, dipped behind buildings, through alleys, across parking lots, and finally to a three-story apartment building.

Christine leaned her bike under the stairwell and knocked on apartment 1H. A good-looking young man opened the door and greeted them warmly. He had that boy next door look—baby face, crooked smile, dimples, freckles, and kind eyes.

"You must be Claire," Christopher said. "Come in."

The three of them settled into the living room where Christopher presented a platter of finger foods and an assortment of chocolates. Claire's eyes lit up.

"Wow," Christine said, "yum!"

Claire sat down and put a large helping of crackers, cheeses, fruits, salami, and chocolates onto her plate. She needed no invitation and was glad Christopher didn't make her feel guilty for diving in. While Christine and Christopher made small talk and caught up on life, Claire scanned the small apartment to see what intel she could gather. Pictures of Christopher and a pretty woman sat everywhere, showing them camping, river rafting, hiking, hugging at a beach, and kissing over a glass of champagne.

Claire liked the corner unit Christopher had. It was on the ground floor overlooking the courtyard and had one small bedroom and a bathroom near the entrance. He had decorated it simply and kept it clean and tidy. The only sign of a woman's touch was the plants and potted flowers throughout the place.

"I better get going," Christine said. "I gotta ride back and be home before Grandma gets there."

"Call me when you get home so I know you made it," Christopher said.

Alone in the apartment, Claire suddenly felt awkward. She had barely said anything to her host, managed to eat most of his food, and hadn't thanked him for his hospitality. "Thanks for letting me stay here."

"Sure," Christopher said. "Let me get you a pillow and blanket. You can crash on my couch for a few days until you figure things out."

"So what do you do for a job?" Claire asked.

"I'm a manager at RadioShack. It pays the bills."

"Where's your girlfriend?" Claire asked. "She's pretty."

Christopher sat down in the chair opposite the couch and didn't answer right away. With his head bent, he rubbed his palms against his knees, and when he finally looked up, his eyes were wet. He cleared his throat and took a deep breath before answering. "Chelsea died seven years ago in a car accident."

Claire gasped and swallowed the knot in her throat. "Oh, I'm sorry, I thought . . ."

"We were engaged, and then one day . . ."

"You don't have to talk about it."

Christopher nodded. "She was the love of my life. I miss her every day."

For the rest of the evening, Claire and Christopher watched TV and distracted themselves with *Diff'rent Strokes* and other sitcoms. By eleven, it was lights out, and Claire had the best sleep she'd had in months.

#

Before long, Christopher and Claire talked about her moving on. Three weeks had passed, and Christopher handed her twenty dollars and a pocket knife. "Claire, I'm sorry, but you can't stay here any longer. Take these, and hopefully, it can get you by for a bit." He handed her the bill and showed her how to use the knife. "Listen, the cops are looking for you. There are flyers posted with your face around town. I can get in trouble for harboring a runaway."

Claire held back the tears. She had known her stay was temporary, but the false sense of security felt real. In her heart, she had hoped things would change and she could stay with Christoper indefinitely. She would never forget his kindness, and for a moment in time, her faith in humanity . . . in men . . . was restored.

Back on the streets, Claire returned to what she knew, grabbing food from Taco Bell's value menu, getting bean burritos for fifty-nine cents, taco supremes for seventy-nine cents, or chicken meximelts for ninety-nine cents. The bathrooms in the fast food joints became her solace when she needed a little break from the world or to unload the bean burritos souring in her gut.

The days turned to nights, and nights warped into days. Time blurred together, and when the sun was just above the horizon, Claire second-guessed whether it was sunrise or sunset she was observing.

If it hadn't been for Christine and Jackie's charity, there was no way Claire would have survived as long as she did out on the streets. She took naps at Jackie's house when Mrs. Clemmons was out and crashed hard at Christine's house after her grandma went to bed. Both friends snuck her food to sustain her and helped stretch the money she had in her pocket. On the nights she couldn't take shelter at someone's house, Claire roamed the streets and stayed in the shadows, away from people and streetlamps.

"Hey!" someone shouted. "Hey, girl . . ." A car rolled slowly alongside Claire as she walked near Mayo High School. "You okay? You need a ride somewhere, amiga?"

Claire looked at the Hispanic man in the Pontiac Firebird TransAm. He reminded her of Jalisco. She had forgotten about her Mexican friend, Jalisco, and the other truckers she met at Motel 6 . . . HotLinx and his daughter, Grasshopper, and the Asian man who made rice wine . . . This stranger calling her amiga triggered a memory that had long been forgotten.

"Amiga," the man said, "it's cold outside. I'm not going to hurt you. C'mon, you want a ride?"

Claire simply didn't care anymore what happened to her. Perhaps it was a death wish, but she didn't have an opinion on whether she lived or died. A part of her knew it was reckless to get into a car with a stranger, but she also wanted to get out of the cold. *If he tries anything, I'll fight back.* Claire touched the pocket knife in her coat pocket and ran her thumb over the stainless steel. *I'll bite him, scratch him, kick him in the balls, gouge his eyes out, and make him bleed to death.*

"Yeah, sure," Claire responded.

He stopped the car, and Claire got in.

"Want a beer?" he asked.

Claire shrugged. She had no plan. She had nothing to live for. She hadn't gone to school for two months. She remembered how it felt being drunk on vodka and Kool-Aid and didn't mind getting a buzz on. It would bandage the misery she felt.

They pulled into a convenience store, and her new friend returned with a six-pack of beer. They drove to a barren parking lot and cracked open the beers. "I'm Miguel, by the way. What's your name?"

"Claire."

"So, Claire, what the hell are you doing out here? I mean, you're just a kid. Where are your parents?"

"Fuck my parents."

"Whoa, all right. I see you're hurting, but you don't understand the risk you're putting yourself in. Someone could hurt you. You could die out here."

"Maybe I want to. Maybe I don't care anymore."

"I could kill you," Miguel said. "I'm not going to hurt you but—"

"What does it matter?" Claire asked. "I'm not going to live long anyway."

"What the fuck? Girl, don't say that."

"Why? It's true. I'm never going to make it to twenty."

"Please, go home," Miguel said. "I don't want to hear about you in the news."

"You don't know what I've been through. You don't have a clue. I'm not going home."

"Why don't you tell me? Maybe I can help."

Claire opened the door and got out. It was abrupt, she knew, but she also didn't want to divulge her life story and share her woes with a total stranger, even if he was kind and meant well. "Thanks for the beer. I gotta go."

A couple of days later, on a particularly warm winter day, Claire was stripping off her coat and hat to shove them into her backpack when she heard an unfamiliar voice call her name.

"Claire!" A woman approached her and introduced herself. "I'm Jeannie. We've been looking for you."

Claire pivoted on her heels to run, but it was too late. Two police officers stepped out of the patrol car and loomed over her. Claire didn't put up a fight. She was too cold, tired, and weak to outrun them.

"Where are you taking me?" Claire asked.

The woman, whom Claire found out was with social services, had spotted her ten minutes ago and called the police. She now sat next to Claire, hands folded on her lap, smiling like she was about to collect a reward for capturing a fugitive. "You're going home, honey."

28. MISFITS

Rolling through the neighborhood and getting out of a police vehicle reminded Claire of the time she was escorted home from the women's shelter after Gisela tried to leave her dad. This time, she didn't feel embarrassed. Rather, she felt frustrated, dreadful, and disconnected.

Bryant opened the door and swept Claire into a bear hug. "Thank God you're okay."

Claire was unmoved. She stepped over the threshold into the house and gave Shana a blank stare. In her arms was baby Jason. A rush of warmth swept over Claire as she peered at his sweet face. Seeing her brother made her realize she had missed him.

As soon as the officers left and the door closed, Bryant's mouth went a mile a minute. "What happened?" Bryant asked. "Where have you been? I don't understand why you ran away. Do you know what hell you put us through?" Bryant pulled Claire into his arms and squeezed. He kissed her on the head.

There were so many things Claire wanted to say, like, "What's there not to understand? You beat the crap out of me on the night I was raped. You forced me to go out with a stranger when all I wanted to do was stay home. I can't trust you anymore. You don't listen to me. You don't have my back. You don't protect me. I was your sunshine until I wasn't. What the hell?"

Instead, Claire clamped her mouth shut. She stiffened her posture and stepped out of his arms.

"You've always been a good kid," Bryant said. "Then you go and run away? Skip school? You're throwing your education away, and that's the most important thing!"

Claire gave him the silent treatment. She let her face do all the talking. Narrowing her eyes and thinning her lips into a rigid line, she glowered at Shana and Bryant before pivoting to head to her room. Claire held her breath, expecting any moment now her father's fingers would wrap around her wrist and spin her around. She braced herself and prepared to plant her body firmly centered on the floor should a blow behind her head come. But nothing came. No push. No slap. Not even a scream. Claire held her head high and continued walking. Adrenaline kept her alert in the days that followed.

For the first couple of weeks, Bryant was loving and sweet. He brought home a key lime pie knowing it was Claire's favorite. He stopped at yard sales and purchased books or cassette tapes he thought she'd enjoy. He had Shana do all the cooking and cleaning so that Claire could focus on her studies and catch up with the curriculum at school. Never mind that Shana complained she couldn't be a full-time mother and a maid at the same time.

School life resumed for Claire, but it was far from the normal routine she'd once had. She returned not as the quiet, flat-footed mouse but as a serpent whose razor-sharp, wicked little tongue and beady, cold eyes could tear anyone down to their knees.

"Well, if it isn't Coppertop, back to grace us with her stench," Paul Bergerhackle said. His friend Nick Darling stood beside him, smirking as if he was entitled to front-row seats at every show.

"Dude, your mom would be so proud of what a little bitch her daughter is," Claire fired back.

Paul, Nick, and their posse of rejects relentlessly harassed Claire whenever they had the chance—in the hallways, in class, and off school grounds. Calling Claire Coppertop after the Duracell battery was their favorite nickname for her, and it stuck for the rest of the year. The demeaning insults became a daily battle, and Claire relished belittling them right back. As much as she wanted to lash out violently, she swore she'd never be like Gisela.

Losing control and unleashing her rage would only turn her into a monster. Claire believed her fury, if not checked, would send her to prison. Memories of throwing knives at Gisela reminded Claire she needed to internalize her feelings and control her temper before she lost people she cared about. Never seeing Ton-ton, Shannon, Benji, and Barry again was one of the greatest losses and biggest regrets in Claire's life. So Claire's tongue became her strongest artillery.

Not only did Claire's attitude change but so did her attire. She threw out all her dresses and skirts— a symbolic ceremonial burial to the good people-pleaser little girl she once was—and got jeans so tight she had to use pliers to zip them up. Her clothes had to feel like armor and be hard to get off.

Claire no longer sought her dad's approval nor did she need everyone's acceptance at school. Her teachers all loved her, though, because Claire respected her teachers and spoke kindly to them, which earned their trust and adoration.

The only solace Claire had was when she spent time with Christine, Jackie, and their circle of misfits. There were eight of them. After school, the gang often got together at Rick's house.

Rick Maynard lived with his mom. She was white. His dad was Black and Hawaiian. That made Rick the butt of every racially-motivated joke. To make ends meet, Rick's mom spent her waking hours hooking. Word spread like wildfire that Rick was the son of a prostitute. Of course, Paul and Nick fanned the flames with their relentless assaults.

"Hey, Ricky Dicky," Paul once said, "what's it like being a trash whore's mutt?"

Nick would join in too. "Speaking of trash. My dad thought he was taking out the garbage last night; turns out it was your mom!"

"Fuck off," Rick retorted. "You both should look in the mirror. Bastards!"

Claire felt sorry for Rick and couldn't resist a good jab at the rich Mayo kids. "So, Nick, you're saying your dad's the real-life Hester Prynne?"

"What?" Nick asked.

Claire laughed. "Pretty boy here is too dumb to get the insult. Oh, if you only had a brain."

"Shut up, Coppertop," Nick said.

"Make me, Scarlet Seed!" Claire flipped Nick and Paul off and walked backward a couple of steps. "All of Daddy's money can't buy you smarts." Claire swiveled around toward Rick and gave him a high five. And that was how they became friends. Claire felt good that day having one-upped the other two in insults, but she quickly felt the sting of the irony. She was no better than any of them.

Rick had an older sister named Mary, but she was in high school and was rarely home. It was only natural that the hangout spot became Rick's house where there was no adult supervision.

"Hey, Red," Rick said one afternoon, "ya wanna come over and get stoned?"

"Sure," Claire said. "Can I bring my friends?"

"Yeah," Rick said. "Any time. I always have people over."

Claire brought Christine, Jackie, and their other friend Melissa to Rick's house. He lived two miles from Claire's in a cobalt blue house with gray trim on a small corner lot fully enclosed by a chain-link fence. Out front, a tire swing and old sandbox reminded her of days gone by when children used to laugh and play there. Now the sandbox was infected with dandelions and rocks, and the swing sat lopsided on a frayed rope.

"Is this the right place?" Melissa asked. "I thought Rick lived near the church."

Melissa was a sweet girl, but she had always been meek and guarded. Claire hoped her grit would rub off on Melissa so that her friend could be brazen and more rebellious.

"This is the right place all right," Christine said. "There's his face in the window."

Rick's face quickly disappeared behind the curtains and reappeared at the front entrance. "Come in, bitches." He gave an exaggerated bow and opened the door wider.

The four girls walked up the steps and into the house. It was dark inside. All the windows were covered. The air smelled damp and tasted stale.

"You really should open the windows and let some air in," Claire said.

"It's raunchy in here," Jackie added.

"Whatever," Rick said. "We're going to be in my room anyway, so who cares."

They followed Rick through the yellow kitchen where dirty dishes piled high and covered every countertop nook and cranny. Fruit flies buzzed around a basket of overly ripened fruit. Claire noticed the trash overflowing with soda cans and Hungry-Man TV dinner trays. It made her think of Grandma Sharon and Grandpa Harold with their beer cans and frozen dinners.

"My room is downstairs," Rick said.

"Geez," Claire said, "don't you ever clean up after yourself?"

"Why?" Rick asked. "That ain't my job. That's girls' work."

Claire and Christina looked at each other and rolled their eyes.

"Yeah, but it smells like wet dog in here," Melissa said and then immediately covered her mouth as if her insult would get her kicked out.

Claire smiled. She patted Melissa's shoulder. "Yup, smells like wet dog and Rick's used tampons."

The girls giggled. Rick shot them a scowl.

Music wafted up the stairs along with several distinct voices. At the base of the steps, the room opened up to a space of about four hundred square feet. Rock and roll pounded through the speakers. Four boys around thirteen or fourteen years old sat smoking, drinking, and bobbing their heads to the beats of Rick Springfield's "Jessie's Girl."

"Wow," Jackie said, "you can fit two cars in here."

The guys looked up and nodded to the girls. Claire recognized two of them.

"Do you all know each other?" Rick asked. No one responded. "Guys, this is Claire, Christine, Jackie, and Melissa."

"Hey" was the unanimous response.

Rick pointed to each of his friends. "That's Ray, Billy, Jackson, and Taylor."

"Jeez," Claire said, "all you guys need now is a one-eyed bulldog."

What?" Rick asked. "I swear, Red, you never make sense."

"That's because she's too smart for you," Christine said.

"I don't get it either," Melissa said.

"You gotta be into country music to understand," Claire said. "There's this guy named Billy Ray. My old man told me Billy and his brother, Kevin, have a band called Sly Dog, named after their dog, Spike."

Jackson lit up a cigarette and offered one to Claire. "Enlighten us, oh wise one. If their dog is named Spike, why wouldn't they just call themselves Spike? Or the Bulldogs? Or One-Eyed Sinners?"

Claire accepted the cigarette. She felt grown up hanging with these teenage boys and didn't want to be a priss.

"Yeah," Billy said, "Why Sly Dog? Makes no sense."

"Oh, I like the sound of One-Eyed Sinners," Melissa said and sat down next to Jackson.

"Oh really?" Jackson said. "I've got a one-eyed sinner right here." He pointed at his crotch. Everyone laughed.

Taylor offered Claire a lighter. Claire pulled a long drag like she'd seen her dad do and inhaled the puff. Immediately the burn of nicotine and other carcinogens seared her throat, nostrils, and chest. Claire coughed hysterically. The boys laughed.

"Easy," Jackson said. He stood up and loomed over all of them. He handed Claire a Tab soda.

Melissa patted Claire's back. "You okay?"

"Not such a big shot, are ya?" Taylor, the strikingly handsome blond one in the group, laughed. "Try again, but take it easy on the draw!"

"So you're a country music fan?" Rick asked. "I knew you were weird."

"I'm all about metal, myself," Christine said. "Oh, the big hair and tight pants. I don't know, there's something hot about dudes—"

"Looking like ladies?" Taylor asked. "Long hair and makeup? You dig that?"

Ray laughed. "What are you, Tayor, Black or something? No one says 'dig' except those nig—"

"Hey," Christine yelled, "what's wrong with that? I can dig it."

Taylor got up and saddled the chair next to Christine. "All they do is scream and smash guitars," Taylor said.

"Yeah, but they got the vocals," Christine said. "You got pipes like that?"

Claire was content sipping her Tab soda and watching Taylor and Christine debate the pros and cons of heavy metal. Sitting separately from the group was Jackson, smoking his cigarette and drinking his beer. He got up only to change the LP, take a piss, or grab another beer. Billy and Ray threw the football around in the room and talked about girls and sports like typical jocks.

"Earth calling Coppertop," Rick said.

Claire snapped at him. "Don't call me that."

"Whoa, somebody's sensitive."

"I'm just tired of everyone calling me names," Claire said.

"What's your deal anyway?" Rick asked. "I mean, you act all smart and better than the rest of us—"

"I do not!" Claire crossed her arms in front of her. "What makes you say that?"

Rick shrugged. "I don't know. You're intense. And you give off these vibes."

"What vibes?" Claire asked. By now she was getting used to the cigarette and felt high from the nicotine. Claire took Rick's beer and chugged it. It was bitter, but she liked the lightheaded effect it had on her.

"I can tell you're hella smart. You use big words that half of the school doesn't understand. The teachers like you, and the kids hate you, so . . . that makes you a mystery. And who the hell likes country music?"

Claire laughed. It was nice having someone to talk to. Before she knew it, she had told Rick all about her traveling days with her dad singing outlaw country songs and performing at taverns. She divulged parts of her life living with Gisela and the terror her stepmother brought. Claire skipped the sexual assault stories but shared how her dad was the ultimate Jekyll and Hyde.

"You know," Claire said, "growing up, my dad never baby-talked me. He always spoke to me like he was talking to an adult, so I guess I got my vocabulary from him. He's really smart and articulate . . . a real charmer . . . sweet-talks his way out of everything."

"Sounds like a textbook narcissist to me," Rick said.

"Yeah, but he's a drunk most of the time. He can barely hold a job, and yet he comes down hard on me about getting through school to support myself. He acts like he's this protective, caring guy, but he turns a blind eye when his friends try to molest me. One time, this guy named Floyd burst into our house and started feeling me up. He was drunk as fuck. I told my dad about it, and he just made excuses for him! He said, 'honey, you have to understand, he has a wet brain.' My dad's got a wet brain! When he drinks, he gets crazy and violent. He'll be sober for months and then go on a horrible bender. Then he has these angina spells that land him in the hospital. He isn't faithful to his wives either, always chasing after threesomes. I wouldn't be surprised if I had brothers and sisters I don't know about."

"Wow, your dad's a real winner," Rick said. "Sounds like my mom. She's always sleeping with different guys. Sometimes she brings them home, and I hear them moaning and screaming and knocking over shit. I've walked in on my mom a dozen times spreading her legs for every hairy dicky-do out there."

Claire giggled. "Dicky-do?"

"You know? When your gut sticks out further than your dickies do."

Claire chuckled and snorted. "Oh my god, that's gross."

"Tell me about it. Ever walk in and see your dad doing the dirty deed? Because I see my mom all the time with her ass against someone's cock or her legs sticking up pointing toward Jesus, screaming, 'I've been a bad girl.'"

Claire couldn't hold in the laughter anymore. She hugged her stomach and let out a loud burp, scrunching her nose as the carbonation bubbled up. Everyone was in stitches at that point.

As the hours wore on, the group continued to hang out and get to know each other. They got high, binged on junk food, played games, and listened to music. They laughed and chastised one another, even flirted a little. Claire learned the guys all knew each from being on the football team at Mayo High School. Rick was the youngest who had recently turned fourteen. He met Taylor, Jackson, Ray, and Billy through his sister, Mary.

As the school year progressed, it became routine to hang out after school. Sometimes it was all of them; other times only a few of them . . . on rare occasions, it'd be Claire, Ray, and other faces who came and went but were not part of the core usual suspects. Separately they were all misfits from different walks of life, but together they lorded over their parents and challenged authority figures. Over time, Claire got used to Rick's rough edges. He had no respect for women in general, probably because his sister and mom were never around, and when they were, according to Rick, they were mean and demeaning to him. And even though he was often rude to Claire, Christine, and the others, he was also rude to his friends, so it normalized his behavior. Claire shrugged it off as boys being boys. That was just how Rick was wired. It was like how all of them were wired. Every one of them had a secret story they buried to forget. In time, Claire let her guard down around Rick, Taylor, Jackson, Ray, and Billy.

It was the biggest mistake she'd ever made.

29. BREAKING POINT

Claire's thirteenth birthday came and went. Even she forgot about it until Christine brought it up two weeks later.

"I got you something," Christine said.

"For me?" Claire asked. "How come?"

"Uh, duh! For your birthday! Sorry, it's late." Christine scurried off her bed and opened her closet. They had been hanging out in Christine's room for thirty minutes smoking pot, munching on Cap'n Crunch cereal, and writing poetry in their journals with MTV playing in the background.

"Okay, close your eyes," Christine said.

Claire did as she was told. She sat up on the bed cross-legged, giggled, and opened her mouth.

"What are you doing?" Christine laughed. "You look like an idiot."

"Is it cake? Or pie?"

"Better. Open your hand."

Claire felt something small, lightweight, and plastic placed in her palm. It had a little bit of weight to it. Curious, she curled her fingers around the items and crinkled the plastic. With her eyes still closed, Claire smelled it but couldn't make sense of it.

"Can I open my eyes already?" Claire asked.

"Yup. Open." There were two small baggies in Claire's palm. One was a tablet, and the other was powder. "So this," Christine pointed at the tablet, "is MDMA. It's like the hottest thing right now. Everyone says it makes you feel good and lovey-dovey with no side effects. Total rage at the parties. And this one," Christine picked up the other little bag, "is a gift from my dad. It's cocaine."

"From your dad?" Claire asked.

"Yeah, well," Christine said, "my dad lives in Columbia. He's got another family there. I have a half-sister I've never met. Anyway, every once in a while he just randomly shows up and stays for a few days."

"And your mom?" Claire asked.

"Mom married someone else and lives in Chicago," Christine said. "She didn't want the responsibility, so here I am with Grandma."

"Is your grandma your dad's mom?"

"Yeah," Christine said. "Hey, how much money have you saved up from babysitting?"

"Well," Claire said, "right now I'm broke. I just got a record player with a built-in radio."

"Oh man, I thought we could go to a concert together. Bon Jovi is coming to town. Maybe we can go see White Snake or Kiss later this year. They're coming too. Save your money, okay?"

Claire nodded. "So are we going to try one of these?" She held up the two plastic baggies.

Christine pointed to the powder. "You'll like the cocaine. It gives you tons of energy. Whenever I feel tired and need a burst, I take a little bit of it. Let's save the pill for when we go to a party."

"So you've had cocaine before?" Claire asked.

"Yeah, a few times. My dad gives it to me when he comes. Did you know that a tiny bit of this stuff is like brain tonic?"

"What do you mean?" Claire asked.

"Well, it's one of the ingredients in Coca-Cola. It's supposed to cure headaches and upset stomachs. So it's good for you. Do you know how Coca-Cola got its name?"

"No, but I have a feeling you're going to tell me."

"Well, the name Coca has to do with the extract of coca leaves. And the other ingredient comes from kola nuts, so there you go. Coca-Cola. See? You're not the only brainiac here."

"What are kola nuts?" Claire asked.

"Hell if I know," Christine said.

The girls burst into laughter. Claire followed Christine's lead and snorted a tiny amount. The powder smelled sweet and tickled her nose at first but then burned her nostrils. The discomfort was worth it because, almost instantaneously, a surge of euphoria exalted throughout her senses. There was clarity in every detail around Christine's room, from the flowers on her blanket to the cracks in her bedroom wall.

Claire jumped off the bed and turned the volume up on the television. The two danced to MTV music videos and talked incessantly about school gossip, boys, which band member they wanted to marry, and the jobs they'd have when they got older.

By 5:45 p.m. Claire left to go home. Christine's grandma usually came home around six. As she pedaled her bike home, Claire pushed herself to go as fast as she could and thought she could ride all the way to Illinois.

#

At thirteen, Claire felt different than when she had turned eleven or twelve. There was a newfound fierceness that came with knowing she'd soon be a freshman in high school. She now had friends. Her best friend, Christine, was her everything, and she loved her so much. Life at home was tolerable only because she was rarely there and had little interaction with her dad or Shana. If she wasn't babysitting, she was with Christine or over at Rick's.

"Hey, Claire." Rick caught up to Claire and gently bumped into her on purpose. "Wanna come over tomorrow and hang out?"

"Saturdays are not good," Claire said. "I usually have to babysit."

"Well, get out of it. I got Twisted Sister's newest album."

"*Stay Hungry*?" Claire asked. The *Stay Hungry* album had been released two weeks prior, and Christine had been talking about it.

"It's pretty good," Rick said. "See you tomorrow."

Rick darted across the street before Claire could confirm.

The next afternoon, having nothing better to do, Claire grabbed her sweater and bounded out of the house.

"Where do you think you're going?" Bryant asked.

Claire stopped and simply said, "Out."

"I want you back in two hours. Shana and I are going out, and we need you to watch Jason."

Claire looked at her watch. It was almost three o'clock. "Fine," she said. "I'll be back at five."

Claire rode her bike the two miles to Rick's house. The usual crew was there—Taylor, Jackson, Billy, and Ray—plus one other girl Claire didn't know.

"Glad you could make it," Rick said. "This is Ashley, my sister's friend."

"I can only stay an hour," Claire said. "I have to be back by five."

Claire took off her sweater and settled downstairs in Rick's room with the rest of them. She opened a can of beer and chitchatted with Ashley while Rick took out the Twisted Sister album and showed it to everyone. On the cover was lead singer Dee Snider dressed in black and hot pink holding a bone.

Rick played side two starting with "I Wanna Rock," and by the fifth song, Ashley got up and said she had to go.

"I better go too," Claire said.

"Oh, come on, you don't have to leave for another half hour," Rick said. "You haven't listened to the other side yet."

"Next time," Claire said.

Jackson shot up and handed Claire a beer. "At least stay for another beer."

Taylor smiled at her and said, "All the good songs are on the other side, like 'Burn in Hell.'"

Claire couldn't resist his good looks and caved in. "Fine."

"Stay Hungry is a good one," Billy said.

"And of course, 'We're Not Gonna Take It,'" Ray added.

Claire said goodbye to Ashley as Taylor walked her out. Rick flipped the record over to side one. "Stay Hungry" was the first track.

Taylor reappeared downstairs in the room. He closed the door, and Claire noticed he turned the lock. The hair on her arms and neck raised. She stood ramrod straight and looked wildly at the boys. "What's going on?"

Rick seized her wrist and jerked her forward. Her body slammed into his. She felt the hardness between his legs and knew instantly what he had in mind.

Claire yanked her arms back to free herself, but his grip was too tight. An arm slithered around her waist from behind her and crushed her ribs. Jackson. He hoisted her off her feet and thrust her onto the bed.

"Fuck you," Claire screamed. "Let me go!" Claire thrashed her body to get some leverage, but Ray pushed her chest down and pinned her to the mattress. The look in his eyes scared her. He took hold of her left arm and pulled it hard straight up above her head. Billy grabbed her other wrist and pinned it down while Taylor and Jackson each grabbed her ankle and spread her legs apart.

Claire squirmed and tried biting Billy and Ray, but they were both out of reach. Rick stood at the end of the bed and unzipped his pants. He pulled his jeans and underwear off and stood erect with his penis hard and throbbing. Claire was able to free one of her legs and kicked Rick square in the testicles.

Rick winced in pain and doubled over. "Damn it, Jackson, hold her tight." He climbed onto the bed and tried to unbutton Claire's pants. "Fuck," he said as he struggled to unfasten them and pull the zipper down.

In the background, Twisted Sister screamed out the lyrics of "Stay Hungry" while Claire racked her brain to find a solution out. The boys overpowered her with their size and strength. There were five of them, and no matter how hard she twisted and turned, no matter how loud she screamed, cursed, and begged, they didn't stop.

Rick pulled her pants and underwear off and quickly mounted her. His thrust inside her was deep and hard. He panted and fumbled as his fingers undid her shirt. Midway through he got frustrated and ripped her shirt apart. Buttons flew, and Claire lay flat on her back, breasts exposed. Rick leaned over and bit Claire's nipples. She wailed in despair. He bit so hard he left teeth marks and blood.

"You fucker!" Claire screamed.

"That's what you get for kicking me in the balls, you slut," Rick yelled.

"Mother fucker!" Claire exclaimed. "Fuck you all." Claire spit in Rick's face and headbutted him.

He rubbed his forehead and sent a flying fist at Claire's face. "How does that feel, bitch?"

Rick drove faster and harder until he came and shook violently. He nodded to Taylor, and the two traded places. In the few seconds it took for them to maneuver, Claire kicked Taylor and then Jackson in the head. It stunned them both. She pulled her arms out from Ray and Billy's grip and leaped off the bed.

Claire grabbed a couple of beers and threw them at the boys. She darted toward the door and felt a cold can hit her at the base of her neck. Someone hurled the beer back at her. Another hand grabbed her hair and pulled her to the floor. Claire screeched in agony, her scalp feeling like a thousand needles entering her head. She fought with all her might, grabbing anything she could to throw at them. She kicked and punched, bit and scratched, but she was outnumbered, outweighed, and outmaneuvered. The guys lifted her off the floor, each carrying an arm or leg, and tossed her on the couch like a bag of dirty laundry.

On the turntable, Dee Snider's voice screamed "We're Not Gonna Take It" just as Taylor took his turn with Claire. Over and over, Twisted Sister proclaimed, "We're not gonna take it," and after Taylor finished, it was Billy's turn.

After Billy, it was Ray. Their hands were rough. Their bodies were wet from sweat as they gyrated and thumped against her, bruising her body and giving her a rash against the fibers of the couch and floor. Ray's breath was the worst, and Claire was sure she was going to vomit. A huge cramp developed in her stomach, and pain shot up and down her spine. Unlike the last time when she disassociated, this time, Claire was wide awake and alert. Her mind raced in circles trying to figure out what she could do or say, but her body went limp.

The constriction in her throat reduced her screams to grunts. Claire stared at the ceiling and cried, but the tears didn't flow. Her legs cramped up, and the excruciating pain of having her knees pried open made her grind her teeth. She bore down and arched her back to give some relief to her hips. A chill ran down her legs. Her feet and hands went numb. Claire thirsted for water. Her lips were dry. She closed her eyes and focused on her breathing. Deep breaths, in and out.

Inhale. Exhale. Repeat.

Time stood still for Claire.

Twisted Sister continued to scream on repeat.

Inhale. Exhale. Repeat.

"Is she dead?"

"Shit."

"She's not blinking."

"Yeah, but she's still breathing."

"Guys, I don't know . . ."

"Why is she so stiff?"

A sharp sting reverberated across Claire's face. She refocused her gaze on Taylor. He slapped her cheeks again and shook her.

"She's back," Taylor said.

"That was close," Rick said.

"That was hella weird, that's what that was," someone said. Maybe it was Billy.

The last person left who had waited for his turn was Jackson, the tallest of them all. The one who always fetched the beers. The one who sat away from the rest of the group and only got up to go to the bathroom or change the music.

The two of them locked eyes. A hint of kindness and pity shined in his yellow-green irises. The longer Claire looked at him, the bigger the orbs around his pupils got.

"Out," Jackson said. "Everyone out. I can't do this with you all staring."

"I don't know man," Rick said. "You gotta watch out for the redheads. She's a spitfire."

"Go," Jackson said. "Don't worry. I don't think she has any fight left in her."

The gang grumbled, but they all exited. Alone in the room with Jackson, Claire sat up and pulled her knees to her chest. She wrapped her arms around them and hyperventilated.

"Calm down," Jackson said. "It's almost over. I'll be quick and then you can go home."

"Fuck you," Claire whispered. Feeling weak, physically and emotionally drained, she couldn't run if she tried. The pain between her legs subsided to a dull throb. Her heartbeat pulsated rhythmically with her breathing, and all Claire could think of was scratching Jackson's eyes out.

"Listen, the sooner you let me, the sooner this will be over."

"Why?" Claire asked.

Jackson pulled his pants down and exposed himself inches from Claire's face. He didn't say anything. Instead, he pulled her head toward him and forced her mouth open. The longest forty minutes of Claire's life took place downstairs in Rick's bedroom, and when Jackson finished, he got dressed like it was another ordinary Saturday.

Claire put on her clothes and ran out of the house. She slowly pedaled home and let the wind suffocate her feelings. It didn't feel real that she had just been gang raped by five guys . . . boys whom she thought were friends.

Claire didn't think she could feel any dirtier or more broken than she already was, but that day was the breaking point. There was no chance of recovery.

30. FROM ALL SIDES

Claire came home to an empty household. Bryant had left a note on her bed demanding to know why she was late. Didn't she have any respect for them? Because of her tardiness, they had to find a last-minute babysitter. She crumpled the note and went straight to the bathroom. She had a black eye and bruises all over her body. Claire got into the shower and stood staring at her feet until the water ran cold. Back in the familiar haven of her room, Claire lay in bed for days. Nothing her dad did or said could make her leave her bedroom. She skipped school for a week, and when she finally went back, nothing mattered anymore.

At lunchtime, Christine and Claire skipped their afternoon classes and went to Christine's house. They made themselves a sandwich and turned on the TV.

"Okay," Christine said, "what happened? You haven't been in school, and you're acting funny, like someone pissed on your grave or something. And I see your black eye. It's faint but I see it."

Claire didn't know where to start. She hesitated to tell Christine what had happened even though they were best friends. Claire felt guilty. There must have been something she could have done to prevent the incident. What did she do or say that made Rick and the boys attack her? Why didn't she see it coming? Was she that damaged that they thought they could do whatever they wanted with her? She asked a thousand questions but each time came up short of answers.

Christine sat next to Claire and rubbed her back. "Hey, are you all right? Did your dad beat you again?"

Claire shook her head. "Something happened at Rick's house."

"What?" Christine asked. "When?"

"A week and a half ago," Claire said. "I went there on Saturday to hang out and listen to the new Twisted Sister album."

Christine perked up. "Oh yeah? Did you like it? I heard it was good. I can't wait to—"

"Chris," Claire said, "they attacked me."

"What?"

"Rick and Taylor . . . all of them."

"What do you mean, they attacked you?"

"Exactly what I just fucking said, Chris!" Claire screamed. "Jackson, Billy, Taylor, Ray! All of them. Fucking Rick and the guys jumped me. They locked me in the room and forced themselves on me."

"They wouldn't do that," Christine said. "Why would they do that? They're our friends."

"Well, they did," Claire said. She got up and put on her shoes.

"Where are you going?"

"Home." Claire grabbed her sweater and slipped it over her head. "I just want to be by myself."

Claire left in a hurry and rode her bike across the park. Her stomach churned and felt bloated. She imagined pedaling as fast as she could into a tree or right in front of a car to end her misery. If her best friend didn't believe her, who would? *Where's a cliff when you need one?* Claire wondered. She thought adults were predators, but kids her age too?

Claire pulled back on the brakes and came to a screeching halt on her bike. She let out a blood-curdling scream. *Why was this happening to me? Why were all the guys so damn horrible?*

#

By the end of the school year, Claire's grades had gone downhill dramatically, from As and Bs to Ds and Fs. So derailed in life, she threw common sense out the window and flushed any dreams she ever had down into the sewer. When she tried to tell Melissa about the attack, Melissa let out an incredulous gasp and then dismissed it. She didn't bother telling Jackie, and so she spent the entire summer getting high and shoving her emotions down deep to forget. Claire and Christine spent every day together doing drugs, getting drunk, binging on junk food, and listening to music as loud as their ears could handle.

One day that summer, Claire was over at Christine's house for a sleepover. Christine's dad was visiting. Eduardo's Colombian features were very prominent, and Claire saw where Christine got her good looks. He had thick wavy black hair, a strong square jawline, and a dark complexion that made Claire think of him as exotic.

The three of them played cards in Christine's room while father and daughter caught up on life and got reacquainted. Eduardo did most of the talking and asked a lot of questions. Claire wished that her father was as genuinely interested in her life as Eduardo seemed to be in Christine's.

"Seeing any boys, Chris?" Eduardo asked.

"No," Christine said.

"How's school?"

"It's summer, Papá."

"I know, *mija*," Eduardo said, "but are you looking forward to ninth grade?"

Christine shrugged. "I guess."

"You're growing up so fast, blossoming into a beautiful young lady right before my eyes."

"She's the prettiest at our school," Claire said. "She could have any boyfriend she wants."

Eduardo frowned. "Remember, Chris, you're my princess. No boy is allowed to touch you or kiss you. Only your *papito. ¿Comprendes?*" He gently lifted Christine's chin to meet her eyes and winked at her, then patted her thigh. "Go downstairs and get me a beer and some chips and salsa."

Christine made eye contact with Claire and pursed her lips. She rocked back and forth and curled a strand of hair around her fingers. Claire cocked her head and arched her eyebrows. Christine parted her lips slightly as if to say something but left the room quietly. Claire didn't understand what the look was about. As soon as Christine was downstairs, Eduardo leaned across Claire and flipped the light switch off. Claire felt the temperature drop and the air sucked out of the room. Eduardo's hand crawled its way to her breast. He pinched her nipple and kissed her on the mouth. Claire froze. His pass came out of nowhere, and she didn't know what to do. This wasn't a stranger; this was her best friend's dad. It took Christine less than five minutes to retrieve the beer and snacks, but in that time, Eduardo's hands had already mapped out the contours of Claire's body. As the footsteps got louder up the stairs, Eduardo seized his wandering hands and flipped the light switch back on. He resumed his position and talked to Claire about school just as Christine reentered the room.

The card game resumed as if nothing had happened. Claire wondered if Christine's dad was this way with his daughter too.

Each time Claire came home, she headed straight to the bathroom to throw up all the crap she ate at Christine's house. Soon, she took to cutting. At first, she placed an experimental cut here and there on her leg with her razor, and instead of hurting, it felt good. Really good.

The initial slice was intense, but it was kind of like scratching an itch from a hundred mosquito bites, or maybe it was like getting a tattoo. Claire imagined this was what it felt like to have a needle go up and down 3,000 times a minute when you're getting ink injected into your skin. The harder and deeper she went with her razor blade, the more relief she felt. In some odd way, her skin felt like it was on fire, but it hypnotized her into a meditative state. Soon, she was an artist, carving patterns on her legs to turn her pale canvas into a red motif.

That summer Claire and Christine went to the county fair. Some of the carnies invited them to an after-party. The drunk fest quickly spiraled out of control. One of the carnival employees kissed and groped Claire feverishly and wanted to have sex.

"I can't," Claire said. "I'm on my period."

"Give me a blow job then until I come," he said.

Claire backed away. "No."

He punched her in the face so hard she thought her jaw had cracked.

"I told you, you're going to suck my dick off until I come, and you're going to swallow every bit."

Claire tried to leave and find Christine, but he blocked her exit and forced her to give him oral sex. Her jaw ached, and she wanted to bite down hard but gagged at the thought of the mess in her mouth.

While Claire wrapped her life inside a cocoon and buried her emotions into the abyss, the only way to know she was still alive was through self-harm. By turning inward, Claire lost sight of the outside world. Getting high with Christine and chain-smoking cigarettes went together like peanut butter and jelly. The drugs led to starvation to the point where having an apple a day was too much food. At night when she felt the loneliest, Claire took to cutting. This became her life. The nightmare played in a loop from self-destruction to reckless sex with anyone who wanted it.

By ninth grade, Clair had fallen into her rhythm. She took more risks and slept around with adult men. There was never a shortage of business owners who solicited her or married men who wanted her as their mistress.

It all started with a Mayo Clinic doctor who asked if she wanted to party. She was fourteen. They went to his house and blew cocaine. Claire partied, drank, and took drugs to numb it all out. Of course, the doctor got frisky and wanted to get laid. He knew how old she was but begged for it anyway. Claire quickly learned that she had power over men—rich, powerful, desperate, gullible men.

Claire ruined them all by telling their wives. Vengeance was sweet, and the men all deserved to have their lives unraveled. The richer they came, the better it was so that she could bury them deep in their pile of misery. She played the game, and she reveled in it because it gave her control over them. Men in their twenties, thirties, and forties, all having sex with young teenagers—this disgusted Claire, knowing they preyed with no remorse on young girls while being unfaithful to their families.

The worst one she met was a young single man, or so she thought, who took her back to his place, and after hooking up, Claire noticed a framed photograph of a woman on the fireplace mantel—his wife, who was in the hospital having his baby. Claire was sickened by his vile deception. It took her two months to track down the wife, and when she did, she divulged everything about the affair.

Sometimes she'd call the men's wives over the phone and tell them about their cheating husbands. Sometimes she'd send a greeting card in the mail and include a memento of evidence. These confrontations always left her heart jackhammering against her chest like she had just run a marathon. Claire believed she was doing it for justice for herself and all the young girls who were getting hurt. She was convinced all adult men wanted to be with little girls. At least now, she was in control. Sometimes she put herself into really bad, dangerous situations because she did stupid things, but that was her reality.

#

Abuse and dysfunction came at Claire from all sides, whether it was at home, at school, or out in her community. One day, Claire found out from Melissa that another girl—a popular girl from a good family—was also raped by Rick and his friends. Claire smirked and said to her friend, "Now you believe me?"

Freshman year of high school was mayhem. Christine and Claire's lives spiraled out of control. They added shrooms to their charcuterie of drugs and wine coolers to their elixirs. Christine shared with Claire that Eduardo had been molesting her since she was a child and continued to do so whenever he was in the country.

She believed her sister in Colombia was likely getting raped also. In solidarity, the two girls threw caution to the wind and did whatever they wanted. "Fuck authority" was their war cry.

Planned Parenthood soon became their saving grace. Neither of them wanted STDs or pregnancies, so they made appointments with the clinic even though it was way across town.

"We gotta ride there as fast as we can," Claire said to Chris. "Dinner is at six."

"We can make it," Christine said.

The girls didn't anticipate how long the wait would be even though they had an appointment. By the time they got checked in and seen, got their birth control pills and a handful of condoms, it was close to 6:30 p.m. They rushed back home, and as soon as Claire walked through the front door of her house, Bryant was all over her.

"Where the fuck have you been?" Bryant yelled. "It's past seven."

"I lost track of time," Claire said. "Sorry."

Bryant bolted out of his chair and stormed toward Claire. She smelled the booze on his breath. He grabbed her by the hair and dragged her through the house. Bryant's nostrils flared as he picked Claire up and heaved her across the living room, over the couch and the La-Z-Boy chair. She hit the back wall and screamed in pain.

"You're grounded," Bryant said. "And you," he pointed at Christine, "get the hell out."

The violence at home was more incentive for Claire to stay away. Her father's threats and demands fell on deaf ears. Even though Bryant nailed her window shut, Claire came and went as she pleased, sneaking out to party until morning with Christine, Jackie, and Melissa.

On the weekends, the girls got smashed on bottles of Bartles and Jaymes or tanked on Bacardi 151 as they cruised the mall to kill time. Christine's favorite place to sit and sober up before heading home was inside the JCPenney department store. The lighting wasn't as bright as the other parts of the mall, and the soft seating was near the bathrooms.

One night, the police picked Claire up while she was out partying and took her home. The officer handed Claire over to Bryant and said, "She looks a little young to be out this late."

Bryant thanked the officer for getting his daughter home safely and immediately went into a rage.

"You goddamn whore," Bryant said. "You're just like your mother."

"What did I do?" Claire asked.

"You're heading down a bad path, Claire. You're going to find yourself pregnant at sixteen."

Claire stomped up to her room and tuned her father out. Bryant could be cruel in other ways. One Saturday morning, while her dad sat around with his friends, drinking a gallon of whiskey, he called out to her to come downstairs.

Bryant tossed Claire a T-shirt. "Read what it says for all of us."

Claire read the shirt silently to herself and said, "No way in hell."

"Read it!" Bryant yelled. "Hold it up. Let us see it."

Claire draped the shirt in front of her and mumbled, "President of the Itty Bitty Tittie Committee."

Her father and his friends lost their composure and howled with laughter. She flung the shirt at her dad and ran to her room, slamming the door as hard as she could. She stayed in her room and did her own thing, listening to music or reading a book. Music, especially, was therapeutic.

At school, things weren't any better. She was always showing up bruised or with a hangover, which made her easy prey. Girls picked fights and provoked her to get a rise out of her. Rumors spread that Claire was a slut and slept around with everyone.

The Wednesday before Thanksgiving break, Claire wanted to spend time with her friends. She hadn't seen them for a while since she was serving another lifetime sentence of being grounded. Claire told Bryant she had detention that day. After school, she went to the hill behind the school and sat with Christine and Jackie to catch up.

"Hey, what's new?" Claire asked

"Well," Christine said, "my grandma has been making me go to AA meetings."

"Oh shit," Claire said. "That sucks."

"Tell me about it," Christine said. "It's stupid. You're supposed to sit around and share your fucking kumbaya stories, and there's this twelve-step nonsense you're supposed to go through."

"What are the steps?" Jackie asked.

"I don't know. I'm still on the first one—admitting I'm powerless over my addiction and that I can't manage my life," Christine said.

"How is it?" Claire asked.

"Lame," Christine said, "but guess who I ran into? Christopher!"

"No way," Jackie said. "The guy Claire stayed with when she ran away?"

"Yeah," Christine said. "It's sad. His girlfriend's death really messed him up."

"Wow," Claire said, "that's sad. Chelsea died like seven or eight years ago. I hope someday someone will love me like that."

"So . . . changing the subject," Jackie said. "There's a rumor going around about you."

"Me?" Claire asked. "Let me guess. I'm having an affair with a married man who has three children. Oh wait, I've got something better. I stopped sleeping with all the teachers, and that's why I'm failing all my classes."

Christine cleared her throat. "They said you lost your virginity to some guy named Mark."

"Yeah, at a biker party," Jackie said, "and that you had sex in exchange for drugs."

"In Oronoco," Christine said.

"At some trailer park," Jackie said, "and that you manipulate guys with sex for drugs and money."

"Are you kidding me?" Claire asked. "Who's spreading all these rumors? I bet it's Paul or Nick . . . or maybe Rick and his shitshow friends."

"Kimberly," Christine said.

"The new girl? My next-door neighbor? That Kimberly?"

"Where would she get that idea from?" Jackie asked.

Claire sighed. "Because I made the mistake of telling her I had been raped. I didn't give her any details except to say it was by an adult. Shit."

"Then how would she know about the biker gang and the trailer park?" Christine said.

"I don't know," Claire said. "Enough about my rosy life. What's going on with you, Jackie? Any plans for Thanksgiving?"

The three of them talked for ninety minutes, and once again, Claire lost track of time. She ran into the school to grab her book bag before heading home when the vice principal stopped her.

"Your dad was just here looking for you," Mr. Lee said. "He was pretty upset."

Claire bolted home and ran the whole mile without stopping. The moment she stepped inside the house, she braced herself.

"Sit down," Bryant growled. Claire did as she was instructed and sat on the couch.

"What do you have to say for yourself?" Bryant asked.

"I was talking to my friends and just lost track of time."

"Bullshit," Bryant said. "I talked to the school. I know you didn't have detention, and the whole school was cleared out half an hour after the bell rang. So don't you sit there and lie to my face."

"I'm not!" Claire said.

Bryant jumped over the coffee table onto the couch where Claire sat and whaled on her. He pinned her down and straddled her. His two hundred pounds was no match for Claire's one hundred. He hammered her head, neck, face, and chest. He broke her glasses and sliced her eyelid open.

Claire screamed and feared her father would bludgeon her to death. She clamped down and ground her teeth to brace the impact. In the process, she also bit her cheek at the same time Bryant's fist clocked her in the jaw. The inside of her mouth was cut up. She tasted blood.

"That'll teach you," Bryant said and walked out the front door.

Claire looked at Shana, who witnessed the whole thing. Shana looked frozen in time, forever petrified and in shock. She didn't say a thing, didn't call the police, and never tried to stop the beatings. To Claire, Shana was yet another adult in her life who had failed her. For that, she resented Shana and treated her as nonconsequential.

#

Not too long after that incident, Bryant came home drunk and marched straight to Claire's room where she was listening to music on her Sony Walkman with the headphones on. He lunged at her and ripped the cassette player out of her hands. He slapped her and smashed her Walkman to pieces—the Walkman she had purchased with her hard-earned babysitting money.

"You're just like your mother," Bryant screamed. "You're a no-good lying slut." He gripped Claire by the hair, and with his face inches from hers, said, "You ever test me in any way again, you're dead. I'll bury your ass." Bryant surprised Claire with a gun and shoved the barrel into her mouth. "I brought you into this world, and I can take you out."

Claire sank into her bed and closed her eyes. She didn't dare move. She had no idea what had provoked him. Bryant removed handcuffs from his back pocket and locked them into place.

"My god," Bryant said. "What a tramp you've become. I'm going to straighten you up even if I have to kill you to do it. I'll stick you in the trunk until we get to Wyoming. I'll leave your dead body out there where no one will find it. Or maybe you should go live with your mother and be a whore."

Bryant stormed out of the house and left Claire imprisoned in her room for a good hour before Shana came to check on her.

"Shana, get me out of these things," Claire said.

"He'll kill me," Shana whispered.

"Please," Claire said. "My wrist hurts. My legs are cramping up, and my hands are numb. And I have to pee."

Shana looked at the doorway and back at Claire before nodding. "Okay, but if I set you free, you have to promise not to come back."

"Don't you worry. I am never coming back."

31. ALCOHOLICS ANONYMOUS

Claire rode to Christine's house, and an hour later, Child Protective Services picked her up to take her downtown. When she arrived at the Department of Social and Health Services, Bryant was there. The fury in her father's eyes freaked Claire out. His body trembled as if so engulfed in rage that his whole being would explode.

A diminutive lady escorted Bryant and Claire to a room down the hall and motioned them to sit.

"Mr. Baker, Claire, my name is Lacey. I'm with the Behavioral Health Administration. I'll be conducting the intake interview and handling your case."

"This is bullshit," Bryant said. "You can't hold us here." Bryant rose to leave.

"Sit, Mr. Baker," Lacey said. "The sooner we clear this up, the sooner you can go home. Your daughter has been in the foster care system before, and unless you want the state to file civil charges against you, I recommend we all come to an understanding on what's to happen next."

Bryant let out a gruff exhale and sat back down.

"Now, Claire," Lacey said, "why don't you tell me what happened."

"I'm never going back," Claire said. "You can't send me back. Otherwise, I'm as good as dead."

"That's right," Bryant said. "Don't send her home. I'll kill her."

Lacey maintained eye contact with Claire and asked, "Has your dad ever sexually abused you?"

"Now wait a min—" Bryant said.

"Mr. Baker, you'll have your turn. Claire?"

"No," Claire said, "but his friends try to." She went on to explain what it was like living with a drunk father and how toxic her home environment was.

When it was Bryant's turn to give his statements, he made excuses for everything. He described himself as a recovering alcoholic and claimed he had his drinking under control. He confessed to beating Claire because she was into sex and drugs and he found contraceptives in her room.

In the end, Lacey assigned Claire to the Pitrillo family. Lacey recommended a chemical dependency evaluation for Bryant and asked that he set up an appointment as soon as possible. Both father and daughter were required to go to counseling for thirty days and talk through their issues as well as attend Alcoholics Anonymous meetings. After thirty days, the court would decide on next steps.

#

The first counseling session was a joke. Claire and Bryant sat far apart from one another and barely spoke.

Midway through the session, Isaac, their therapist, asked, "Bryant, name two things you love about your daughter."

"Well," Bryant said, "she has a beautiful voice. She's in choir."

"Great," Isaac said. "What else?"

"She's intelligent."

"What about you, Claire?" Isaac asked. "What do you love about your father?"

Claire looked at Bryant, then back at Isaac. She struggled to find something good to say. Bryant was once her world, until he wasn't, and she could barely remember what he was like when she was three and four years old. He used to keep her safe and spoke kindly to her. There once was a sparkle of pride in his voice, but the man before her now was unrecognizable. The years of alcohol abuse, high blood pressure, and angina spells had aged her father quickly. He was five feet, ten inches, and 200 pounds. There was nothing she loved about him.

"Claire?" Isaac asked. "Anything you like about your dad?"

"Well, when he's sober, he can be very loving and reasonable," Claire said. "When he's sober . . ." Claire couldn't think of anything else.

Isaac nodded and smiled. "Bryant, you have a lot of work to do. She almost couldn't come up with anything, and if she hadn't, you would have never had a chance. It's going to be up to you as to whether you can fix this because your relationship is as tenuous as it's going to get."

Isaac turned to Claire, "Why don't you tell your dad what's on your mind?"

Claire looked directly at her father and didn't back down. She felt strong having an authority figure in the room who was in control. "I don't have any respect for you. You said I was a slut, and you call me a whore. You accuse me of selling out the family name, yet you go and sell the family name all the time. I don't respect the hypocrisy. You don't get to hold me to a higher standard. I'm a kid. I'm supposed to make mistakes. You're supposed to help me. Instead, you punish me and chastise me and make me feel lower than dog shit. Why would I respect you? When I need you, you beat me. You punch me and knock me across the room. What the fuck?"

"Do you think you can rebuild your relationship with your dad?" Isaac asked.

Claire glanced at her father before answering. Bryant sat stoned-faced. She wanted to see a glimmer of kindness, some sign to show that her words penetrated his armor, but she saw nothing. "I don't know. I really don't. I hate him."

That was the first and last counseling session they had together. Bryant convinced DSHS and the court that he didn't need supervised visits with his daughter and that he would meet with Claire regularly in a public space to work out their relationship.

Their second therapy session was at an ice cream and coffee shop. They talked about their relationship for an hour, every week, for a few months. During this time, Shana and Bryant welcomed their second son into the world and named him Jack. Claire adored her little brother as much as she did Jason.

Sitting with her father talking about life events seemed surreal. In Claire's mind, her father never allowed himself to be vulnerable. He didn't admit any wrongdoing or apologize for beating the crap out of her or sticking a gun in her face.

In the last meeting they had before Claire was due to come home from foster care, she opened up about the night she was raped by Mark.

"Remember when you sent me out with that drug addict for pizza and a movie? And then you backhanded me when we got home? You were screaming at me, and you asked me if I had anything to say for myself. Laurie was standing right there, and I tried to talk to you, but I didn't want to talk to you in front of her."

"Yes, so?" Bryant asked.

"She took me to a party and had me raped," Claire said. "She wanted drugs and used me as payment!" Claire divulged what happened and keenly observed her father's reaction.

Bryant sat sipping his coffee and didn't utter a word. After Claire finished talking, Bryant simply said, "Well, maybe next time you'll know better how to protect yourself."

In that instant, Claire knew she could never trust her dad again. She grabbed her purse and slid out of the booth. "You have no idea how to be a parent, do you?"

#

For the next year, Claire remained in foster care. When she finally went home, she was once again delivered to the front steps of her house by a police officer.

Bryant received his daughter with open arms. "Oh my God, I've missed you. It's so good to have you home."

Claire knew her dad was putting on a show for the cops, and that made her revolt with hatred for him.

The time spent with her foster family, the Pitrillos, was smooth except for one incident when Claire tried to kill herself by overdosing on sleeping pills. They rushed her to the hospital, where she recovered and came home with the jitters. The Pitrillos family did their thing while providing a safe shelter for Claire, and Claire did her thing while continuing with counseling and AA meetings.

That first night home, Claire took a good look at herself in the mirror. She didn't want to end up like her dad—end up in dysfunction and poverty. She made a promise to herself to try to do better, and that meant removing herself from her dad's wasteland.

Claire stormed to Bryant's room. "You have twenty-four hours to find my mother—otherwise, I'm out of here."

Bryant stared blankly at her, and for two minutes father and daughter were at a standstill. Then Bryant got up and, within ten minutes, had Claire's mother, Janet, on the phone.

You son of a bitch. "You knew all along, and you kept her from me?" Claire took the receiver from her father. "Hello?"

"Claire!" The voice on the phone was high-pitched and loud. Janet spoke animatedly nonstop without taking a breath. "Oh my god, I can't believe it! Sweetheart, the last time I saw you, you were four. Do you remember? I was on my way to Missoula, and I've been here ever since, hoping your dad would come back or that you'd find me.

"Your brothers and sisters are dying to meet you. And Mark, your little brother, do you remember him? You used to call him your baby dolly. He hasn't forgotten you. I talk about you all the time. You'll have to come to Montana for the weekend this summer after school is out. Lonnie is getting married. Say you'll come!"

Claire looked at her father, who was standing inches from her, eavesdropping on their conversation. "Mom, of course, I'll come." She challenged Bryant with her steely gaze and dared him to say otherwise. It was settled. They'd see each other in a few months.

#

There were two types of AA meetings—open and closed. In the open meetings, anyone could show up and talk about their experiences or how AA helped them. Relatives, friends, and anyone interested in Al-Anon were welcome to attend. The closed meetings were for recovering alcoholics only. Christine and Claire started going to the closed AA meetings together at the community center. Occasionally, they ran into Christopher.

All the meetings were the same, and even the faces were the same. Some went a few times a week, others went a few times a day. On one particular evening, Christine, Claire, and Christopher were all there. The three of them were animated, as it was good to be among friends. They were quickly asked to find a seat so the meeting could begin. In the middle of the semicircle sat a woman in her thirties. She was the chairperson.

"Welcome, everyone," the chairperson said. "My name is Doris. I've been an Al-Anon member for seven years and just commemorated five years of sobriety." A few people clapped. "Thank you for being here. We're going to start the evening with a short opening prayer."

As the group lowered their heads in prayer, Claire looked around the room. Thirty people filled the room, an even mix of men and women with the majority being teens and young twenty-year-olds.

After the Serenity Prayer, a portly man in his sixties, about five feet, nine inches, stood and introduced himself as Wally. He read the preamble. Another person read the Twelve Steps and Twelve Traditions.

Then Doris asked, "Do we have any first-time attendees here tonight?" Two people raised their hands. "Welcome. Please be sure to pick up a twenty-four-hour chip tonight as a symbol of your commitment to stay sober for twenty-four hours. Tonight we are going to discuss step one, admitting we are powerless over our addiction, and that our lives have become unmanageable.

"Please work with your sponsor on each of the twelve steps, and if you do not have a sponsor, we can help you find one. I want to remind everyone that anonymity is critical, meaning we do not discuss anyone's sharing or identity outside of tonight's meeting. Now would anyone like to share their experience, strength, or hope relating to this step?"

The first to go was a businessman named Bob, who was in his forties. "Hi, I'm Bob. I'm an alcoholic."

The room responded. "Hi, Bob."

"I own a dealership on the edge of town," Bob said. "My job is stressful, and when I spend two hours trying to close a deal only to have the customer walk away, it pisses me off. Whiskey calms me down and releases tension. By noon I want to have a shot of it with my coffee, and before I know it, I've gone through the whole bottle. I've tried tossing the bottles into the trash, but afterward, I'm mad at myself for throwing away my hard-earned money.

"Sometimes I dig the bottle back out of the trash, or if I've dumped it down the drain, then I run to the store and buy more. I'm smashed by closing time. Even though I try to present myself as sober and in control, I'm paranoid that the customers smell it on my breath. Some days I barely make it into the office. My business is afloat because I have good employees, but they're going to walk once they find out I spent their commission on booze. Anyway, I continue to be powerless over my addiction, and my life has become unmanageable. That's all I have to say."

"Thank you, Bob," Doris said. "Anyone else?"

The person next to Bob raised his hand, and Claire heard the timbre of his voice before she noticed his face—a smooth baritone so silky she thought he couldn't possibly be a smoker or drinker. His rugged good looks took Claire's breath away and reminded her of a young Timothy Dalton. If she had to guess, she would peg him as eighteen or nineteen years old. His shoulders were wide, and as he talked, his Adam's apple bobbed up and down as if dancing to Disney's Fantasia. He wore tight blue jeans and cowboy boots. Claire felt a stirring in her body and thought she could saddle up with this James Bond cowboy.

"Hello. I'm Jonathan, and I'm an alcoholic," the James Bond cowboy said. "Bob here is actually my dad. What he forgot to mention is that his wife, my mother, was killed by a drunk driver two years ago, and ever since that we've been grappling with her death. Well, at least I am. My mom and I were close. She . . ." Jonathan's voice cracked, and he choked up.

His lips trembled, and when he spoke again, his voice was a little higher in pitch. "Sorry. It's been hard. My mom was the kindest, most loving woman. She . . . always knew how to make me laugh and turn a sour day into a sweet evening. I . . . ." Jonathan wiped his eyes.

Doris encouraged him to continue.

He took a breath and continued. "I've thought about taking my life several times so I can be with her, but . . . well—" Jonathan chuckled "—I guess I'm a little bit of a mama's boy, and she'd be very disappointed in me." He let out a nervous laugh, and a few people tittered with him. "Anyway, I don't want to let her down. I know the irony in both of us being here, fighting our demons, when my mom was killed by a drunk driver. This is why I have to get better. I don't want to be that drunk guy that accidentally kills someone." Jonathan rested his elbows on his knees and clasped his hands. With his forehead on his knuckles, he said, "That's it for now."

Claire wondered how she would feel if her dad died suddenly or if he killed someone while in a drunken stupor. Would she feel relief that he'd be out of her life, whether dead or in prison? Or would she mourn and forgive him for his mistakes? She wondered what his story was and how he got to be such a hot mess. Claire shuddered and pushed the thoughts aside. Maybe one day they would reach a point in their relationship where they could have a serious, adult conversation about their differences and troubled life. A few more people shared their stories, and the last person to speak was Wally, the older gentleman who had read the preamble at the start of the meeting.

"Hello, I'm Wally. I'm a recovering alcoholic. Next month will be my four years of sobriety." A few people cheered and clapped for Wally. "I say recovering because it's work every minute of every day to not fall off the wagon. It stays with you, you know? Once you've had a taste of the elixir, you want more of it. But it's toxic. It kills you from the inside out, and after it pours out of you, it seeps back in to poison you some more. And then the cycle starts again. For me, anyway . . . but I found my reason to stop drinking and stay sober. If you can find your why, you're on the right path to being clean and living a healthy, happy life." Wally patted his belly and continued. "Okay, sorta healthy. I'm still fighting the cheeseburger addiction." This resulted in a rise in the audience. "Step one? Admit I was powerless over my addiction and that my life had become unmanageable. That took me a good three or four months to get to that step."

"What was your 'why' that got you committed to getting sober?" Christine asked.

"My reason isn't the same as your reason," Wally said. "That's up to each of us to figure out for ourselves. But, yeah, for me, my illness destroyed my marriage. My wife took the kids, and I haven't seen them in years. I miss them. They're my why. I want to see them again someday and earn their forgiveness. And now, I spend my days driving buses. It's a motivator to continue staying sober, and I spend all my free time helping teens with their addictions. My son and daughter were teenagers when I started down this road of destruction. I destroyed their youthful years, and I feel like if I can help other teens with their problems . . . if I can save them . . . then in some way, I'm making up for the havoc I caused with my kids. So, as Doris mentioned earlier, if you don't have a sponsor to help you along your journey to a new you, then get one. And I'm happy to sponsor any young soul out there who doesn't mind a stocky, hamburger-loving, bus-driving old fart like me. Thank you."

The AA meeting went for ninety minutes, and afterward, a third of the group met up at a nearby diner for the "after-meeting" to connect, talk, and be in the company of others who had the same struggles. Wally volunteered to drive the teens who wanted to come but didn't have rides. Only one boy volunteered to ride with Wally. Claire and Christine had no money, plus they had ridden their bikes to the community center. It was already eight o'clock. The girls wanted to get high and grub on some cold, leftover pizza at home. Then Wally made an offer they couldn't refuse.

"I can put both of your bikes in my truck," Wally said. "It's dark and not safe, so why don't you girls come with us? Food is on my dime, and I'll even take you home."

Claire wavered, not ready to trust this old man, but then she overheard Bob and Jonathan, her James Bond cowboy, saying they'd meet everyone at the diner.

"I'm in," Claire said. "Come on, Chris. We gotta eat. And as my best friend, you're obligated to come to make sure I'm safe. And do you really feel like riding your bike? And do you really want to go home early on a Friday to hang out with your grandma?"

Chris cracked a smile, and Claire knew she had hooked her best friend. Off to the diner they went, along with a boy named Dan, in Wally's truck. During the short ride, while Wally was chatting it up with Dan and Chris, Claire sat half-listening and half-thinking . . . what was her *why*?

That night, the group sat at a large booth and chitchatted over chicken pot pie and ice cream. It was one of the best nights Claire'd had in a long while.

32. WALLY

In the winter of 1986, when Claire was in tenth grade, life got a little better. People at school left her alone, and she wasn't getting harassed on the daily. Her grades still suffered, but at least she wasn't fending off bullies. She had been going to AA meetings almost daily, and while she was still drinking, partying, and doing drugs, she could look back six months and give herself credit for being less impulsive and more intentional.

Men came and went in her life, and oh, how she loved ruining them. She remembered watching a documentary on PBS Nova and National Geographic about the praying mantid species. She loved that they were able to rotate their heads 180 degrees so they had a wide range of vision. Even more fascinating was, despite their size, they could ensnare small birds, reptiles, or mammals and eat their prey alive. She remembered seeing a praying mantis catch a hummingbird and eat it to death.

Claire imagined herself as a praying mantis who, while small, could bring down someone larger than her. In the mantid world, the males died after mating, which tickled Claire to no end. Like the females, she, too, enjoyed killing her mate's livelihood after copulation. She relished in destroying every sick pedophile out there.

Although she was still promiscuous and only a hundred pounds soaking wet, she felt better about herself. Having Wally as her AA sponsor had helped, and even her relationship with her dad improved. Bryant had been going to AA meetings, and the two of them continued to keep the lines of communication open.

During the first couple of months of AA sessions, Claire discovered her "why" for wanting to be sober.

Christine's grandmother put Christine through a drug treatment program, and after getting out, Christine was told she couldn't hang with Claire anymore.

"I'm sorry," Christine said. "My grandma forbids me to see you again. She says you're a bad influence. She doesn't want me around you because you're using drugs and—"

"Then I'll quit!" Claire said. "Chris, I need you more than I need the drugs. Please! Let me show your grandma." Then it dawned on Claire what her reason for getting clean and sober was—it was her best friend. She couldn't lose Christine.

Claire continued to go to AA meetings without Christine. She spent more and more time with Wally to work on the twelve steps, even though she was still hung up on step two: Came to believe that a Power greater than ourselves could restore us to sanity.

To believe that no human power could relieve her afflictions was absurd to Claire because, as she interpreted it, that meant only a supreme being like God or some extra-terrestrial, supernova, universal energy was the divinity. Claire couldn't accept that. She believed in the power of mind over matter, sheer human willpower, and the resiliency of people. After all, she had survived multiple rapes, anorexia, cutting, suicide attempts, violent beatings, and more, yet she was still standing, still breathing, and still functioning. If any power greater than herself could restore her to sanity, it would be Wally.

The first time Wally picked Claire up at her house to take her to an AA meeting, Bryant was upset. Claire suspected her dad was jealous of her relationship with Wally. The two of them were getting close . . . closer than Claire and Bryant were.

"What the hell do you want with my daughter, you creep? She's fifteen!" Bryant yelled.

"Whoa," Wally said. "It's not like that. I don't look at your daughter that way. I promise you, I've never touched her and never will. That's not what I'm here for."

"You keep your hands in your pockets," Bryant said. "If anything happens to her, I'll break your neck and put you in a wheelchair for life. You'll be cross-eyed and shitting sideways for the rest of your life."

"Well, I don't want that," Wally said.

That night, Wally drove Claire to an AA meeting forty-five minutes away so they could have a long talk in the car.

"Let me tell you a story," Wally said as he drove out of the neighborhood. "I graduated with a Ph.D. in chemistry. Now I know what you're thinking. A good-looking stud like me has looks and brains? No way! I know . . . too good to be true, but I'm telling the truth."

Claire giggled. "Only one Ph.D.?"

"Who says I'm not working on my second?" Wally said, the corner of his lips lifting ever so slightly. "I worked at a lab in Atlanta as a chemist. Well, I climbed the corporate ladder and got burnt out. The drive was gone. The long hours and constant traveling, going to conventions and giving presentations . . . it all put a strain on my marriage. I was always eating out, entertaining partners, and drinking every day . . . not what you imagine a chemist doing, right? I told you, it's because of my debonair looks that I got invited to all these functions."

Claire laughed. "You just keep believing that. So is that how you got hooked on booze?" Claire asked.

"It played a role, but the catalyst was when my wife had a miscarriage. She just never recovered from it, and I was never there to comfort her or mourn with her. My job kept me away for days at a stretch, or I'd pull all-nighters because I was on the verge of some breakthrough. We each coped in different ways. I turned to vodka. My safety blanket. My binkie. We became strangers, and instead of using the precious hours we had together to talk and share our feelings, we argued and blamed one another for not being empathetic enough. Anyway, we divorced. She took the kids and turned them against me. I left Atlanta and moved back home to Rochester to take care of my mother. She's eighty-seven, you know."

"Wow," Claire said. "How's she doing?"

"Ah, you know, her body is all mashed potatoes, but her mind is tough and chewy like an overcooked steak! I have to use a meat mallet to break her down into submission."

"Oh, stop!" Claire laughed.

Wally chuckled. "She's the sweetest sauerkraut you'll ever meet and still twists my ears when I misbehave." Wally winked, leaned over, and whispered, "Which is all the time. My brother and I would squeal like pigs whenever she got a hold of our earlobes! Anyway, the point of my story is . . . my mother is the power. She is who restored my sanity. And you want to know how?"

"How?" Claire asked.

"Through storytelling. Stories connect us. They humanize us. They help us understand that it's not 'what's wrong with you?' but 'what happened to you?' that makes us the way we are. So when we come to understand behaviors through another person's lens, we find it easier to forgive the hurt they inflict on us or, better yet, understand the hurt we inflict upon ourselves."

Wally certainly gave Claire some things to think about. All this time she had felt that the second step in AA had to do with a higher power, but that power could come from anywhere or anyone.

"So . . . believing that a power greater than ourselves could restore us to sanity doesn't allude to God being the greater power?"

"For some, yes, but it's how you interpret it that matters. Claire, I don't know what religion you associate with—"

"Not Seventh-day Adventism," Claire said. "I detest organized religion. I once had a stepmom, Gisela, whose family were Seventh-day Adventists. They were so rigid, especially on Saturdays, the Sabbath day. No talking, no TV, no eating, no—"

"No farting," Wally added.

"Oh, definitely no farting," Claire said. "That would get you the belt."

Both of them had a good laugh at that one. Wally went as far as to mimic some flatulence noises. Claire laughed until she had to pee and made Wally promise not to crack any more jokes. Her bladder couldn't afford a tinkle.

"Okay, so back to higher powers," Wally said. "Would you consider yourself spiritual then?"

"For sure," Claire said. "Definitely not religious. I hate God. The whole 'God is merciful' thing is smoke and mirrors."

"If you hate God, then you must believe he exists. Right? Otherwise, how can you hate something that isn't real?"

Claire wasn't sure how to respond to Wally's question. She was pensive until Wally broke the silence.

"Claire," Wally said, and gently patted her hand, "to be spiritual is to be in tune with the ethereal, whatever or whomever that celestial being is to you. And God can mean different things to different people. But think of it this way. God is like the wind. You can't see the wind, can't touch it or taste it . . . but you can feel it and sometimes you can hear it. This is how you know it exists. It's like that with God.

"So the next time you feel alone or scared and you want to bounce ideas off of someone or confess something, or just get something off your chest, talk to that spiritual being. I mean, what do you have to lose? And who knows, maybe someone out there is listening. There's something magical about serendipity. The laws of the universe are unknown, and anything is possible."

They finally arrived at the AA meeting in some podunk part of Olmstead County. The paint on the old and rickety barn peeled like a blistered sunburn. The hour dragged by slowly as farmers sat around talking about their wives leaving them or dying. Claire couldn't wait to get out of there. There was an after-meeting at the local church no bigger than three lean-tos slapped together with rusty nails. When no one was looking, Claire mimicked getting hanged by a rope, and Wally nodded in agreement. It was time to get the heck out of dodge and head home.

#

Just when Claire and Bryant's rocky relationship began to mend, Bryant faltered and slipped back into his old ways, binge drinking, demeaning Claire, cheating on Shana, soliciting threesomes . . . With every two steps forward, it was one slide back to start.

Meanwhile, Claire tried to get healthy, stay sober, attend regular psychology appointments, get off drugs, go to work, and make an effort in school. She started working at Bob's dealership on the outskirts of town washing cars in her bikini. The job paid a lot more than babysitting and came with a steady paycheck plus some perks like free snacks and occasional tips from customers. Surprisingly, most of the tippers were women. Bob and his son, Jonathan, the Timothy Dalton lookalike, were still in the AA program and attended regularly. Claire often hitched a ride to the meetings with them after she got off work. She still crushed hard on Jonathan but knew he was out of her league. Jonathan was five years older than her and had a girlfriend. Still, she enjoyed flirting with him and admiring him from a distance.

Alcoholics Anonymous and Wally soon became Claire's life. One day Wally invited her to a family function.

"Want to come over for dinner?" Wally asked. "My mom is itching to meet you. My brother and his family will be there too."

"It depends. Are we having hamburgers or cheeseburgers?" Claire asked, knowing how much Wally loved burgers.

"Oh, neither. You know how much I detest burgers," Wally declared. "No, we're going fancy—bleu cheese with a side of double-stacked beef patties, cooked to your order, bookended with a soft, pillowy bun, and topped with sesame seeds. And for the pièce de résistance, a generous serving of 'Pardon Me, Do You Have Any Grey Poupon' mustard, imported from Dijon, France," Wally said as he took a bow.

Claire heartily accepted the invitation and rode with Wally to his house. When they arrived at the charming two-story A-frame home, who should open the door but . . . Wally? Claire did a double take. Standing in the foyer was a Wally look-alike, only a bit thinner.

Wally's twin smiled and shook Claire's hand. "I'm Wiley. It's nice to finally meet you. My brother talks a lot about you."

In the kitchen were two women, an elderly woman whom Claire took as Wally's mother and a middle-aged brunette. Wiley introduced Claire to his wife, Rita, who wiped her hands on a towel and embraced Claire with a soft squeeze.

"*Siéntate*." Rita motioned to the chair next to the matriarch of the family and invited Claire to sit.

Delores Jennings sat with her cane resting against her thigh. She wore a green velour tracksuit and one brown orthopedic shoe. Her other naked, bunioned foot rested on her knee.

"Sit, child," Delores said. "Goodness, you are skinny. Rita, let's feed this poor girl. Come a little closer so I can get a good look at you. My eyes aren't what they used to be."

Claire felt at ease with Wally's family and wondered if this was what a normal family looked like. She yearned for this and hoped she'd have a couple of sons someday as kind and smart as Wally and Wiley. Claire scooted closer to Delores, who immediately caressed her cheeks and squeezed her arms. It tickled, and Claire giggled.

"Mrs. Jennings, thank—"

"Oh, Lord, who's Mrs. Jennings?" Delores said. "Rita, you see a Mrs. Jennings here?"

"No, *Mamacita*, I do not," Rita said.

"Call me Delores, dear," Delores said. "Better yet, call me Dottie. Now I know what you're thinking. Dottie is short for Dorothy, not Delores, but I don't give a rat's turd about that. I always liked the name Dorothy ever since I saw *The Wizard of Oz* and asked my momma, may she rest in peace, why she didn't name me Dorothy instead of Delores. My, that Judy Garland. She was something!

"Do you know what *delores* mean in Spanish? It means pain, as in sorrow and melancholy. I shit you not. My momma gave me that name after the Virgin Mary, but who wants to be named Sorrow?"

"*Sí*, Maria de los Dolores means 'Mary of the Sorrows,'" Rita said and placed a plate of freshly grilled jalapeños, a bowl of tortilla chips, pico de gallo, and guacamole in front of Claire.

Wally and Wiley flocked to the spread and got their hands slapped by Dottie. "Where are your manners, boys? Ladies first," she said. "Please, Claire, you are our guest."

Claire grinned and put a little bit of everything onto her plate. "Thank you, Dottie. Rita, this looks so good."

"*Claro*," Rita said. "Of course, it's fresh and homemade, even the tortilla chips. The best way to have guacamole is tableside, no?"

As the evening wore on, Claire learned a lot about Wally and his brother. Wiley also had a Ph.D. and worked for the government as a chemist, serving the black ops team off the grid. He, too, became an alcoholic and went into treatment to save his marriage.

Claire found that fascinating. "What do you do now, Wiley?"

"Ah, I drive buses now, just like Wally," Wiley said. "Only I don't do tours or coaches as he does. I just do street driving. I'm a married man. I can't be leaving for long stretches, or Rita here will find another husband."

Rita playfully punched her husband and kissed him on the cheek. "The first chance I get, *mi amor*."

"So how did you both do it?" Claire asked. "How did you overcome your addiction?"

Wally got up to make himself a second cheeseburger, and as he constructed his sandwich, he said, "That's where step three comes in . . . deciding to turn your will and your life over to the care of God as you understand him. The first three AA steps are designed to shift your way of thinking and empower your mind to be strong. When we give in to our vice, we have the illusion of being in control. We think we can control how much we drink or how we behave while drunk. You now know firsthand, Claire, your dad's frame of mind when he's sloshed."

"Yeah," Claire said, "and I don't want to be like him. I have a bad temper. I know that if I allow myself to lose control, the rage will consume me."

"You're not alone," Wiley said. "Give your burden over to God or to whatever higher power you believe in . . . something that ignites your passion to live a life of sobriety."

"That's right," Wally said. "Visualize what your life would look like if you were free from addiction. Once you have that picture in your mind, hold onto it. Then, and only then, can you turn your life over to this higher power."

Claire thought about what her perfect life would look like. She imagined herself married to a strong man, someone who made her laugh and showed her tenderness. She pictured a big house with a beautiful garden, a couple of dogs, and two or three children. They would travel to places like France and Greece, maybe Italy and Spain too. In this new life, her dad and she reconciled and were living a healthier lifestyle. She didn't need much though. She just wanted to be happy and at peace.

33. DOWN THE SAME ROAD

Wally had given Claire a lot to think about, and she looked at her father in a different light. The two of them sat down for an ice cream sundae one afternoon to talk. Claire's mission was to learn more about her dad.

"What do you want to know?" Bryant asked.

"Everything," Claire said.

"All right, well, I was born in Michigan on June 20, as you know. We moved to Texas when I was little. In my late teens, we moved to California where I lived until I met your mother. What else?"

"What was it like for you growing up?"

"So," Bryant said, "I'm the oldest of three kids. My childhood wasn't anything to brag about. My dad beat the living daylights out of me—"

"Wait," Claire said, confused. "Grandpa Harold?"

"No. Grandpa Harold is your grandma's second husband."

Claire was shocked. What else did she not know? "Go on."

"As I said," Bryant continued, "my old man was merciless. He beat all of us."

"Grandma too?"

"Yes. Your grandma is tiny. She's only four feet, eleven inches, and he threw her around like she was a ragdoll. Anyway, one day when I was sixteen, I stood up to my dad. He knocked me around good and banged me against a wrought iron fence. He beat me to a pulp. I thought I was going to die, and if I was going to go down, I was going down swinging.

"I couldn't take it anymore and left home for good. Your grandma left shortly after and, years later, married your Grandpa Harold. She was in her thirties. They've been together ever since."

"I want to see them, Dad. After school gets out. Let's do a road trip across the country like we used to. You and me, Shana and the boys. I bet Grandma and Grandpa would love to meet little Jason and Jack."

Bryant hesitated for a moment but surprised Claire by agreeing.

#

In school, Claire's English teacher assigned the class homework. The essay topic was "Who am I?" Claire put pencil to paper and gave some thought to who she was and what she wanted to become.

Who am I? That's a good question. Now let's find out. My name is Claire Anne Baker. I am fifteen years old, five feet, four inches, and weigh 110 pounds. I have green eyes and copper-colored hair. They say redheads have quick tempers. That saying certainly fits this redhead. I have little control over my temper, and I become very angry easily. I can be very cruel to those with whom I am angry. When I don't have a hold on my temper, it can and has led to many difficult situations and problems. I am very impulsive. Many times I have acted without thinking of the consequences of my actions.

I tend to want to be in control in many situations in which I am working so that I may improve. I am a very stubborn and independent individual and cannot stand any violation of my independence. I've been told by many people that I am sensitive and intuitive to other people's needs. I love to help people with problems, and I am a good listener. Because I have been all over the United States, I am very adaptable to almost any situation.

I like to think of myself as an intelligent person who uses her intelligence to the best of her ability. I have been through more stress than any teenager I know. I think my life has made me a stronger person because of the problems I have had. I try to give others the hope and encouragement to do the same. I am very outspoken and outgoing, but I can be shy at times. I usually don't mind saying what I feel about a subject that is highly controversial if I feel strongly about it.

The most important person in my life is my father. My parents got divorced when I was six months old, and after five months in court, my father got custody of me. I only saw my mother once when I was four years old, and I remember that day as clearly as if it were yesterday.

My father and I did a lot of traveling when I was young, and we shared a closeness because of that. Yet we are so alike at times that I feel he is sometimes the hardest person in the world to get along with. Other times we are so close it almost hurts. If he died any time soon, I would be crushed. When he does die, I know I will go through a pain unlike any I have ever experienced. My father taught me a lot about life, love, hope, values, happiness and so much more. I love that man.

To me, happiness comes to things with love and security. I think happiness is a very important part of life. If somebody gave me a million dollars, I would pay my bills, buy a new wardrobe, and put the rest in the bank for my future.

My most valuable possession is my stereo because, above all, my greatest passion is my need for music. I couldn't live without it. I love to sit and reflect over the day while listening to the radio or tapes or records. Singing and dancing are a big part of my life. The conditioning of my voice and body, the nervousness of getting up in front of hundreds of people to perform for them, letting music seep into my very soul, and becoming the music. There is nothing so grand as standing on stage and getting a standing ovation. I feel if I can make a person ridiculously happy over a song or cry over a heartbreaking song, the whole thing was worth it.

My stereo helps me practice, and although it may not be worth a lot of money, in my heart it is worth more than gold. Even though singing is very important to me, that's not what I'd want people to remember me for. I want people to remember me for my honesty, sensitivity, my willingness to listen, and for helping people whenever I can. I guess what I'm saying is that I want people to remember me for my love of life and people.

Maybe now we both know more about me than when I started. I hope I never stop learning about myself.

Claire read her essay several times and tweaked it here and there. It was a wonder her outlook on life and her father had changed so much. She had Wally to thank for that. He was a constant positive force in her life, helping her to see her life from thirty thousand feet up and analyzing her decisions based on thoughtful scenarios. He was like a father to her, and she knew he would always be in her life.

#

That June, they all piled into the car and drove from Minnesota to California. Claire was beside herself with excitement. She didn't let the fatigue of the road trip dampen her spirits.

It had been ten years since she last saw her grandparents and her aunt Samantha. Her cousins must be all grown up. Bryant reminded Claire of her cousins' names—Brandon and Tom—and Aunt Samantha's husband, Brandon Sr.

Two days later, they arrived in the San Fernando Valley. Driving along the highways and through the dry terrain stirred a nostalgic feeling in Claire. When they pulled in front of the small, one-story stucco home in the Sun Valley neighborhood Sunday evening, the memories flooded her with warmth and peace. Not much had changed from what she remembered. The lawn was a little overgrown but green. The larkspurs were in bloom. Claire grinned and jumped out of the car, arching her back with her arms in the air to get a good stretch. Jason clambered out of the back seat while Shana scooped baby Jack into her arms.

Grandma Sharon ran out of the house with her arms flapping as she squealed, "I can't believe it!" She reached Claire first and grabbed Claire into a tight embrace. Sharon rained kisses all over her face as the tears streamed down both their cheeks.

Grandpa Harold was right behind Sharon, along with Aunt Samantha and her husband, Brandon.

"Move over, bacon," Grandpa Harold's gruff voice boomed. He gently pushed Grandma Sharon aside and, still strong as a buffalo, lifted Claire off her feet. He swung her around, then patted Claire's head and rubbed her cheeks. Claire didn't hold back and returned the gesture. She cried with tears of joy and rested her head on his tank of a shoulder.

Aunt Samantha cocked her head, smiled, and opened her arms. Claire folded into them and got a good whiff of sweet perfume.

"Sweet Jesus," Aunt Samantha breathed. "You're all grown up, little one." She fluffed Claire's hair and marveled at how copper it was. Samantha playfully punched Bryant in the chest and hugged him, then scowled, "Ten damn years, Bryant!"

"Don't you start with me," Bryant said. He smiled and introduced Shana and the boys to the family.

Uncle Brandon helped bring the bags into the house and cracked cold beers for everyone, including Claire. Even though a decade had passed since she was last there, and she had left under traumatic circumstances, none of that mattered now. They were together as one happy family, letting bygones be bygones. Grandma Sharon oohed and aahed over the boys and couldn't keep her eyes off Claire. She kept touching Claire as if she didn't believe Claire was real.

"We've got some fun plans for the next five days," Uncle Brandon said. "Six Flags, street races, boating . . . Claire, your cousins, Tom and Brandon, are going to join us. We all took time off of work."

"It's not every day there's a Baker family reunion," Aunt Samantha said.

The house buzzed with activity as everyone talked and tried to recap the past ten years in three hours. Eventually, it was time to retire for the night. Aunt Samantha and Uncle Brandon went home, promising to return in the morning to join them for breakfast before heading to the amusement park.

Back in Claire's old bedroom, she tried to remember what it had looked like many seasons ago. She gazed out the window and recognized the lemon tree in the neighbor's yard. Claire held little Jack in her arms and pointed to the tree. "See that? I used to pick lemons from it, and one time, I jumped down onto an ant hill."

Claire's brother Jason sucked in his breath. "Oh no."

"Yes, a bunch of fire ants crawled up my legs, and I cried because it hurt so much."

Claire put her brothers to sleep on the bed and curled up behind them. As tired as she was, Claire was wired from the excitement of being back in California. There was magic here, and she decided she'd move to Los Angeles one day.

#

The week flew by as the family enjoyed outings together. Claire got to know her cousins, who were in their twenties now. Both of them were single and getting started with their careers.

Brandon had followed Grandpa Harold's path and joined Boeing as an engineer. Tom worked at the CBS television network as a production assistant coordinating scripts, selecting footage, organizing and distributing tapes, and performing clerical duties as assigned.

By the time Saturday morning rolled around, it was time to say goodbye. It was the trip of a lifetime for Claire, who promised to write and keep in touch now that she had Grandma Sharon's address and phone number. Once again wetness rippled in rivulets down Claire's face as she hugged her grandparents, cousins, Uncle Brandon, and Aunt Samantha. Good times were had by all. Jason and Claire took home a nice souvenir mug and pin from Six Flags Magic Mountain, the perfect gifts from Grandpa Harold.

Back in Rochester, Claire met up with Christine, Jackie, and Melissa to tell them all about her trip. She resumed going to counseling and AA meetings, gushing with Wally about how amazing LA was. And at work, she was in such high spirits that even Bob and Jonathan at the car dealership noticed.

One weekend Claire was outside in her bikini, washing cars at Bob's car dealership, when Bob called her into his office. Thirty minutes remained on the clock before Claire's shift was over. She wrapped a towel around her body and went inside the main building.

Bob sat behind his desk, coffee mug in hand, as he poured over invoices and paperwork. Claire knocked lightly, and without looking up, Bob answered, "Come in and close the door."

"You wanted to see me?" Claire asked.

Bob removed his glasses and smiled. "Business has been good at the car wash, and I think a lot of it has to do with you."

Claire noticed the sly glance Bob gave to her thighs, and she sat down so the towel draped over her knees. "Thanks," Claire said. "This summer has definitely been busy."

"You deserve a raise."

"Oh, wow. Thank you."

"You earned it. Effective next week you'll be paid $3.50 an hour, and if you want to pick up more hours here and there, that can be arranged. I know school is starting back up next week, so instead of the car wash, I'm moving you to administration. I need a part-time assistant to help with some accounting work, answering phones, filing, that kind of stuff. You think you're up to it?"

"Absolutely." Claire was delighted she could cut back on babysitting and make more money at the dealership.

"There will be times, especially month-end, when you might be required to work late."

"Sure," Claire said. "No problem."

"Good." Bob stood up and took a sip of his drink. "I'll walk you out." He quickly stepped around his desk and stuck out his hand for a handshake. Claire extended her right hand and was immediately pulled in for a kiss.

"What the fuck?" Claire hissed.

"How about a kiss to seal the deal?" Bob said.

"Fuck you," Claire said. She moved toward the door and was blocked by Bob's imposing stature.

"Listen," he said, "I know you like my son, but I told Jonathan to stay away from you because you're mine."

"I'm almost sixteen, and you're what? Forty? Forty-five?"

Bob grabbed Claire's wrist and pushed her against the wall. He tugged at her towel and let it fall to the floor. He kicked Claire's legs apart and rubbed his genitals on her body as he drove his tongue into her mouth.

Claire relaxed and kissed him back. She unzipped his pants and pulled them to the floor. He stepped out of them, and as she stood up, Claire kneed him hard in the nutsack.

Bob howled in pain and swore like a sailor.

"I quit!" Claire screamed. She grabbed his pants and ran toward the door. "I don't work for you anymore. You'll never fucking have me." Claire opened the door and snarled at Bob, still bent over in pain. "I never had a chance with Jonathan anyway, you sick fuck." Claire slammed the door and ran back to the lockers. She tossed Bob's trousers in the dumpster on her way out.

She had been down the same road one too many times. Enough was enough. *Watch out world*, Claire screamed silently, *because I'm fucking coming for you!*

34. STEAKS AND CAKES

Wally presented Claire with a dinner invitation to celebrate her progress with Alcoholics Anonymous.

"Wear something nice," Wally said. "We're going to get gussied up."

Claire didn't own anything fancy and stressed over what to wear. She had tossed all her dresses a long time ago, and even if she'd still had them, she wouldn't fit into them. Shana came to the rescue and loaned her a long, flowing, floral-print maxi dress. Claire smiled, thinking how far Shana had come with the way she dressed. She wore a bra consistently when in public now and chose long skirts or dresses instead of T-shirts and jeans. Shana and her father's relationship was still rocky at times, but they hadn't had a flare-up for three months. Claire thanked Shana and waited for Wally to pick her up.

"Where are you going?" Bryant asked.

"Wally's taking me out for my birthday," Claire said. "Somewhere fancy."

Bryant's eyebrows puckered. "What's going on between you two? He's an old man. He shouldn't be hanging out with teenage girls and taking them out to dinner."

Claire wondered if the look on her father's face was one of jealousy or disapproval. "It's not like that," Claire said. "He's like a dad to me." As soon as the words came out of Claire's mouth, guilt settled in her throat, especially since her father winced and got off the couch to go into the kitchen.

Headlights shined through the curtains, and Claire drew back the drapes to see Wally pulling into the driveway. Claire ran out to save him the trouble of parking and coming to the front.

Wally smiled. "Ready?"

"Yes," Claire said. "Where are we going?"

"You'll see."

They drove to downtown Rochester and parked at The Kahler Grand Hotel. Wally escorted her inside the beautiful hotel and toward Lord Essex, a fancy steakhouse. Visions of steaks swirled in Claire's mind and brought drool to her mouth. The hustle and bustle of the wait staff, the sizzle from the kitchen, the buzz of the well-dressed patrons, and the smell of the food were sensory overloads to Claire's young, impressionable mind.

The host took Claire's and Wally's coats and hung them in a closet. Wally complimented how radiant Claire looked.

"And you look so dapper, Wally!" Claire exclaimed.

He presented his arm, and she gladly took it. They followed the hostess, turning heads as they walked. People smiled as they passed by their tables. Claire did not see any judgment in their eyes. Perhaps they thought she was Wally's daughter rather than a young female companion. Their acceptance of her made her walk a little straighter with her head a little higher. In the far corner of the restaurant, they were seated, and Wally graciously pulled out her chair for her.

As they poured over the menu, Wally said, "Every young lady should experience fine dining."

"So tonight's lesson is about fine dining etiquette?" Claire asked.

"Tonight is about you," Wally said, "but maybe we'll both learn a few things along the way."

They placed their order with the waiter, and when the basket of bread arrived, Wally placed his napkin over his lap. Claire did the same. She observed Wally closely and took his subtle cues, noting not to put her elbows on the table and moving slowly and deliberately when she buttered her roll or sipped her water. The waiter came back with their Shirley Temple drinks, and Wally winked at Claire. "We can pretend it's sparkling celebration juice. Cheers to you, my dear. Happy birthday."

"Cheers," Claire said. "Thank you."

Over their medium rare steaks, haricot verts, roasted rainbow carrots, beet salad, and mushroom risotto, Wally and Claire engaged in topics ranging from her choir concert to sports.

"I'll take you to Twin Cities this season for a baseball game," Wally said. "Good ole American pastime."

"That'll be fun," Clair said. "You know when we first met and you were shuttling all of us to the AA meetings, I thought you were a weirdo."

Wally stopped cutting his steak and looked at her with surprise. "What do you mean?"

"I didn't think you liked me. I mean, I'm used to every man wanting something from me and making passes at me. I've slept with so many guys, half of them I don't even remember their names. And I get a high out of destroying them. You, on the other hand, took me out to eat and did all these nice things for me, even including me in your family get-togethers, yet you've never tried to . . ." Claire lowered her voice. ". . . to touch me."

"Claire, I've worked with a lot of troubled teens in the past few years. None of them are as obstinate as you, and I mean that in a good way, because there is strength in you that will get you through this hurdle in life. Of course, I like you. You are not weak in character and have something that's hard to teach—common sense. Somewhere along your journey, you've lost your way, and it's because of what happened to you. Your emotional intelligence is as high as your intellectual quotient. You're strong and beautiful, inside and out, but you need to learn to respect yourself. I hope one day you'll see yourself the way I see you."

"I don't know if I'll ever get there," Claire said. "Sometimes, right when I make progress, something happens and sets me back a few notches. It's so hard to climb out of my shithole. And when I want to trust someone and believe in them, they betray me."

"It worries me that you and Christine are still drinking, doing drugs, partying, and being promiscuous. You're going to be eighteen in a couple of years, and then life is your choice. You can get healthy. You have the agency to live life on your terms. You can go anywhere and do anything you want, be whomever you want to be, but the road to get there is not for the faint of heart. How much do you want it, Claire?"

"I'm a fuck-up. I always relapse."

"Do you want to run toward disaster or a better life? You don't have to be a victim forever. You're getting your strength."

"At the last Al-Anon, we talked about step four, 'searching and making a fearless moral inventory of ourselves.' I don't even know what that means. Like, where do I start?"

Wally flagged down the waiter and asked for more salted butter for his bread. He placed his hand on the table, palm up, and Claire slipped her hand on top of his. He held it gently and squeezed. "My dear, I'm proud of you. I don't know if anyone tells you this enough, but if you look at yourself compared to where you were a year or two ago, would you say you've grown for the better?"

Claire gave it some thought and nodded. She still had a long way to go to get healthy, and at times she wanted to quit therapy or kill her father, but yes, in general, things were better. She was better. "Yes," Claire said. "But I—"

"No buts," Wally said. "From now on, you're going to cut that word out of your vocabulary, and you're going to replace it with the word *and*. Now . . . regarding step four, the main goal is to help you gain a better understanding of yourself during treatment. Your inventory is a list of your resentments, fears, guilt, and hate."

"So, basically, all the hang-ups that are getting in the way of me becoming healthy, sober, and happy?" Claire asked.

"Exactly," Wally said. "It's more a list of your reactions than of what actually happened. The intention is to examine your character and behaviors. For example, this need you have to be vindictive against the men who've lied to you or hurt you."

"Well, they deserve it," Claire said in defense. "If they didn't cheat on their girlfriends or wives . . . I mean, these sickos are chasing skirts that were in diapers when they were full-grown men, old enough to vote, to become doctors, to go to war . . . It's filthy and disgusting, and they need to rot in hell."

"Why do you feel you have to be the one to send them there?" Wally asked.

"I can't just turn the other cheek, Wally. If I don't, another girl will be made a victim, and that girl may not be as tough as me. If I can teach these men a lesson first and prevent them—"

"How can you be sure they won't do it again anyway?"

"Well, I guess I can't, but—"

"And," Wally reminded her.

"Okay, I guess I can't, *and* I can slow them down." Claire smiled. "That sounds weird."

Wally chuckled. "Yeah, a little bit."

The two of them finished their meal, and the waiter brought out a slice of lemon cheesecake frosted with lemon curd. There was a candle on the cake.

Wally reminded her to make a wish before blowing out the candle.

Claire closed her eyes and wished for "more steaks and cakes and fewer fakes and mistakes." She blew out the candle and then blew Wally a kiss.

He pocketed the air kiss and asked, "So when are you meeting your mom in Missoula?"

35. THE TRUTH

Claire crashed to the floor. She scrunched her face and screamed at the severe pain in her stomach. This was the third time this past month that the excruciating jab in her abdomen had crippled her. The doctors couldn't make sense of what was happening, and Claire feared the worst. Maybe she was dying. Perhaps she had contracted HIV. People everywhere were dying of AIDS. Had her promiscuity caught up to her?

Bryant rushed to help Claire stand up. "My god, you're burning up."

Claire wailed in agony. Bryant carried Claire to the car and sped to the Mayo Hospital. He parked illegally in the red zone and hoisted Claire out of the car. Inside the hospital, Bryant fluttered around his daughter and snatched a wheelchair. Instead of using the wheelchair, she dropped to her hands and knees to crawl the rest of the way in. She was immediately admitted to the emergency room.

"You're so fucking stubborn," Bryant growled.

A nurse checked her temperature. It was 106 degrees Fahrenheit. She placed an ice pack on Claire's lower stomach, forehead, and chest. After a full body scan, the doctors talked about getting her into surgery.

"Mr. Baker," one of the doctors said, "I'm Dr. Chadwick. Your daughter's fallopian tube has twisted into a knot. It's filled with fluid and about to burst. We're prepping her for the OR immediately."

"How long is she going to be in the hospital?" Bryant asked.

"A week or so," Dr. Chadwick said.

Claire said goodbye to her dad as a resident wheeled her into the operating room. Dr. Chadwick had her count backward from ten, and when she regained consciousness, she was in a small, sterile room. Bryant sat next to her with his head in a book. Claire closed her eyes and dozed.

#

The murmur of voices slowly brought Claire back to consciousness. She blinked to gain clarity of her surroundings. A man's face came into focus—her surgeon, Dr. Chadwick. Claire tried to sit up to see if her dad was there, but Dr. Chadwick held her down. She strained to listen for her dad's husky alto tone, but he was not present.

"You have PID," Dr. Chadwick said. "Pelvic inflammatory disease. There's a lot of damage and scars in your uterus. Your fallopian tube was sixty percent blocked. I removed it. You're really lucky. I wanted to give you a full hysterectomy, but I didn't. I wouldn't want you to come back and sue me later. Girls like you shouldn't have babies."

"Girls like me?" Claire knew she was a mess. She was trying to get healthy. Her body was scarred from the rapes. She was sure of it.

Dr. Chadwick continued. "The chances of you having a baby one day are very slim, and for someone who is as promiscuous as you are . . . well, I'm setting up an appointment for you to see a psychiatrist."

"I'm not going to see a psychiatrist," Claire said.

"Yes, you are. You're going to see a shrink and—"

"No."

"Claire, I can make you go."

"But you can't make me talk."

"In all my life I have never seen tissues so inflamed and infected as yours. You need to stop having sex before it kills you."

"Don't judge me. You have no idea what I've been through."

"I'm not releasing you until—"

Claire grabbed her food tray and threw it at Dr. Chadwick's head. "I told you I'm not going," she screamed. "You're wasting your time."

Dr. Chadwick pursed his lips and wrote feverishly in her chart, glancing at her after every few pen strokes.

"You don't know your own mind," the doctor said.

"The hell I don't!" Claire screamed. "I don't know the psychiatrist you are recommending, and I am not going."

Dr. Chadwick didn't utter another word. He stared at her for a solid five seconds before leaving the room in a huff. He took no care to close the door gently.

Claire cried her heart out. The thought of never having a family devastated her. She wanted children one day. Her dreams dissipated along with her hopes of ever finding a husband who'd have her knowing he could never carry on his family name.

Claire finished feeling sorry for herself and shuffled slowly to the toilet to urinate. When she lifted her hospital gown, she discovered they had shaved her pubic hair for the surgery.

"Fuckers," Claire said, feeling violated and duped.

#

Wally visited Claire the next day and brought her flowers, a book, a box of cassettes, batteries, and his Walkman for her to borrow.

God, how Claire loved this man. "Thanks, Wally. You're so thoughtful and sweet."

He gave her a peck on the forehead and grabbed her chart. As he read it, he raised an eyebrow and chuckled. "It says here you have anger problems. What happened?"

Claire told Wally everything that happened. Over the next ten days, Wally visited every day. Sometimes his brother, Wiley, and Wiley's wife, Rita, came too. Wally's fatherly AA sponsor hat never came off. They continued to talk about the direction Claire's life was heading and what she could do to heal, which involved accepting what had happened to her and learning to love herself, to forgive her aggressors as well as her mistakes . . . All easier said than done and, in theory, sounded great. However, in practice, that proved to be a total failure.

After ten days in the hospital, Claire was released. Not once did Bryant visit her in the hospital. Claire, disheartened that her father would abandon her at this crucial time, simply gave up on him. She was foolish to hope he could ever be the father she needed him to be. Whatever his shortcomings and insecurities were, that was for him to deal with. Claire was done trying.

Bryant reappeared at the hospital to take Claire home, and during the ride back, he asked, "So what happened?"

Claire explained the dire status of her uterus and cried that she couldn't have babies, that it would destroy her body even more.

"Don't let that make you feel any less of a woman," Bryant said.

"Oh, really, Dad? Get a vasectomy, and then let's talk."

"Oh, well, that's different."

"How so? You don't believe in birth control—"

"That's right. I'm not wrapping this rascal. How am I supposed to feel anything?"

"Seriously, how many women have you slept with?" Claire asked. "How many did you get pregnant?"

Bryant shrugged. "I don't know."

"I want to know. Take a guess. Ten women? Twenty?"

"At least that many," Bryant bragged. "Probably a hundred."

"Wow," Claire said. "Let's do the math. Let's say ten percent of them got pregnant with your child. That means out of a hundred I have at least ten siblings. You and Gisela had Tanya and Shannon. You and Shana have Jason and Jack. What about you and my mom?"

"No, you are the only baby from that marriage, but your mom had four from a previous marriage."

"Wow, so I have at least eight half-siblings between you and Mom that I know of. And at one of your parties, I heard you say to Lloyd you once had two women pregnant in the hospital at the same time having your baby. So we're at ten now."

"That sounds about right," Bryant said. "Yeah, my first wife, Margaret, and my mistress were both at the hospital at the same time. It was your aunt Samantha who found out. She went to the hospital and said she was visiting 'Bryant Baker's wife' and they took her to my mistress's room."

Unbelievable, Claire thought. "I'm curious how many of your threesome side chicks you got pregnant. And how many marriages have you had?"

"What's with all the questions anyway, Claire?"

"I know nothing about you, Dad. I want to know how you got to this point in your life. Were you married before you married Mom?"

Bryant pulled into the driveway of their house. He turned off the engine but didn't open the door to get out. "My first wife was Margaret. We had five kids together."

"Whoa!" Claire shook her head. "What were their names?"

"The oldest is Patricia Jane. We called her PJ. Then came Bryant, named after me, then Tricia, Ron, and Jacob."

"Dad, you have a lot of kids!" Bryant reached for the door handle, and Claire quickly apologized. "I'm not judging. I just want you to be honest with me and share your life with me. Help me understand. Please."

Bryant settled in his seat and said, "Honey, I have thirty-two kids. This includes stepkids and at least twenty who are biologically mine."

Claire was stunned that he had kept track and had a profound number to brag about. She didn't dare say a word for fear he'd stop talking.

"One day I found Margaret in bed with another man. Turned out to be a cop. I couldn't beat the shit out of her and couldn't beat the shit out of him, so I left and didn't look back. Margaret filed for divorce, and I married your mom, Janet."

"Do you think Margaret cheated on you because you had a mistress in the hospital having your baby at the same time she was having your baby?"

"I guess. I dumped the side chick to save my marriage, but that backfired."

Claire studied her father. He was known to tell outlandish tales, like how he served in the Vietnam War and earned a purple heart when, in reality, he had never left the United States. It was all plausible, and he could very well be telling the truth. "Did you ever see your kids again?" Claire asked, to which Bryant said no.

"When you dropped me off at Grandma Sharon's and disappeared for a year, where did you go? Why did you leave me?"

"I was seeing someone then. Her name was Cindy. She was a waitress at a diner. You met her once, although you probably don't remember her. She wanted to be with me but wasn't ready for motherhood. So I took you to your grandparents in California. Cindy and I married, but funny thing was, she later wanted kids and I didn't. I came back for you because Grandma Sharon was trying to get custody of you."

Claire tried to absorb all this information and was thankful her dad was willing to open up. "Whatever happened to Gisela? She was a real bitch. You have no idea how abusive she was with me."

"All I know is Gisela moved to Montana and remarried," Bryant said.

"Well, knowing what I know now," Claire said, "I think Gisela took her anger and frustration out on me because she couldn't on you. You were horrible, Dad. You handed over all the parental responsibilities to her, and then you went and had affairs behind her back, forced threesomes on her, got drunk and beat her, got in trouble with the law, and lost jobs. I don't condone what she did to me, but you didn't make it easy on her either. Plus she had Benji and Barry, Tanya, me, Shannon . . ."

The two of them sat in silence for a while, thinking about the past. Claire tried to connect all the dots and make sense of how her life had become so messed up. She finally broke the silence. "How come you and Mom divorced? How'd you end up with custody of me?"

Bryant cocked his head and scratched his brow. He took a deep breath, and instead of answering her, he said, "That's enough for now." Bryant got out of the car and walked into the house without another word.

#

Two days after Claire returned home from the hospital, she ended up back there. The antibiotics given to her weren't strong enough. This time, a different doctor treated her. He had a better bedside manner and was empathetic to her situation.

"Claire," Dr. Jackson said, "I think therapy can help you."

"I already have a counselor," Claire said.

"Yes, good, but I think a psychiatrist can add another layer of value as you continue to heal and get healthy, not just physically and spiritually but mentally and emotionally as well."

Soon after, Claire began therapy with Dr. Kae. At first, whenever Dr. Kae asked a question, Claire laughed and deflected to protect herself and not show vulnerability. Dr. Kae suggested Claire keep a journal and pour all her emotions out on the pages. Claire took her advice, and over time, she was able to open up and share with Dr. Kae exactly what was on her mind.

Claire realized that holding back would only slow her progress. She understood that the more she got things off her chest, the more she was releasing the years of pent-up anguish, fear, guilt, shame, and poison that were harbored deep inside her psyche. Every pen stroke symbolized a thin layer of trauma peeling away and being released into the world so it would no longer be her burden to store. It was freedom.

36. THE REUNION

Before summer ended, Bryant and Claire got on the road and drove from Rochester to Missoula to see Janet. They made arrangements for Claire to stay with Janet for three days while Bryant camped nearby. The road trip was reminiscent of the old days when Cowboy and Sunshine cruised from one mile marker to the next. They headed north on US-52 then west on I-90 all the way to Missoula.

They crossed three state lines in two days while harmonizing to outlaw country music greats like Willie Nelson, Waylon Jennings, Kris Kristofferson, and David Allan Coe.

Snuggled in the Northern Rockies of Montana, surrounded by wilderness and rivers, Missoula was absolutely breathtaking. Claire made a mental note to come back one day to check out the terrain and perhaps do some hiking, kayaking, and fishing.

Along the drive, Bryant opened up about his first crush, his wild teenage antics, and how the army taught him to be regimented about order and cleanliness. Claire found herself enjoying her dad's company again. She wished he was always sober because when he was clean, he was kind, fun, and a great conversationalist.

As they neared Glacial Lake, Claire saw smoke in the distance and smokejumpers parachuting in to fight the wildfires. It was quite the sight to behold.

By five o'clock that Wednesday, they finally pulled into the parking lot of Blue Ribbon café. Claire's palms became clammy and she was dizzy with nervous energy. Inside the café awaited her mother and Claire wasn't sure she wanted to go in. They didn't drive 1300 miles to back out now.

"Are you coming in with me?" Claire asked.

"I'm not sure I want to see your mother," Bryant said. "It's been a long time and we didn't part on good terms."

"Well I haven't seen her since I was four," Claire said, "so you have to come in and help break the ice. You owe me."

With that, the two got out of the truck and slowly walked into the restaurant. Bryant spotted Janet right away and lead Claire to the round table near the restroom.

Claire gasped. *Oh my god, she's fat!*

There sat a middle-aged woman with five other people ranging in age between middle grade and adult. *They must be my siblings.* For years, Claire imagined this moment and sketched in her mind what her mother looked like. She dreamt of meeting a slender woman with copper hair, long and wavy like hers. She'd have green eyes, too, and look like Claire only older with a few character lines around the mouth and eyes, perhaps a raspier voice as well from smoking. In Claire's imagination, her mother would be slightly heavier given motherhood blessed her with five children. The woman in front of her was nothing she pictured. Instead, she was morbidly obese with dyed blonde hair.

Janet struggled to stand up but when she did, she reached out her arms to hug Claire.

Claire stepped back from the embrace and made an excuse not to hug her mother. "Sorry, I smell from our travels and need a shower." Claire gave her a weak smile. She did not want to lose herself in the folds of the 400-pound stranger before her. Janet's flabby arms looked like they weighed as much as two Claires.

Bryant said hello and made a mad dash out of the restaurant, saying he'd see them in three days. He didn't even try to be cordial or stick around to make small talk.

Coward.

Janet introduced Claire to her brother Michael, who was the oldest and looked to be late twenties. He had brown eyes with specks of dark green in them and when he smiled, his whole face lit up. Next was Lonnie, who was nine years older than Claire in her mid-twenties. She was the one getting married that weekend. Cheryl and Katie were three or four years older than Claire and the last to be introduced was Mark, who wasn't a baby dolly anymore. He was eleven.

Claire squeezed in between Mark and Katie and kept her eye on the menu to avoid talking. She simply didn't know what to say and became mute. Luckily, Janet did most of the talking.

"You should try the blue ribbon trout," Janet said. "It's amazing. Goodness, Claire, I'm so happy to know you now. We all are. I've missed you. I was devastated that your father took you away from us all these years."

"It's true," Michael said. "Mom's been crying and pining after you all this time. The last time I saw you I was around thirteen. Your dad just took you and ran off and we didn't think we'd ever see you again."

"What do you mean?" Claire asked.

"It's true," Janet said. "You were abducted."

"Dad told me you divorced when I was six months old and it took another five months for the courts to grant him custody of me," Claire said.

"You know," Katie said, "let's enjoy our dinner and our first night together. There'll be time to catch up on the past later."

They were fifteen minutes into their reunion and Claire felt overwhelmed and distraught. She wanted to call her dad and go home. Unfortunately, he was going off the grid and planned to camp in the wilderness for three days.

Mark scooted close to Claire and pointed to her sourdough. "Are you going to eat that?"

One look at his baby face and Claire melted. "You can have it," she said. *You can have anything you want, baby dolly.* It was so surreal to be sitting there with her family, meeting them again after all this time. Tomorrow was Thursday and there would be things to do to prepare for Lonnie's wedding on Saturday, but at that moment, it was all about getting acquainted - learning surface information like what school Claire attended and the classes she enjoyed. They talk about hobbies and jobs, favorite colors, and inconsequential things.

#

On Thursday, Katie took Claire to the laundromat. While they waited for the clothes to wash, Katie opened up about the day Bryant disappeared with Claire.

"I was too young to remember the details," Katie said as she pulled her long, brown hair into a ponytail, "but Michael and Mom talked about it a lot. For years they relived that day over and over. Mom was a mess. It destroyed her. She was six months pregnant with you when she married your dad, but then they separated when you were six weeks old."

"Why did they separate?" Claire asked. She had a suspicion it had to do with her father's drinking but maybe he was a different man then. After all, she had fond memories of them traveling the country, performing at bars, and talking to truckers on the CB radio.

"Well," Katie said, "Mom said she let herself go after she had you. She was in her thirties and her body didn't bounce back. She was depressed and took to drinking and it was probably a combination of things that made your dad fall out of love with her. She suspected him of having an affair too and says it's because she refused to have orgies."

Claire smirked. "He does have this obsession with threesomes."

Katie continued. "Well, you were eleven months old when your dad kidnapped you. I guess he busted into the house and locked all of us in the bedroom. Mom said there was a screaming match that escalated into a physical match. Your dad kicked her head through a wall, grabbed you, and walked out the door. Michael climbed out of the bedroom window and saw you disappear down the road. He went inside the house through the front door to find Mom unconscious, her head bleeding, and things smashed everywhere."

"Holy cow," Claire said. "That must have been so traumatic for Michael... for all of you."

Later that night, the family gathered around the dinner table and talked some more. Janet opened up and shared how she was married to her first husband when she was seventeen.

"I had Michael when I was nineteen," Janet said. "Then I married Jerry and had Lonnie, Cheryl, and Katie. I cheated on Jerry with your father and left Jerry for Bryant."

"How did you meet my dad?" Claire asked, fascinated to learn all this history.

"Your dad moved to California when he was a teenager. I was a nurse working the graveyard shift when we met. I just lost myself in his presence. He was so handsome and charming. I left Jerry and traveled around with your dad to South Dakota and then Minnesota where you were born. After your dad and I parted, I went back to South Dakota for a while."

"And you and Dad kept in touch all this time?" Claire asked.

"Let me tell you, Claire," Janet said, "your dad is an ass. He kept tabs on me and whenever he swung into town, he demanded sex in exchange for me to see you. He's got a perverse sex addiction. I mean, when I was in labor with you, halfway to the hospital, he pulled over and pretty much raped me. He wanted to know what contractions felt like on his dick. I was like, what the fuck. Yeah, he forced me."

Claire cringed, not wanting to know more details of her father's sex life even though she knew enough. She felt like she was going to vomit.

"Anyway," Janet continued, "we used to party hard back then. Michael, Lonnie, Cheryl, and Katie watched over you when we were out. Those were the days. We both drank heavily then. I smoked a lot of pot which your dad hated. He thought it was worse than alcohol."

Janet went on to share that Bryant filed for divorce and she remarried only to find out he lied about the divorce being final. He threatened her saying he had her for bigamy and used that as an argument for taking Claire.

"I told him I was never giving you up, but he stole you from me. I was afraid of him and couldn't do anything to get you back. I tried to get pregnant right away to fill the void but I had a stillborn daughter. I was drinking like a fish. Then along came Mark. I was on my way to Missoula when I met up with your dad in Billings. That was the last time I saw you, over ten years ago. I don't know if you remember that.

"I do," Claire said. "I remember it clearly."

"I never left Missoula. I figured eventually I'd hear from your father and would see you again. I'm so happy you found me."

"So where's Mark's dad now?" Claire asked.

"He went to prison for robbing a bank."

Claire couldn't believe the twilight zone she was in. There was dysfunction at every turn. She couldn't wait until the weekend was over.

Friday was nonstop with wedding preparations, last-minute changes, adjustments, and deadlines to execute. Everyone had a role and there was little time for the family to sit and chat. Claire was assigned all things related to food and beverages, being the point of contact for the restaurant and dinner reception, running interference for any mishaps, and making decisions on the fly based on what little knowledge she had about the menu and food allergies. In the end, the wedding on Saturday was lovely. Lonnie was beautiful in her gown, her hair pinned around a halo of gerbera daisies. Love was in the air and Claire yearned for a slice of that happiness pie.

Sunday arrived and Bryant picked Claire up early in the morning. It was a tearful goodbye as Janet and her children hugged Claire, making her promise to visit again next summer. It was a mad dash to get home and

Bryant did it in one stretch, driving nonstop to get back to Rochester for his job at a construction site.

Father and daughter talked about their time in Missoula during the drive. Bryant caught some trout and found bars nearby to occupy his time. Claire mostly talked about the wedding which Bryant feigned interest in. The long road home was pensive and dull.

37. LETTERS

Claire turned sixteen on October 24, 1987. Her birthday wish was to put in motion plans to move to Los Angeles when she graduated high school. That meant saving money, getting good grades, and getting healthy . . . none of which was easy to do. Whenever she brought up the topic of moving to LA, Bryant would shut it down.

"No, you're not," he'd say. "You're going to live here in Rochester."

She continued to see Dr. Kae and kept a journal every day, safekeeping her thoughts in a shoebox hidden deep within her closet. Day-to-day living had its challenges, especially when her dad lapsed back to his benders. It was a vicious cycle for Bryant. If work was stressful and things didn't go his way, he turned to the bottle to comfort himself, which in turn caused problems at work. Bryant got into a big argument with his boss at the construction company and decked his supervisor in the jaw. He left his manager dazed with a broken jaw and left himself bereft of another paycheck and benefits to support his family. Back on the welfare wagon they went.

Claire and Christine continued to stick together, but their relationship became strained at times. While Claire worked hard to shift her mindset, find her voice, and protect her body so she could get healthy, Christine slipped back into the rabbit hole.

Christine eased off on going to Alcoholics Anonymous meetings and drifted away from Wally, saying she didn't need a father to give her advice on what to do and how to live her life.

Claire suspected Christine's father continued to abuse her, leaving her in a fragile state of mind. As hard as Christine's grandma tried to help, she never got close to the root of the problem with her granddaughter. Instead of opening up and seeking the sun for energy and healing, Christine saw the sun as a ray of burning light, exposing all the shame she wished to hide. The more her best friend stayed hidden in the shadows and recesses of her turmoil, the more helpless Claire felt.

Claire loved her best friend, however, and she needed Christine like she needed air and water. They found common ground with cocaine, weed, rum, cigarettes, and music—the perfect concoction for a good time. They dated guys and fought whenever one of them felt left behind and their lives weren't in sync. The two girls slowly drifted apart during their junior year of high school. Writing letters to one another and passing notes in class became the preferred mode of communication.

Claire,

Hey girl, how's it going? Me? Much much better. Last night I got home from my meeting with John (counselor) and took a two-hour nap. Got up at about 6:00 p.m. Went out to eat with Grandma. Watched Rags to Riches, which was really good. Watched Remington Steele. He's such a fox. Then went to bed. Grandma and I got along really well. I couldn't believe it. I overslept. It was 7:45 on the button. I just thought oh shit. I got to school during the second hour, and Dr. Jordan wanted to see me. All I could think was just fucking great this is going to be a shitty day, but everything turned out fine. Grandma knows I cut the first hour Friday, and she didn't really say much. I had some chick write me a note so I got excused. I told Dr. Jordan that I overslept this morning. I figure she'd give me ASC (after-school class suspension) but all she said was not to let it happen again. I'm off the hook for now. I'm feeling pretty decent today too. I'm going out for lunch with John today, so I won't be seeing you. That's why I'm writing this, so you know I haven't forgotten you. What are you doing tomorrow after school? I don't have anything planned until 5 when I have to go see my social worker. Yay. But if you're not busy, do you think we can do something? I want to get those pictures developed while I've still got some money left. I almost forgot. Hey, you skinny redhead, smile. That's better. Smile if you're horny. Hahaha. Well, I don't know what else to say, so I shall say no more. I can't spell sianara. See? I told ya. But I can spell later. I love ya. Take it easy.

Chris

#

Christine wasn't the only one who wrote letters to Claire. Her father did too. They spent less and less time together as Claire's days were filled with school and homework while her evenings were filled with making money, seeing her therapist, and attending AA meetings with Wally.

Claire,

Since I am not getting the help I need from you in keeping this place clean, I will have to say the hell with it and let it stay dirty. I'm sorry you won't help, but I'll accept it. Can you accept that I'll no longer buy your cigarettes, give you rides, or stay at home to try to be with you when you show enough downtime for me to do it? We can live together, but you won't share your time and labor with me, and I'm very unhappy about it. If your word is no good to me, why try?

Dad

The correspondences continued, and it became convenient to drop letters instead of talking.

Dad,

I know you love me, but I can't allow you to parent me. You're sick, and you need help. I plan to move out and get an apartment with Melissa. You can support me by signing the agreement. The landlord is agreeing to rent to a minor if you sign the lease.

PS: Sorry about the report card. I am trying.

Claire

Bryant and Claire were passing ships in the night, both consumed with their own problems. Whenever they intersected it was "Really, Claire? Two Fs?" and "Shut the fuck up, Dad, you don't know anything—you don't understand where I'm coming from," to "You're sixteen. What is there to understand?" and "Whatever!"

#

That year while sharing an apartment with Melissa, Claire wrote to her mother, giving Janet her new mailing address and making plans to come to Missoula after she graduated high school. Eventually, she planned to live in Los Angeles but would love to spend the summer after high school with Janet for a while to figure her life out.

Claire didn't want to stay in Rochester for the rest of her life, sucked into the vortex of sex, drugs, and dysfunction. Her life was a wasteland of mayhem and disingenuous people who had no problems throwing friends under the bus to climb to the top of the social ladder. The gap between the rich and the poor stretched wider every year, and Claire was anxious to start anew. Other than Wally, there was no reason to stay. And while Claire's life was progressing in the right direction, it seemed like everything in Rochester stood still or went backward. The country was moving at supersonic speed, and Claire was missing out, stuck in Olmstead County.

Dear Claire,

 I was so excited to get your picture, and it's beautiful. You are just gorgeous. I know you don't have a phone anymore because I called on Thanksgiving. I was just worried that you had moved again. I was relaxed and happy when I got your letter. I was disappointed that you can't come for Christmas. Maybe next year. After all, we have a year to plan for it. I'll miss you though. I will send presents next week. Can you have someone take pictures of you opening them for me, please?

 Your sister Cheryl now lives in South Dakota but was here for three weeks, and we had a really nice visit. I think we got real close again. It helps to ease the disappointment of you not being able to come for Christmas. Katie and her children may be here for Christmas, and she will help too. God, I miss you. I can't wait for summer to get here. I want to see you so bad.

 We put up our tree. It looks really nice. I'll send you some pictures of our Christmas so you can feel a part of us, okay? I was glad to hear you have a new boyfriend, but don't let yourself get hurt. You have to watch out for those older guys, but you seem to know that. I just wanted to remind you. He sounds nice though. It sure would be great if your dad decides to move to Great Falls next year.

 We can see one another more and that would mean the world to me. I am praying that you do so and so is the rest of my family.

 I got a letter from Olmstead County the other day asking me to pay child support for you, and as I have only been allowed to see you for three days in the last ten years, I don't think they can press it, and as I only get $286 a month to live on (welfare), I don't think that they can make me either. I was surprised that your dad had them get child support from me; after all, he never did when he was keeping you from me.

So much for that. I'm sorry I poured out my feelings on this subject, but I thought you'd like to know. I hope you like what I got you for Christmas. I will be mailing it in two days. Please write soon, and call me collect on Sunday before 3:00 p.m. I'll sign off now. Love you.
Mom

A week later, cookies and miscellaneous items from the Dollar Store—hand towels, soap, a candle, dish soap—arrived at her apartment.

By the time eleventh grade came around, Claire had gone through the twelve steps in AA with Wally and clocked in nearly 900 hours of meetings. She wrote a declaration to herself and kept it in her purse everywhere she went, often pulling it out to read whenever people tested her patience or situations anchored her back to old habits and destructive thoughts.

Declaration

I will not allow myself to be hurt anymore by any person, and in doing so I will never allow myself to be vulnerable to anyone. I must remain calm and cold even to those I continue to care for. I will not have relations with any man of any kind except in a strictly social and platonic way nor will I even start or maintain a friendship with any man lest it is misconstrued as a more intimate relationship. I will not have sexual relations for at least five years; therefore never again will I place myself in a position where a person I care about can say that I am beneath them and accuse me of having no morals or that I copulate with anything that moves. I'm not a whore and never again will be accused of such actions of flaunting myself and my affairs in front of others. In doing so I will dutifully complete my studies until the time henceforth I have a graduation certificate from John Marshall High School. I will remain cold and aloof in any social functions until such time that I can go to college and complete my musical theatrical education. I will also be cautious and wary of any females I even consider allowing to be more than a casual acquaintance. I have only myself to rely on, and I must always remember that.

Dutifully signed,
Claire Anne Baker

38. LOS ANGELES

Grandpa Harold died of a massive coronary when Claire was seventeen. The news devastated her and brought guilt upon Claire. She wished she had been able to get to LA sooner. The farfetched notion that she could have saved him or prolonged his life had she been there was preposterous, she knew, but Claire couldn't help thinking maybe there was a slim chance she could have influenced the outcome. She would never know. He was the only grandfather who mattered and who truly loved her. They weren't blood relations, but he was the love relation that gave her a home, and love was thicker than blood.

Shortly afterward, Aunt Samantha's marriage to Uncle Brandon fell apart, and they divorced. Grandma Sharon turned her spare room into a haven for Aunt Samantha, and the two of them had each other to lean on.

At home, Shana and Bryant's marriage teetered, which sent Bryant back into drunken brawls, job terminations, and insatiable demands for rough sex. He often came home smashed, sometimes too intoxicated to gracefully get out of the car that he'd crash into the concrete. On one occasion he stopped breathing, and Claire administered CPR.

When high school graduation came, Claire said goodbye to Christine and cried until she couldn't cry anymore. Melissa gifted Claire the book *Alcoholics Anonymous*, and Claire promised to never lose it or give it away. Jackie and her mom, Mrs. Clemmons, threw a small, casual party for the girls, with Italian food, movie rentals at Blockbuster, and a sleepover. They watched *Dirty Dancing*, *Breakfast Club*, and *Footloose* back to back until the wee hours.

In the last counseling session with Dr. Kae, Claire was gifted *The Courage to Heal,* a book for survivors of childhood sexual abuse. It became the staple read, alongside the *Alcoholics Anonymous* book, that Claire referenced time and time again.

The toughest part of leaving Rochester was leaving Wally, the portly man in his sixties who went from reading the preamble at an AA meeting to reading Claire like an open book. Wally, who took her under his wing, introduced her to his family, took her out to sporting events and bus tours, introduced her to fine dining, visited her at the hospital, and above all, showed her unconditional love without judgment or expectations. He gave her a map to life and let her draw the path she wanted to take to go from damaged to determined. Their farewell didn't end in tears but in laughter.

"Think of me the next time you have steak and lemon cheesecake or burgers and bleu cheese," Wally said as he imparted his last words of wisdom.

"I'll be eating steak and lemon cheesecake every day then," Claire said. "You're in my heart and will always be in my life. I'll take you everywhere with me. And one day when I get married and have children— because I will, Wally, I am never giving up on that dream—you're going to be right there with me to celebrate those milestones!"

"Well, I'm sixty-five years old now, so hurry up," Wally said, "but don't rush either. I'm not going anywhere. Seeing you walk down the aisle with the man of your dreams is on my bucket list."

#

Bryant drove Claire to Missoula and dropped her off at Janet's house. He had no choice. If he didn't drive her, she was going to hitchhike or take the Greyhound. With all the serial killers on the prowl and nutjobs on the buses, Bryant conceded to delivering Claire safely to Montana for the summer before she continued to California.

In the three months Claire lived with her mother that summer, she concluded her mother was an unethical and deceitful woman. Claire never thought she'd say this, but she was glad her father had taken her when she was eleven months old. The way Claire rationalized it, despite her father being a violent drunk who had his demons to overcome, at least he didn't do drugs, and was kind, smart, talented, and fair when he was sober.

Claire's mother, on the other hand, was a hot mess every second of every day. She was difficult and irrational whether drunk, sober, or high. She had double standards, buying Claire lingerie and encouraging her daughter to make money using her sex appeal, while at the same time scorning Claire for using her body to manipulate boys and accusing Claire of whoring herself out.

The positive side of being there in Missoula, however, was getting to know her siblings and learning more about her past.

"When I was around ten and you were maybe six months old," Lonnie said, "Mom went out partying, and when she got home, she went straight to bed. She didn't wake up in the morning, and you were crying your lungs out, starving. Michael and I looked for milk and baby formula, but there weren't any, so I got orange juice out of the fridge. I held you and fed you your bottle, and you slept for hours. Your dad came home and went ballistic. I was so scared. I didn't know what was happening. I later learned the orange juice was filled with vodka, and you had alcohol poisoning from the screwdriver cocktail. You almost died. I felt awful."

"It's okay, Lonnie," Claire said. "You were just a kid. It wasn't your fault. How were you supposed to know?"

#

Over the Labor Day weekend, Aunt Samantha's ex-husband, Brandon, drove to Missoula to collect Claire and bring her to LA. Claire found a waitressing job and signed up with a talent agency. She saved her money in the hopes of moving out on her own. Knowing that her father's first wife, Margaret, and their five children lived in California, Claire looked them up in the phone book and focused on the male names, speculating the women may have changed their names if they were married. She found her brother Robert Baker first, and from there was invited to meet the family. They embraced her with open arms and accepted her as part of the pack like a long-lost sister.

Peggy Jane, called PJ for short, was the oldest and the perfect blend between Margaret and Bryant from her facial expressions to her mannerisms. The eldest son, Bryant, who was named after their father, looked more like Margaret with his thick lips and wispy hair. Tricia and Ron were opposite-gender versions of one another. Put a wig and lipstick on Ron, and he could pass for a pretty girl, while Tricia could have passed for a boy with her androgynous haircut and preppy clothes. The youngest was Jacob. He was the last person Claire met.

"C'mon," Ron said, "I'll take you to meet Jacob."

They drove to a suburban neighborhood, and Jacob's first comment was "Oh Ron, she's hot. Girl, you gotta give me your number."

"She's your sister!" Ron said.

In the months that followed, Claire got into a routine and ping-ponged between spending time with her grandma's side of the family and Margaret's side.

Shortly after Claire's eighteenth birthday, her sister Katie moved to San Diego with her husband Rich and their kids. Claire moved in with them. She slept on their couch.

Katie went to school during the day while Claire watched the kids. In the evenings they had sister time together. Claire eventually got a job at a twenty-four-hour diner in National City and worked the graveyard shift at 11:00 p.m. She slept from 4:00 p.m. until 10:00 p.m. in the kids' room when Katie got home from school, then woke up with enough time to get to work at the diner. The first adult thing she did as an eighteen-year-old was to buy a car for eighty dollars. The Oldsmobile Omega was shit brown, and Claire fondly named it The Brown Turd.

Things were falling into place. Claire slowed down on her drinking, mostly because she was either working, sleeping, or taking care of Katie's kids. Gone was the constant need to numb the pain with drugs or put up her defenses from scuzzy men. Claire had a new family, a healthy and normal one, to lean on. She called home to Wally often to keep him in the know, and she checked in on her dad every so often. Christine and Claire continued to write letters and sent greeting cards on special occasions, usually tasteless ones that would make the other laugh.

Sometimes Claire had triggers, like if she heard a Twister Sister song. It immediately took her back to Rick's room where she was fighting off five teenagers who raped her one after the other. With each episode, she woke up with a jolt, her sheets soaking wet and her jaw sore from clenching it in her sleep. If a closet door accidentally closed on her or she found herself in small spaces, she was transported back to her eight-year-old self, trapped in a dark, locked closet or the rat-infested attic, with Gisela's distorted face coming through the darkness into her mind's eye. When these triggers happened, Claire retreated into her fear and refused to be around people for fear they'd call her crazy.

Oatmeal and chicken frying in hot oil also triggered Claire, taking her back to when Gisela forced her to eat her vomit and regurgitated oats and getting burned at the Love Homestead when the oil splattered on her body from Gisela's carelessness. Sometimes there was nothing to do but cry and ride through the roller coaster of emotions. She often punched and kicked in her sleep, waking up to find pillows on the floor and blankets knotted around her body.

The worst trigger of all, which always came unexpectedly, was when she'd get a scent of grease combined with a whiff of wet dirt. Walking past mechanic shops after a rainfall especially reminded her of the stranger who kidnapped her and tortured her for five hours in the open fields. She'd shiver uncontrollably, even if it was a hot summer day, as her body remembered the frigid night and damp earth. It was a wonder she was alive. Being introduced to sex at the age of eleven years old in such a violent way would always haunt her. During these episodes, Claire chained-smoked through two packs of cigarettes a day. She'd hyperventilate and call Wally. Journaling, praying, and reading self-help books were all she had to help her cope.

In Southern California, there was no deficit of good-looking people aspiring to be models, actors, and musicians. Claire was one of them. Without a college degree, Claire hoped her looks would land her in film or her voice would put her in musical theatre. They were pipe dreams, but she had nothing to lose. She certainly didn't want to be waitressing her whole life.

And then one day the talent agency called. Hollywood had a role for her, and she should audition.

39. THE CATALYST OF CHANGE

Claire used a Thomas Guide map to get around LA. During the first three years, Claire worked at restaurants and went to auditions whenever the talent agency set one up for her. She landed small nonspeaking roles and was hired as an extra on several sets. Claire loved working on film sets, but there was a lot of idle time in between scenes, which bored her to tears. Every time she got to the studio, she'd be raring to go only to twiddle her thumbs while people set up a shot. It was not uncommon to work for an hour and then sit around for four. Oftentimes it took hours to set up a shot to capture two to four minutes of film, adjusting the lights, filters, props, camera angles, and so on. There was nothing to do but go to the craft services table, which was the food table, but in Hollywood, you can't eat for fear of looking fat on camera.

On some sets, there was a basic kitchen food truck. Claire usually ordered one egg white with sauteed mushrooms and a bottle of water. Rather than sit around and do nothing, Claire volunteered to help the second assistant director with errands and general tasks during her downtime. Occasionally, Claire served as a stand-in for a leading character and walked through the whole scene as that character.

Many of the big stars were assholes with massive egos. Attitudes ran unchecked as they strutted around with an air of "I'm too good to talk to you. You're not in the same league to be talking to me."

Claire once worked on the set of *Beverly Hills, 90210*, an American teen drama television series produced by Aaron Spelling. One of the cast members was an entitled prick. One time, he was playing basketball in a big square, and everyone sat around bored. Claire watched him toss the ball around with the rest of the others until the actor came up to her and said, "What are you looking at? Don't you dare look at me." He turned to the showrunner and screamed, "Get her out of here."

Claire later worked on the set of *Calendar Girl* with Jason Priestley. She got there midafternoon and checked in with wardrobe. They spray-tanned her and outfitted her with a coconut bra and grass skirt. It was a themed pool party scene at night at one of the big houses on the hill. They filmed all night in drizzly, windy, sixty-degree weather. At one point, the main actor walked up to Claire and said, "Ooh, got milk?"

Claire responded, "Ooh, fourteen?"

His friends laughed at him and said, "Oh, that's good! She got you back!"

One of the biggest sets Claire worked on was the third *Lethal Weapon* movie. During the filming of the hockey scene at the LA Kings arena, the lead actor took a megaphone and yelled to 4,000 people, "Who stole my fucking paper? Bring my fucking paper back right now." Someone had walked away with his newspaper on the set. Little things upset him, and he was a jerk to everyone around him.

On April 29, 1992, when Claire was twenty years old, she got called to be in an American sports comedy-drama movie with Louis Gossett Jr. called *Diggstown*. She drove The Brown Turd through downtown LA, where a riot erupted. Four white police officers had been acquitted that day over the beating of a black motorist named Rodney King. Claire saw the videotaped beating several times on every news channel and was sickened by the police brutality. Because of the acquittal, citizens took to the streets to let out their anger and frustrations. The protests turned into a long day of looting and burning. Streets were barricaded, cars and businesses were ablaze in flames and smoke, and windows got smashed with gunfire, baseball bats, and rocks. People ran about carrying televisions, cameras, jewelry, food . . . anything they could carry. Driving through the unrest in South Central Los Angeles was terrifying. Not only was Claire navigating through unfamiliar parts of the city, getting derailed due to road closures, but she had to drive with her head down, all the while praying The Brown Turd didn't break down in the middle of the crossfire. A few people wore T-shirts that read "Gates Must Go," referring to Daryl Gates, the LAPD police chief. Many activists held signs in solidarity to support ending racism. They cried for justice for Rodney King and his family.

Claire eventually rolled up to the *Diggstown* set but wasn't sure if she was at the right place. A big security guard confirmed she was and let her through the gate. She worked the set until three in the morning and then drove home. The looting lasted for over five days. Over fifty people died, thousands were injured, and about a thousand buildings were damaged, resulting in over a billion dollars of damage to the city. California declared a state of emergency in South Central LA.

Working on *Diggstown* was great. Even The Brown Turd had a cameo in the film. Hollywood paid her $75 a day to park her car inside the set. The director used her car whenever they needed to set up a street view.

There were a couple of guys in Hollywood Claire wanted to date, but she had committed herself to not dating anyone for a while. While she truly enjoyed acting and being on set, she didn't like the Hollywood culture of sex, drugs, and starvation. Speed and coke were everywhere, and women starved themselves, being told to lose ten pounds when they were already 105 pounds. Claire was no exception to the rule, even though she was just a stand-in. She was told the camera added fifteen pounds, so she needed to lose some weight. Claire was already a size two and was told she'd look better as a size zero.

In addition to her weight "problem," she also had a "face" problem.

"You've got a great expressive face, and you'd be a great actress," the photography director said, "but you need to get your jaw fixed and straightened. If you don't want to be a stand-in forever, you have the chops to be an actress. You just have to get surgery."

Claire knew she had uneven features. After all, her jaw had been cracked on more than one occasion from years of abuse. One side of her face was longer than the other.

While there were a lot of pros to being an actress, there were three times the cons. Producers propositioned her, and one went so far as to say, "I need a nanny and a mistress. Why don't you come to work for me? You'll do."

Every wrap party on the Hollywood scene reeked of drugs and alcohol. Cocaine was Claire's weakness because it gave her nonstop energy and made her lose weight, but she knew she'd have a heart attack and die, so she did not want to get addicted.

Claire knew she couldn't stay healthy in this environment even though she liked what she did. She also wanted to have children one day and believed getting her mind, body, and spirit healthy was the key to stability and happiness. Claire decided she'd had enough and walked away from acting for good.

#

The US Travel and Tourism Administration hired Claire to work for their market research company. She started out doing phone interviews and was really good at it. She was given an opportunity to do coding and was even better at that. A lot of part-time coders worked there, but Claire was the only full-time coder on the payroll. The job involved pulling data on outbound flights from the US to multiple countries and picking a sample size of 2,000 flights a month going from every major airport in the country to another airport internationally, e.g. Seattle to London Heathrow or Miami to Rio de Janeiro or LA to Beijing. The survey was done in fourteen different languages. Every questionnaire had an English side and then a foreign language side, asking "What city are you visiting?" or "What was your experience here?" There was a very thick book with all the cities in the world listed, and each city corresponded to a number. The data entry people would key in the numbers, and Claire spit out statistics. There were numbers for customs, rental car companies, hotels, etc. Her job was to turn the questionnaire into numbers, and another department keyed in the numbers so that they could pull statistics to analyze. When Claire's boss went on maternity leave, Claire ended up running the coding department for six months.

After five years of turning information into numbers, Claire learned a lot about herself, from her work ethic to setting boundaries. She worked hard and earned good wages. The output equaled the input, and life treated her fairly. She began respecting herself enough not to get into casual relationships. As Claire worked on getting her life in order and figuring out who she was and who she wanted to become, she made a conscious choice to not only address her childhood trauma but to stop the cycle of abuse in her family. More than anything, Claire wanted the American ideal of a healthy marriage to a respectful, loving husband, a couple of kind, well-adjusted kids, and maybe a dog or cat. She dreamed of falling in love, buying a house with land, vacationing every year to some adventurous destination, fine dining on caviar and champagne, and being at peace with herself.

Claire had notes everywhere reminding her that the cycle of substance abuse and physical or sexual abuse stopped with her and that she was the catalyst of change for the future. The last thing she wanted to become was a narcissistic alcoholic like her dad. She started paying attention to her mental health and read a lot of self-help books. Wally remained in her life with his nuggets of wisdom and an endless supply of encouragement. Slowly, Claire began dating again and opened herself to long-term relationships. Most of them failed before they even began, and at one juncture, she thought she had found her mate. Claire put plans into motion to start a family, but miscarriage after miscarriage ensued, and the relationship unraveled. Claire couldn't understand why she could conceive but not carry the pregnancy to full term. The man she was with dropped the devastating news that he had never wanted children anyway and hoped Claire would let go of her dreams of motherhood. It was another one step forward and two steps backward for Claire.

Claire prayed for strength and accepted that it wasn't meant for her to be with this man who had strung her along and given her hope. In the end, she was glad she didn't have children with him because he'd likely abandon their family when the going got tough.

To fill the void, Claire entered chat rooms and spoke to strangers online. That was where she met Drake.

#

The year was 1997. Yahoo chat rooms were all the rage. Everyone was online messaging each other, meeting new people, and discovering new cultures. Claire created an account and had the option of either using a profile picture or building an avatar for herself. She chose one of the photos she had from the talent agency.

Drake and Claire casually conversed in a group chat. He lived in Maryland. She lived in San Diego, California. Claire enjoyed having someone to talk to without any commitments, expectations, judgments, or romantic interests getting in the way. She was upfront about not wanting to hook up or have a boyfriend, as she had just gotten out of a relationship. Drake applied no pressure, and they formed an easy friendship online. Eventually, they broke off into ICQ, an instant messaging service, and chatted privately.

Conversation flowed smoothly between the two as they talked about politics, entertainment news, music, food, and travel. Claire enjoyed friendly debates with Drake and looked forward to their chats.

February 1997

Drake: Hey, Claire. What's new?

Claire: I spent Christmas in Seattle with my sister, Katie. She's begging me to move up there.

Drake: Gee, California or Washington. Hmm. Definitely Cali.

Claire: Right? Temecula isn't San Diego, but I'll take the sunshine over the rain any day. Katie hates the weather. Her husband and his family are from there, and he got stationed there, but he's out to sea. Her kids are acting out, so she feels alone and exasperated.

Drake: That's tough.

Claire: Yeah. Seen any good movies lately?

July 1997

Claire: Haven't talked to you in a while. Guess what? I just moved to Seattle! My brother-in-law drove down to help me move up. The weather's nice in the summer. What have you been up to?

Drake: Working. School. Information technology stuff. Boring.

Claire: Do you ever miss the military?

Drake: Once a marine, always a marine. Hoorah!

Claire: Send me a picture of yourself in uniform.

Drake: Sure, but be careful. You might just fall for me.

Claire: Ha!

Drake: So are things better for your sister?

Claire: I guess so since I'm here now. Her daughter, Carrie, is having a tough time adjusting. Her middle child, Jeremy, is a hellion. The youngest, Robbie, so far seems normal and sweet.

Drake: Your sister has her hands full. Glad she has you now. I have friends in Seattle. Maybe I'll come to visit, and we can meet. You seem cool. I mean, you don't seem like the serial killer type.

Claire: Yeah, that would be great to finally meet you after all these months. I've been meaning to try out the new ax.

September 1997

Drake: Wazup? I got your letter yesterday. Nice picture!

Claire: Awesomesauce! I got yours too.

Drake: I got my tickets. Think you can handle me for ten days? J/K. No pressure. If it doesn't work out and you end up finding me repulsive, haha, I'll have my buddies' shoulders to cry on.

Claire: Funny.

Drake: Actually, one look at me, and you're going to fall head over heels for me.

Claire: As if. I already know what you look like. It's going to take more than a uniform.

Drake: Ouch. Well, for what it's worth, I think you're pretty fly.

Claire: Yup, all that and a bag of chips.

Drake: Whoa, I just heard your ego knocking at the door. Better check yourself.

Claire: Eat my shorts.

Drake: Okay.

Claire: Oh my god, you're such a flirt.

Drake: Changing the subject. I'll be staying at the DoubleTree by the airport. Any chance you can pick me up and take me to the hotel?

Claire: No problem. Hey, I gotta bounce. Send me your flight information.

40. NEW BEGINNINGS

Drake stepped out of the terminal and greeted Claire with a hug. In person, he was taller and more handsome than she expected, with broad shoulders and kind eyes. The only photo she had of him was his US Marine photo where he looked like a deer in a spotlight with his blank stare and rigid expression. Claire could tell she impressed him as well by the way he kept looking at her with tenderness and curiosity.

"How was the flight?" Claire asked.

"Not too shabby," Drake said. "Smooth landing, good food . . . even got mints with my pillow."

"Really?" Claire asked. "That's phat."

Drake chuckled. "Psych. But maybe the Doubletree will put mints on my pillow with their turndown service."

"Fo' shizzle. I hear they give warm chocolate chip cookies too," Claire said.

"Bitchin'. Maybe I can convince them to give me two. You know, for serving our country and all."

Claire marveled at the ease with which she could talk to Drake. It was strange seeing him in the flesh, watching his lips move when he talked instead of staring at the blinking cursor when he was about to type a message. That evening they shared a nice dinner and talked about everything from movies to books, social justice issues to second amendment rights, and military life to family dynamics.

Claire ended up staying with Drake for two nights before going back home to grab some stuff to stay with him the rest of the week. It was Drake's first introduction to her family. This would be the true test of whether he was scared easily.

While Claire packed her things in her room, Drake made small talk with Katie and her husband, Rich. Suddenly, Claire's niece, Carrie, kicked in the bedroom door.

"You know, you haven't been out of a relationship for very long, Aunt Claire," Carrie said. "You have to wait for four years before you can get into a relationship."

"Carrie," Claire said, "I love you, but you don't get to dictate my life. I am going to love you no matter what, and I am not going to abandon you, but you don't get to dictate my life."

"I hate you!" Carrie exclaimed.

"That's okay. I love you anyway," Claire said.

Carrie ran to her room, and Claire shook her head. *Teenagers*, she thought. They never made sense.

Drake and Claire left the house and headed back to the hotel, or the "crib" as Drake called it. Claire observed Drake closely, looking for signs that her family may have freaked him out. She was sure he'd take one look at them and run back to Maryland.

"What was up with your niece?" Drake asked.

"Carrie is kind of a mess. She acts out for effect and attention. My sister coddles her, but not me. Not her aunt Claire! And for some reason, her juvenile mind thinks I'm not allowed to date until four years between relationships."

"Oh, so now we're dating are we?" Drake teased.

"Oh, please," Claire said. "Talk to the hand. You wish."

Drake laughed, and Claire giggled. "Tell your niece I'm not a scrub," Drake said.

Claire and Drake spent the entire ten days together, eating, drinking, sightseeing, and making out.

At one point, Claire said, "You're da bomb," and she meant it. "When I saw your picture, I thought you were funky-looking."

"Wow," Drake said, "don't hold back now!"

"Seriously," Claire said, "the photo you sent me with your dead eyes and frozen smile . . . you looked scared of something."

"You asked for my picture in uniform, and you got it."

Claire giggled. "I'm just saying!"

Claire slapped Drake's chest playfully, and he caught her hand. He held it to his chest and leaned in for a passionate kiss, gentle enough to be seductive, long enough to be alluring, and deep enough to show he meant business. Claire responded to his kiss and knew he was the one.

The night before Drake flew home to Maryland, he asked Claire to consider an idea.

"Would you ever consider moving to Maryland?"

"I can't," Claire said, "at least not any time soon. Carrie needs someone stronger than her mother in her life. If I left now, she would feel abandoned. My niece was molested when she was younger, and I know how important it is to have a strong positive role model, because . . ."

Claire choked and was hesitant to share parts of her past with Drake. It frightened her that she might lose him if he knew about her past, of the rapes, the abuse, the promiscuity, the drug and alcohol dependency.

Drake caressed Claire's face and stroked her hair. His touch reassured her that there was something real and magical happening between them.

"Listen," Drake said, "the past is the past. You can share with me in your time when you're ready. We all have monsters in our closets. What's important is what's before us and the people we choose to be going forward. I want to give us a shot."

"What's holding you back in Maryland?" Claire asked. "I mean, would you move to Seattle?"

"My mother lives with me. I'm just going to tell her I'm moving to Seattle," Drake said. "She can either move with me or to Florida and stay with my sister."

Ultimately, after a long conversation, they agreed that Drake would finish school before moving to Seattle. Claire had a few months to prepare for his arrival. Claire's moving out drove a wedge in her relationship with Katie. The timing was right, though, as Carrie became increasingly destructive and manipulative, accusing her father of sexual abuse, which opened an investigation by the military. Claire stated that Rich was abusive, but there was no evidence of him sexually abusing Carrie. A mandate was made that Carrie would go into foster care, and this ripped Katie's heart to pieces.

Meanwhile, Jeremy, the middle child, ran amuck with a butcher knife, chasing Carrie and slashing the couch, being completely destructive and antisocial.

"Katie," Claire said to her sister on the day she moved out, "I love you, and if I am to continue loving you, I have to move out. I cannot continue to live in your home. This is not working out."

At Christmas of 1997, Claire flew to Maryland to help Drake finalize his move. When Drake told his mom he was moving to Washington, she lost her mind. Claire might as well have been evil incarnate taking her son away from her after spending only ten days together. This didn't stop Claire from interviewing Drake's mother, his best friend, his niece, and his sister about his character and feelings on fatherhood. Claire was leery, naturally, but their testament of his character appeased her worries.

Claire was upfront with Drake about wanting to have kids and planned to never give up no matter what havoc it would wreak on her body. Drake suggested they consult a fertility specialist.

They drove back to Seattle and stopped in Rochester so Drake could meet Claire's best friend, Christine, who was married by then. Drake also met Wally and finally, Claire's father, who had a new wife and four rugrats.

When asked what happened to Shana, Bryant confessed he had cheated on her with Torrie and so Shana left him. *Good for her!* Shana had finally had enough of Bryant's disrespect and infidelity. Bryant and Torrie wed shortly after the divorce and yadda yadda yadda, four kids came into the equation.

Drake and Claire moved into their apartment in Kenmore, Washington, and rang in 1998 with a commitment to start a family after they got married. Drake's marriage proposal was perfect, with no flair or fanfare . . . just the two of them opening their hearts to one another and promising to stand by one another through everything.

Sadly, Grandma Sharon passed away from colon cancer shortly after Drake and Claire got together. It took some time for Claire to mourn and feel ready for the big leap. She took it slow and wanted a long engagement. Too slow, apparently, because Claire's nephew, Jeremy, asked Drake, "Are you ever going to marry my aunt Claire or what?" to which Drake answered, "Jeremy, I promise, if I do, you'll be the second to know."

In August 2000, the two of them tied the knot. Wally flew into Seattle to walk Claire down the aisle. His slender, warm hands covered Claire's shaky ones right before the wedding processional.

"Claire, everything will be all right. He is a good man. I know you're worried—"

"You would think that after going around the sun twenty-eight times, I would have met more than one man who hasn't failed me," Claire said. "So far, you're the only man who hasn't let me down."

"Drake will not fail you," Wally said. "I see the love he holds for you. Marriage has its ups and downs, but I believe you two were meant to be."

"It's not just Drake I worry about," Claire said. "What if I fail him? I can't have children, and he will be the last to carry his family name."

"Before you can live your truth, you need to tell your truth," Wally said.

"I have," Claire said. "And he still wants to marry me."

Wally kissed Claire on the forehead as the music queued the walk-in song. "Then lean into it, Claire," Wally said. "I've watched you fight your demons these past years and witnessed you rise from the ashes like a phoenix. You are a miracle, my dear. I'm so proud of you."

Claire took Wally's arm and began the walk toward Drake. As she took her steps, Claire thought, *My heart beats stronger for you, Drake, than any other. Here you stand before me, giving me your love and honor, about to promise your devotion until death do us part, and all I can give back is my undying devotion and gratitude. Thank you for betting on us.*

THE END

AFTERWORD

In the Spring of 2013, T-Mobile, the telecommunications company headquartered in Bellevue, Washington, became a publicly-traded company. John Legere was named CEO of the company and a new team was formed under the Legal Affairs department to manage board and committee meetings, annual shareholder meetings, retreats, SEC filings, board portal management, and a plethora of other responsibilities. Lynn Thomas and Amy M. Le were hired to support the attorneys, C-suite leaders, and Board of Directors for all things Corporate Governance and Securities related.

One night, after a rough eighty-hour work week in New York City, Amy invited Lynn down to the hotel bar for an impromptu post-mortem meeting. They decompressed over Macallan 18 and talked about how the board retreat went. Both Lynn and Amy opened up by sharing parts of their personal traumas.

The two women worked together at T-Mobile for four years and became best friends who shared everything from their taste in food and drinks down to the flat iron they couldn't live without. On one particular trip, they both brought the same John Frieda JFS1B flat iron with titanium plating to straighten their hair! It was uncanny they both preferred scotch, neat instead of on the rocks, seafood of all kinds, spicy foods, and of course, foie gras. When it came to wines, they were both redheads, loving Cabernet Sauvignons and despising Chardonnays. Frequently they would order food for each other, confident the other would approve, everything from medium-rare wagyu to Kumamoto oysters.

In February 2017, Amy's mother passed away from lung cancer and her world shattered. She quit T-Mobile to write her mom's story as a way to honor her mother's legacy. Lynn asked Amy if she'd help write Lynn's story as well. In September 2018, they began recording their conversations as Lynn drummed up the horrors of her past. Thus began Amy's ghostwriting project, The Copper Phoenix.

Lynn worked at T-Mobile for another six years after Amy left and then retired a few months before this book was published. Amy's autofiction novel, Snow in Vietnam, debuted in May 2019. It was at that point that Amy began writing The Copper Phoenix, transcribing the recordings onto a sketch pad or Microsoft Word.

As one can imagine, the project was traumatic for both Lynn and Amy. There were long periods when Amy couldn't type a word and so she focused on her second book, Snow in Seattle, the sequel to her first novel. When Amy wrote chapter nineteen of this book, titled How Stars Died, it took her a month to harness the mental willpower to address the chapter, and it took thirteen hours of not eating to write those seven pages. She admitted she was a crying mess during that time. The chapter almost didn't get written. Not only was it a tough one to write, but Lynn had kept that first rape a secret. It wasn't until after Amy probed further about the details of Lynn's story that didn't add up that Lynn confessed to getting kidnapped and left for dead in a big field when she was eleven years old.

Today, Lynn has been married to the love of her life for twenty-three years. It wasn't always easy. There were times her husband triggered some of her trauma without understanding how or why. Keeping the lines of communication open was the key to healing. Lynn's husband provided a safe space for Lynn to talk without feeling judged or ashamed.

Time and time again, Lynn has proven that there is light at the end of the tunnel if one is brave enough to face one's demons. Despite multiple doctors telling her she'd never have children and that she should stop trying because the irreparable damage to her body made her at high risk of dying during delivery, Lynn never gave up on having children. Lynn and her husband have two wonderful sons who are thriving in life and three sweet Labradoodles who are spoiled rotten.

"Never again was I going to let someone else dictate what I could or couldn't do," Lynn said.

"Her grit and tenacity make her the most resilient woman I know other than my mom," Amy said. "That inner strength fuelled Lynn's drive to change the course of her life, break the cycle of dysfunction in her family, and be a beacon of hope for others. She's stubborn as hell, too, and would give you this Bert stare if you said something that chapped her."

For someone who went through so much unspeakable affliction, Lynn remains kind, selfless, happy, successful, loving, giving, funny, and talented.

"There are no words to adequately describe the wonderful person Lynn is. In my heart, I believe she is a being not of this world but an angel sent to show us love, forgiveness, and compassion," Amy said. "There is nothing ordinary about Lynn. She puts the *extra* in ordinary."

Many who are lucky enough to know Lynn on a deeper level would agree. Lynn Thomas, aka the copper phoenix, is extraordinary.

Thank you for reading The Copper Phoenix. Please consider writing a review on Amazon, Goodreads, Bookbub, and Barnes and Noble to help other readers discover The Copper Phoenix. You can follow Quill Hawk Publishing, Lynn Thomas, and Amy M. Le on the following pages:

https://quillhawkpublishing.com/

https://www.facebook.com/CLynThomas
https://www.instagram.com/coppertoplt/

https://www.facebook.com/authoramymle
https://www.instagram.com/amy_m_le/
https://www.linkedin.com/in/amymle/

AMY M. LE

Amy M. Le is a Vietnam War survivor and Congenital Heart Disease (CHD) warrior. She is the CEO of Quill Hawk Publishing, a hybrid publishing company dedicated to amplifying diverse voices. Amy also co-founded The Heart Community Collection, a resource for the CHD community. Snow in Vietnam was her critically acclaimed debut historical fiction novel. Amy resides in Oklahoma with her husband, son, and pets.

LYNN THOMAS

Lynn Thomas is currently retired and lives in Kansas. She is a wife and mother of two grown sons and three Labradoodles. In her past corporate career, she was a highly sought-after Sr. Legal Analyst and Corporate and Securities Paralegal. Her greatest joy is spending time with her family, traveling, and demonstrating her culinary prowess in the kitchen.

Made in the USA
Columbia, SC
07 April 2023

14607383R00183